A NOVEL

YEAR OF THE GOOSE

CARLY J. HALLMAN

The Unnamed Press
Los Angeles, CA

Unnamed Press
P.O. Box 411272
Los Angeles, CA 90041
www.unnamedpress.com

Published in North America by The Unnamed Press.

1 3 5 7 9 10 8 6 4 2

Copyright 2015 © Carly J. Hallman

ISBN: 978-1-939419-51-4
Library of Congress Control Number: 2015955220

This book is distributed by Publishers Group West
Printed in the United States of America by McNaughton & Gunn

Designed & Typeset by Scott Arany
Cover Design by Jaya Nicely
Interior illustration by Zejian Shen

For my family

YEAR OF THE GOOSE

FAT PEOPLE FAT CAMP

When our ducks grow fat,
our stomachs growl happily!
But then our children grow fat,
and our nation's heart grows heavy!
—CHINESE FOLK BALLAD

If you're a fatty and you're ready
to make a change, come on down
to our fat camp today!
—CHINESE RADIO COMMERCIAL JINGLE

WE NEED MONEY AND WE NEED IT NOW

KELLY HUI, THE TWENTY-FOUR-YEAR-OLD DAUGHTER OF BASHFUL Goose Snack Company's founder and China's richest man, Papa Hui, strode through the Jiangsu government building's entrance, gave her name to the teenage security guard, and plopped herself down on a rickety chair. The meeting she was waiting for, certain to be a snore-fest, was tragically the most exciting work-related thing she'd done since her father had made her the head of corporate social responsibility—a department in which she was the sole employee— two years before. To be fair, this was also the only work-related thing she'd done.

She rummaged through her Hermès bag, found her iPod, stuck her earbuds in her ears, and put on a Radiohead song. She tapped her foot in rhythm on the floor. She listened to another song, and then another, and then another. Swatted at a fly that buzzed around her head. Glanced down at the time—ten past—and sighed loudly. The guard, a scrawny kid who couldn't have been more than seventeen and who, Kelly thought, probably spent most of his day secretly masturbating under his little podium, looked up. That's right, she thought, flipping her hair over her shoulder, store this one away for later.

Then she thought: Did I really just invite a teenage peasant to deposit my image in his spank bank? Did I really wake up at seven a.m. to ride all the way out to this craptastic Communist-era building with no air-conditioning to meet with a government official who is probably just going to ask me for some sort of favor but who can't be bothered to show up on time to do so? Did I really study my ass off at USC to head up a nonexistent department in a polluted city that doesn't even have a California Pizza Kitchen? Did I really think

Papa Hui was going to set me up in a decent job, train me to run the company, and then, ha, leave the company to me? Do I still think that? Do I still hold on to this false hope? Why? Why am I here? What am I doing? Is my iPod going to run out of battery?

She began to sweat slowly, drop by drop, and then profusely. Breathed in, out. Removed a tissue from a small pack in her purse and dabbed her forehead. Turned off her iPod. Just as she yanked the buds from her ears, the guard barked her name.

She rode up in the wobbly metal box of an elevator to the eleventh floor, where a serious-looking middle-aged official with an unnaturally lustrous head of hair met her. He led her down the dim hallway. A sour stench, not unlike that of rancid meat, hung in the air. She held her breath and wondered why these assholes couldn't bear to spend a little money sprucing up their workplace; heaven knows they spent enough on their cars and women and watches and weird medicinal foods.

"How is your father?" the official asked. He stepped briskly in his crocodile-skin shoes.

"Healthy as an ox," Kelly answered, and wasn't that the truth. At almost sixty years old, his cholesterol was lower than hers, his skin showed not a wrinkle, and he'd jetted off to Cuba the previous year to have his heart preemptively replaced with that of a twenty-two-year-old. "Yeah, he's sure going strong," she added in a tone that did little to hide her disgust.

The official paid this tone no heed. "Good to hear," he said. They entered his dusty closet of an office. He sat down behind a cheap laminate desk and gestured for Kelly to sit across from him. The chair creaked under her weight. I know I've packed on a few since L.A., she thought, but come on.

The official cleared his throat into his hand, obviously a rehearsed gesture that provided him an opportunity to flash his Rolex. "Now look, I respect your father a great deal, and I don't wish to waste any of your time, so let's get down to it, shall we?"

Kelly nodded. Here it comes.

"As I'm sure you've heard, our great province recently made national headlines for having the chunkiest children in all of China."

Yeah, she'd heard and vaguely remembered; it'd been the talk of Jiangsu social media for a few hours, until some other headline came along and then that became the talk, and then another headline, and on and on.

The official continued. "Obesity has many causes. For instance"— he counted them off on his fingers—"pregnancy, laziness, capitalist greed, drinking too much cold water, being born under an inauspicious moon. But doctors agree that the most prominent cause of obesity is consumption of fatty junk foods."

Beads of sweat burst from Kelly's forehead, and a tremble seized her hands—this was why he'd called her here. Of course. He was going to blame the Bashful Goose Snack Company for childhood obesity and try to force it to pay what would surely amount to a hefty fine, and Papa Hui would be furious at her for agreeing without his consent to attend this meeting. His majesty would, of course, refuse to pay the fine (he viewed all fines as bribes, and not paying bribes was one of his "core principles"), and then the government would shut the whole empire down, and then what would she do? Return to America and attend graduate school on high-interest student loans? Stay in China and be forced to move in with her newly impoverished family in a one-room hovel in the countryside where she'd be pecked to death in her sleep by that damn goose?

Sweat oozed from her skin, and she could feel the color draining from her face and her mascara bleeding into and stinging her eyes, and she reached into her bag to dig for another tissue, and she considered just running away, hauling ass for good, but she feared if she stood she would faint and—

The official, looking concerned, pulled a bottle of Evian from a pack under his desk and handed it to her. She unscrewed the dusty cap and took a big gulp.

"Now, don't worry," he said. "The last thing we want to do is to shut anyone down over this. After all, I myself know that the occasional Bashful Goose Chocolate-Cream-Filled Snack Cake or, say, the rare Bashful Goose Fried Corn Dough Ball in the context of an otherwise healthy diet is a perfectly reasonable indulgence.

"In fact," he went on emphatically, "Bashful Goose treats are my personal favorite brand of snack food. When my wife and I got married many moons ago we decided to forgo the wedding candy and instead serve our guests Bashful Goose snack cakes. Now you may ask: Why tempt fate in that way? Why throw caution to the wind in the face of such dire potential consequences? But to that I say: you must do what you love, and to hell with tradition and superstition and the rest of it. And, I'll tell you, my wife and I are still together to this very day."

Kelly tried not to snort. Ha, and exactly how many mistresses do you have? How "together" are you, really? She couldn't quite bring herself to speak these thoughts aloud though; in all her days, she had never seen a government employee appear this excited about anything.

The official stared past her with dreamy eyes, thinking fondly of either his wife or processed balls of carbohydrates. The tiniest bit of drool gleamed in the corner of his mouth and then Kelly knew for certain which one it was.

"Cool story," she said dismissively. Her sweat production slowed. She glanced down into her bag at her iPhone, at the time. She had a hair appointment in the afternoon, and if the official kept on like this, she wouldn't make it and she'd be left to go about her life with ratty-looking extensions until Stefan, who was quite booked up these days, could find another slot for her. "Now, what is it that my company can do for you?"

The official ran his fingers through his own gorgeous head of hair. His Rolex reflected a flickering beam of fluorescent light. "Well, it's safe to say that all of us here in Jiangsu Province have lost a fair bit of face in this obesity crisis, wouldn't you agree?"

Kelly nodded. Sure, yeah, cut to the chase.

"And so we in the government have decided the best way to save face is to save our children from being swallowed up by their own hungry mouths! And that is where you come in." With flourish, the official yanked opened his desk drawer and removed an old, clunky Dell laptop, which he opened to reveal a slow-loading PowerPoint presentation. "We would like to invite you, the Bashful Goose Snack Company, to donate funds to start our province's very first government-certified weight-loss reeducation center!"

Thoroughly convinced of the rightness of it all, and with a couple of hours left until her hair appointment, Kelly ordered her driver to deliver her to Bashful Goose headquarters, where she would ask Papa Hui himself for the funds. The city went past in a blur, all skyscrapers and steamed bun shops and trees and Volkswagen taxis. She sprawled out in the backseat of her Audi, stuck her earbuds in, and hit Play on a guided meditation track she'd downloaded. Prompted by a soothing female voice, she tried to focus on all things good and pure: this project and what it could mean. The state-of-the-art fitness facilities, the virtual reality weight-loss visualizer, the flown-in European chef. Rehabilitating the province's fattest kids as an act of charity, as an act of kindness, as an act of selflessness. Proving herself capable to the old coot, proving to him that she should be the one to someday run the company.

And keep focusing on those positive things, keep focusing, the voice said, *stay with it, stay with it.*

But at that, Kelly's thoughts shot to the reason she was listening to this stupid hippie's amateur track in the first place; to the reason she played host to all these anxieties, and she always burst into nervous sweats, and she insisted on living across town from her family in a shitty neighborhood her mother didn't feel comfortable in, and she normally avoided going to her father's office at all costs—why her life, her miserable excuse for a life, had long ago taken a turn for the pathetic: the goose, that bashful goose.

THE LEGEND OF THE BASHFUL GOOSE

FROM THE BASHFUL GOOSE SNACK COMPANY OFFICIAL WEBSITE:

ONE AFTERNOON, MANY YEARS AGO, WHEN OUR GREAT NATION HAD officially opened up but most of us still toiled in her fields, Papa Hui, our company's dear founder, found himself strolling around the willow-lined Three Horse Lake in his hometown of Old Watermelon Village.

Yes, Papa Hui stepped forward, crunching autumn leaves beneath his feet. But philosophically, he found himself at a standstill, at a crossroads in his life. He had just paid off the 20,000 yuan loan he'd taken out to open Papa Hui's Snack Shop, Old Watermelon Village's first grocery-like store. In this way, he was a free man. But, as the saying goes, when life removes one set of chains, it usually, and happily, snaps a new set into place: the local doctor had just confirmed that his beautiful young wife, Mama Hui, who had missed her visiting aunty for the second consecutive month, was indeed pregnant with the couple's first child.

With a child on the way, Papa Hui pondered as he strolled: Can I really just go on selling dusty bags of State-owned-factory-produced snacks? Don't I owe the next generation something more, something better? Is there a kingdom I can build, he mused, worthy enough for this child to someday inherit?

Tangled in his thoughts, Papa Hui hadn't heard the footsteps that had been following him for some time—until now. Startled, he whirled around, but whoever, or whatever, it was ducked behind a willow branch. Never mind, Papa Hui thought, it's just some devilish child playing pranks, maybe one of those Wang children, whose parents had miraculously avoided fines or forced sterilization despite their blatant violations of family-planning laws.

Papa Hui, tickled by the thought of one of those little buggers hiding, cried out, "Bashful child, come out, come out!"

But no child emerged; no child answered these shouts.

He slapped at a mosquito that landed on his arm. A breeze rustled the willows, and a dark cloud moved across the sky.

Papa Hui's thoughts took a sinister turn. He contemplated other potential pursuers: Another aspiring snack-shop entrepreneur who hoped to kill off the competition. A weirdo from a neighboring village who had decided to take a step up from torturing field mice and try his hand at murdering thirtysomething men. The Gang of Four. The Hong Kong mafia. An escaped convict. A Soviet spy. And if it is someone dangerous, he thought, what then? Who am I to fight off such an enemy? I am no one, just a simple man; I am no one.

Resigned to this fate, he turned back around—his helpless body trembling, his shoulders slumped in defeat—and continued on his walk... toward what?

And again, he heard the footsteps. He paused. A sliver of golden sun peeked through the clouds and shone down on him. Enveloped in this light and warmth, a sense of bravery flooded his body. I am not no one, it struck him, I am a father-to-be, I am the boss of Old Watermelon Village's most successful snack shop, I am a husband, I am a man, I am a Chinese, I am someone! He shook out his trembles. He pushed back his shoulders. Bursting with pride in his own humanity, which he felt then for the first time, he charged toward the nearest willow branch and, with both arms, swept the leafy limb aside. Nothing. He swept aside another droopy branch, and another, and another, until at last he found his pursuer.

Papa Hui, looking down at the little devil who'd caused him so much fear, couldn't help now but laugh. "Bashful goose, come out, come out!" he said, and the goose did come out, and it followed him home.

"Good night, bashful goose!" Papa Hui called out the window that night to the bird. Mama Hui just rubbed her belly and rolled her eyes.

From the other side of the window, nestled in the dirt, the goose honked in response and bashfully covered its face with its wing, in what is now the bashful goose's most famous pose, pictured in our great company's logo.

The next morning, our dear founder Papa Hui set off to begin his first debt-free day at the snack shop.

"Good-bye, Mama Hui!" he called. "Be safe!"

"Good-bye, bashful goose!" he called, opening the door. "Be good!"

But as soon as he had taken a step out, that bashful goose lunged at his canvas-clad legs. Papa Hui slapped the goose away, but it only came back at him more aggressively. It pecked. It bit. It honked.

"Bashful goose, what's wrong with you?" Exasperated, Papa Hui bent down and looked directly into those beady little eyes. "Why are you suddenly so outgoing?"

In place of an answer, the goose hid its face behind its wing, honked, and then took off in a waddle-run toward the field that led to Old Woman Wu's house.

Old Woman Wu once had a reputation as a very skilled baker, and in the old days of revolution and reeducation, she had generously baked for the ravenous village children all manner of pies and cakes spiced with creative famine-time ingredients including but not limited to: grass, tree bark, pond algae, and sparrow's feet. But when her husband died in a railway construction accident, Old Woman Wu devolved from her cheery, anything-is-possible self into a weepy recluse. Her long raven-black hair turned gray, and the now well-fed children took to calling her "Witchy Wu."

Papa Hui chased after the goose, running and running across that field, sweat sprouting from his pores, all the while trusting fully, inexplicably, in this goose and where it would lead him.

The goose at last stopped at Witchy Wu's gate, honking furiously and flapping its wings. Papa Hui bent over at the waist, clutching his knees, panting. He looked up just in time to spot Witchy Wu throwing open the door, seeking the cause of the commotion that had violently woken her from her midmorning nap. When Papa Hui's calm eyes met her frantic ones, they both knew it was fate that had brought them together.

The rest, as they say, is history. Papa Hui joined forces with Witchy

Wu and rebranded the store with a new mascot and a new name. The two tossed out those dusty, old packages of State-owned-factory-produced snacks and began developing and producing their own original snack products to wild acclaim. Villagers simply couldn't get enough of Bashful Goose Snack Company's Watermelon Wigglers and Tangerine Crumbly Cakes (one whole tangerine in every bite!), among other delights. The company's good luck turned to great luck when Papa Hui took a bet on a new form of advertisement—a TV commercial, one of the very first in a nation where the hottest new must-have product was a TV set. The Bashful Goose logo soon became as iconic as Mao's portrait at Tiananmen Square, and the first Bashful Goose jingle, a catchy ditty composed by Papa Hui himself, became the anthem of a generation with money to burn. Factories were erected to meet the surging demand and trucks were dispatched and the snacks were soon available in all corners of our great nation, from the ports of Shanghai to the grasslands of Inner Mongolia to the mountains of Tibet.

In the late 1990s, Witchy Wu sold her shares of the company to Papa Hui and retired with her many-decades-younger boyfriend, a former Australian soap opera actor, to Canada, where the happy couple still resides today.

Thanks to that fateful encounter with that bashful goose, Papa Hui is now the richest man in China. And to this day, the goose who led him to his fortune continues to follow him everywhere he goes...

ENOUGH ABOUT THAT DAMN GOOSE!

WHAT CUTESY, QUAINT LORE, BUT THAT WASN'T THE GOOSE KELLY knew. In the backseat and now just mere kilometers from headquarters, hyperventilation seized her.

This "bashful" goose had brazenly tormented her throughout her childhood—pecking at her armpits, biting the backs of her knees, yanking out her hair, shitting in her bed, tearing her homework to shreds, and cleverly framing her for a variety of devious acts (including but not limited to: smashing a precious Ming dynasty antique vase and clogging the toilet with the jagged pieces, eating four tins of expensive caviar that had been given to Papa Hui by Boris Yeltsin, leaking information to the press about possible insider trading committed by some of Papa Hui's New York friends, scratching Dr. Dre lyrics into the paint of Mama Hui's Lamborghini, and purchasing marijuana from a Nigerian drug dealer [how the goose pulled that one off, she still wasn't sure]).

Trying to explain to her parents that none of this was actually her doing had proved an impossible task. Any time she even so much as hinted that the goose might not be a perfect angel, Papa Hui burned red in the face and shouted about what a spoiled girl she was, and how things were different when he was growing up, and how they wouldn't have any of this—not the cars, not the apartments, not the vacations, not the hired help, not the electronics, not any of it—if it weren't for that goose, and *"Don't you dare blame the goose!"*

Frankly, Kelly had been relieved when, following the marijuana incident, her fed-up father made the decision to send her to Los Angeles for high school. She lived there in a big, empty house in Culver City with a nanny who spent most of her time either on the phone yapping in a baby voice with her boyfriend back in China or working to improve her English by watching endless episodes of *Law and Order*; attended a snooty school for rich troubled girls who found her dull and called her "Slanty-Eyes McGee" and "Sucky-Sucky Blow Job Five Dollar," among other charming names; slouched on city buses beside men who reeked of urine and women who muttered incoherently to themselves—and these were the moments that comprised the best years of her life. This was her era of safety, of stability, of freedom, and then when she went on to USC and ditched the nanny and moved into an off-campus condo, she felt even freer still.

Why she'd chosen to leave that paradise of palm trees and traffic jams, and why she thought there would be anything here in China for her, she still didn't fully understand, but she inhaled deeply, got out of the car, and began the long but pleasant enough journey through the headquarters grounds, passing fountains, multiple goldfish ponds, a bamboo forest, and then, at the front of the building, a gigantic gold-coated statue of enemy number one.

From behind the mahogany desk he'd had custom crafted in Sweden, Papa Hui greeted his daughter with a terse, "In a moment." Kelly shut the door and stepped inside. The old man was hard at work on a Sudoku puzzle haphazardly torn from a newspaper—a sizable corner of the puzzle was missing, rendering the thing unsolvable. Kelly shook her head. Why on earth did he not just buy a book of them? Or get an iPad and download an app? Or at least hire someone with better ripping skills, or perhaps, you know, just employ a pair of scissors to properly remove the puzzle in its entirety?

Principle, that's why. Here was a man whose net worth was in the billions, but who often humble-bragged to the media about spending less than one hundred renminbi a day. Fifteen bucks. Yeah, sure. She always shook her head when she skimmed such articles—such a limited budget was easy to adhere to for someone whose meals were provided for him at the office by the country's top chef, and who had a driver so therefore never had to pay cab fare, and who had already purchased everything he could possibly need, and—

Kelly jumped involuntary, her legs jelly. A familiar honking sound snipped its way into her thoughts. The goose waddled up from behind her and nipped at her calf. She swatted its beak away, shouted, "Off!" The goose ducked and lunged for her fingers. She threw her hands up in surrender, took a few careful steps back, and lowered herself to sit on a chair, the goose standing its ground, watching her with unblinking eyes.

In all this commotion, her father, still concentrating on that unsolvable puzzle, never once looked up.

HAIR EXTENSION APPOINTMENT—KELLY HUI—THREE P.M.

"So yeah, my dad agreed to give the money. And I think this is going to catapult me to fame. It could, I mean." Kelly studied the way her face moved in the salon mirror as she spoke. Her eyes appeared dead and dull as she delivered this information, very unlike those glitzy girls on TV— so she wasn't quite ready for her close-up. Oh, well. She would get there. There was always something new to work on, a million yet-untraveled roads to self-improvement.

Stefan smiled and nodded.

Kelly continued: "Imagine, I could host a weight-loss TV show. Help children shape up in front of a live studio audience. You could come to the studio and do my hair. Maybe the network would hire you on full-time as, like, a staff stylist. I don't know. Maybe your job now is better. I'm just throwing out ideas."

Stefan smiled, snapped a cape around her neck, and pumped up her chair—a comforting routine. Her once-thick mane had never fully recovered from a goose-related "accident" many years before, and instead of struggling through life a victim of partial baldness, she relied on Stefan, who in his docility had also become a close friend and confidant, to add both length and volume with top-notch extensions. These babies today were from the Lulu batch—much coveted and cut from the head of the girl with the loveliest locks in all of China. As the old saying goes, a woman's power resides in her hair. And if you can't make your own power, make do. Yes, Kelly was soon to be set. The best of the best.

"And all of those losers I grew up with, they're going to be so sorry. I mean, what are they doing now? Crashing their Ferraris into overpasses? Snorting horse tranquilizers? Dancing the night away in the same clubs they've been dancing all their nights away in since high school? Oh, and that Jenny Tao—her dad is the CEO of Happy Mart— all she's doing is directing dumb art films that her parents fund and no one goes to see. I heard her dad tried to pay Spielberg to meet with her to give her career advice, but Spielberg refused, even though he was going to pay him, like, ten million dollars just to have coffee with her."

Stefan raised an eyebrow, lifted the corners of his mouth, and then ran his fingers through her hair. "So, let's get these old ones out first, and then we'll see what we have to work with." His whispery voice tickled her ear canals. She nodded in response, shut her oversharing trap and her eyes, and let him begin his work in peace.

A pair of tiny scissors slicing through elastic string. Fingers untwisting, tugging. An MGMT song from her hooked-up iPod played softly on the speakers. Stefan's was a totally private salon, owned by China's number one hair extension company and catering to those who sought and/or required total privacy: film stars, pop stars, national icons. She belonged here. The best of the best.

She relaxed. Relaxed, relaxed, relaxed.

Until that meditation track began to echo through the blankness of her mind—*breathe in, breathe out*—and then a goose honking in rhythm in the background, and anxiety shot up from her finger-tips and from her toes, and she opened her eyes and grabbed for the distraction of her iPhone to run a few research-related searches. Childhood obesity. Risk factors. Basics of nutrition. Fitness for beginners. She read and read, scrolled and scrolled, and she wouldn't let herself stop reading and scrolling until a phone call came through. She picked up, and the person on the other end answered before she could say a word. "Hello? Is this Kelly Hui?"

"It is."

"This is Government Official Fang. Were you able to meet with your father?"

"Yes," she said, looking at herself in the mirror. Her old extensions were all out. Stefan was examining her natural roots. "And I think we have a deal."

The official inhaled sharply, excitedly.

"On one simple condition," she added.

The official cleared his throat. "What's that?"

"I want a hands-on role in running the camp."

Silence.

"Hello?"

"While we appreciate your generous financial contribution, Ms. Hui, the actual administration of the camp is a very gritty and diffi-cult job, and one that I'm not sure somebody like you would actually be interested in."

Stefan met her eyes in the mirror.

"What does that even mean?" Kelly rolled her eyes, making her best are-you-kidding-me? face for Stefan's benefit. He winked back at her, cheerfully humming softly along to the one guilty-pleasure Lady Gaga song she'd loaded on her iPod. Fucking shuffle. "Somebody like me?"

The official cleared his throat. "My meaning is that you seem like a very busy and very classy woman. Based on our research and the experience of some of my colleagues, fat camps can be very ugly, very stressful places." Perhaps sensing skepticism in her silence, he added, "Let me put it this way. Have you ever had a two-hundred-pound child bite your ankle because you wouldn't allow him an extra ration of dressing with his lettuce?"

"No," Kelly said. "But one of my classmates in Los Angeles had her arm licked by a crazy guy on the subway and—"

"Well," the official interrupted, as though he hadn't even heard her, "this very thing happened to a man my colleagues met in their research. Let's call him Mr. Li. This Mr. Li served as a first-time fat camp administrator at a private camp in Shanghai—he was hired with experience as a hospital dietitian. On only the fifth day of the camp, when Mr. Li refused to allow one of the children to add extra salt to his boiled vegetables—"

It was Kelly's turn to interrupt: "I thought you said it was dressing on lettuce."

"Look, what it was is irrelevant. The point is the child became bel-ligerent, falling to the floor, kicking, screaming, carrying on, before savagely sinking his teeth into Mr. Li's ankle. The child's jaw had such a hold on him that it took four counselors to unhinge it. Mr. Li was then rushed to the hospital where he had to undergo rabies vaccination, which, as you may know, is a series of shots that takes two weeks to complete. And he still has the incisor marks on his ankle, and, ahh, don't even get me started on how much the hospital bills came to—"

"Oh," Kelly grunted, adjusting her posture in the mirror. She eyed Stefan's extension handiwork, which was coming along quite beautifully if she did say so herself. "Well, rest assured that if I am savagely bitten by a rabid little rascal, I can certainly cover my own medical expenses. As you may be aware, in addition to being 'busy' and 'classy,' I am also very 'wealthy.'"

"Indeed," the official said flatly. He audibly yawned. Kelly thought she could make out the sounds of an action movie playing in the background. Was he speaking to her from a cinema? No wonder they didn't care what their offices looked like—they didn't actually work there. Or anywhere.

Kelly sighed. Her scalp was uncomfortable. Her ear was getting sweaty. "So, how about we arrange for transfer of funds and then you send me all the details about date and location and so forth."

"Ms. Hui, look, what I'm trying to tell you is—"

"No address, no money." Kelly hung up to the muffled boom of an explosion.

KINDHEARTED BOY LOOKING FOR NICE GIRL! ENJOYS SURFING THE WEB. CHATTING WITH FRIENDS. AND COLLECTING SEASHELLS...

A COUPLE WEEKS LATER, ACROSS TOWN, ZHAO, THE TWENTY-NINE-year-old son of a cleaning woman and a late construction worker, sat at his bedroom desk, opened a web browser, and entered the address of the dating website he frequented. He'd not yet sent any messages to any girls, but he felt confident that he might soon work up the courage, or cowardice—whichever it may be—to do so. He browsed a few profiles, all pretty and therefore all out of his league, and then stood up and smoothed out his shirt. Oh, well. It wasn't the day for finding a girlfriend anyway. Today was the day of his big interview.

He'd been matched to the position by an online agency he'd registered with out of desperation a few weeks before. Sure, it was paying for a job (the agency guaranteed placement within three months), but wasn't it true that everyone had to pay for his job in one way or another? Money was at least a clean way of doing so—this method didn't involve unethical acts or shady dealings, just a simple online escrow payment.

And anyway, he needed this: two months before, he'd walked out on his job as an assistant at a fitness equipment sales company. He was far too old to still be a mere assistant—all the other assistants were girls fresh out of college. He'd been promised promotion eight years before when he was hired; however, he was overlooked time and time again. He was a good worker, efficient if not sharp, and therefore attributed his lack of upward mobility primarily to his appearance—deep acne scars pocked his face, his front teeth were turned in at an odd angle, and no matter how hard he washed he always gave off the impression of being deeply unclean. Regardless, it was humiliating being left behind, and on a day like any other, a Tuesday, the absurdity of it all hit him. Very suddenly and for no instigating reason, he snapped. He walked into his boss's office and issued a firm "I quit." That was all he said. His boss, young and handsome and therefore valued by the world, didn't ask why or any other questions. He offered a pleasant, "Okay," and that was that.

On that Tuesday like any other, Zhao gathered his belongings from his desk, shoved them inside his bag, and left without saying good-bye to anyone, not even the mousy accountant whom he'd had a crush on for over a year and who earned three times his salary. He spent the subsequent weeks "sorting things out." He locked himself in his room for days at a time, reading the news on the Internet and following with interest a great number of microbloggers who spewed on the topics of politics, social issues, and cute animals. He became deeply engaged in a few TV series set in various dynasties. He bought a potted plant and tended to it daily. He quit smoking. He got back in touch with his mother, whom he had begun officially totally ignoring a couple years before because she nagged him to an annoying degree about why he hadn't bought an apartment, why he hadn't found a wife, why he wasn't a top-level executive, and so on. He called her up (not at all surprised that she had the same phone number all these years later—she never let things go) and told her he'd quit his job, and that he was still renting that crappy room in that crappy shared apartment, and that the future still looked uncertain, and that the only women he'd ever slept with were prostitutes or otherwise irreversibly ugly and/or deformed. Oddly enough, his mother hadn't seemed to mind all of these highly inappropriate confessions. In fact, she only grunted in response, told him to take care of himself, hung up, and then picked up their relationship right where it had left off—sending snapshots of eligible bachelorettes in the post, calling to gossip about the nouveau riche whose houses she cleaned, e-mailing links to travel agency websites (she'd developed a fondness for spaghetti and dreamed of being sent on a senior citizens tour to Italy), and so forth. Three weeks after he'd first called, she even made a trek into the city to stay with him a weekend. She scrubbed and reorganized his room, cooked hearty meals for him and the surprisingly friendly flatmates he'd never really spoken to before, and told him, albeit in a vague way, that she was proud that he was her son and happy to have him back in her lonely life.

And then she was gone again. His plant grew. His TV series turned to reruns. This two-month period of his life had been nice, had been necessary, but he knew it couldn't last forever.

Dressed in his crispest button-down shirt, a Playboy bunny belt buckle, and navy-blue slacks, Zhao lumbered down the dusty stairwell to the street, planted himself on the sidewalk, and flagged down a taxi. He arrived at his destination twenty minutes early, paid the driver, and got out. He paced before the bleak white structure, Communist-era architecture at its finest.

So there was the job, this tangible possibility here before him, but there was also the feeling of wanting to be somebody, a sense of this being a last chance, and there was the weight of guilt at the pit of his stomach and the desperation of wanting to be rid of this weight, unburdened. To be employed at all wasn't ideal; employment meant setting an alarm and getting properly dressed every morning and spending less time surfing the Internet, and it meant letting go of all the tiny freedoms that he had so recently fallen in love with. But he could waste his whole life away floating in ideals, freedoms. He could wake up a ninety-year-old man, unmarried and unaccomplished—with nothing to show for himself and no one there to love him—and say, "Well, at least I stayed true to my ideals." But where was the freedom in that?

The very next week, the government officials who would be overseeing his position invited Zhao to a restaurant to make their formal employment offer. His eyes skimmed the contents of the contract. *Hereby referred to as the employee. Can do. Can do. If this contract is broken, a penalty of 100,000 yuan will be assessed. Boring. Boring. Over the course of the summer, the employee must rehabilitate a minimum of two fat kids.*

He glanced up from the printed pages and into the stale eyes of the government officials sitting around the white-clothed table. The waitress, a dark-skinned country girl with shapely legs, brought a plate of salted duck's feet and set it before the men.

"If my wife would allow it," one of the officials said, eyeballing the waitress, "I would take that one home and keep her." The men laughed collectively. The waitress blushed and scurried away. Another of the officials, an older fellow with crinkly skin and beady black eyes, poured Zhao's cup full of rice wine. Zhao nodded, acknowledging this act, and then felt his phone vibrate against his leg. He slipped it out under the table as the old man filled the others' cups. His mother. He rejected her call and shoved the phone back into his pocket.

The waitress brought another dish, fried peanuts. "Zhao here could take her home. No old lady to worry about, is there?" The first official socked Zhao in the arm. There was laughter, and there was a glint of envy in each of the laughing officials' eyes. Zhao did not notice this glint. He only heard the laughter and then felt, again, a vibration on his leg. He slid his phone from his pocket. A text message from his mother. It read, "How about her?" Embedded within the text message was a blurry photo of yet another anonymous woman's face, probably snapped at the supermarket or the Grand Ocean department store or in line for a five-*mao* public restroom. A wave of regret washed over him; he was sorry he'd ever taught his mother how to use her phone's camera function.

"Now, you do understand, Zhao, that if you fulfill the terms of the contract, there is an opportunity to move up the ranks. It's not usual, to skip the test, but these are special circumstances and this is a club, you see, and in a club, members make the rules, but we can also break them."

Zhao nodded. A set-for-life cushy government job? No Party exam necessary? Yes, please.

Satisfied with his mute response, the officials returned to their chatter. Zhao excused himself. He strolled into the bathroom, pissed, rinsed his hands in the sink, and studied himself in the mirror. His perfectly round face housed eyes so deeply set that they verged on sunken in. He stroked his cratered, stubble-less chin with his hands—he couldn't grow a beard, but his toes were coated in hair. He took a step back and eyed his figure—not exactly an ideal shape: extraordinarily slim in the limbs, sure, but playing nurse to an ever-growing gut akin to that of a pregnant woman.

But oh, well, and never mind.

Zhao inhaled and mouthed, "You deserve this," into the mirror. He puffed his chest and sauntered out, passing the waitress. She leaned against the wall outside the private banquet room in limbo between the kitchen and the officials' table. Zhao studied her: thin arms that jangled from her body like those of a marionette, slight overbite that forced her lips into a perpetual pout, shiny black hair slicked into a bun, skin the sandy color of unfinished plywood. He thought, Me and this waitress, we could be good together. He briefly entertained snapping a quick picture of her with his phone and sending it to his mother with a text that read, "Her."

He didn't. He sat down. The men chattered on. He stared, still, at the waitress.

"Zhao, what do you think?"

The chatter stopped. The air was thick, silent. The officials, each one a door to a new life, sat before him, sat around him, awaiting his answer.

A voice from the kitchen shouted in a countryside dialect, and the waitress disappeared.

Zhao cleared his throat. "Yes," he said, and he felt freedom flee his body. He said, "Yes. We have a deal." He felt his phone vibrate again. She was relentless. He slipped it out and rejected the call. The waitress returned with two dishes—real dishes, not appetizers or snacks, but wonderful, steamy, spicy Hunan food. The crinkly official, the one who'd poured the wine, removed a pen from his shirt pocket and placed it in Zhao's hand. Zhao signed the contract and stuffed himself full. And he drank. And they drank. And they drank and they drank.

2.

THEM FAT KIDS AIN'T HERE

Fᴀᴛ Pᴇᴏᴘʟᴇ Fᴀᴛ Cᴀᴍᴘ ᴄᴏɴᴠᴇɴᴇᴅ ɪɴ Jᴜɴᴇ ᴡɪᴛʜ ᴀ ʜᴜɴᴅʀᴇᴅ ᴏᴠᴇʀ-weight campers from every corner of Jiangsu Province, all in dire need of direction and rehabilitation. The camp was held on the Wuxi High School for Exceptional Students campus. Five amphetamine-swallowing counselors and one cook served as Zhao's staff.

Zhao floated through days one and two of camp like a tycoon in a dream. The campers exercised. The counselors encouraged. The cook steamed vegetables. But Zhao was born under an inauspicious moon. The first days passed easily—too easily—and he felt an acidic burn in his gut, and he knew that his luck would not last.

Day one of Fat People Fat Camp, and Kelly, wearing her new Lululemon yoga pants and slurping down a healthy breakfast smoothie, bounded out to the waiting Audi. She'd packed an over-night bag with a few changes of clothes in case she needed to stay on the campus. She tossed it into the backseat and climbed in. Thirty minutes of stop-and-go traffic later, her driver located the outskirts-of-town address the officials had given her: not a bustling camp, but an open field.

A few spins around the adjacent dusty roads later, Kelly realized she'd been had. She dialed the official, who apologized profusely and insincerely, and who, over an odd ringing sound (which reminded Kelly an awful lot of slot machines she'd unprofitably played in Vegas all alone on her twenty-first birthday), gave her the "new" address, which of course also turned out to be a sham—another empty field. This wild-goose chase continued for two days, leading Kelly and her driver on a thorough and exhaustive tour of Wuxi and its surrounding areas, until, over the squeals of either an aroused woman or an ailing pig, the annoyed official gave Kelly the address of what turned out to be a chicken farm.

The chicken farmer, a crinkly old man with rascally eyes, informed Kelly that two days before a busload of fat kids had indeed turned up at his farm, but that they were then promptly bused to another top secret location. If any of their parents knew where the children were, he painstakingly explained, they'd inevitably send care packages full of contraband or perhaps even attempt to tunnel under the ground using Democratic People's Republic of Korea–patented techniques to deliver to their children the snacks they so craved, and such parental meddling could completely derail all weight-loss efforts.

The farmer then proudly announced he had been given fifty yuan by a government official for use of his land and address as a "confusion point." Kelly, reading between the lines, stuffed a red hundred in the farmer's hand. The farmer promptly pulled from his pants pocket a thin stack of folded and sweaty photocopied papers, including the administrator's résumé and a document that listed another address (Wuxi High School for Exceptional Students, a nonoperational school that famously lost its funding halfway through construction when its wealthy underwriter was killed in a paragliding accident in Hawaii [some suspected foul play] and his widow [a B-list Korean actress] refused to pay the bribes necessary to continue the school's construction).

With some useful information finally in hand, Kelly and her driver sped off, leaving the farmer in a cloud of dust, happily clutching his hundred-yuan note. In the backseat with the air conditioner on full-blast, Kelly read and reread Zhao's résumé. This, she stewed, *this* was the man they'd deemed worthy to be in charge of this project?! A man with an associate's degree from some third-tier city's unaccredited no-name university? A man whose only real professional experience was working as a low-level assistant for years and years without any promotion in a crap fitness equipment company that she was pretty sure was a pyramid scheme? The small head shot that accompanied the résumé showed a man who verged on hideous: eyes too close together, cheeks too fleshy, mouth big and meaty, skin pocked—but maybe it was just a bad Xerox. Either way, she thought as she stole a look in the side view mirror at her own face (symmetrical enough to be a spokesmodel, if not beautiful enough to be a supermodel), this? This was the face of the war on obesity?

Her car slowed and soon stopped. Through the tinted and shut windows Kelly heard the unmistakable shouting and grunting of fat children. She thanked the driver and told him she'd call when she was ready to be picked up. She grabbed her bag and marched into the half-finished school, with its roofless hallways and exposed pipes, and located a small office—the only room with its door open—where the man who must have been Zhao sat playing solitaire on his computer.

"Excuse me," she said. She dropped her bag on the floor and placed her hands on her hips.

Zhao frantically clicked out of his game and spun around. He was as terrible looking in person as he was in his photo. Worse maybe. "Oh, hello," he said in a voice that could turn off Helen Keller. He looked Kelly up and down with lascivious eyes. "Not a camper then?"

Refusing to acknowledge this, she furrowed her brow. "My name is Kelly Hui, and I am a representative of the Bashful Goose Snack Company."

Zhao squinted at her, clearly taken aback by her authoritative tone. He stood up slowly, leaning his body away from her. "Um, okay. Is there something I can help you with?"

This was one question (and she'd played over many in her head in the past few days driving in and around Wuxi) that she didn't have an answer to. She hesitated awkwardly and then said, "No, I'm here to help you." She remembered one of the lines she'd rehearsed in her head. "Bashful Goose Snack Company believes that obesity is a most dire problem for China's youth. At this camp, we aren't just saving calories, we're saving lives."

Zhao screwed up his face. "Huh? Sorry, who are you exactly?"

"I'm Kelly Hui, head of corporate social responsibility at Bashful Goose Snack Company."

Zhao grimaced—or maybe that was just his unfortunate default facial expression—and shook his head.

She dropped her arms to her side. "The company that's sponsoring this camp?"

He shook his head again.

Hopeless, incredibly and undeniably hopeless this one was. "Never mind. I looked over your résumé, and your, shall we say, lacking qualifications speak to the need of some corporate management intervention. I'm here to help *you*."

Zhao squinted, squirmed, and then his eyes finally lit up in recognition. "The company that makes Watermelon Wigglers?" He shimmied his chest and burst into song, one of many of the company's commercial jingles. *Bashful Goose snacks, eat 'em right up / They're so delicious, they'll make you fall in love!*

Kelly nodded. Zhao snapped his fingers loudly—Kelly, startled, jumped back. "Yes," he said. "Ah, yes. Now, sorry, why'd you say they sent someone from Bashful Goose here?"

She inhaled deeply. "Bashful Goose put up the funds to sponsor this camp. We are the sole financial backer."

"Oh," Zhao snorted, and took on a sarcastic tone. "I understand."

"What's that supposed to mean?"

"I don't mean to suggest that I'm not doing well with what I've been given. You'd just think a big company like that would've been a bit more generous is all."

Kelly tried to hide her disgust. This, she thought, *this* is exactly why I hate this country. Give a little, give a lot, it doesn't matter; they want it all and then some. "If three million yuan isn't generous, isn't enough for you, I don't know what is, and—"

"Look," Zhao said, jamming his index finger knuckle-deep into his nostril. "I don't know what three million you're talking about. I'm working with a very small budget." He pointed at the same computer monitor he'd been playing games on only a moment before. He motioned for her to sit down at the desk and take a look for herself. Careful not to touch this booger picker's mouse or keyboard, she studied the spreadsheet he'd opened, the numbers contained therein. She pointed to the figure in the "total budget" column. "That's it?" she asked. A tremor started in her arms, making its way down to her fingertips. Her forehead popped with sweat. "That's your total budget?"

"And they said if I could do it for less, it'd be better."

"We gave three million," she said. "You were supposed to have three million. So where did that money go?"

They met each other's eyes. "The officials," they said simultaneously.

YEAH. YEAH. THAT'S FINE. THE MONEY'S ALL YOURS

KELLY THOUGHT BACK TO THAT DAY MANY WEEKS BEFORE WHEN SHE'D proposed her grand plan, when she'd marched into enemy territory and asked her father for the money. He hadn't, as she'd anticipated, questioned or doubted her. He'd just (eventually) pushed aside his doomed Sudoku puzzle and listened. Listened intently as she described the proposed facilities, the expert counselors with higher degrees from top universities, the vision she had to make China a healthier, fitter place one child at a time. Listened, cocked his head, and listened some more.

But the Papa Hui she knew was abrasive, crude, my-way-or-the-highway, dismissive of her, always irritated with her, burdened by her.

She thought he'd peered back at her that day with a sort of recognition, of pride. She foolishly thought he'd seen something in her eyes, some glimmer of hope that he recognized from his own days of aspiration, of youth.

Because without any fight at all, he'd agreed to hand over the money.

But Papa Hui was no idiot and was, despite the company's lore that profitably stated otherwise, hardly an idealist. He was the country's richest man and he knew, better than anyone, how China and the world worked. When he'd looked at his only daughter looking starry-eyed, he wasn't looking on with pride, but with pity. Please, he saw the future: government officials running riot through Macau's casinos, forking out for bottles of Johnnie Walker and elaborate fruit platters in ornate nightclubs, recklessly spending on iPhones and iPads and electronic wine bottle openers and exotic animal parts believed to increase sexual potency. And he saw her future too, which was obviously synonymous to him with her present and with her past: as a powerless little troublemaker who would never, ever be as good as a goose.

AND TAKE ME ON THE GRAND TOUR
AND SHOW ME ALL THE THINGS I LONG TO SEE

KELLY, SILENTLY RAGING AT HER FATHER AND FLOATING IN A STATE OF disbelief, ordered Zhao to lead her on a tour around campus. She stepped heavily, angrily, in her new Nikes. Everyone knew officials were corrupt, so why did she believe their pitch? How had she fallen for this? And why hadn't she realized that her old fuck of a father would go to any lengths, including spending three million yuan, to humiliate her?

There was supposed to be an Olympic-sized swimming pool, state-of-the-art fitness facilities, and world-class chefs. Instead, there was a sewage-like stench hanging in the dense air.

Kelly crinkled her nose. "Is there something wrong with the pipes?"

Zhao shook his head. "No, I think you're smelling lunch."

They lingered for a moment longer in the dining hall, a dimly lit room with low ceilings that may or may not have been pocked with black mold. "Onward," Zhao said, and led her to the kitchen, which Kelly noted was definitely the source of the stench and where the cook, not stopping to look up at them, diligently chopped vegetables.

Kelly watched, mesmerized by the rhythmic *chop, chop, chop* of the cleaver.

Zhao's voice cut into the beat. "Gym next?" She followed him across the courtyard to a small building, which housed the indoor fitness facilities—a sorry scene. On one side of the room stood a dusty treadmill, a torn vinyl bench, and a single barbell. On the other, an instructor bounced before a cracked floor-to-ceiling mirror, crying chipper instructions and encouragements. Tinny pop music blasted from a cell phone speaker, and a dozen or so fat kids, all with identification numbers worn around their necks, lazily swung light dumbbells about and stepped out of sync. The instructor waved at Zhao, dropping her own small dumbbell on her toe. She winced slightly, but then picked it up, forced a grin, and carried on.

This is war, Kelly decided, watching that pained smile relax into a more natural one. If she could rehabilitate these lazy-ass children, make them thin despite the stolen money, the corruption, the derelict surroundings and inadequate equipment, Papa Hui would be made a fool. He'd be sorry he ever doubted her, sorry he tried to humiliate her, sorry for everything. Not that his opinion would matter then anyway. Not when she proved herself a national hero, and one who didn't need fancy flourishes to make a difference. All she needed, and all she had, was little more than savvy, prowess, and a big heart.

As the kids continued to exercise and as Zhao muttered rude half-formed thoughts about cellulite under his breath, Kelly whipped out her iPhone and texted her driver not to worry about picking her up, that she'd definitely be staying the night. She slid it into her pocket and then ran her fingers through her silky extensions.

"Hey." Zhao nudged her arm. She instinctively recoiled. "There's a pool down there," he said, pointing to a stairwell in the corner. "But we can't use it because the construction workers who were building the school were using it as a toilet. Still sort of stinks."

Vomit crept up her gullet. She swallowed the acidic liquid down, took a few deep and burning breaths, and followed Zhao through the nutrition classroom (where a group of children sat uncomfortably at rickety desks chorally reciting lines from a Chinese translation of a Weight Watchers pamphlet), the activity room (where students crafted what Kelly first mistook for bracelets, but what upon further inspection turned out to be colorful ball gags), and the camper dormitories (where a few students lounged on cot-like bunk beds, snoring, biting their fingernails, and flipping through high-fashion magazines, among other approved leisure-time activities).

Finally, they stepped back outside, where a pack of children sat in a poorly formed circle on the basketball court, singing, *Oh, how bad to be thick, oh, how good to be thin! / Oh, eat a lot of food is for pigs, eat a little bit is for kids!* Their harmonious voices drifted high above the trees, and Kelly couldn't help but picture the people in the surrounding apartment blocks, the old aunties washing dishes and the teenagers studying for university entrance exams, pausing and craning their necks for a better listen.

Pride overtook heartburn and welled up inside her. What she was going to do could really make the busy nation stop and pay notice. Could make her father drop dead of a shock-induced heart attack. Could make everyone say, "Hey, this girl could really be someone! She's changing lives here! She can move mountains!" Oh, there would be articles in the airline magazines, interviews on all the top websites, TV specials profiling formerly fat children whose lives the one and only Ms. Kelly Hui helped rebuild from flabby rubble, best of the best...

A deep voice spitting, "Hey, fatty!" ripped Kelly from her daydreams. At once, the children stopped singing. Zhao glared down at a chipmunk-cheeked, blank-faced girl. He lightly kicked her in the back, and she spun around to look up at him with wounded eyes. Zhao knelt down beside her, his hideous face centimeters away from hers. She crinkled her nose and shrunk from Zhao's rotting breath. "Why weren't you singing with the rest of them?" he spat.

The girl didn't speak. She blinked. Tears welled up in her eyes.

"Sing!" he shouted in her face. A solitary tear rolled down her crab apple cheek, but she didn't open her mouth, just stared back at him. He calmly stood up, clapped his hands against his thighs. "Now get back to it!" he called to the lot of them, and then blew the whistle he wore around his neck.

On cue, the children resumed their song, but it sounded different now, its joyful spirit sapped. Anger welled up inside Kelly again, temporarily replacing her pride and ambition, and she fiercely shook her head—not only was this blockhead inexperienced and unrefined, but he was also a bully, and in her mind, there was little worse. Her nostrils flared and she took an aggressive step toward that ugly Zhao, who had begun slogging back toward the office. She advanced quickly up from behind him, jabbed him hard in the kidney with her pointer finger, and lowered her voice so that the children wouldn't hear. "That's a human being you were talking to back there."

Zhao spun around, all bulging eyes and outrage, all puffed-up chest. "Yes? And?"

Carbohydrates are for energy! Protein is for muscle! / If you eat too many of any, you better start to hustle! To burn! TO BURN! TO BU-BU-BU-BU-BURN!

"It's pretty inappropriate to speak to anyone, and especially a child, like that." Her voice came out louder, meaner than she intended. Despite her intention to keep this confrontation subtle, under wraps, the children took notice and cut short their song. Oh, well, she thought, let them hear. This was for their own good. Who knew what damage he'd done already? Who knew what horrible words he'd spat at these delicate souls? Who knew how much weight loss had already been hindered thanks to this bully of a man-child?

A dozen sets of eyes darted between the pockmarked administrator and the moon-faced heiress.

"What, are you sent from the public manners bureau?" Zhao spat. He made no effort to keep his voice down. "And anyway, those 'human beings' are here to lose weight. I'm only trying to encourage 'thin behavior.' That is my job."

"You wouldn't have a job if it weren't for me." Kelly narrowed her eyes. "And whether you like it or not, I'm in charge here now, I'm your boss, and—"

But she never finished her sentence. A bell's shrill ring sliced through the thick afternoon air, and the voices of all the campers formed into a collective bellow: *"Luuuuuuuuunch!"*

"Take cover!" Zhao shouted, and yanked Kelly across the courtyard and into the nutrition classroom's doorframe. The ground trembled and then full-on quaked as a hundred pairs of thick legs raced down the stairs, bolted across the courtyard, and streaked toward the cafeteria. Kelly squeezed her eyes shut and jammed her fingers into her ears. An iPad-sized chunk of plaster shook loose from the corner of the ceiling. Zhao shielded Kelly's head with his arms. The plaster shattered against the floor, narrowly missing them both.

A moment later, the rumbling stopped. The air fell still. Kelly opened her eyes and removed her fingers from her ears. Peace and silence had been restored.

"Shall we?" Zhao asked.

Realizing she'd been holding her breath, she exhaled deeply. Her stomach rumbled; all she'd had for breakfast was a small bowl of muesli. But despite her empty stomach, her soul swelled with satisfaction—she'd stood up to Zhao, put him in his place, established herself as the alpha wolf. With numbskulls like him, a few harsh words were usually all it took.

"We shall," she said. She walked with rapid, determined, triumphant steps toward the cafeteria.

LEADERSHIP IN SEVENTEEN EASY STEPS: LEARN TO MANAGE OTHERS BY MANAGING YOURSELF

LEADERSHIP IS THE CORNERSTONE OF EFFECTIVE MANAGEMENT... SO IT went, and so went a line in one of the many self-help e-books Kelly downloaded during her era of freedom and stability. She arrived at age fourteen in Los Angeles, no friends, no social life, nothing but incredibly fast Internet. She sat inside, air-conditioning blowing and blinds shut, as the sun rose, sweltered, and set outside. She ate granola bars, drank massive quantities of Mountain Dew, logged on to chat rooms, logged out of chat rooms, obsessively read fan fiction, obsessively wrote rude comments about aforementioned fan fiction, turned the computer off and watched endless episodes of *Blind Date* on TV, turned the computer back on and sparked short-lived affairs with shooter RPGs, Napster, strangers' LiveJournals, fetish porn, and The Sims. Finally, she landed on the wide world of web-based self- and professional-improvement. Finally, she was home.

Upon completing the exercises and self-inventories in a number of e-books, Kelly concluded that it was not simply "bad luck" or "fate," but her own failure to establish herself as a dominant player in her myriad relationships (father-daughter, mother-daughter, goose-human, et cetera) that had placed her in her current predicament. Shut in her new bedroom, hunched over her Toshiba desktop computer, she also learned that it was never, ever too late to change. Armed for the first time with any semblance of self-awareness and with techniques to help quell her anxiety, Kelly decided to undertake an experimental project to henceforth establish herself as the alpha wolf in all of her American relationships.

August melted into September, and after weeks of careful plotting and strategizing, she set forth with her leadership crusade, first taking on the Los Angeles Academy for Wealthy Young Ladies. Although her tactics for exuding dominance (including: hacking teachers' blogs and other online accounts to post and send sexually provocative information, photographing classmates through the cracks in the bathroom stalls for blackmail purposes, and periodically setting pet-store-purchased gerbils loose in the locker room) didn't win her any friends, the other girls (who, during the course of their high school careers, were so incredibly vicious as to drop a bucket of red paint on one leather-jacket-wearing classmate's head in a politically correct reenactment of *Carrie*, to somehow change one classmate's submitted Yale essay to read only "I has special needs thanks you to read this," and to purposefully run a Mercedes SUV over another classmate's foot in an In-N-Out Burger parking lot) left her be save for a few unfortunate albeit unoriginal Asian-stereotype-derived nicknames. Kelly, no stranger to bodily harm and sabotage thanks to the goose, was relieved not to suffer through such physically violent incidences here. A few stupid words she could deal with.

With her status securely locked in at school, Kelly soon spread her wings, pursuing in the "real world" other minor conquests, which most notably included intimidating Prada and Coach store employees into giving her unheard-of discounts, intimidating bouncers into allowing her access into twenty-one and older nightclubs, and intimidating a chiseled Tommy Hilfiger model into giving her his cell phone number and that of his coke dealer.

But the home front was where Kelly waged the real war.

Papa Hui had hired a nanny to accompany Kelly to America and to serve as her live-in guardian. This "nanny," a twenty-four-year-old peasant named Aunty Minnie, had no actual training in education or child care. She was the daughter of one of Papa Hui's drivers, and the old man told her to take the job or lose her father's. But it wasn't all blackmail. There was also a hefty salary, an extended stay in the United States, and the prospect of landing a Hollywood husband who would finance the breast implants she so desperately wanted/needed—this sugar daddy dream existing despite a bespectacled boyfriend who worked as a computer repairman back in Shanghai.

Kelly, unwilling to follow orders from such a sorry character, systematically executed a number of carefully planned tactics, including but not limited to: forwarding flirtatious e-mails (both real and fabricated) to and from other men to Aunty Minnie's boyfriend in China, planting duck hearts procured in Chinatown in Aunty Minnie's "delicates" drawer, paying a foster kid she met at the public library to rob Aunty Minnie at knifepoint in the front yard, emptying a bottle of vinegar into Aunty Minnie's blueberry juice jug, and threatening to report Aunty Minnie to the authorities for not having her "papers in order," the punishment for which, Kelly informed her, was indefinite detainment at Guantánamo Bay, where phone calls were not permitted and where immigration offenders were forced to help the authorities torture terrorists (Kelly remained proud of herself for spinning this particularly convincing tale).

Within a matter of well-played weeks, Kelly earned free run of the house—if she craved dumplings exactly like Grandma used to make, Aunty Minnie would dress up just like Grandma—gray wig, dentures, and all—and make them. If Kelly needed someone to complete her homework for her so that she could play Dance Dance Revolution at the mall arcade for hours, Aunty Minnie would circle multiple-choice answers until the sun came up. If Kelly needed an advance on her allowance, or someone to arrange the purchase of Adderall, or most frequently of all someone to just leave her the hell alone and get out of her damn way, Aunty Minnie was her girl. And if Kelly, on her eighteenth birthday, needed someone to leave America, return to China, marry a wiry computer repairman-boy with thick glasses, and never speak of her trying time in America or of the spoiled sociopath who robbed her of her chances of riches and foreign citizenship and of the desire to ever bear children of her own, well...

WHERE'D THEY GET THIS COOK? A PRISON?

KELLY AND ZHAO REACHED THE FRONT OF THE LINE, WHERE THE COOK plopped a ladleful of steamed vegetables and a second ladleful of some unidentifiable gelatinous material onto their plates.

"Yum," said Kelly. Facetiously, of course. Zhao grunted.

There wasn't enough space around the few shoddy tables to seat all the campers, so many stood, shoveling food into their faces. Others squatted. Still others plopped themselves down on the tile. Kelly and Zhao maneuvered their way through this multilevel maze of flesh and fat and took a seat at the counselors' table in the corner. Kelly introduced herself to those seated as "Kelly Hui, Bashful Goose Snack Company. I'm here to help you with whatever you need. We're a team here. We must work together," before launching into the same short speech she'd given Zhao about saving not only calories, but lives.

The counselors nodded, smiled—no teeth, all pursed lips—fidgeted, picked at their food.

Kelly pushed her own food-like substances around her plate with her chopsticks. The blob left a slime trail. *A successful leader speaks from the heart, makes him- or herself relatable to others.* "Where'd they get this cook?" she said to the table, trying to lighten the mood. "A prison?"

Everyone around the table, with the exception of Zhao, emitted robotic laughter.

Kelly, failing to notice their insincerity, grinned. "And if so, then I'm going to hope for the death penalty!"

Zhao picked up a piece of his gelatinous blob with his chopsticks, held it up, studied it intently. "Delicious food is what got these kids here in the first place."

Kelly dropped her chopsticks and returned her hands to her lap, balled into fists. Yes, her jokes were incongruous, but they were nonetheless chuckle-worthy, hardly deserving of such a stark response. Hey, hey, the nimrod was back for round two; not going down without a fight. Well, she'd give it to him. "Yeah, well, starvation isn't the way to go about it," she snapped. "Their metabolisms will shut down. It's better that we teach them healthy eating habits and to eat sensible portions of nutritious foods." She looked to the others for backup. They all chewed their lips, played with their food, peered down at their trays.

Zhao placed his chopsticks beside his tray. "I didn't realize you were a medical doctor." He picked at a whitehead on his jawline.

"No, but I have the Internet and something called common sense. Have you heard of either?"

A half-dozen set of eyes darted between the thick-maned heiress and the balding administrator.

Zhao dabbed his ooze-gushing zit with the side of his hand. He picked up his chopsticks, used them to maneuver the gelatinous blob into his mouth. "Extreme obesity calls for extreme solutions."

"Oh, so you have heard of the Internet. Fantastic. And you've read the back of a Miss Mian's Laxative Tea box. Correct me if I'm wrong, but I do believe that's their official slogan. *Extreme obesity calls for—*" Zhao's cheeks flushed red. Flustered. She was getting to him.

"Yeah, well, I made some of my own slogans too: fat kids grow into fat adults, so let's cut down the weeds before they spoil the garden." As he spoke, she caught glimpses of that nasty blob resting on his white-fuzz-coated tongue like a tumor, like some rare disease. "And then—"

Another bell rang, thankfully cutting short his foray into *Mad Men* territory. Prepared now for the worst, Kelly instinctively covered her head and ducked under the table. But this time there was no earthquake. The ground was still. The others remained unfazed. She waited a moment—safety first!—before she crawled out and retook her seat. Campers lazily stood and lumbered toward the doors, some lingering only to steal a few last licks from their trays. The counselors returned their own trays to the kitchen and left without a word.

Peace and quiet. Absence. Her stomach growled. Kelly poked her own gelatinous blob with her chopsticks. She'd dealt with Zhao, his insubordinate attitude, satisfactorily. Now she needed another form of gratification. She lowered her voice and leaned toward him. "Hey, so you must have some real food in your office, right?"

Zhao nodded. His cheeks had taken on a greenish hue. Kelly realized that he still hadn't brought himself to swallow the blob and couldn't spit it out now in front of the cook, who was intently pushing in chairs the campers had left askew. Zhao stood, wobbly on his feet. "Let's go," he murmured, his words slightly garbled. "It's growing in my mouth."

Kelly followed Zhao to his office, where he shut the door and spat the blob into the wastepaper basket. He sputtered, hunched over the basket, strings of blob-infused drool falling from his mouth before finally wiping his face on his sleeve and composing himself. He marched over to his desk and unlocked one of its drawers, revealing an impressive stash of cookies, chocolate bars, and potato chips.

"Is this stuff you've confiscated from campers?"

"Contraband, yeah. Some of it," Zhao said. He tore open a bag of Lays. "Some I bought myself."

Get to know your people. The best managers become actively involved with what their people are trying to accomplish.

Kelly narrowed her eyes. "Can I ask you something?"

Zhao set the open bag of Lays down on his desktop. He sat. He shrugged.

"Why are you here? Was your old man owed a favor by someone in the government or something?" A mocking tone seeped into her voice—she didn't want to be this, she was losing control, she was better than this. "Was your dad one of those guys who refused to let the government tear down his shit-hole of a house to build a shopping mall, claiming unjust compensation and to 'stand for something' until the government upped the price a bit and offered his son a job in return? Or was he—"

Zhao stopped her, saying softly, "My father is dead."

Kelly tossed her hair over her shoulder. She tried her best to appear unfazed. "Yeah, okay, whatever. So I'm just so rude now, aren't I? You probably think, Oh, why is she criticizing me when she's not qualified either. Well, I am qualified. I have a business degree from America and I am the head of—"

"Corporate social responsibility at Bashful Goose Snack Company," Zhao finished her sentence.

She crossed her arms, puffed out her cheeks, and stared down at him. He leaned back in his chair. Sighed. Leaned forward again. Tapped his fingers on the desk's edge. "Look, I know what you're thinking. I'm hardly qualified for a position at McDonald's, much less here. I'm a loser. I'm hideous."

She uncrossed her arms. She wasn't expecting him to come over to her side so easily.

"But if you must know, I got this job through an agency. I don't know why they hired me, okay? There looked to be several other attractive, more authoritative applicants waiting when I went in for the interview. Why they chose me and not them, I'll never know. But I'm glad they did. I'm glad to have a paycheck is all I mean. And, hell, a little prestige. But truthfully, I hate working. It's exhausting. I'd rather be watching TV or fucking around on the Internet. But no one gets paid for doing that, do they? That doesn't earn anyone any respect."

But of course people got paid to do that—how about that government official, living it up right this minute in Macau's ornate casinos; how about her father doing Sudoku puzzles at his gold-rimmed desk; how about the past two years of her own life?

"So," he continued, "I wasn't going to question their decision. Why would I? I accepted happily, gratefully. Not because I'm passionate about weight loss or because I thought I'd be the best person for this job or even because I think I know what I'm doing, but because I needed the money, and I also needed to get my mother off my back. That's it. That's all."

Kelly, noticing another swivel chair against the wall, wheeled it over to Zhao's desk, dusted it off, sneezed, and sat down. She leaned forward and rested her elbows on a stack of papers. "Look, I didn't mean to go off on you like that. I can be, well, I can be pretty ambitious sometimes, and I'm not really used to talking to people much anymore, and sometimes I say things I don't mean. Okay?"

"Oh. Is that supposed to be an apology?"

Kelly shrugged. A moment of silence. They both looked everywhere but at each other.

Finally she spoke. "I can understand what you mean about your mother. I think."

Zhao, probably relieved more by the silence ending than by Kelly finding him relatable on one very basic level (they both had parents!), said overeagerly, "Your mother is a nag too?"

Kelly shook her head. "No, my mom—she's fine. Well, actually she's terrible, but harmless. It's more my father. He's the head of Bashful Goose Snack Company. Papa Hui, you know. China's richest man. The nation's most beloved tycoon. Whatever."

Zhao nodded gingerly, muttered some indiscernible interjection, perhaps aware for the first time of what an important and wealthy person she was—perhaps in awe.

Kelly went on, again losing control of her mouth. "And he's not so much a nag as he is neglectful. He sent me away to the U.S. when I was only fourteen. At the time, I stupidly convinced myself that he'd made that decision so that I'd get the best possible education and then come back to China where he'd start training me to run the company. And of course I was more than happy to go to California, pay my dues in school, and also get away from—" The goose's beady, demonic eyes—eyes that glowed red in the dark. A tingle down her vertebrae. "Never mind. But yeah, after I came back, I realized he probably just sent me overseas to get me out of his hair. I wasn't cute anymore. I was all, like, chubby and zitty and fourteen. I wasn't useful. Anyway, so obviously I grew out of that—the physical awkwardness, I mean. Not the uselessness. Here I am with this stupid job title, running 'corporate social responsibility.' Do you want to have a guess at how many 'responsibilities' there have been in the past two years?"

Zhao made an I-don't-know face, which turned his ham lips out at an angle Kelly found truly revolting. She looked away.

"None," she spat. "Not a one. Corporations here don't give a shit about anything but money. Did you know that in America, almost all companies give money to charity? A lot of them even run their own charities."

Zhao furrowed his brow. "Isn't that just so they can evade taxes?"

Kelly, genuinely surprised that he possessed even this fleeting awareness of the outside world, sighed, resigned. "Yeah, well. At least it gives their CSR departments something to do." She cradled her head in her hands, her gaze traveling the chipped laminate desktop. "Sometimes I wish the old man would just die already." She jerked and abruptly looked up, straightened her spine. Her voice changed, deepened. "But you know I don't actually mean that. Please, as if. He hasn't formally left the company to anyone yet anyway—really pisses his lawyers off. I think he thinks he's immortal or something. Hell, maybe he is. He's healthy as a twenty-five-year-old, his doctors say. His cholesterol is lower than mine. And anyway, that's terrible, isn't it? Wishing my own father dead? To be honest, I'll probably die first, at least metaphorically, of embarrassment. He's been doing all these interviews lately with business magazines. And when I come up in the interviews, all he says is that he hopes I'll find a husband soon. Like my education, my charity work, my management philosophies don't mean a thing to him. All he wants is for me to find some man and to get married and to pop out a baby. I mean, what century is this? Should I ask my waxing girl at the salon if anyone there can bind feet?"

Zhao—half listening, staring out the window at a pecking bird, at fatties strolling past, at fatties also eyeing that pecking bird—nodded sympathetically.

She slapped the tops of her thighs. "Sorry to unload. All I'm really trying to say here is that I really care about these kids"—she gestured toward the window—"and I want this camp to be successful. I *need* it to be."

Zhao nodded again.

Kelly's voice strengthened. "So it's imperative that we run a well-oiled ship." Sharefest was officially over. But it had been necessary, that bonding. "Even if we may have our disagreements on *how* things should be done, we must work together. We share a common *why*."

An effective leader doesn't lead from a podium, but from the ground below his or her people.

"Okay," Zhao said. "Sure."

Kelly held her hand up for a high five. Zhao stared blankly at her, at her hand. A few century-like seconds later, his eyes lit up with recognition and he slapped his palm against hers. A gust of wind through the window rustled the Lays bag. Zhao's gaze first met the bag and then Kelly's face. Her gaze had also settled on the bag.

They both retracted their hands, placing them at rest on the desktop.

"We shouldn't," she said. "We should just phone in an order somewhere. Some rice and vegetables. Something nutritious. We've got to set a good example."

"The local government has warned all the restaurants in town not to deliver here under any circumstances. Violators face hefty fines or jail time."

"Well, I suppose that's a sensible policy, isn't it?" Kelly snorted. "Ha, couldn't be bothered to actually fork the money over, but sure as hell could find the time to fine people and create new rules. Death and taxes, eh?"

Zhao nodded. "So back to the cafeteria then? I'm sure the cook's got plenty of leftover blob."

They both looked down again at the chips. And then at the still-open drawer containing cookies and crackers and a delightful assortment of high-calorie, high-deliciousness snacks.

MEANWHILE IN LOVELY FIVE-STAR MACAU...

THE OFFICIAL ADJUSTED HIS ROLEX, RAN HIS FINGERS THROUGH HIS thick head of hair, inhaled deeply, and considered the range of decisions that spread out before him. In this life, there were so many decisions, and each came stuffed with so many consequences.

He stood under low-wattage bulbs. He stood in his Armani suit. He stood and he thought.

He thought not of Zhao, whom he trusted fully to rehabilitate the minimum of two fat kids, and not of that pushy heiress, who had at last stopped calling to pester him for the address, probably turning her attention instead to the latest trend in pubic hair grooming or some other equally serious issue. He thought not of his wife at home, puttering around in overpriced dresses and nagging everyone within a hundred-meter range, nor of his mistress watching TV and drinking supermarket wine and running the air-conditioning 24/7 in the apartment he paid for. He thought not of those fat children, mere statistics, who would soon be cured of their ailment anyway. He thought not of the other officials and the warden who sat around a table nearby, awaiting his return.

No, he thought of food, just food: of the platters of sashimi before him, of these elegantly displayed, beautifully cut pieces of raw fish; of the drool that pooled around his gums. A woman bumped into him as she reached for a plate, bringing him to his senses. He was fixating too much on this spread before him. He was being shortsighted. There were places to go, places to be. Naan, hairy crab, curry, sushi, sea cucumbers, chocolate, dim sum—platters and plates and pots and spreads as far as the eye could see.

He snatched up the tongs and loaded his plate with fresh tuna, salmon, eel. He loaded and loaded and then hesitated, considering adding more to the precariously stacked mountain on his plate, but then he thought, Fuck it, this is a buffet; there are stacks and stacks of clean plates. I am a free man, I am a hungry man, and I can come back as many times as I want.

...AND THE DAMAGE DONE

AFTER ALL WAS SAID AND DONE, IT WAS UNCLEAR WHOSE HAND HAD reached into the bag first. And it was also unclear into which of the two mouths any individual snack item had disappeared, but based upon the pile of discarded wrappers in the wastepaper basket, in a matter of minutes, Zhao and Kelly had collectively consumed seven Dove chocolate bars (three white, two milk, and two dark), five bags of flavored Lays (two cucumber, two shrimp, one barbecue), two sleeves of Chips Ahoy! cookies, one packet of Bashful Goose Seaweed Bites, sixteen White Rabbit candies, seven Bashful Goose Red-Bean-Filled Snack Cakes, thirteen Watermelon Wigglers, one Bashful Goose Sesame-Paste-Filled Snack Cake, twelve spring onion crackers, six egg yolk moon cakes, one loaf of French-style baguette bread, and three boxes of caramel popcorn. Their bodies screamed out with discomfort, their stomachs distended, and they both leaned back in their swivel chairs and dropped off into coma-like sleeps.

MEANWHILE. ACROSS CAMPUS...

WHILE KELLY AND ZHAO REMAINED COMATOSE AND LOST IN DREAMS, Camper Fourteen, a boy with cystic acne and grease-heavy hair, undressed and waddled into the boys' communal shower. The day sweltered, and he was dripping with sweat following participation in the optional post-lunch digestion walk. He turned on the water. He squeezed a bar of soap between his sausage fingers and the soap became goo. He rubbed this goo across his chest and into his armpits, where hair had only just begun to sprout. He grunted; the water was too hot. As he shifted his weight and reached out to adjust the faucet, he lost his footing and slipped on the wet floor. His arms flailed, grabbing out for something, but there was nothing. His head cracked against the tile floor.

He lay there for many minutes, and in one of those many minutes, his ghost left his body.

Less than an hour later, Fourteen's bunkmate, Camper Nine, his eyes still crusty with sleep from his post-digestion-walk optional recovery nap, stumbled into the shower and planted his bare sole directly into a squishy pile of Fourteen's brains.

AND THIS IS HOW IT STARTS...

A SHRILL SCREAM BLASTED THROUGH THE OFFICE WINDOW, AWAKING both Zhao and Kelly from their food comas with a start. Zhao's eyes popped open. He cocked his head, attempting to trace the scream's origins. "The showers," he mumbled, his eyelids falling shut again.

"What?" Kelly slurred. She rubbed her temples. The room spun.

The insides of his eyelids changed color, and the immediacy of the situation struck Zhao with great force. He jumped up, brushed the crumbs from his crumpled shirt, and darted out the door. A second later, Kelly, coming to her own wits, followed.

Sprinting, sprinting, and at last they reached the dormitory and the boys' shower room. Zhao knocked, but there was no answer, just the soothing sound of running water.

Kelly, stricken with a cramp, was bent over at the waist and clutching her side.

Zhao rapped again to no answer. "Hello? Is anybody there?" He grabbed his own stomach, also cramped, and shot Kelly a look. "Owww," he said, and then again, "Is anybody there?"

There was no answer. Zhao cracked open the door.

There, in the center of the shower floor, stood Camper Nine, naked as the day he was born save for the number necklace he wore around his neck. His mouth hung agape, his body trembled, his fat rolls jiggled.

"What's wrong?" Zhao asked, stepping into the shower room. "Was that you screaming? Say something!" He lifted his whistle to his lips.

Kelly watched from the hallway as Camper Nine pointed. On the wet floor below, at the corner shower, lay Camper Fourteen, water weakly streaming over him. His brains, like bits of ground beef, had leaked out onto the floor and were inching their way toward the drain.

Zhao dropped the whistle, which fell, bouncing against his chest.

Camper Nine shut his mouth and then opened it again, releasing the beginning of what would've surely been another long scream had Zhao not tackled him to the ground, pulled a small club from his pocket, and whacked him in the head. The boy's eyes drooped shut; he went quiet.

The hot water heater hummed.

Kelly placed her hands on her hips, assuming a dominant stature. "Why the hell did you do that?" she said.

Zhao ignored her. He said, "Stay here with him."

In shock and unable to muster up further words of protest, Kelly stepped inside the room as Zhao stepped out. "Lock it," he ordered, and shut the door behind him. "Showers are closed!" she heard him cry to someone in the corridor. His footsteps faded. Her gaze shot from the two billowy bodies to the mildewy walls to the crusty showerheads to the dripping ceiling tiles. There was no place to settle. She didn't belong here. She turned the lock.

There was silence, and there was sweat popping from all of her pores, and she felt everything slipping away from her—her vision, her plan, her redemption, her fame, her greatness. And then there was a moan. She looked down again at Camper Nine, whose eyelids twitched ever so slightly. He blinked a few times, shut his eyes, and then opened them again. Kelly watched gradual recognition of the situation creep over his face. Suddenly he jerked, grabbing for her, trying to pull himself upright. Panicked and remembering what the government official had said about rabies shots, Kelly backed up, pressing against the door.

The boy continued to struggle on his back. "You bitch," he hissed. "You fucking bitch."

Kelly's stomach tumbled in cartwheels around her abdomen. She took a deep breath. She rolled her eyes. This was a child she was dealing with. Only a child. "Oh, please. Look, we're not trying to do you any harm here. There's been an accident. Administrator Zhao has gone for help. Stop trying to move. You could hurt your spine."

Nine quit struggling and stared with clarity directly into her eyes. "Accident? He was the one who hit me."

Wheels turned, cartoon light bulbs dinged. She stepped over to him, squatted down, and stroked his wet hair. "No, no. Why would you think that? You don't remember, do you? Poor boy. You came in and saw your friend and you had such a fright that you passed out. We came to help you."

Camper Nine squinted and rolled his eyes back in his head, considering this possibility. There was a knock on the door then and Kelly jumped up, accidentally nicking Nine's forehead with the tip of her shoe. "Ouch," he whimpered.

"It's me," called a voice from the corridor. Kelly opened the door and opened her mouth to ask Zhao to back up her story and tell Camper Nine all about how they were only there to help him, but she hadn't spoken but a couple of these words when Zhao whacked the kid again with the club, knocking him unconscious for the second time.

No. Kelly rocked on her heels. No, no, no. She drew the edge of her hand into her mouth and bit down to stop herself from screaming. The dead brains kid, that was an accident, something they might be able to wash their hands clean of. But now it looked like a cover-up. Now they'd physically abused another kid—

Zhao, all unruffled and cool, interrupted her train of thought. "So I started a rumor with the counselors that the screaming was due to these two getting into a fight over a piece of contraband, specifically a Banana Peel Popsicle."

Kelly, momentarily intrigued by Zhao's indication of a plan, removed her hand from her mouth. She nodded and then, feeling that urge to scream bubble up inside her again, shoved it right back in. Bite.

IN LOVELY FIVE-STAR MACAU, THE GOOD TIMES NEVER END...

THE OFFICIAL ADJUSTED HIS ROLEX, RAN HIS FINGERS THROUGH HIS thick head of hair, inhaled deeply, and sipped from a glass of Johnnie Walker Blue. The room—dizzying patterned carpet, dangling chandeliers, leather sofas, karaoke TV screens—spun in amazing acrobatic feats. His phone buzzed in his pocket. He'd successfully ignored the buzzing all day. He pulled it out now. Numerous missed calls (including one from his wife and another from his mistress and yet another from a curvaceous young lady he'd met the week before at a banquet) and also a number of new text messages, including one from that damn heiress that read, "Despite your best efforts, I found it."

His blood pressure shot to the sky. Compression in his chest. He'd assumed that the cessation in her pestering phone calls had just meant she'd given up, but this little rich girl was more insistent and more annoying than any other woman he'd known, and he'd known a lot of annoying women. He certainly hadn't counted on her personal interest in this fat camp endeavor. She was bound only to get in the way. Wasn't receiving an enviable salary for doing nothing good enough for her? Why couldn't she just leave well enough alone? He stared blankly into his drink, wondering if he should say something to the others, who were singing their hearts out while he mused pathetically in the corner, sinking into this overstuffed sofa, wondering if that damn heiress hadn't just blown everything.

Sensing his despair, a girl in a skintight, sparkly black dress half walked and half danced over to him. "Why so sad?" she asked with a pout. "Your friends having too much fun without you?" She batted her long, thick eyelashes.

He looked past the girl and at the other officials and the warden, who were falling over one another, all limbs and pinstripes and hair plugs, and pawing at similarly slight and pouty young women, and wailing syrupy ballads into booming microphones. "There is so much love," one of them slurred in impromptu spoken word. "So much."

The official willed his blood pressure down to what he was sure was an acceptable figure. He hazily considered the definitions of the word "acceptance" and the word "fate" and decided then and there that whatever happened, at least he would have this one last trip to remember. At least he'd lived a life full of women and full of fun—unlike that of, say, Zhao and of all those other men in this country and this world too timid to ever treat themselves to a taste of success. And at least he'd established this connection with the warden, which might get him out of truly hard labor, if it really came down to that. But it probably wouldn't come to that.

The official slammed his empty glass down on the table, stood up, grabbed the girl's delicate hand, and marched over to join the others, losing himself to the singing, to the drinking, to the love.

WE'VE GOT A BIT OF AN ACCIDENT ON OUR HANDS

In the shower room, Zhao wiped his sweaty palms on his pants and, from somewhere Kelly couldn't discern, produced a rope, motioning toward Camper Nine. "We've got to tie him up. We can't have him escaping and talking before we figure things out," he said. His voice was calm. "Help me."

Kelly, at a loss, obliged. When fifteen minutes later they'd finally managed to tie the girth of the kid up completely, they slid side by side down the wall, exhausted, panting, their guts cramping, burning.

"What now?" Kelly asked. She would allow Zhao a little wiggle room. He was measured, rational, and she was a bundle of nerves, not thinking straight. She would let him make a few decisions, and then she'd manage the execution of his decisions herself. This illusion of control would make him feel important, and it would help them both get things done.

Zhao, clutching his stomach, turned to her, his eyes radiating pure panic. "What do you mean?"

"You said you told the counselors there was a fight. I thought you had a plan."

Zhao shook his head. "No. I mean, you're the boss, right?"

Kelly shut her eyes and rubbed her temples. "Okay, um, how about we wait until the others are all in the cafeteria to sneak these two guys over into the storage room. That will get them out of the way and give us more time to think this through. We'll keep Nine unconscious for now, to keep him quiet, but we'll obviously need him later to testify that Fourteen's death was an accident." She fingered the ends of her hair. "Yeah, we can work together; carry one body at a time. They may be fat, but they're only children. They can't possibly be *that* heavy."

Zhao nodded. "Good thinking. And then if we need to bide more time, I'll call the cook, tell him to get the stash out of my office and start distributing."

She glared at him. Give a little bit of freedom and get a whole truckload of idiocy back. "We ate the stash," she said coldly. "Where have you been?"

"There's more," said Zhao. "The entire filing cabinet."

Kelly shook her head; the sneak had been holding out on her. Casting her annoyance aside, she pulled her iPhone from her pocket to check the time; just five minutes until dinner.

In sync, they both took a few deep yogic breaths, and then Kelly stretched out her hand for a high five, which Zhao responded to more quickly than before—he was learning. Becoming increasingly aware again of her physical self, she noticed that the backs of her pants were quite wet despite their moisture-wicking properties, and that when she stood up the water reached nearly to the tops of her Nikes. She glimpsed over at the drain, which had become clogged with brains. She fixed her stare on Zhao, who was simultaneously coming to the same realization—and not just about the drain. She shoved her hand into her mouth.

Zhao hopped up and rushed over to Camper Nine. During the course of their discussion, he had somehow regained consciousness, flipped onto his belly, and attempted to wriggle from one side of the shower room to the other, tried to escape.

Not moving, not breathing.

Together, Zhao and Kelly struggled to flip the body over.

Face: blue. Skin: cold.

"Somehow I don't think anyone is going to believe that this one was an accident," Zhao muttered. A cold, invisible finger traced a line down Kelly's back.

There was a knock on the door.

"Showers are closed!" Zhao cried. He excelled under pressure, she had to admit. A natural.

They listened to the dimming footsteps. They exhaled. Zhao placed a quick call to the cook, telling him about the stash. Just as he hung up, a bell rang. There was a collective shout, *"Dinner!"* and the floor quaked. This time, they did not seek refuge, did not run for a doorway, did not squeeze shut their eyes or jab their fingers in their ears. Kelly and Zhao stood in the center of the room in a literal flood, barely balancing themselves, with only each other to hold on to until the shaking stopped.

HERE IS WHAT THEY WOULD HAVE SEEN...

INSIDE THE CAFETERIA, GELATINOUS BLOB WAS DOLED, VEGETABLES were plopped, and campers chowed down.

If any one of those campers had looked up from his or her tray and out the murky windows, he or she would have seen, in broad but waning daylight, the figures of Zhao, their dear administrator, and Kelly, their dear underwriter, struggling to roll the corpse of one of their dear fellow campers, Camper Nine, toward a storage closet, where his body would be hidden away to protect the futures and aspirations of the aforementioned administrator and underwriter.

Yes, if any one of these campers had looked up, he or she would have watched on in horror as Kelly and Zhao successfully stuffed Nine away in the storage closet and then returned to the boys' dormitory building, where they emerged mere minutes later dragging the corpse of another of their fellow campers, Camper Fourteen, and then rolling him too across the courtyard where his body would meet the same fate...

But all of this is not mere speculation. At this exact moment, a few campers, who had finished gobbling up their dinners, did sluggishly drag their gazes away from their plates. And at this exact moment too, the cook, bless his soul, came to the rescue at Zhao's phone-barked orders, tossing bags of contraband high into the air. The enthused campers leaped and bounded, tackled and wrestled, punched and kicked, performed all of these calorie-burning motions in order to acquire bags of Bashful Goose Coconut Meat Treats, cans of pizza-flavored Pringles, boxes of chocolate-filled Hello Panda Bites, and on and on.

It was by far, one of the counselors quietly noted between dainty nibbles of gelatinous blob, the most exercise any of the kids had gotten since the camp had begun.

AND STILL THERE SHONE A GLIMMER OF HOPE

Outside, Kelly and Zhao successfully dumped Fourteen's body beside Nine's in the shed, wiped the sweat from their brows, clutched their burning bellies, and trudged across the courtyard to the cafeteria where they expected one of two scenarios.

Scenario One: The campers would be shoveling down their practically inedible dinners, utterly oblivious to the tragedy that had occurred.

Scenario Two: The cook would be doling out contraband using the method Zhao suggested, which involved a friendly competition/game with junk food prizes awarded to the winners. The campers, delighted and drooling with anticipation, would remain utterly oblivious to the tragedy that had occurred.

What they did not expect was what they found: overturned tables, smashed plates, splattered blood. A war zone—a silent, eerie, human-less war zone.

Kelly's eyes bulged. She turned to Zhao. "What the hell?" she muttered to herself, to him, to no one.

She took a slow, stunned lap around the room, pausing to assess individual pieces of damage: a fork stuck in the wall at a ninety-degree angle, a tray cracked into a dozen jigsaw-like pieces on the floor, a large clump of hair trapped beneath a table leg. What the hell had happened indeed. An image of Papa Hui laughing played on infinite loop in her head, with that bashful goose honking in victory as the sound track, overlaid with gritty footage of herself serving time in a gulag. She began to sweat. She squeezed her hands into fists, jabbing herself in the palms with her own fingernails, resulting in a sharp pain that did, she was pleased to note, take some of the edge off.

"Where are the kids?" she heard Zhao ask, but his voice did little to shake her from her spell.

"Don't even want to speculate," she heard herself reply.

Rustling from the kitchen—a sign of life. They both rushed over and through the door. Inside, the cook paced behind the prep table, humming a frantic tune under his breath.

"What's happened?" Zhao asked.

Sweat poured from the top of the cook's shaved head, rolling in beads down his shiny face. He pointed at the floor, where beside the prep table lay two fat bodies, their clothes blackened with footprints. Zhao nudged a limp arm with the inner edge of his own shoe.

"Trampled," the cook said, still pacing. His words fell out quickly, one on top of the next: "I was just doing what you said, trying to give out the food in an orderly way, but then as soon as they caught sight of it, they went mental, all of them lunging at me at once, and I don't know what the hell happened, I was just—"

"All right," said Kelly. Surely it wasn't too late; surely they could still make it out with their reputations unscathed. There had to be a way. There was always a way. There was hope yet. "Now let's not panic."

The cook looked between them with crazy eyes. He didn't shove his hand into his mouth. He just perspired more and more profusely, a fountain of a man. "What do you mean?"

"Just stay calm, we can handle this." Kelly nudged Zhao, who nodded in agreement. They were in this together now. "Okay, where are the others?"

"I had the counselors take them outside. They're running relay races."

"They shouldn't be running right after eating," Kelly spat. "That's a surefire recipe for vomit. Where did they find these people anyway? Did any of them even pass basic PE?"

As if on cue, a counselor barged through the door. "We need someone out on the track now," she announced shrilly. "We have an emergency!"

Zhao told her they'd be out shortly and handed her his club. "For protection," he said. She took it and departed, the door swinging shut behind her. Kelly knelt down beside one of the trampled bodies and felt for a pulse. Nothing—but she wasn't a trained medical professional and thus her reading probably wasn't accurate. This girl couldn't be dead. Kelly stood up, squared her shoulders, raised her chin, tousled her hair. She had to act like she knew what she was doing. Best of the best. "Put them in the freezer for now."

"Even the live one?"

"What?" Kelly and Zhao coughed out simultaneously.

The cook pointed to the kitchen's back corner, where a fat child sat crouched next to a melting industrial-sized tub of sugar-free ice cream, alternating between taking greedy bites of the ice cream from a bowl and sucking his thumb.

Kelly placed her hands on her hips. "Why's he here and not out running relay races?"

"Saw me drag the bodies in and started asking questions."

Another lightbulb. She couldn't suppress a giddy grin. "Wait, so no one else noticed these trampled ones?"

The cook shook his head.

Kelly exhaled deeply; there really was still hope. "Keep giving him ice cream. Keep him quiet. We'll be back in a minute."

The cook nodded, and Kelly and Zhao darted from the kitchen, through the wrecked cafeteria, and to the track around the basketball court, which was strewn with a number of freshly dead bodies, along with the remnants of all that "hope."

From what Zhao and Kelly were able to piece together, Camper Thirty-Two had suffered a heat stroke during one particularly grueling leg of the relay races. His best friend, Camper Three, a boy from Nanjing with shifty eyes, tripped over Thirty-Two's unconscious body, fell at an odd angle, and broke his arm. This fractured ulna prompted Three to emit a cacophony of screams, cries, and shouts, which the counselors agreed sounded subhuman, satanic, and terrifying, and which one of the counselors may have accidentally permanently silenced with the use of Zhao's "protection" club. This violent act set off a few other screamers, whom the counselors may have treated with similar, irreversible vocal cord relief. That, they determined, was how it must have happened.

But what happened next?

The remaining living campers stood huddled and petrified at the edge of the field surrounded by counselors, who appeared oddly at ease with everything. No one said a word. Kelly thought she recognized one of the counselors from somewhere—he reminded her of a famous artist who'd long ago been arrested. Not that it mattered.

All eyes settled upon the fair-skinned heiress and the beastly administrator.

Zhao took a brave step forward, and then Kelly stepped up beside him, nudged him with her elbow. *Train your people well, and then trust your people.* Zhao cleared his throat.

"We shall..." he announced. The children waited with bated breath, and Kelly too; they awaited a speech, a plan, something to save the situation, something to deliver them from this evil. "... take them to the infirmary!" he concluded grandly.

Kelly spoke out the side of her mouth: "There is no infirmary, is there?"

Zhao shook his head ever so slightly. He whispered back, "To be fair, I did ask about it. The officials told me it was an unnecessary expense." A whiff of his rank breath shot into her open mouth, and her stomach seized up in response. He raised his voice and continued his announcement: "When I count to three, everyone will run to the other side of the courtyard where your dear leader, Ms. Kelly, will deliver a speech that will rival that of the greats. And afterward, you will all be given the opportunity to answer listening comprehension questions. Those who answer the questions correctly will be rewarded with contraband!"

There was an excited buzz among the campers.

Kelly's jaw dropped. She opened her mouth to ask what the hell she was supposed to talk about and why the hell he volunteered her for that, but before she got a chance to speak, he hissed, "I need to go and figure things out. Distract them." He quietly ordered one of the counselors to his office to pick up the remaining contraband.

He cleared his throat, and his voice rose again. "One. Two," and on three, there was a small earthquake as the campers shot up and barreled toward their destination.

AN EXCERPT FROM KELLY HUI'S ADDRESS
TO THE DISTRESSED CAMPERS

Dearest campers, I want to add that I understand thoroughly the struggle you have faced and continue to face. Dear campers, when your parents say, "You're fat and you must lose weight, you're not good enough the way you are"... when they rip that hamburger out of your hands... when they refuse to let you add even the tiniest bit of peanut sauce to your hotpot meat... don't you think, May heaven strike you down?!

I want to reassure you that it's only human to think that way. It's natural.

After all, these are the people who can give us what we want, but that means too that they intrinsically possess the ability to take it away. They hold in their greedy hands all the power in the world and they tease us with the possibility of handing it over, but they never do, do they? They hold it above our heads, turning it over and over again in new lights, eternally finding fresh ways to use it against us. So have there been times, dear campers, times when I wished my own parents dead? Sure, but who among us hasn't felt that way?

ONCE UPON A TIME IN GREATER LOS ANGELES...

A SEVENTEEN-YEAR-OLD KELLY STROLLED LEISURELY DOWN THE SIDE-walk, past vintage stores and cafés, past other young people who apparently lacked a productive way to spend a sunny Tuesday after-noon—no jobs, classes, or hobbies aside from shopping and eating for this bunch. She clutched a cup of gelato, banana pudding fla-vored, that she'd convinced the out-of-work actor/apron-wearer who worked there to give her for free. She wasn't supposed to be strolling or eating semi-stolen gelato. She was supposed to be in a psychia-trist's office. She'd set up an appointment with the guy, Dr. Shapiro, from the backseat of a taxi in the immediate aftermath of an ER visit a few days before. The nurses there had assured her that she was not having a heart attack but a panic attack, and some joke of a doctor looked at her for, like, ten seconds, reaffirmed the nurses' diagnosis, and prescribed her enough Valium to tide her over until she could sort things out with a therapist. Clearly, this ER doctor was one of those dunderheads who believed everything could be solved with expensive pharmaceuticals and a few heart-to-heart conversations, and after the metaphorical smoke cleared and she was back home feeling quite relaxed indeed, Kelly decided that she wanted no part in telling her so-called issues to some shithead therapist, who—if movies had any basis in reality—would probably just wind up raping and/or killing her anyhow.

And anyway, she knew enough about herself to know that her anxiety as of late had been caused by the looming end of high school and by the total lack of response from the universities to which she'd applied. Her grades weren't great, and Papa Hui refused to pay her way into a school, insisting that she "get by on her own merit." Unfortunately, her subsequent revenge-motivated attempt at donating a large sum of her father's money to Stanford failed when one of his accountants noticed a discrepancy and alerted him before the transaction was finalized. With everything now uncertain and completely out of her hands, the idea of college, of working hard and reaping the benefits, became vividly and startlingly real to her. High school was stupid, obviously. But college could make or break her. There, she'd at last get to focus on business and management and psychology, and all the things she actually felt interested in, and all the things that might lead her somewhere worth going.

She licked the final melted remnants of gelato from her spoon, tossed the plastic cup into a recycling bin, and then stepped into a vintage store, where she killed a good hour browsing, trying on, and finally buying a few dresses. As the shop's door rattled shut behind her, Kelly, who was no longer thinking of the "future" so much as how *Ghost World* and amazing her new dresses were, looked down and noticed a very thin girl with sandy dreadlocks sitting on the sidewalk, her back against the store's brick wall. Beside the girl sat a well-worn backpack and a Starbucks cup—a receptacle for what would clearly become drug money.

A tingle shot up from Kelly's toes. She'd developed an interest in striking up conversations with homeless people and weirdos, and it was a hobby she admittedly enjoyed in part for its perceived riskiness. Anyone with any authority or sense would deem it "unsafe" for a young girl to just mosey around chatting up creeps, but Kelly enjoyed the mostly fucked-up and sometimes funny things these "creeps" had to say, and it was also a trip to play up being the more sane, powerful, and wealthy person in the relationship.

Vying for a high on this otherwise boring afternoon, Kelly squatted beside the girl. The sun beat down on the pavement, warming it pleasantly. She lunged at the girl's Starbucks cup, snatched it, and caught a quick peek inside. Probably less than a dollar in change. The girl scowled at Kelly and yanked the cup from her hands, slamming it back down on the sidewalk. The coins jangled.

"Get fuckin' lost," the girl said, her hand wrapped possessively around the cup. Kelly didn't budge. The girl stared straight ahead. A hip young couple in tight jeans walked past, their hands in each other's back pockets, probably all clammy and gross.

Kelly poked the girl's bare leg. Her skin was soft, covered in short pale hairs. "Still a bit chilly for shorts. What drugs are you on?"

The girl burst out laughing and then shook her head. "Jesus. What's your problem? Fuckin' people all have a problem."

Kelly leaned into the girl's arm and looked at her with a well-rehearsed wounded expression (the same one she so often used on Aunty Minnie), until the girl finally met her gaze. "Why you gotta be so weird? Get out of my face."

"Sorry," Kelly said. She softened her voice. She sounded more sincere that way. "I didn't mean it."

The girl shrugged. "Yeah, all right." But she kept her death grip on the cup.

Time ticked on. They both looked everywhere but at each other. "Hey," Kelly finally said, her voice still softened. "Are you hungry?"

The girl cocked her head, furrowed her brow. "Nah, I'm just sittin' here with this fuckin' cup for shits and giggles. I got me a whole kitchen full of yuppie food back home."

"Do you want me to buy you dinner at a restaurant? That's all I mean. I'm going to eat now anyway. So you can come or not. It's up to you."

The girl studied Kelly. Her eyes darted from side to side and then up and down, and finally she exhaled a white flag and said, "Yeah, okay."

The sun dripped like slimy egg yolk into the horizon. The guy who worked in the vintage shop with the comic-book dresses turned the sign in the glass door around to read closed. The girl dumped the change from her Starbucks cup into her backpack, zipped it up, shoved the cup into a side pocket, and set off after Kelly, who had set off in search of grub.

"Is this place okay?" Kelly asked, stopping in front of a retro-y diner brimming with denim-clad, baseball-cap-wearing part-time production assistants who paid rent from trust funds. The girl nodded, but it wasn't really a question, and what choice did she really have?

Inside, in a vinyl booth, over cheeseburgers and arugula salads and Sprites and, finally, cheesecake slices, Kelly lent an ear to the girl's woeful tale.

Like so many of the other homeless freaks Kelly had spoken with, this girl had been raised primarily in foster care. She spewed on the typical slew of shady characters—"parents," "brothers," and "sisters"—all of whom stole from her and/or abused her and/or molested her. There were, of course, a few decent humans too, who'd gone out of their way to protect and care for her, but the girl didn't dwell too much on that good fortune. Why would she? There were other terrible and far more interesting topics to explore: alcoholism and crystal meth addiction and the "things some girls do for money," which she herself even admitted to sometimes still doing, when times got tough.

Kelly thought it odd that this girl, a perfect stranger—and one who, with her coherent speech and relatively refined mannerisms, didn't seem hopelessly mentally ill—was so eager to volunteer all of this traumatic and often incriminating information to another perfect stranger. She stared across at this girl, anxiety rippling up from her fingertips. Why, she thought, does she trust me? Why, she thought, does anyone trust me?

The girl drew her napkin—the same one she'd used a moment earlier to blow her nose—to her face, wiped her mouth, and turned the conversation to Kelly. "So you from Japan or what?"

Kelly slowly chewed the last bite of her cheeseburger. "China. I'm Chinese."

The girl nodded. "Well, it's basically all the same, right? You're here in America now is all I mean."

Kelly shrugged—what could she even say to that?—and the girl dove into a long, rambling story about how before she went into foster care, her biological mother dated a Korean man, and about how he had a terrible gambling problem, and how his kitchen smelled really funky, and how he was a grade-A asshole. Kelly drifted in and out of attention, bored now with this insipid girl, and thinking about those college decision letters, about her future. She thought about only this as she handed the waitress her debit card, signed the bill, and stepped down to the sidewalk beside the still-yapping girl. She was so lost in thoughts of admission letters, of test scores, of transcripts that she hadn't noticed how far they'd walked—out of the gentrified area and into a more sparsely populated stretch of road near Griffith Park.

Under a streetlight, Kelly stopped. It was time to make a break for it; time to head home and see what that Aunty Minnie was up to, and if nothing amusing, maybe time to pop another of those leftover Valium and go to bed. "All right then. Where are you going?" she interrupted the girl, who was now blabbering on about some lovable Rottweiler in one of her childhood foster homes who was run over by an eighteen-wheeler, "flat as a fuckin' pancake."

The girl pointed into the park: dark trees, hills. "I'm meetin' a friend over there sometime tonight. If he decides to show up. His name is Eddy—I think you'd like him. He's wicked hot, everyone says, but not my type. Maybe—"

Kelly nodded. "Okay," she said. "Take care." But she hadn't even taken a full step before the girl's voice, tinged with desperation, rose up from behind her.

"Hey, how about a little cash?"

Kelly stopped in her tracks. She spun around slowly. A flash of red.

"Just a few dollars? I need me some bus fare."

She squinted. The girl was a silhouette now. Not a girl anymore. A shadow. "Oh," Kelly said, her soft voice quavering. "That's interesting. Why do you need to take a bus? What happened to Wicked Hot Eddy?"

She wasn't a shadow. She was real, in focus. The streetlight shone strangely on the girl's pale skin, making it appear green, decayed.

"The park is right here," Kelly said. "Why do you—"

"Come on, bitch, a few dollars ain't gonna make no difference to you."

A red curtain dropped over Kelly's eyes; she knew somewhere in the core of herself that this wasn't a real curtain, but her perception was colored by it all the same. What was real? What was a curtain, even? After everything she'd done, this was how the nasty skank thanked her? After buying her what was probably the nicest meal she'd had in ages? After sitting there and politely listening to her vapid sob stories? She had the audacity to ask for money on top of everything?

The curtain grew thicker, velvety, thicker still, until nothing was red, until nothing was there at all.

That night, even before she popped a Valium and drifted into a silent void, Kelly couldn't recall what had happened in the minutes that followed, but she vaguely recalled a struggle, the girl's soft skin against her palms, a faded sensation of hatred and a stronger sensation of total indifference. The power of squeezing, denying breath; the freedom of running. And she read later a few news articles about a dead vagrant found in Griffith Park, but she never spoke to the police and she never went to jail, and anyway that evening, before the Valium, when she'd returned to that big, empty house in Culver City, she'd found a thick envelope on the kitchen counter printed with three big maroon letters: USC.

MY CULINARY ARTS EDUCATION
HARDLY PREPARED ME FOR THIS

Dearest campers, it is only human to want to protect yourself, and it is therefore only human to sometimes wish others harm. So when your mother slaps your chopsticks out of your tubby little hands, when your teachers stop their lessons to reprimand you for stealing bites of that piece of cake you sneaked from home, when—

Kelly, startled at the touch of a fingertip on her shoulder, stopped speaking and spun around. The counselor Zhao had sent to his office leaned in and whispered, "There's no contraband left. The cook distributed all of it."

Kelly nodded. Dozens of sets of eyes, and it seemed too the ghostly eyes of those missing, stared back at her. In the not-so-far distance, under a setting sun, Zhao and the other counselors struggled to roll a body into the storage shed—and there were still two more bodies left on the basketball court.

"Okay," Kelly said. "The end! Questions will come shortly. But first, a different game, a sort of intermission if you will."

The campers cheered.

"This game is called Statue. If you want to win some food, you must sit still, and I mean *completely* still, until I return."

The campers, saliva glands audibly gushing and gleeking, went motionless. The courtyard looked like a sculpture garden at a modern art museum. If only she were sipping a latte at the Getty and not running around like a madwoman in this goddamn concentration camp. Kelly wove her way through the children-cum-statues to the dining hall and back into the kitchen. She pounded on the now-locked door, shouting at the cook to let her in.

He answered the door with his cleaver raised. He exhaled, lowered the cleaver, and stepped aside.

"I need food," Kelly panted. "Any food."

The cook shook his head. "Fresh out." He set the cleaver down on the prep table. Blood glistened on the blade.

Kelly's eyes widened. "What happened to it?"

"Damn kids ate it all."

Sweat seeped from her palms. She took a wide stance. Control, control. "No, I mean the cleaver—what's the blood from?"

"Oh." The cook blushed, hemmed, hawed. "Well, uh, it's a funny story. I was scooping ice cream out of the tub for that Number Seventy-Four, keeping him quiet like you said, but I couldn't scoop fast enough. I started sweating even worse. My arm went all limp like a noodle, and I started to see all these funny things—not hallucinations, mind you—but more like thoughts that were pictures. I saw myself being eaten alive. All sorts of weird things. Did you know that people and bananas share fifty percent of their DNA?"

Kelly shook her head—what did that even mean? He sounded like a nutjob, a lunatic. Maybe her jokes were on point and he had actually served time in prison—that was, after all, where so many of the mentally ill wound up. "I did not know that about bananas, no."

"My culinary arts teacher always told us that, the point being to teach us to respect food and—"

"Maybe your culinary arts teacher should have spent less time pontificating about fruit DNA and more time teaching you how to cook," Kelly spat. The cook cocked back melodramatically, like this was the Three Stooges and she'd just slapped him with a dead fish or something. A sensitive soul. It didn't matter. She didn't care. Focus. "The cleaver. Why is there blood on the cleaver?"

"Well, I'm getting there. So I'm scooping away, never scooped so hard in my whole damn life, when suddenly I hear a bit of a ruckus coming from over near the window. I turn my head real quick and look over and see this kid, I think it was Camper Thirty-Five or Fifty-Two—who can tell any of these rascals apart?"

"That's why they wear number tags."

The cook shrugged. "Yes, well, anyway, I realize that this camper has chewed his way through the screen like a billy goat and is trying to climb in through the window! Slippery melon thinks he can tiptoe away from the rest of the group and help himself to a little snack. I swear, give these kids one millimeter of freedom and they take a whole hundred *li*."

"The blood. Get to the blood."

"So I told you I was already in a bad state of mind. A frenzy really. What with all the deaths, the cover-ups, and so on. So I dropped the ice-cream scoop in the tub and ran over to the window. I spotted his fingers on the ledge, those fat little sausage fingers, and I hacked them clean off with my cleaver." He pointed across the room, where ten stumpy fingers lay scattered on the floor.

Vomit lurched up Kelly's throat. She reached out and grasped the prep table to keep from keeling over. "Where is the rest of him?" she asked weakly, but truthfully, she didn't want to know.

The cook blushed again, and his quivering lips surrendered to a sheepish grin. "Outside under the window." He paused. His smile fell. "Uh, well, look, after I chopped off his fingers, I may have sort of, um, beheaded him."

Kelly felt the blood drain from her face in one whoosh, like a toilet flushing. "What? Why?"

"No reason really. I just sort of lost control of myself for a moment." He laughed. His eyes shone with a familiar reddish light.

Kelly worked to keep her own expression stoic. "Okay," she said calmly, cautiously. "Well, where's the ice-cream kid?"

The cook instantly perked up, eager to redeem himself. "Oh! After I beheaded that fingers kid, I jammed ice-cream kid in the freezer with the dead ones to keep him quiet until you came back. Stuck him in there with the scoop and the tub. Give him a little DIY time. Give my poor arm a break."

Kelly stepped over to the freezer, her feet concrete bricks, knowing but dreading what she was to find.

A moment later, she and the cook dragged the unconscious ice-cream kid's body onto the kitchen floor. They crouched over him, his blue lips, his darkened eyelids.

"Hypothermia," Kelly said, rubbing her icy hands together. "How is that even possible? How cold do you keep it in there?!"

"You were droning on out there for a damn long time."

"Oh." She did a double take. She flipped her hair over her shoulder. She batted her eyelashes. She stood. "You heard my speech?"

The cook nodded. "And to be honest, I've heard better." He rose, stepped away from the body, picked up the cleaver, and inspected the blood. "Oy, guess I should clean this up."

Just as he finished his sentence, the ice-cream kid's corpse opened his eyes, and the cook gasped, hopping back unsteadily, spooked at this sight. The cleaver slipped from his hands and landed, blade down, on ice-cream kid's throat, slicing it clean through.

NEVER TRUST A FAT KID FARTHER
THAN YOU CAN THROW HIM

As Kelly dealt with the kitchen and Zhao rolled the last body into the storage shed, a camper, whose file showed that he suffered from ADHD (diagnosed the year before by a doctor in Shanghai) in addition to obesity, was physically unable to sit still any longer in Kelly's Statue game and cocked his head slightly to the left, but not so slightly that he couldn't see Zhao and the counselors maneuvering his dead bunkmate's body. Realizing at once that his bunkmate was irreversibly dead and not actually being taken to an imaginary infirmary, he let out a yelp, which startled many of the children-cum-statues into turning around themselves to see what the matter was.

The counselor who'd been left in charge immediately "scolded" these rule-breakers for their disobedience with slurs such as "silly geese" and "doggone rascals." The children paid no mind to her cheery, somewhat psychotic form of authority. Soon, others, their curiosity devouring their desire to win an arbitrary game, began to turn around too. Some shouted. Some tittered. *"Have you seen So-and-So? I think So-and-So is dead!"* Some just shook their heads, tut-tut.

The slur-slinging counselor, threatened by this uprising, armed herself with the flashlight/Taser combo she'd found in Zhao's office, where she'd been sent to search, in vain, for contraband. (She was usually terrified of weapons, preferring to use poisonous substances as a means of control and revenge, but she had also heard many stories of fat children viciously attacking their minders, and had herself once witnessed what she considered to be one such event long ago, before her imprisonment, in a Wuxi Pizza Hut when a child threw a bowl of potato bacon soup in his mother's face after she refused to let him order a third brownie à la mode.) The counselor, who had only ever administered physical punishment to ex-lovers via pesticides, began tasing those children who moved, zapping them into unconsciousness (this Taser, acquired at a black market army/police supply store, had an unusually high/deadly voltage) and scaring the others into inanimate submission. Soon, the crowd was under control, there were no whispers, and there was no movement. There was just the sound of cicadas chirp, chirp, chirping.

MEANWHILE, BACK IN THE KITCHEN...

ZHAO BURST THROUGH THE DOOR. "THEY KNOW," HE SAID. HIS EYES darted around, and he moved his head to and fro, as though expecting a fat kid to pounce on him at any second.

"What? Who knows what?" asked Kelly. Her head was swimming, woozy. She leaned with her back against the prep table, clutched her stomach, stared down at the poorly laid tiles on the floor, and wondered what the hell she'd done to deserve this. Just steps away, the cook held his cleaver under the faucet. He hummed an old Communist ditty. The water ran red, then pink.

"The kids," Zhao said. He grabbed his stomach. "Ow. They know something is amiss. They started talking. What are we going to do?"

Kelly bit her lip—how long could they keep doing this? "Um, well, I suppose we can continue to distract them until we figure something else out, right? It's supposed to be movie night. How about we do that? Act like everything is normal, act like it's movie night."

Zhao sighed. "I don't have a better idea." He cast his gaze to the floor. His cratered cheeks glowed green. "Where—where did those fingers come from?"

Kelly opened her mouth but, not knowing where to begin, left him hanging, and bolted outside to deal with the campers, whose faces lit up at the sight of her.

"Who's the winner?" Camper Ninety-Four cried. "Is it me?"

"Um." Kelly fingered the ends of her hair. "You're all the winners."

"What about them?" another said, pointing at a grouping of bodies the counselor had tased. "They didn't stay still."

"Um," Kelly said. "If you 'fell asleep'"—she pronounced those two words with a certain euphemistic emphasis that told the children not to question—"then you're not a winner and you can stay here and sleep outside tonight." She raised her voice, addressing the dead: "Did you hear that sleepyheads?! It's outside for you tonight!!"

Camper Sixteen, a known smartass and always in the front row, piped up. "If they're asleep, then why aren't they snoring?"

Kelly "accidentally" stomped on Camper Sixteen's hand, effectively shutting him up, and announced, "All right, let's go. I'll, uh, order pizzas for all the winners."

The kids, forgetting their questions, burst into whoops and applause. They stood, wobbly on pins-and-needles legs, and made their way to the activity room, where Zhao was preparing that night's film, *Your Body and Global Warming*. Kelly derived comfort from watching his methodical movements; it all appeared so normal, removing the disc from the sleeve, placing it in the flimsy drawer, pressing the buttons, adjusting the volume.

The campers made themselves comfortable on the floor and stared up, mouths agape, at the screen. Zhao and Kelly sat beside each other in chairs at the back of the room, clinging to their ribs and guts, trembling, sweating. *If you're like most people,* the narrator boomed, *you probably think: What does my fat ass have to do with these burning rain forests?* Monkeys screamed. Smoke rose. Indigenous people, thin arms flailing, fled. Images appeared on the screen of french fries, oil spills, whale blubber, billowing clouds of pollution.

All was normal, but all was not normal. An uneasiness plagued the remaining campers—some rocked back and forth, some drooled, some wept quietly into their own hands, and one young girl, Camper Sixty-Eight from Suzhou, who always wore her hair in two knobby pigtails, began nervously gnawing at her own arm. By the time anyone noticed, the credits were rolling and she had ingested fifteen pounds of her own flesh. Surrounding campers, no longer distracted by the film, leaped up in panic, in disgust. Some slipped on the mixture of saliva and blood, and many others began tripping over the first fallen. Thinking quickly, Zhao clambered up on top of a table and out of harm's way. He grabbed Kelly's hand and yanked her to safety with him. Helpless, they watched from above. Campers attacked other campers. Campers attacked counselors, who attacked right back. Fat limbs and a few thin ones slipped and slid in every fathomable way and direction, at every fathomable speed. There were shouts, there were screams, there was chaos, and at the end of it all, only Zhao and Kelly, clutching their burning stomachs and cowering atop the table in the corner, were left alive...

...or so they thought.

LADIES AND GENTLEMEN, THE FAT CAMP RUNAWAYS!

THREE A.M. A CICADA CHIRPED. THE MOON SHONE WEAKLY, BARELY visible through a thick blanket of smog. Peng, one of two remaining campers at Fat People Fat Camp, jogged slow circles around the basketball court. He burned calories, and as he burned calories, he waited. A cicada chirped.

From the darkness, a figure emerged. Peng stopped; his belly continued to jiggle. The figure—full, voluptuous, meaty—approached and wrapped its thick arms around Peng's wide frame. It was Ming. A cicada chirped.

Peng whispered into Ming's ear, "In this material age, we can only hold each other."

Ming's thin lips curled into a smile; Peng held her too closely to see this with his eyes, but he could sense it. The two bodies formed a single massive silhouette. Ming whispered into Peng's ear, "If it were daytime, we'd blot out the sun."

A shrill whistle slashed through the thick summer air.

Zhao shone his flashlight on the dark blot, revealing two faces, two connected figures, rolls upon rolls of fat. Zhao's plastic whistle fell to his chest. Before he could speak, his cigarette dropped from the corner of his mouth. His phone vibrated in his pocket. He cast his eyes toward the ground, trying to catch the half-smoked cigarette before it went to waste, trying to see who was calling, trying to stop the drool from seeping out the whistle and leaving a sloppy wet spot on his shirt.

A cicada chirped, and into the darkness, the full figures fled.

✳

Peng and Ming panted. They'd lumbered from the fat camp's basketball court to Wuxi train station, a distance of three kilometers. Side by side, they leaned against the building's wall and slumped down to sit on the concrete, four legs sprawled in opposite directions in a cellulite compass. Ming looked into Peng's eyes. She said, in her gentle baby-doll voice, "Love is not a vice," and she took his hand into her own.

A legless beggar, riding a makeshift plywood skateboard, wheeled over to the pair. He offered a nod and said, "Ah, you must be the Fat Camp runaways."

Peng replied, "We are."

Ming punched Peng in the arm, unhappy with his disclosure. She didn't know how the man knew who they were, why he cared; all she knew was that they had been running, running not to lose weight, but to save their own lives.

The man nodded his head again, vigorous this time, and nearly lost his balance on the skateboard. "Media's on alert. Camera crews are on their way."

Peng wiped his nose on Ming's sleeve and eyed the man suspiciously. "How did you lose your legs?"

"Factory accident."

"That's a shame." Peng jammed his fingers into his pocket to try to dig out some change, but before he completed the task, a massive gang of ill-groomed, dark-eyed people with cameras and camcorders and notepads and tape recorders appeared behind the beggar. He wheeled through their leather-clad feet and into what remained of the night's shadows.

"Why do you think China is facing this childhood obesity epidemic?" a voice cried.

Flashes went off. White spots lingered in their fields of vision.

Someone shoved a microphone into Peng's armpit. "Who sent you to fat camp?"

A photographer snapped a picture of Ming's kneecap. "When will your wedding take place?"

A reporter jotted down the words "plagiarism" and "dizzy."
A man adjusted his thick glasses and feigned concern. "How will you cope with the humiliation of being a fat camp dropout?"
From the darkness, the legless beggar reappeared on his skateboard with a notepad, joining the rest, shouting, "What do you believe to be at the root of your weight problems?"

ZHAO. YOU'LL DO ANYTHING
FOR A LAUGH

AROUND FOUR THIRTY A.M., KELLY, PHYSICALLY EXHAUSTED FOLLOWing what she claimed felt like a heart attack (and refusing, to Zhao's simultaneous terror and relief, to seek medical attention), collapsed into a deep sleep on the office floor. Zhao, unable to even fathom sleeping with such a stomachache and with such adrenaline coursing through his veins, watched the rise and fall of Kelly's chest until he could watch it no longer. He stood. He crept from the office and into the courtyard. He peered at the storage shed, barely visible under the dim lights. He felt drawn to it, like he'd left something there, lost something. He jogged over, opened the door, and felt around in the darkness. Pungent air, sticky-sweet, with overtones of old cheese, rotten eggs, dead blubber.

Over the course of the summer, the employee must rehabilitate a minimum of two fat kids.

He hadn't caught them, those last two, those runaways, thanks to his mother's ill-timed call. She'd woken from a nightmare and sent him a text message summarizing it after he'd failed to pick up. She'd dreamed that her dear son had gotten stuck in an elevator and that no one could get him out. Not an unlikely scenario in the grand scheme of the world, considering loose fire codes and bribery-aided inspections, but not here. He replied, "There are no elevators here. Go back to sleep," and that was that.

And now, this was this.

He couldn't locate the light switch—just flesh, hair, fat. What was he even doing here? In this shed, and in this job? His legs trembled and acid seared his stomach, and he longed to run away, or to vomit, or to die, but he remembered something his mother always said, one of a million things she always said: "Lose your mind, and that's just fine. But lose your job, and you'll lose everything."

He'd lost—well, given up—his job once before. And look where that had gotten him. He couldn't risk his future yet again; he was too old, too ugly, too pathetic to take any more chances.

That hope that had electrified his body when he was offered this position, when he signed that contract—that hope had abandoned him, left him for dead.

If this contract is broken, a penalty of 100,000 yuan will be assessed.

All he'd had to do was rehabilitate two of them. That was it. A 2 percent success rate. It should've been easy.

In his head he ran through all the ways to cover this up, to escape the crippling fine and assured career destruction, the government officials' power-backed punishments, the probable jail time. He thought up places where he and Kelly could go into hiding, live out their days. Surely she had access to money, to plane tickets and phony passports. Maybe they'd get married. She wasn't a knockout, but she wasn't hideous either. She had nice hair. Maybe they could flee to somewhere in South America or Africa, or maybe Vietnam— yes, they'd blend in better there.

Breath held hostage in his lungs, he traveled the walls, the air, with his hands, but still couldn't find the light switch, only darkness. He gave up—what was he even looking for? what did he even want illuminated?—shut the storage room door and locked it, strode back to his office, stepped over Kelly and her puddle of drool, stared at his phone and wondered when it would buzz again, wondered when the two fat runaways would tell the world everything they knew. He waited, and as he waited, he smoked an entire pack of cigarettes, lighting each new one from the dying embers of the last.

Hours passed. Dawn broke. Zhao stepped over Kelly to retrieve the newspaper from the doorstep, but there was no newspaper. This was modern times. He left the door ajar. A bird chirped. He turned on the computer and loaded his favorite news website, one he'd refreshed fifty times a day back in his golden era of unemployment. "China's Fattest Couple!" read the main headline. He spat on the floor. His phone buzzed. He picked up. It was his mother. He listened, hoping for something new, something enlightening. She did not deliver. He screeched into the receiver, "I am at work! No, you absolutely will not fix me up with my own cousin! No!" He hung up.

The phone buzzed again. Unknown caller. Either his mother had figured out how to block her number or... He picked up. The voice on the other end was low, decidedly not maternal. "Come to the Old Meeting Place Restaurant tonight at six."

Before he could respond, the line went dead.

He set down the phone and picked up the empty cigarette box. He shook it, hoping for a miracle. He peered inside. Still empty. In a former life, he'd quit this disgusting habit. Who was he then? Who was he now? Was there any correlation? He stood, shut the office door, and unzipped his pants. He remembered the pretty waitress the night he'd signed the contract. Her plywood skin. Her thin limbs. No, he couldn't. She was holy. He glanced over at Kelly, sprawled out on the floor, still snoring, her long hair a splattered halo—here was a woman right before him. Yes. He tried to make the best of it, tried to imagine what it'd be like to be with her, but the shrill voice of his mother echoed in his head, and his dick went limp in his hand.

SHANGHAI IN THE AFTERNOON

Four p.m. A car horn blared. Peng and Ming had freed themselves now not only from the camp and its overexcited counselors and under-flavored food, but from the media and its nosy reporters and their even nosier questions.

Hand in hand, they wove through Shanghai's traffic and skyscrapers and trees and crowds. They squeezed their eyes shut, and no one could see them. As the sun moved across the sky, their fame gave way to anonymity. There were new stories to follow: wars raging in far-off lands, and an old man who bit the heads off live chickens in Guangxi, and stock markets collapsing and recovering, and children in Yunnan who had been buried alive in their shoddily constructed school, and on and on.

The sun set behind the smog, and the city lit up. Somewhere beyond the lights, they knew there were stars.

They ducked into a restaurant in the French Concession. They ordered salads with dressing on the side. They ordered Coca-Colas. They ordered slices of cheesecake. They ordered french fries. They ordered hamburgers. They ordered escargot. They chewed and they smiled and they giggled, and all manners of things went into their mouths, but never once did a word come out.

EXTRA. EXTRA! READ ALL ABOUT IT!

THE BETTER PART OF AN HOUR LATER, ZHAO MUSTERED UP THE COURage, or cowardice—whichever it may be—and clicked on the article, first examining the photograph of the blubbery couple stricken with deer-in-headlights expressions. He then skimmed the text, written in childish, tabloid-y prose... *These two little whales escaped from a fat camp somewhere in Jiangsu or Anhui Province. They are deeply and obviously in love, and although they refused comment on wedding plans, by the looks of things, they'll be eating their wedding candy soon enough. And what a massive load of candy it is bound to be!*

On the floor, Kelly smacked her lips and opened her eyes. She sat upright and slipped her phone from her pocket. Zhao couldn't wait to tell her the good news, but he wanted to be sure of it first. So he read on. And on. Nowhere were there mentions of deaths, tasings, tramplings, drownings, beheadings. His heart fluttered. Why weren't the little fatties talking? Why weren't they telling the world what they knew? Could these kids truly be so selfish? Could it be that now that they'd escaped, now that they'd made it out alive, their only motive was to obtain and secure their own freedom? That all they wanted was to protect themselves?

After a few final nods and smiles, they were off on an eastbound train. Their exact whereabouts are currently unknown, but they have certainly charmed our China on this day of slow news!

Zhao came up for air, a giant grin plastered across his face, his stomach pain milder, his heart racing in a new direction, but Kelly was already gone.

OUR DEAR HEIRESS MAKES HER ESCAPE

A BLACK AUDI SCREECHED TO A HALT BEFORE THE CAMP GATES. KELLY, overnight bag in hand, hopped in, breathing a sigh of air-conditioner-induced relief.

"Thanks for getting here so quickly on such short notice," she said to the driver.

He nodded at her in the rearview mirror. He said, "Of course."

This driver had been with her for two years. He had, in that time, done everything she'd ever asked. She knew that if she so ordered, he would have her at the international airport in thirty minutes flat; would drive her across the border into Tibet or Mongolia or North Korea; would, if she so ordered, probably even drive them both off a cliff. He was, after all, loyal in the way that only money could buy, and now she herself, for the first time, wasn't.

"Where to, Ms. Hui?" he asked, his gaze not leaving the road.

She exhaled from her diaphragm and ordered the poor loyal bastard to take her to the only place in the world she wanted to go: Bashful Goose Corporate Headquarters.

After a sepia-toned stop-and-go drive, she bid the driver farewell, slammed the car door behind her, and made her way through the grounds, marching through the bamboo forest, which led to fountains that shot up, synchronized to elevator-music versions of various Bashful Goose jingles, including one she herself, at age eight, had composed. As she walked, that now-familiar burning welled up in her abdomen, not unlike heartburn, but with bleak emotional over- and undertones.

She rode the elevator up and up to the top floor.

"Is my father in?" she politely asked Papa Hui's receptionist, a thirtysomething woman with a sleek bob and a round face. She wondered if ol' Papa had ever hit that.

"He's down at lunch right now, but he should be back shortly," the woman answered in a cheery voice, and then looked back at her monitor—probably, Kelly thought, at some very kinky pornography.

Kelly flipped her hair over her shoulders and, not bothering to turn to see if her assumption was correct, strode into her father's office. She shut the door softly behind her, and then took a seat in his overpriced chair at his overpriced mahogany desk, dropping her bag down on the plush carpet. She settled in. Atop his desk sat two gold-framed photos: one of himself with his arm around Kelly's mother on their honeymoon trip to Beijing, and one of him standing with the goose next to a small lake back in Old Watermelon Village. She picked up this second picture and traced her fingers along the goose's neck.

Thanks to that fateful encounter with that bashful goose, Papa Hui is now the richest man in China.

Why, she wondered, in that story about the damn goose, why does he always attribute his success to that stupid animal and not to me?

Don't I owe the next generation something more, something better? Is there a kingdom I can build, he mused, worthy enough for this child to someday inherit?

A voice outside. Footsteps. The door opening. Kelly fumbled to set the picture down, dove out of the seat, crouched below the desk, and as quietly as possible unzipped her overnight bag. She removed the cleaver, which she'd pried from the cook's surprisingly strong dead hands, by its handle. She looked down at her own trembling hands, soft and weak, and wondered, for just a brief moment, if this was the right thing to do—but that wonder was almost instantly replaced by the thought of the many lives that could have been saved had she only done this sooner. She listened as the footsteps drew nearer (breathe in, breathe out), and then she jumped to her feet.

I JUST FLEW IN FROM MACAU.
AND BOY. ARE MY ARMS TIRED!

ZHAO, WHO HAD BATHED IN THE GIRLS' SHOWER ROOM AND CHANGED into fresh-ish clothes, strolled into the Old Meeting Place Restaurant. Its decorations were not ornate. Its walls were white. Its tile floor scuffed. Its tablecloths glowed an atrociously bright shade of yellow.

A waitress, the same waitress who had waited on him at the other restaurant the night he'd signed the contract, the same waitress he had refused to fantasize about, appeared behind the hostess podium. She said, "Oh. Hello."

Zhao tried to hide his surprise, his pleasure that she'd remembered him. "You work here now? Small world."

"Jobs come and go," she said with a smile. Then, back to business, she said, "Follow me, please."

Zhao obliged, simultaneously awed at this lucky coincidence and scared to death at the prospect of this mystery meeting. As he followed, he stared down at her legs and found comfort only in the tiny flexes of her calf muscles.

The officials sat around the table, stern expressions painted on their shiny faces. Zhao mentally rehearsed his self-criticism speech and awaited the verdict, the scolding, the shame, the demand that he pay the 100,000-yuan penalty. Better, yes, than a death sentence, better than prison, better than becoming a media pariah, better than dealing with this joke of a legal system—but, still, maybe he should have run after Kelly. Maybe he should have fled toward whatever freedom she left seeking.

One of the officials, a man with an unnaturally lustrous head of hair, cleared his throat. "Zhao, what you have done—"

Zhao felt his cell phone vibrate against his leg (surely his mother calling).

"—is remarkable."

The phone continued to vibrate.

"'Rehabilitated' all but two campers!" The official pronounced the word with a certain euphemistic emphasis. "A record, Zhao. A glorious and remarkable achievement!"

Each of the officials picked up a shot glass, stood up, and cheered. They clinked their glasses together.

Zhao didn't cheer, didn't stand up. He sat, stunned, as the waitress entered the room with a tray stacked high with huge cuts of meat.

The men began to feast.

Zhao's phone continued to vibrate. He looked at the unidentifiable meat and then at each of the officials' faces, which looked now not like doors, but mirrors, and then he reached down and slid his phone from his pocket, dropped it into his soup, and pushed the steaming bowl away. He sat back in his chair and felt, once again, that burning in his stomach. He recognized it now as hunger. He picked up his chopsticks. He ate and he ate and the burning faded, and the delicious, fatty, juicy meat soon disappeared, and the waitress took away the last plate, and Zhao felt lucky—luckier than he'd ever felt and bound only to be luckier still—so he shouted over the din of the chattering officials, "Bring that back, lady legs. I wanna lick the grease!"

iN THE NEWS

BASHFUL GOOSE HEIRESS KILLS FATHER. GOOSE. RECEPTIONIST IN SENSELESS ACT OF VIOLENCE

WUXI, CHINA —...while across the country, mourners take to the street to weep and wail...

May our great nation find the strength necessary to carry on without guidance from its most powerful and beloved tycoon!

THE LEFTOVER WOMAN BEHIND THE CLEAVER: PROFILE OF A COLD-BLOODED MURDERESS

WUXI, CHINA —...Ms. Hui, a 24-year-old bachelorette, was educated in Los Angeles, California. Unable to secure a boyfriend, fiancé, or husband in the United States, despite its abundance of eligible and wealthy men, Ms. Hui returned, single, to China two years ago. Upon her return Ms. Hui was appointed head of corporate social responsibility at Bashful Goose Snack Company. This reporter was unable to unearth information about any charitable projects undertaken during Ms. Hui's employment at Bashful Goose—by all accounts, it appears she squandered much of her time and her enviable salary on dining out and purchasing pirated DVDs...

In an April interview for Asia Business Monthly, *Papa Hui indeed referred to his daughter as a "royal pain" and asserted he would "personally kiss the hairy ass cheeks" of any man foolish enough to take Ms. Hui off his weary hands...*

BASHFUL GOOSE SNACK PRICES SKYROCKET AMID RUMORS

WUXI, CHINA —...a spokesperson for the Bashful Goose Snack Company insists that the company will not shut down or slow production. He urges consumers to remain calm...

However, as one netizen posted on his microblog, "How can we trust anyone anymore? Children killing parents! Heiresses killing tycoons! I for one am stocking up on Tangerine Crumbly Cakes..."

KELLY HUI NAMES HAIR TYCOON WANG XILAI AS COCONSPIRATOR IN PAPA HUI MURDER

SHANGHAI, CHINA — Ms. Kelly Hui, accused of the murder of Bashful Goose founder and CEO Papa Hui, has named Wang Xilai, a hair tycoon headquartered in Shanghai, as a coconspirator. According to Ms. Hui, Mr. Wang approached her last summer in a dark alley. There, he allegedly offered her a large sum of money to murder her father...

JIANGSU CHILDHOOD OBESITY FIGURES PLUMMET

NANJING, CHINA — Government officials were pleased to announce at a press conference Friday afternoon that Jiangsu is no longer China's fattest province...

AT THE ROOT OF IT ALL: THE MEMOIRS OF A CHINESE HAIR TYCOON

You cannot prevent the birds of sadness
from passing over your head, but you can prevent
them from nesting—and shitting—in your hair.
—ANCIENT CHINESE PROVERB

YUNNAN, CHINA

I AM A SIMPLE MAN. I WAKE WITH THE DAWN. I TAKE A BRISK WALK around my house to stretch my legs. I linger at the window, staring out at sweeping fields, orange orchards, the gold-tinted horizon. I prepare my breakfast, a plain rice porridge, and I boil water for my morning tea. Aside from the clinking of the pan, the whistling of the kettle—all of these homey, comforting noises—it is quiet. I live alone. I haven't spoken to anyone I would consider a friend in a very long time. Most days my voice goes unused.

I finish my meal and wash my dishes in the sink. This house, for a country house, is well outfitted. I've got running water, a bathtub, a washing machine. This is not a farmer's house. It is a retreat for an overworked city man with soft hands and black circles around his eyes. I was once such a man, and I suppose, in a way, still am. But what do bank accounts and investments matter out here, in the countryside, in Yunnan, a province all but forgotten by those great shakers and moneymakers in Beijing, in Shanghai, in Guangzhou? I exist now not among neon lights and constant construction and golden toilets and *da hong pao* tea. I exist among the forgotten in the cast-aside home of dozens of ethnic minorities—non-Han Chinese—under a slice of the only clear blue sky we have left. But I'm not political and I'm not some environmental nut, and that's not why I'm here. It's more about the thought that after I'd acquired everything, after I'd achieved what I set out to achieve, that there was nothing else left. "What next?" is the most terrifying question in the world when answers cease to be.

I go for a stroll through the orange orchards. Birds flutter above in the sky, white clouds above them. I've spent the past month— or maybe it's longer now, maybe it's been nearly a month and a half—here, walking these paths, sleeping in that simple house. I have a car, my Bentley, parked in the driveway, but I have no reason to use it. I have nowhere to go. I have my groceries and supplies delivered from Kunming. The man who used to bring them in his bread-loaf van was young, not much older than myself, maybe twenty-six or twenty-seven. He made mention once, upon my noting the birds singing outside, of having a deaf three-year-old son. He found a way to bring this up again each subsequent visit, and I came to understand that he was not trying to share intimate details of his life for friendship's sake, but rather in hopes that I'd take heart and offer money for a surgery or for the little guy's tuition at a special school. All I could feel at this realization was selfish pity, shame that I'd never be able to escape myself. People still knew who I was; will always know who I am. How couldn't they? My photo was plastered in magazines, in newspapers, all over the Internet. And what about that car in the driveway, the clothes in my closet, these parts I hadn't wanted to escape, these parts I'd taken with me? Maybe I wanted them to know. I couldn't fault this sad-eyed father for trying anyway, for his son's sake; some might even call his effort admirable, so I gave him some money, a large chunk of money, and then I dismissed him from the job.

Now the man who makes my deliveries is older, in his forties, bald and gruff. He came yesterday. He isn't one for small talk, producing at most a grunt in response to anything I might say. If he knows who I am—or who I was, to be more accurate—he doesn't show it. He hauls in bags of rice, crates of eggs, boxes of vegetables. He leaves them on the floor for me to put away. He doesn't linger. He doesn't hold up any mirrors. He leaves.

Left alone, here among rows and rows of evenly spaced orange trees only a little taller than me, I stop and remove my shoes, dangling them on my fingers as I continue. I've taken to walking barefoot on the soil, despite the risk of parasites, of ringworm, of heaven knows what else. There isn't broken glass here like in the city, smashed beer bottles and car windows. There are rocks, caterpillars, mushrooms; there is energy, uncorrupted energy. I think so often of people in those cities, how so many of them live in high-rises, and how many of them wear shoes outside, and, accordingly, how many of them reside in bodies that never touch the earth. How can you feel connected to anything when you're floating on rubber soles and concrete slabs, when you're perpetually passing through? Everyone is a stranger in the city, and it's no wonder we have customers trampling customers in foreign hypermarts, entitled businessmen ripping babies from strollers and slamming them down against the pavement, women tearing out each other's hair over the rising price of vegetables.

Thank heavens I am removed from all that now. I am connected; I live and I walk on the ground. Sometimes I think this earthing therapy is working, is grounding my psyche and lifting my spirits. But then midafternoon hits and I have nothing to do, and this depression washes over me, the typhoon of meaninglessness that inundates me with the feeling that all my life has been wasted and that it will continue to be wasted.

I step over a sharp-looking pebble and I notice something on the ground, maybe two meters ahead, that interrupts my thoughts. I approach with trepidation. There are people who might want me dead, after what they think I've done, what I didn't actually do. But as I draw nearer, I see that this foreign object is not a bomb or a booby trap or anything of the sort. It is a laptop computer. My laptop computer.

I begin to tremble, to sweat.

The little things I could dismiss as delusions. When I found my lost watch on the outside windowsill with all its numbers carefully removed, when I found a human tooth on my pillow one morning but no missing teeth in my mouth, when I saw a fly that looked to be carrying a folded note but was unable to reach for it before it flew away. But this is my laptop and it is sitting in an orange orchard and I was not the one who put it there.

I carry it inside, sit down at the table, open it. There is no message that pops up, no warning, no clue. I perform a thorough check of all my folders and documents and find nothing unchanged. I stare into space and try to recall a specific physical sensation, pain or something, from the exact moment I saw the computer in the orchard and in those moments that I carried it back inside. Nothing springs to mind. I lift the computer and check the bottom for dirt. There is none. I suppose it's entirely possible that I've made the whole thing up, that the computer was here on this table all along. I don't realize until now that I've been holding my breath. I exhale.

I pop in the Ethernet cable, and I open a browser and wait for a page of celebrity red carpet photos to load. This is a daily practice, searching famous heads for my trademark hair extensions. The Internet here is painfully slow, but I suppose I've got nothing else important to check anyway and plenty of time to waste. There are fewer and fewer new search results, fewer and fewer articles and blog posts to read. The media is losing interest in me. It was another story entirely a month ago when all the headlines read, "Tycoon's Nervous Breakdown." Netizens and experts alike engaged in analysis and frank conversation about our country's lacking mental health services. While happy to open the floor to such important discussion, I also couldn't help but feel it wasn't really me they were talking about. This, I learned from their discussions, is called disassociation.

I knew I was in trouble well before the alleged "breakdown," when I started hearing voices at night. I'd clap out the lights in my apartment and lay down in bed and then they'd start. They were never evil or demonic, never told me to "kill, kill, kill" like they do in the movies. But they were hardly kind. They were critical, harsh, honest. They said, "You don't deserve this," and "You know nothing about friendship, about people, about love," and "You will die alone," and other such gems, and I used to lie there paralyzed, with damp palms, too frightened to move, to clap the lights back on. I used to squeeze shut my eyes and pray silently that my grandmother's ghost would make an appearance and demand that those voices leave me alone. My grandmother was the only person I think ever truly loved me, who ever made an effort to understand me. She died when I was twelve. Now that my mental health is improving, I think maybe she was there after all, that all of those voices were actually hers.

The pictures never load, and I give up, shutting the laptop. I stand up to stretch, and go over to the kitchen but decide I'm not hungry enough to bother preparing lunch, and resolve instead that today I will sing a song. Believe it or not, I've never sung a song before. I was a prodigious child with a mind tuned solely to success. If I wasn't good at something the first time I tried it, I wouldn't do it again. Early on, I determined that music wasn't my strong suit, so I just halfheartedly mouthed along to the words in nursery school—no one noticed my lack of voice in such a big crowd. That's how I got by in my early years, and then after that, there was no need, no requirement to sing.

No one can hear me here, so I am safe from judgment, but I am unsure of where to begin. Standing on the cool tile before the stove, I open my mouth. I shut it again. I know I've got to start somewhere though, so I start to hum. This is easy enough. I hum a tune by a famous singer who used to wear my hair. She had mental problems too—it was rumored that she was a victim first of her father, who molested her in her youth, then of a volatile and abusive relationship with a music executive. Later, after that executive's lethal overdose, she turned the violence on her manager, savagely attacking him with an ax. He barely survived. This song though, it gives no indication of any such brutality. It is beauty, pure beauty, and then, recalling the words, I open my mouth again, and this time I sing.

I am halfway through the song, really belting it out now, when there is a knock at my door. I freeze mid-note, my mouth agape. My gaze darts over to the window, through which I see a figure, dressed all in black and wearing a ski mask, running to a red sports car. The figure pulls open the driver's side door and then, a moment later, the car speeds off. I creep over to my door, my heart pounding. Who was this figure? Why didn't I hear the car approaching? Who, besides the grocery deliverymen, knows where I am? Is this another mental break? Have I not escaped the voices? Have they grown bodies now? I pull open the door, afraid of what I might, or might not, find.

It's amazing how long it takes to tell a story, or to listen to a story, or to read a story, or to write a story, and then, once stored in the brain, how quickly, instantly, that story can be remembered. Memory is, despite all connotations otherwise, not connected to time. A second, a story, and a lifetime take up the same amount of space in the brain and can therefore be remembered all at once, without sequence or pacing, just all at once.

In the time it takes me to undo the lock, turn the knob, and open the door, a story comes to mind, one my grandmother's mother, a wrinkly old raisin with bound feet, told me a very long time ago: "When I was a child in the Dragon Mountain Village, we had a neighbor, Village Witch, who gathered herbs and plants in the forest. She used her gathered materials, along with some form of magic, to concoct potions. I know she was a true witch because she once cured my father of a fever so terrible that we were certain he was going to die. With only one sip of her potion, his health was completely restored. Yes, she saved many lives and cured many villagers, and because of this, she was so beloved that no one dared question her odd lifestyle—Village Witch had no husband, no relatives, only a child, named Witch Daughter. From the time Witch Daughter could walk on her own, Village Witch schooled the black-eyed girl in her magical and medicinal ways. For all those years, Witch Daughter never left her mother's side, so it came as a great surprise to them both when one month Witch Daughter's blood didn't come. Village Witch dismissed it as an anomaly—after all her daughter was just sixteen and maybe her moon cycle was still adjusting. But the next month there was still no blood, and the next month still none, and Witch Daughter's belly grew full, and Village Witch cornered her daughter in their home, shook her by the shoulders, and demanded that she tell her who had done this to her. Witch Daughter didn't speak, didn't speak, didn't speak, and then finally said, only, 'No one.'

"Now this confession frightened Village Witch, who had herself gotten pregnant under similarly mysterious circumstances, and whose own mother, disbelieving, had disowned her, forcing her to walk a great distance to find a village where she could be a stranger, a village that might take her in. And she'd found one. Yes, many years ago, these Dragon Mountain villagers had accepted one unwed mother, but were they ready to accept another?

"Bogged down by these thoughts and questions and by the stress of her daughter's virgin pregnancy, Village Witch made a mistake in her scavenging and accidentally cooked a poisonous mushroom into one of her potions, killing an old villager. His family was livid. That very same month, a doctor—a proper doctor trained under French missionaries, a doctor who dismissed what she did, calling it 'hocus pocus'—began making what would become regular rounds to the village. Village Witch knew now for certain that Dragon Mountain, having no use for her, would never accept her daughter and the baby that grew inside. She had her answer.

"Frightened by a looming future, Village Witch forced all manner of tonics and potions down her daughter's throat to try to rinse the baby out. Nothing worked. In fact, these poisons only seemed to make the baby stronger. Resigned now to their fate, the inevitability of this baby's birth, the two witches locked themselves inside their gates. No one thought this troublesome or suspicious—that murdering witch, the villagers said, she was lucky they were all so civilized, lucky they didn't slay her and that fat, googly-eyed daughter too. But my father, despite the other villagers' unkind words and despite the recent availability of modern medicine, still felt he owed his life to Village Witch. He took pity on her. Locked in that house, they ran out of food, and Village Witch was too afraid of meeting an angry mob to go out and scavenge in the mountains, so my father and I slipped rice, leftover vegetables, and bits of cooked bird meat under their gate. Sometimes Village Witch would meet us there, and through the stones' cracks she told us all about her daughter's strange and stubborn pregnancy, and many months passed this way, and then, come autumn, I was woken in the night by a cry. The time had come. I hopped up from the kang, my parents and my brothers still snoring, holding each other tight, and I raced outside, where there was no more crying. I stood under the cover of our pomegranate tree and watched Village Witch on the roof of her house, her silhouette cast against the full moon as she held a smaller silhouette by its ankles and then dropped it headfirst down the chimney shaft. And that was the end of that.

"Village Witch told my father and me when we brought her food the next day that Witch Daughter had suffered a miscarriage and that as soon as she was well again, they were planning to set out to a different village where no one would know them, where they could be strangers, where they could start again. 'We are just two women,' she said sadly. 'Surely someone somewhere will take pity as you have.' I knew she was lying. There was no miscarriage. I had seen the baby with my own two eyes, heard its cry with my own two ears. But I was afraid and it wasn't my business, so I spoke nothing of this to my father.

"Not more than a week later, Dragon Mountain Village got its own strange visit. I was in our garden picking herbs when I saw an unfamiliar man, maybe twenty or so years old, amble up. He didn't look like a wanderer, the type who sometimes happened across our village; he didn't at all resemble these holy men with their scraggly beards and raggedy clothes. No, this was a regular farmer, and he sat down at the gate of the witches' home, stared forward for a moment, and then released a scream. Oh, he sobbed, he wept, he wailed, and I jumped up, shaking the dirt from my hands, to get a better view of the scene. As I positioned myself front and center, I caught a glimpse of Village Witch's face peering out the window at the peculiar sight.

Dozens of villagers poured from their homes, from their gardens, and down from the mountains to watch this grown man cry—he'd dry up soon, like a pickled radish, they said, if he carried on like that. The crowd swelled, and the man finally calmed himself down enough to call out Witch Daughter's name, and then he just started crying again. 'Those evil women!' the villagers shouted. 'What harm have they done now?!' Villagers climbed over the gate and pounded on the witch family door, demanding that Witch Daughter show herself to this poor, sobbing soul.

"I imagined the two witches inside, trembling, terrified by this man, by this mob. How sorry I felt, and how confused too.

"Some time later, after the villagers had nearly pounded the door in, Witch Daughter emerged, frail and pale, her mother by her side, and opened the gate. At the sight of her, the man stopped crying. He said, 'You killed me.'

"Witch Daughter's eyes were wild as she looked around—who was this man talking to? Answering her unspoken question, he looked directly into her eyes and said it again.

"'What are you talking about?' Her voice shook.

"'I would have lived to be nineteen years old,' he said. 'If you'd let me live.' He then turned to the village chief, who was now at the front of the crowd. 'Look in the chimney,' the man said. 'You will find me in the chimney!'

"At the angry villagers' demands, the village chief, though confused by exactly what it was he was looking for in the chimney, ordered the village men to break it open. They demolished the structure with their axes, and then held a tiny corpse up by its ankles for all to see.

"At the sight of this dead baby boy, the villagers went mad, shouting and cursing, wielding those axes as weapons now, driving Village Witch and Witch Daughter back into their home, ordering them never to come out again. As this chaos continued—threats soared through the air like sparrows—my father just shook his head and asked the red-eyed stranger if he'd join us in our home for a cup of tea. The man obliged, leaving the scene behind, and followed us home, where my mother boiled water. My father and the man sat down at the table, and they sipped tea, and immediately, something changed behind the man's eyes. 'Where am I?' he asked. He stood up, knocking the cup over, spilling tea. 'Who are you?'

"My father looked up at him. It was as if he was looking at someone entirely different from the man who'd been crying in front of the gates.

"My father explained to the man about the crying and about the witches and about the chimney, and he poured the man a new cup of tea, and eventually, the man calmed down, telling my father that his name was Old Wood Boy and he lived in Purple Moon Village, about fifty kilometers away, and that he couldn't remember any of what my father had told him, nor how he got here to Dragon Mountain Village—that the last thing he could remember was chopping wood and then spotting a weasel. He wondered aloud what had happened to the wood.

"To us, hearing this came as a surprise but not a shock; we villagers all believed that the weasel was a fairy that worked on behalf of dead or lost babies, helping them find their parents. This spirit, we knew, must have possessed the man. My father explained all this. Stunned, the man politely finished his tea, thanked us for our generosity, and set out to begin his long journey home."

My hand pulling open the door, I suddenly have so many new questions about this story I haven't thought of in years: Why was the girl singled out when it was her mother who killed the baby? Why hadn't this man's family sent out search parties to find him? How could a fairy spirit possibly possess a man's body? How did a weasel from fifty kilometers away know of this baby's death? But the only question I asked all those years ago was: "What happened to Witch Daughter?"

My great-grandmother nodded gravely and replied that the witches, shunned in Dragon Mountain Village, fled in the night after the crying man incident. They found a new village, and there, Witch Daughter married a kind man, and her mother died the same year, and the only time Witch Daughter ever returned to Dragon Mountain Village was many years later, for the wedding of one of her childhood friends—to which she hadn't even been invited! Witch Daughter was radiant, my great-grandmother said, and had two beautiful young children in tow, but with the exception of my great-grandmother's family, the villagers all ignored Witch Daughter and her children, as though they were but a tiny tribe of ghosts.

I take all this now to mean that nature and spirits are reactionary. They get their revenge, and they move on. Oh, but people, people do not.

I am remembering this story and my great-grandmother's leathery face and the way her home smelled—like incense and Shaanxi vinegar—as I look down at my doorstep. There is something there. It is a book. I pick it up. My book. Published one year ago, a memoir that I wrote at the height of my success. I brought a copy of it with me here, I don't know why, maybe as a reminder—but of what? I'd been using it as a tray to collect toenail clippings, but last week I shoved it under the too-short leg of my bed to remedy the unevenness. I look over there now. The bed is crooked again, sloping in that one corner. I look at this book's cover, and sure enough there is the circular imprint of a bed leg. Someone—presumably this black-clad figure—has entered my home, stolen my own book from under my bed, knocked on my door, left it on my step, and fled.

I pinch myself. This is pain. I am awake. This is real. I shut the door and peer out the window again: kicked-up dirt swirling in the air, definite fresh tire tracks in the drive. I hold the book open by its covers, the pages facing the floor, and I shake it, hoping for a clue to fall out. There is nothing. I open the book to the first page to see if there is a note. There isn't. It is only just afternoon, but it feels very dark. Gray clouds have rolled in. It looks like it will rain. I am not afraid, just puzzled, so I turn on the light and I turn the page.

MEMOIRS OF A CHINESE HAIR TYCOON, THE BIRTH OF A CAPITALIST

TRY EXPLAINING THE CONCEPT OF CAPITALISM TO A TYPICAL SIX-YEAR-old, and odds are that if he's kind, he'll stomp on your foot and tell you to shut your stupid trap, or, if he's a rascal, he'll run off mid-speech and light a cherry bomb in your toilet to teach you a much-deserved lesson about rattling on. But whittle the same lecture down to a discussion of wants and needs, and suddenly you will find that same little brat very attentively on your page.

You see, prior to my sixth birthday, every two months or so, each member of my family (me, my father, my grandmother) would take our dreaded turn on a rickety kitchen chair as my mother went to town on our hair with the same dull pair of scissors she used to trim the fat from meat and clip from the newspaper articles worth saving ("Girl, 8, Grows Beard after Eating Soviet-Made Candy!" and "Local Grandfather Crowned International Champion of Ring Toss!").

But this routine was broken when a salon opened up near our community. On the day after my sixth birthday, my grandmother allowed me to accompany her there for her very first professional treatment.

A twisting candy cane pole, windows that allowed a clear view of the styling stations, a pink neon sign that read beauty salon, piles of hair forming miniature mountain ranges on the tiled floor, men with well-formed spikes, girls with impossible spiral curls. I felt as though I'd been punched in the back of the knee; I wanted to fall, I wanted to scream, I was so instantly struck by this place's wonder. I didn't fall or scream. I spun in place. I inhaled deeply, savoring the exotic aroma of chemicals, of sprays, of creams.

A stylish man with bleached hair and thin wrists sauntered toward us and, after a few words, led my grandmother to the washing station. I watched intently as he shampooed and conditioned, wrapped a towel turban around her head, and then pushed her down on a swivel chair, snapping a cloak around her neck. I sat in an identical chair at the empty styling station beside them, swiveling back and forth ever so subtly so as not to cause the intimidating man to shout at me. But perhaps I needn't have worried about this; he paid me no mind. Like a wrathful hair-dyed god, he hovered above my grandmother, combing and hemming and hawing and single-handedly determining her fate.

And then he picked up his scissors.

The light caught the silver blades, shooting a glint into my eyes, and I couldn't help myself—my fingers, possessing a life of their own, reached out for them. The stylist, not just a god of appearances, but one of reflexes too, slapped my hand away. "No!" he shrieked. "What, you want me to cut this old bag's ear off?!"

To all of this, my grandma offered no reaction. She, gentle creature she was, never scolded me, never tore me down, never hit me as my cranky parents often did. She sat peacefully, her eyes shut, her head rising from her cloak like a potato uprooted from the earth.

I retracted my hand, placed it in my lap, and resigned myself once again to spectating. But as I watched him snipping and styling, a black screen cloaked my vision, a pollution before pollution, and I couldn't help myself. My hand once again reached out.

The stylist squealed like a pissed-off pig, and my screen dissipated, and he slapped my hand away. "Stop, you devil! These aren't for you!"

Now, this struck a chord. At the time, in the late nineties, when our nation was still emerging from its stagnancy and many of us still lagged far behind, my family lived in a modest home in a Commie block; my parents, a technical school teacher and an HR manager respectively, worked long hours but earned modest incomes. Therefore, the coolest toys weren't for me. Computers weren't for me. Cell phones weren't for me. Taxis weren't for me. Nothing in this city, in this country, in this world was for me. So this effeminate, bleached-blond, black-clad man with his shiny watch and beautifully capped teeth did have a valid point: Why would the scissors be?

Because I fucking wanted them, that's why.

I slipped my hand under the man's sassy slap and grabbed the scissors by their blades. He lunged at me, but I dodged him and charged the door, slamming into its glass with the full weight of my small body. It flew open, greeting bells jangling ("Welcome, welcome!" the receptionist automatically cried out), and I darted outside.

"Come back here, you turtle-egg bastard," the stylist called, hot on my heels, "Give me those—"

I spun around, my eyes wide and crazed, and pointed the scissors at him like a weapon. I heard my grandmother, who'd followed us outside in her cloak, gasp, but all I saw was the metal point before me and the "important" man in front of that, royally irked but also clearly terrified that he might fall victim to one of those killer kids you read about in the papers—the ones who seem like sweet and studious little angels until the day they snap and gouge their mother's eyes out with chopsticks after being told to eat one last piece of broccoli, or "accidentally" electrocute their father with a hair dryer while he's in the bathtub after being ordered to spend less time watching anime and more time training to be an Olympic Ping-Pong champ.

I lowered the scissors. I wasn't one of those kids.

The stylist seized this opportunity. He lunged. Faced with the possibility of being overtaken, my humanness slipped away and I became pure animal. I threw back my head and released a banshee wail. I grabbed on to the candy cane pole and shimmied my way up. With monkey-like stealth I didn't know I possessed, I latched on to the awning above the beauty salon and swung onto a narrow ledge, never once losing my grip on the scissors.

"My baby!" my grandmother cried. "It's not safe up there!" She turned to the stylist, as though all of this were his fault, as though

I could do no wrong, as though she understood and accepted the desire that drove me. "What if he falls?!"

He ignored her. "Come down, you useless beast!" he shouted, stomping his studded black boots on the sidewalk. "Those are my best scissors!"

As the two of them shouted and carried on, my grandmother posing questions about my safety and the stylist cursing my ancestors, a small crowd comprised mostly of hair salon patrons and employees swelled to a larger crowd consisting of passersby, street sweepers, restaurateurs, and children in school uniforms. Before this crowd, feeling powerful for the first time in my short life, I swung the scissors in the air—they were my sword and I was a mighty warrior.

As I bravely maneuvered, twisting and turning on that narrow ledge, I heard speculative voices from below.

"What's he protesting?"

"Who is he?"

"What are his demands?"

But all I saw was a shadow coming from above. I looked up and into this darkness.

To try to describe what I saw here, no matter how many words or languages I possessed and used, would be to say too little, but nevertheless, I will try: a disc, it was, the circumference the length of perhaps five soccer fields. Hovering. Matte white. And from it radiated a warmth, a warmth not unlike that of what I'd imagine a mother's loving hug to be (I wouldn't know—my mother's hugs had always been brief, cold).

Flooded with disbelief, I ripped my gaze away and looked down at the crowd, their weathered faces, their drab clothes, and I knew almost instantly that no one else had seen it, felt it—I knew I was special; this was a secret that had been revealed only to me. I didn't know what the secret was or what it meant, but I understood its specialness at my very core.

When I looked up again, the disc was gone.

I didn't mourn. I knew it'd be back for me. I turned my attention back to earth.

Not missing a beat and in response to the crowd's questions about my demands, about my intent, I shouted, "I'm just one small child!" But was it really the crowd I was talking to?

Police motorbikes and station wagons screeched to a halt in front of the salon, and uniformed officers charged the pavement. Armed with hokey plastic guns, they shot little beanbags up at me, all of which I easily dodged. I was above animal now, above human, above being; I was chosen. I collected the beanbags that landed on the awning and used the scissors to cut them open. I tossed the beans grandly, like confetti, scattering them upon the gaping crowd below.

"Please come down, baby!" my grandmother shouted. The stylist stomped his foot. The clock on the bank building across the street struck five, national dinnertime, and as though being called to prayer, the hungry crowds, stomachs audibly growling, dispersed. The police retreated—no crowd, no show—slamming shut their car doors and speeding off.

Now my grandmother and the stylist stood alone on the sidewalk.

"Please just tell me what you want!" the stylist shouted up at me, his hoarse, shaky voice bordering on a sob.

I bit my lip. To be honest, I was now growing hungry too, thinking longingly about the chicken wings my grandma had promised to prepare for dinner. Aware now of a greater force within the world, aware of my own power, of my chosen status, I was ready to relinquish control of these dinky scissors. I knew that bigger things awaited me.

"Please, anything!" the stylist cried, and peering down at him and his visible-from-up-here bald spot and his scuffed boots and his dye-stained fingertips, I pitied him. I truly did.

I thought for a moment and then spoke my demand.

My grandma shrugged, muttered something along the lines of "Why didn't you just say so?," tore off her cloak, and shimmied up the pole. She collapsed, out of breath, onto the awning and held out a lock of her hair. I leaned over from the landing, opened the scissors and then closed them, taking a slow, careful cut—ah, the music of a man-made metal device slicing through that which is human, pure! In the palm of my other hand, I caught and then clasped the falling black and gray pieces. Tiny motions in the grand scheme of the universe, I know, but with them I became a part of a greater machine, a cog in a ticking clock, a critical circuit in a matte white robot of wants and needs...

So perhaps you could say I was a news-maker from the very start. This first display of bravery earned me an article in the city newspaper: "Local Boy Wields Scissors Atop Hair Salon, Attempts, Fails to Disrupt Socialist Society." My mother used her dull meat-fat scissors to cut out that headline, but never again did she use them on anyone's hair.

LIVE YOUR BELIEFS OR DIE A HYPOCRITE

AWARE FROM A YOUNG AGE OF TRADITIONAL EDUCATION'S POINTLESS-ness, I utilized class time to monitor and record the hair growth of my fellow students. I theorized that boys' hair seemed to grow more quickly than girls', and that the shiniest hair seemed to belong to the most active students, regardless of gender. I made notes about my classmates' strand density, split end occurrences, and variations in natural color. I made diagrams and charts. In the evenings, after I'd completed my obligatory homework and as my grandma watched TV soaps in the other room, I did not join the children in my community in their foolish prancing-and-skipping games. I sat at my desk and studied plucked and fallen strands under a toy-store microscope.

I began to consider what made things grow as well: our parents all constantly pestered us children to drink water, and also often stated that they wanted us to grow up to be big and strong and earn lots of money to fund their retirement activities, such as criticizing others' life choices and taking budget tours of Italy. I therefore surmised that water played a critical role in growth, and to test this hypothesis, I myself began drinking massive quantities of water, filling bottle after bottle from the cooler in the school corridor. The resulting spike in urgent bathrooms breaks led one of my teachers, concerned that I might have developed childhood diabetes, to contact my mother, who, upon her typically late return home from work one evening, confronted me.

"Diabetes!" I scoffed. "No, no, no. Diabetes doesn't cause my pee. Water does. And water is good for hair." I pulled out my hair notebook to show her my latest findings, to fill her in on the intricacies of my life's work, but she wasn't interested. With weary eyes, she shook her head, called the teacher back and told him to mind his business. She fell asleep with the phone against her ear; she fell asleep before she finished talking, before my teacher apologized and hung up.

ALL THE MAKINGS OF A MIDDLE SCHOOL MOGUL

AT THE TURN OF THE CENTURY, EXTENSIONS WERE GAINING MOMENtum, and from the age of nine, I'd made a good living growing and selling my own carefully maintained hair to salons across the city. Occasionally, I'd be out shopping with my grandma and I'd spy a glamorous middle-aged woman or a sexy bargirl sporting my locks, and my lungs would surge with pride—like all of my classmates, I wore the red Young Pioneer scarf at school, but who among them could say they were so patriotic?! I wasn't just reading stories about Lei Feng, hoping that I might someday have the chance to prove myself a worthy comrade by helping a hunchbacked old woman cross the street. I was actually out there in the trenches, improving our nation, making it a more beautiful place! And in doing so, I was also improving my own life. I opened a bank account, which ballooned with each passing year. I was suddenly the kid who, no longer at the mercy of parents' generosity or lack thereof, always had the hottest new sneakers, the latest toys, the newest gadgets.

If I wasn't satisfied with what my grandmother cooked for dinner (though I usually was!), I could just order pizza—and not from lousy Pizza Coming, but from Pizza Hut, where the crust was so thick, it'd constipate you for a week. Life was good, but when my thirteenth birthday rolled around, I knew it wasn't yet the time for contentment—rather, it was the time for expansion. It became my new mission to farm massive crops of the world's most perfect hair for extensions and wigs. Naturally, I worked with the resources available to me, enlisting the help of my aforementioned directionless classmates. I gave them direction. I scoured the halls. I recruited only the students with the finest heads of hair and, more particularly, those with a willingness to invest time and care into their cranial farms and, most particularly of all, those with an awareness of the fleeting nature of the universe—I needed, above all else, to seek out those capable of letting go.

Under my supervision, the Number Seven Middle School became a breeding ground for long, beautiful locks. Each and every day was a new, real-life shampoo commercial. The students not under my care grew jealous all too quickly and improved their lifestyles so as to be permitted to join ranks. Soon, the student body was devouring vitamins as though tablets of fresh mountain air. Desks were streaked with oil from intensive hair treatments and leave-in conditioners. Combs became a form of currency. The cafeteria was forced to adapt to the marketplace and cater to the student body's changing tastes and nutritional requirements—more vegetable oil, less meat fat; more lean protein, fewer sugary carbs. A utopia was established, and at its forefront, there I stood.

But this paradise, like all paradises, wasn't to be eternal. One autumn afternoon, I was sitting in math class, ignoring the lesson in favor of updating meticulous records of each student's hair growth down to the millimeter, when an eerie hush fell over the room. I looked up from my notebook. The teacher, Mr. Deng, a wiry man with thick glasses, stood frozen before a blackboard of scrawled equations, staring in terror at the doorway, where Principal Li stood, his shadow casting its unique brand of darkness over the room. He boomed just three words, my full name, before he turned around and marched out. My classmates gasped. Mr. Deng gasped. A janitor in the hallway gasped. I stood up, shaking, my gaze cast downward, goose bumps rising on my skin, and followed the sound of his footsteps to his office.

I sat down. He sat down. He stared at me for a long moment, not breaking face. He took off his glasses and set them on the desk. "What," he blurted out, and pointed accusingly at my head, "is the meaning of this?"

Behind him, on the wall, I noticed dancing shadows—shadows that looked like those of people, thin people with almond-shaped heads, dancing, dancing; I couldn't look away.

"Meaning of what?" I heard my own voice say. I came back to myself quickly, startled to discover that I sounded brave, and then suddenly I felt brave. I straightened my spine. I looked behind him—the shadows had vanished—and then directly into his eyes, at those expanding and retracting pupils, as he shouted.

"Don't play dumb with me! Of your hair. Of everyone's hair. Don't think I haven't noticed. I've called other students into my office, and they've been obtuse too, but I'm no idiot. All roads lead back to you."

"All roads lead to Rome," I quoted from an imaginative comic book I'd been reading in my self-prescribed thirty minutes of "leisure time," a book in which gladiators went to war against cats dressed as Japanese samurai. It was an odd response, yes, but the situation called for absurdity.

Principal Li's face flushed red. He sputtered, and little drops of saliva flew from his mouth, landing on his cluttered desk. His sputter gave way to a low chuckle. "No, son, that was the past. This is the future. Now all roads lead to Beijing."

I wanted to chuckle too. I wanted to say, "I know, I am the most patriotic of them all. I am the one who will someday lead this great nation forward, who will inspire millions to forge their own paths." Instead I said, "You know what they say about blind nationalism: an eye for an eye makes the whole nation blind. And what can blind people do? In our China, they make excellent massage therapists! It is said that though they lack the ability to see, their sense of touch is stronger than anyone's. So, what then, we all become massage therapists? We all go around rubbing each other's shoulders and feet, and what else? Diagnosing illnesses and maladies based solely on feeling? Is that the future of our great nation?"

To be frank, I had no idea what I was going on about, but it felt right and I kept right on yammering, because what else was I supposed to do? As I veered further into this twisting and turning rant, Principal Li appeared progressively more confused, rolling his eyes back, turning my speech gems over and over again in his head, but despite his best efforts, he remained unenlightened. "Sorry," he finally confessed, interrupting me in the middle of a particularly good metaphor comparing the deteriorating ozone layer to a damaged cornea. "I don't follow."

I smiled smugly and offered no further explanation.

His anger—while hardly subtle before—was now crystalline, unabashed, volcanic, spewing. He spat on the ground and slammed his fist on the desk. "Stop messing with me, you godforsaken bamboozler! Just tell me what's going on here."

I took a deep breath. If I told him the truth, he'd demand a cut of my profits to allow me to continue, and, looking into his corrupt eyes, I swore then and there that I would never run a dirty business. But perhaps there was still a chance, I thought, that he would let me off, view me as an ally, as a patriot. I believed in myself, and above that, I believed in my potential. Whatever was going to happen could happen. Let it be.

I opened my mouth. I told him the truth.

His eyebrows shot up his forehead. "Private enterprise in a public institution!" he bellowed. "The nerve! The audacity! The gall!"

I slouched into the chair, not ashamed but relieved—at least now I knew. And was that really all he had to say?

I cleared my throat. "I happen to know for a fact that you accept bribes from many of my classmates' parents so that they can attend this 'public institution.' Money, dinners, gifts. That gut of yours isn't doing much to hide the evidence. Can't exactly afford to drink Moutai's finest rice wine and munch on sea cucumbers every night on a principal's salary, can you? I'd say you yourself are running your own successful little enterprise here."

His face flushed beet red. He opened his mouth, then clamped it shut, saying nothing.

My chair legs screeched on the floor as I stood up. "Well, then, sir, from one businessman to another, I wish you all the best. May your roads be smooth, may your women be naked, and may our unfortunate political and social climates remain conducive to supporting your terrible, immoral way of life!" I sunk into one step and the next and the next. For flourish's sake, I added a high-pitched "Bye-bye" as I strutted out the door.

News traveled quickly of my encounter with Principal Li. Via QQ messenger and text message, rumors spread and worsened like sexually transmitted diseases. Word on the street was I'd done everything from perform kung fu on the old bastard to curse his ancestors for eighteen generations to threaten an S&M-filled affair with his dog-faced wife. But among these falsehoods, one truth remained evident: my days of farming hair at Number Seven Middle School were over.

That night, I called an emergency meeting at Confucius Temple Park, near my family's new home in a sleek high-rise apartment complex (I'd lent my dad some money for the down payment). I stood barefoot on a large stone, channeling the energy of the ancients. Dozens of my long-locked classmates sat before me on the grass, much to the chagrin of the senior citizens practicing their tai chi, and in direct violation of the "green grass makes a happy world, do not step" signs. We were young, we were rebellious, we were free.

I cleared my throat, summoning spirits. Solemn eyes stared back at me. Worried eyes.

"Friends," I began, "as you've probably heard, Principal Li is onto us. Today I was called into his office, where he delivered an ultimatum."

The Heads, as I'd begun to call them, nodded gravely. Their black hair glistened in the moonlight—what masterpieces, what works of art!

"But before I tell you what Principal Li told me, I first want to thank each of you for your loyalty to me and to your hair and to our great China." I sucked in a shallow, shaky breath. "Unfortunately, Principal Li was able, despite your overwhelming courage and loyalty, to piece things together for himself. He may be a stupid egg, but even a stupid egg finds its way into the frying pan every once in a while, becoming a building block for a wholesome breakfast, chock-full of omega fatty acids."

There was silence, utter silence, until Head Seventy-Two snapped to and elbowed Head Thirty-Three, who forced a weak laugh. Many others followed suit, and uncomfortable, forced laughter rang through the park, apparently disrupting the chi of some of the tai chi participants, causing more than one to fall to the ground. They stood, dusted themselves off, got back to it. I nodded. I continued.

"I am then forced to leave each of you to make a great decision that may well affect the rest of your life. Principal Li has decreed that there shall be no more hair farming on his watch. All students who wish to remain at Number Seven Middle School must cut their hair"—I paused for effect—"and keep it cut."

There was a gasp and then a titter in the crowd, followed by a low hush of whispering.

"While piety is important, my comrades, so is commerce. And although the decision was a difficult one to make, I have decided to quit school and to start farming hair full-time."

I spoke these fateful words with many sets of eyes staring back at me. In those eyes, I saw fear and I saw indecision and I saw uncertainty and I saw determination and I saw hope.

"My friends!" I leaped from the stone onto a bench, and as I did, I raised my fist in the air and I felt like I was flying. "You're either with me, or you're back to school!"

We all know that education is of utmost importance in our China, so it came as no surprise that many of my Heads' parents did not support any such hopes for a prodigious career. It was with heavy hearts and red-rimmed, weepy eyes that these Heads came to me, asking me to reap their final harvest. I cut with steady hands, delivered the hair to local salons, and returned only to distribute payouts at our old after-school haunt, the Yogurt Room. Over cups of unsweetened cultured dairy product, I thanked every Head individually for his or her contributions, handed over an envelope, and wished each one all the best.

My relationships with three very special Heads, however, did not end in the Yogurt Room—they did not end at all. These three made the courageous choice to quit school and accompany me on my path toward greatness. Within a week, I'd found a location for our new full-time farm—a storefront on the first and second floors of an apartment complex, between a small plastic surgery clinic and a shop that exclusively sold blueberry products. I paid the landlord a deposit and the first three months' rent in cash.

The next evening, in my family's living room, I broke it to my parents that I was moving out of their home. My father's face was stern. My mother's didn't move a muscle. I explained about Principal Li's corruption, about wanting to supervise every aspect of my crops, ensuring the organic quality of my product; I explained about my dreams and ambitions and need for a higher profit margin.

At once, both of their steely expressions broke and my stoic parents burst into sobs. I lowered myself to sit on the uncomfortable IKEA sofa I'd paid for, stunned, unsure of how to proceed. I'd never before seen them display any kind of emotion. To be perfectly frank, since I'd started middle school, I'd not really seen my parents at all. Just to talk with them on this evening, I'd had to schedule a meeting via e-mail, and even then we'd gone back and forth quite a few times before we were able to find a time that was convenient for us all.

They sobbed. They wailed.

I cleared my throat. "I'm sorry" was all I could manage. And I was. Never in my wildest dreams did I imagine that quitting school and moving out would trouble my parents so immensely, would cause them such heartache. A tinge of pity plucked at my gut.

Five minutes passed. Five long minutes of wailing and crying. Five minutes with no words to comfort me—my grandmother, I thought, would have known what to say, but she'd died the year before after a thankfully short battle with cancer.

I stood up, and my father snorted what sounded to be a rather juicy load of snot back up his nose. He dabbed his eyes with a tissue. At last, he spoke. "We're just so... so... so proud."

"What?" I shook my head, uncomprehending. "Sorry, what?"

My mother wiped a trail of mucus on her sleeve. "Yes, our son—a successful entrepreneur! This is why we've worked so hard, why we've sacrificed so much! This is what we've always dreamed of!" She burst into tears again, and the both of them knelt down and kowtowed before me. Snot hung in strings from their noses. Tears streaked their faces. I backed away slowly, wary of this mess; I was wearing brand-new Nikes.

YOUTH IS THE SEASON OF HOPE

With my parents' blessing, a small suitcase, and my three special Heads—Twin One, Twin Two, and Kai—in tow, I set off across town on the Number Sixty-Three bus and set up shop in our new location.

On the first floor was a kitchen, where I stored and prepared only the healthiest of meals; a line of barber chairs and mirrors for inspections, trims, and harvests; a mirrored wall and an open space for exercise; a private bathroom where I had a state-of-the-art showerhead installed; and a laundry/sun/vitamin-D absorption room. Upstairs was a small loft where the four of us slept on two identical bunk beds. As Chairman Mao said, great leaders must live with their followers, exist among their ranks. And in that headquarters, we slept, and shat, and shared our dreams for the future—the twins hoped to buy their parents a seaside villa, pay a nationally known matchmaker to find them a set of blond twins for wives, and eventually retire with said twins to Switzerland. Kai hoped to use his savings to emigrate to America, where he'd buy an Olympic-sized swimming pool; as a child, he'd loved diving, but since he'd started farming hair, he hadn't so much as dipped a toe in a pool—chlorine is a dangerous, growth- and quality-inhibiting substance. As for me, I dreamed simply of being rich—of villas made of money bricks, of being matched with more money, of skiing atop mountains of money, of swimming in pools of money, of money, money, money. I wanted only to have so much money that I'd never want for anything.

But dreams were dreams; dreams are like the sky, ever present but untouchable, and dreams remained a distant horizon toward which we continued to run. We lived now in reality. Reality was vitamins; morning, afternoon, and evening calisthenics; boiled free-range chicken and steamed vegetables. Reality was plastic containers of imported yogurt...

SUPPORT THE COMMUNITY
AND THE COMMUNITY WILL SUPPORT YOU

WITH STRICT TWENTY-FOUR-HOUR OVERSIGHT AND CONTROL, THE quality of our product improved tenfold, and we were racing to keep up with orders from the province's finest salons.

One morning, after I'd successful harvested Kai's latest crop and as I was packaging it for shipment, I heard footsteps by the front door. I went to check and found taped to the doorframe a letter from the local neighborhood committee demanding to know what was really going on in my "shadowy" business and threatening to have me shut down for crimes of "spiritual pollution."

My blood, it boiled. Intuitively understanding the importance of transparency from an early age, I raced over to the table where Kai and the twins sat slurping oatmeal and showed them the letter. We ranted together, commiserating: Shadowy?! Spiritual pollution?! Shouldn't those old coots with nothing better to do than attempt to shut down flourishing new businesses go after someone who was actually doing something wrong—say the malpractice-y plastic surgery clinic next door, out of which at least one terrifying, Michael Jackson-esque woman exited every day?! Truly an insult to aesthetics! Or what about that damn blueberry product shop, which was so obviously a front for money-laundering at best and some horrible child-trafficking pit stop at worst! With all of that real spiritual pollution in their midst, why in heaven's name did these old bastards care about organic little us?!

But the thing about most people is that they're very nosy when it comes to things that don't concern them and very bored with the things that do. I didn't respond to the letter, and the next day another envelope appeared taped to the door. For one week, every day I found a new envelope containing a new letter, each more strongly worded than the last. On the eighth day there was no letter. There was a knock at the door. I excused myself, mid-jumping jack, from morning exercises to answer. Three old-timers—two ladies and one man, who, I'd come to find out, composed the neighborhood committee in its entirety—had blessed me on this sunny Saturday with an impromptu visit.

I gestured for my Heads to make a quick escape upstairs—I didn't want my crops to experience any growth-discouraging, cortisol-level-raising stress—and I turned back to the old-timers. "Come in please," I said politely, albeit through gritted teeth.

"You better let us in, you damn pimp!" the apparent leader, henceforth dubbed Old Cranky Lady, shouted, elbowing her way past me.

"Calm down," I said. "Please, take a seat."

She plopped her saggy ass down at the dining table, as did her partners-in-nagging, Old Mr. Wrinkles, who appeared to be half man and half shar-pei, and Old Sassy, a woman with a bad perm who swayed her hips suggestively when she walked and in lieu of speaking just made judgmental clicking noises with her tongue.

I stood before this ragtag bunch, at the table's head, trying despite my annoyance to maintain a stature of authority. This was, after all, my business, my company, my location. I'd signed the lease. I'd paid my quarterly rent installment. I had every right in the world to be there. "Now," I spoke clearly, "what is it you—"

"Whores! You've got a bunch of whores in here!" Old Cranky Lady cackled. "Some of us are trying to raise respectable families and quietly live out our wholesome lives while your cheap prostitutes just laze around in here, filing their nails all day waiting for johns to come poke their Viagra-hard pricks in them. What the hell kind of example does that set for our grandchildren? They're going to grow up thinking, Why should I learn algebra when instead I could just open my legs and—"

A slow, hearty laughter rose from my belly and dribbled out of my mouth.

To Old Cranky Lady, my laughter only further implicated me. "Yes, you pimp daddy, laugh it up, we all know what goes on in here. No sign out front. Long-locked ladies lounging about. The gig is up."

Old Mr. Wrinkles piped up: "Your generation is always rattling on about women's equality and whatnot, and yet, here you are, a young man with long hair yourself, trying to look like some American rock star, all the while exploiting young females—"

"Well, that's all well and nice," I interrupted, "but there are no women here at the moment. Though beautifully tressed, all of my employees are actually young men." I used their shocked silence as an opportunity to shout for the Heads to join us. My three pretties obediently marched down the stairs and stood at attention beside me.

Old Cranky Lady slapped herself in the face. "They *are* men! A homosexual whorehouse! Well, fuck my mother in heaven!" Red marks rose on her cheek, and she clutched her heart as if in great agony.

I bit my lip. "Look, I hate to disappoint you all, but this is no whore house."

Their already sagging faces fell—which, as you can imagine, was a ghastly sight.

"This, my revered elders," I said, with a dramatic sweep of my arm, "is an organic hair farm."

"What's that?" Old Mr. Wrinkles barked. Strings of drool attached his upper lip to his lower one—I wanted to gag, but instead I launched into the explanation: the Heads, the process, the health, the care, the harvest, the profit. At first, the geezers seemed skeptical. I could read the doubt in their eyes. But I tried my best to predict their unasked questions and to provide answers. I spoke of the demand among the nouveau riche for beautiful hair. Of our nation's burgeoning vanity. Of movie stars whose own silky locks just couldn't cut it anymore in our high-definition world. A half hour later, when I finally stopped talking, the coots sat transfixed, as though under a spell.

"Any questions?"

"Yes," Old Sassy spoke for the first time, and her tone was surprisingly measured, reasonable. "How do we get in?"

Though I hadn't been aware of it at the time I'd selected my storefront, the local community, though shoddy on its surface, was home to many wealthy old people with entirely too much time on their hands—there were only so many hours of the day they could spend shucking peas, watching soap operas, and nagging their grandchildren to do homework; only so many public dance lessons, games of mah-jongg, and bus routes to aimlessly ride. These were the sorts who had held on through all the bad China had to offer and, in exchange for blood shed and innocence loss, had been offered apartments in the 1990s when the housing sector was privatized.

Hardly a fair trade, but property is property, and property is money, and money is money, and after a lifetime without...

FINDING TALENT

THESE OLD-TIMERS FORMED A UNION OF SORTS AND APPROACHED ME with their initial investment offer. Cash in hand, I was able to expand my housing units up onto the third and fourth floors of the apartment building. To fill the new beds, I placed ads all over the Internet seeking candidates willing to chop off their beautiful, thick hair and grow in its place new, organic strands. As compensation for their time and effort, Heads would be provided room and board, a modest monthly stipend, and a considerable lump sum each time a crop was harvested and sold.

I received thousands of replies to my ad, e-mails and phone calls at all hours.

Working now not only as a Head but as my head assistant, Kai helped me sift through thousands of digital photos—the ones that had obviously been doctored immediately went in the recycle bin. I wanted photos of roots and of ends, and I wanted to see their hair in action too—I received photos of applicants in front of Tiananmen, crouching on park paths beside cherry blossom branches, smiling in theme parks.

Thousands of photos were soon narrowed down to hundreds. The applicants who made it through the first round were sent an e-mail inviting them to come and interview with me personally at headquarters. I looked carefully at the hair of each, an indication of future product quality, and, more important, at their scalps, which housed all potential.

Of all the heads, a few stood out, and those few were hired on the spot. But no one stood out in the way that a pole star stands out against a dark night sky. That is to say, there were many who were good, good enough, but none who were great.

None, that is, until late Sunday afternoon, the third and final day of interviews. Kai stepped out for a yogurt break. Alone in the interview room, working away, I registered footsteps approaching, but I didn't look up from my stack of papers—there was so much to be done; here I was getting my first taste of what it was not just to be a leader, but to be a CEO. And then, still not looking up, I heard an unsteady voice asking, "Am I too late?"

Into my stack of papers, I muttered, "No, it's fine. Sit."

I could hear the applicant breathing as I continued to rifle through the stacks. I disappeared into a world of words and photos, but was jolted back when a bead of sweat dropped from my forehead onto one of the papers, smearing the ink. It was December, but there was an unmistakable warmth generating from somewhere in the room. I looked up, wondering if this weirdo had brought some sort of space heater with her—it hardly seemed unreasonable after some of the oddities I'd encountered over the past couple of days: there'd been a guy who wore a rainbow clown wig and very seriously claimed it to be his real hair, a teenage girl who wept the entire interview and told us she was planning on taking a lethal dose of sleeping pills if we didn't hire her, a middle-aged woman who tried to sell her graying pubic hair, which she'd already cut and carried with her in a Happy Mart plastic bag. Eyes homed in on the ink-sweat smear, body soaking up that warmth, I was reminded of the flying disc I'd seen as a child standing atop the beauty salon.

And now, as then, I couldn't help but look up.

There was no space heater, no shadow, no matte white disc, nothing strange. The girl who sat before me, whose footsteps I'd heard, whose voice quavered, wore a simple black T-shirt. She had a plain, symmetrical face, the kind of face makeup artists love to paint upon, a runway model's face, the kind of face so nondescript that she just as easily could have had a career in crime. She wore no jewelry, no noticeable makeup, and she wore her hair down.

Her glorious, glorious hair.

MANAGING YOUR HUMAN CAPITAL

ON DAY ONE OF OPERATION EXPANSION, I LED MY ARMY OF NEW recruits downstairs to our newly renovated first floor. I delivered a most rousing speech. I ordered their heads shaved, one by one. There were a few tears, but mostly there was excitement, the electric possibility of fresh lives to be lived, of new pleasures to be had. There was this palatable feeling that we, our feet rooted in the ground and our heads reaching toward an unknowable sky, teetered on the brink of something big...

3.

I STOP READING THERE. I KNOW WHAT HAPPENS NEXT. ALL AT ONCE, I remember the hiccups, the power struggles, the growing pains. The move from Nanjing to Shanghai, the multimillion-dollar investments, the magazine covers, the fame, the glory. I remember it all quite clearly now. I do not need, or want, to read about it any further.

My legs tingle, pins and needles. I stand up, shake them out, and flip through the proceeding chapters. I skim passages, sentences here and there. To think that I thought I was chosen! To think that I thought I had some New Age mandate of heaven! How arrogant I was then, how tragically optimistic! I stare down at the book, and I close it, and it seems to me now like someone else wrote this, a stranger to this self, and I wonder: How many selves are in the self? Are the possibilities finite, predetermined, or are they limitless? How many more versions of me might someday write the future stories of my life?

I rub the cover printed with my name, and I notice the rain pattering on the roof, and I realize it must have been falling for quite some time and I feel tired because of it, so I yawn, and then I go to the bathroom. I relieve myself and wash my hands. I turn off the faucet and then I look directly in the mirror, at something I've been largely unwilling to face: I am losing my hair. No, that's inaccurate. Here it is full-frontal: this hair mogul is going bald.

It began to happen in the months that led up to my breakdown, though I now think it was a symptom and not, as many tabloids noted, a cause. I visited specialists, got second and third and fourth opinions. The verdicts were all the same: I'd exhausted all of my potential. Beyond synthetic options, chemical options, transplant options—options that went against everything I'd ever stood for and grew and knew—there was no hope. For many months, I refused to acknowledge this defeat.

But burying things does not get rid of them; it just puts them temporarily out of sight. I cannot avoid this forever. I watch myself in the mirror as I stroke my hairless patches at my temples, and then I go for the large one on the top.

Floating here in a purgatory state south of admiration and north of disgust, I hear a creaking sound behind me and notice a small flash of movement in the corner of the mirror. My heart skips and I turn around quickly, but there is nothing there. I go from one end of the house to the other, from the fireplace to my bed, but notice nothing out of place.

I return to my computer, open it. There is a new e-mail from my mother. I wait for it to load. My mother is either enviably oblivious to current events or as mentally ill as I'm rumored to be. She writes every week or so as though she thinks I'm still on my way up in the world, that I'm still in my penthouse apartment at headquarters in Shanghai growing my hair and buying a new pair of Nikes every week, that I'm still at heart that same thirteen-year-old boy I was when I left her. I don't have the heart to tell her that her son is in voluntary exile, don't have it in me to shatter her delusion. As cold and distant as she may be, she's still my mother, and my replies are always upbeat but vague, always "I'm doing fine" and "Business is business" and other such nonsense.

Here her latest e-mail loads, and I'm expecting it to be more delusional crap, but as I read, I lean toward the screen, slouching, losing life force. "Your father and I, we spent our whole lives working toward the idea of you. When I was just a little girl I used to imagine someday having a child of my own. It's funny how we're made like that, isn't it? Before we know anything worth passing on, before we have any of the money or resources to care for another human being, before our bodies are even equipped to make one. And then your father and I married because we had four parents total, all longing for a grandchild. He was my first and only boyfriend. It's not so much romantic as sad. If you think we ever loved each other like they do in the movies, you're wrong. We tolerated each other and now we've tolerated each other into an inescapable corner. We are too old and ugly to divorce, and what would be the point anyway? It's alone together or alone alone. Some choice. But I'm sorry to write such a rambling message. All I'm really trying to say here is that many dreams and lives wove together to bring you into creation. Many were crushed. Whatever happens to you next, remember this."

I think about Jesus Christ. I think about Muhammad. I think about Lao-tzu. I think about Chairman Mao. They had earthly parents too. What did these parents think of them? I touch the bald spot atop my head. I tap my bare soles against the floor. So Mom must have finally heard the news, or realized she couldn't keep ignoring it. I curl my toes. I read the e-mail another three times, unsure still of what tone to take away. I drum my fingers on the table. Does she think I did it? Does she actually think I'm a murderer? Is she saying that I ruined her life? That I ruined that of my father too? That my existence crushed their dreams? Or is she simply pointing out the sacrifice and saying it's all been worth it? I bite my lip. Is she angry at me? Disappointed? Sad? Worried? I sigh and surrender my speculation. I notice the date on my mother's e-mail and realize that I am set to appear in court in exactly one week. My nervous heart rattles in my chest. There is another knock. Flesh on wood. My rattling heart drops. I look out the window, but there is no car this time. I jump up and yank open the door. There is nothing on the step this time. I look around. There is no one there. I shut the door. I turn around, walk back to my computer, and that is when I see a new e-mail from an unknown sender. It contains only a link. I know it's not a virus. I know this link. I remember this link. How could I forget?

4.

A MADMAN SPEAKS: THE VIRAL RANTINGS AND RAVINGS OF SUSPECT WANG XILAI

NETIZENS, MY NAME IS WANG XILAI. YOU MAY KNOW ME AS THE founder and CEO of Hair Inc., our nation's most successful hair extension corporation. You may know me as a bestselling memoirist and our nation's most prominent openly gay figure. You may know me as inspiration to millions of marginalized young men and women, as a messenger of hope—I've said it in lecture halls across the country, and I'll say it again now: *With a little hard work and determination, riches are well within your reach!* So reach for them, netizens, take what is yours!

Yes, you may think you know me entirely, that you know all there is to know.

But believing you have it all, isn't this the surest way to fall?

You may be surprised, netizens, to learn that I am writing this from a holding cell. That's right: the man you thought you knew is but a stranger in metaphorical chains.

The police confiscated my phone, yes, but as has so often been the case in my life, they underestimated me. Anyone with half a wit knows that a good businessman always carries a spare. Consider that some free advice, netizens—perhaps, if I'm ever set loose, I will include that nugget in an updated version of my memoir. It is practical advice, to be sure, not high or philosophical, but it is sound, and sometimes the words we need to hear the most are the words that reside closest to the ground: "Look both ways before you cross the street." "Don't eat anything bigger than your own head." "Don't accept rat-poisoned candy from child snatchers who cruise the streets in bread-loaf vans." So on and so forth.

But back to the issue at hand. This afternoon, I was minding my business, going about my day, watching a film in my apartment, when a gaggle of cops burst through the door, pounced on me, slapped handcuffs on my wrists, and hauled me in. I am now being held here on charges of conspiracy to commit murder and accessory to the murder of three individuals: an unmarried receptionist (33), a somewhat anthropomorphic goose (age unknown), and Bashful Goose Snack Company's founder and beloved national figure, Papa Hui (58). Yes, this is the issue at hand.

Of course, netizens, these charges are bogus. I may not be a perfect man, I may not be a holy man, but I am an innocent man. To prove I have nothing to hide, I will lay out the whole story for you, piece by piece. I will type the truth until the crooked cops pry the phone from my unimpeachable hands. I beg of you, netizens, take seriously my cries and spread the word, petition for my immediate release! Alert the media, dear netizens, alert journalists far and wide! Alert the UN, foreign governments, human rights activists, tell everyone you know!

Here it goes: it began with a girl. Her name was—is—Lulu Qi, and she grew some of the best hair my company ever produced, supplied for some of the most famous actresses and models in the world. You've seen her hair in advertisements, in movies, in red carpet photos. Those locks of hers were worth millions and generated millions more. Along with being my top crop and most valuable asset, Lulu became a dear friend. I took special care to ensure that she had the best of everything. She had sessions with a personal trainer, she swallowed state-of-the-art supplements, she slept on the finest silk pillowcases, she drank highly priced soup made from the meat of the endangered pangolin. Okay, I know that's illegal, netizens, and you know what? That's fine. Help get me out of here, and I'll even give up the names of the restaurants and chefs that prepared it for us! Let's take down poachers together, let's save ecosystems, let's set me free.

The year Lulu joined the company was the year we moved head-quarters from that apartment building in old Nanjing to a high-rise in Shanghai... ah, the glitz, the glamour, the garbage. Along with all the other Heads, Lulu and I lived and worked together, and enjoyed afternoon leisure time in my executive break room on the twenty-seventh floor, sipping *da hong pao* tea, gnawing raw almonds, chatting. Lulu was a magical girl, and we had so much in common. We both loved fantasy and science fiction novels, we both loved handsome boys, we both loved sharing fairy tales passed down by our elderly relatives. We never ran out of things to talk about, and leisure time could no longer contain our budding friendship, so while the other Heads attended their daily nutrition and self-care classes, Lulu started joining me for my special tutorials.

I'd hired some private teachers to help guide me with more spiritual matters. It's quite common, as I'm sure you clever netizens are well aware. Most CEOs and people of my status at the very least have someone on payroll to tell their fortune—you know, like which days are auspicious and which days you shouldn't step outside, which days you should burn paper money for your ancestors and which days you should just bugger off because they're on their ghostly menstrual cycles, and so forth. And because Lulu was my friend and because she was inherently interested in such matters, she started joining me for meditation class, astrology class, tarot card readings, fortune stick readings, and earthing sessions. At first, she was an apt pupil. I mean, she'd be quizzing me on the meanings of those tarot cards during leisure time, gazing up at the stars at night and trying to make her own charts, insisting that we go to the park to sneak in extra earthing time.

But a few months or so in, her interest waned. I don't mean to say that one day she was an American cheerleader and the next she was a corpse bride. No, it was more of a gradual—and, I felt, natural—decline. She still attended the classes, but in her free time, she started watching more and more TV, started reading more and more trashy novels, lost that enchanting sparkle in her eye.

During that time, that period of decline, in one of our meditation classes, I received a call and had to scamper off to deal with an emergency—one of my Heads, a very pretty but very silly girl from Guangzhou, had yet again gotten her hair stuck in her hoodie's zipper. I tended to the crisis and then raced back to the meditation room. I paused at the doorway. A hushed conversation was happening inside. Lulu whispered something including the words "hopelessness" and "no point" to the teacher, a Zen master so skilled at meditative arts that he could levitate. The master replied with words that included "believe" and "overcome," but that was all I caught—as soon as they heard my heavy breathing, as soon as they spotted my looming figure, they clamped shut their mouths and pretended to return to their transcendent states, and I settled in on my cushion between them and pretended to return to mine.

Now stick with me here. A day or two after I overheard that conversation, I received an invitation to a dinner banquet to honor the Bashful Goose Snack Company's twenty-fifth anniversary. Naturally, I asked Lulu to be my date. Although it probably would've been acceptable for me to take a male date, I was painfully single at the time, no boyfriend, not even a suitable prospect in sight.

At the time, Lulu was growing a crop for a top actress, who was set to star in an American film. We all felt a special attachment to this crop because this wasn't simply about beauty—this was about patriotism, about glory, about that oft-mentioned "Rising Dragon." These strands would do what diplomats and leaders only wished they could: truly and positively represent our nation abroad.

We spent many months and mountains of money tending to this crop, and under normal circumstances, I never would've allowed a Head out into public on the eve of a harvest, and especially not a harvest as important as this one. Risk management, my friends, risk management—hair can get sucked up like a flip-flop in an escalator, scissor-wielding thieves can have their way, there are car accidents, restaurant fires, oil spills, a million such calamities to consider. Our world is a dangerous one, indeed.

But the Bashful Goose Anniversary Banquet wasn't a normal circumstance. It was a secure circumstance. And I thought it'd cheer ol' Lulu up, attending such an event. Yes, that's what I thought anyway. And that was my first mistake.

As you may have read, netizens, a special banquet hall was erected for the event. This construction project took nearly three thousand workers a year to complete, and rumors buzzed that after the banquet, the structure (designed and then renounced by China's most famous artist, currently on house arrest) would be remodeled into the first Bashful Goose Shopping Mall—it was almost unbelievable! The biggest company in China expanding into a new sector?! Maybe wealth truly was limitless! That's what I thought then, anyway. But those were only rumors, and I digress. That was the future, uncertain, unknowable. The banquet itself? This was the present, tangible as anything.

All the most important people were expected to show. CEOs, actresses, government officials, singers—we were all integral to one another's success; we formed this beautiful spiderweb of prosperity, interconnected, and we all came to pay homage because we knew our web wouldn't exist without Papa Hui. He was the spider that spun us.

Let me make it clear: this was the first time I'd been invited to an event hosted by Papa Hui. Not to say I was left out before—it's more that he wasn't much of a party-thrower. What I mean to say is that this was the first large-scale event Papa Hui had ever hosted.

Had I spoken to Papa Hui before? Not really. We'd exchanged a few words, sure, such as "How are you?," "How's business?," "How's your health?," "Have you eaten dinner?," and so forth. But he is— was—a quiet man, and I'm no real social mover and shaker myself, so I guess the answer is no, not really.

So please see me here, netizens: I'm innocent, truly. I hardly knew the man, and his wealth and power were, and are, of no real consequence to me.

Sure, I remember having all the Bashful Goose jingles stuck in my head as a child, but who didn't? *Bashful Goose snacks, eat 'em right up / They're so delicious, they'll make you fall in love!* Just try to get that ditty out of your head! And, yes, I read his authorized biography in my teen years, and I later read case studies about his company too, learned a lot about marketing, managing human capital, all of that. Even for someone as successful as me, his wealth and clout are, or *were* I should say, unimaginable. Not unattainable, clearly, under the right set of circumstances and with the right amount of optimism... but still, beyond comprehension.

But enough about that. Back to the banquet. Oh boy, dozens of Bentleys and Lamborghinis and Ferraris parked out front like a car show. Plush carpet everywhere. We pushed through the designer-dressed, camera-flashed, bleached-toothed madness that was the foyer, and one of the hostesses escorted Lulu and me through the banquet hall. We followed this lovely creature down a very wide red-carpeted aisle, on either side of which stood dozens of round tables. It was a typical setup, not breaking with tradition, but there were small special touches here and there that let us know this wasn't an ordinary banquet: a Hermès napkin for each guest with his or her name embroidered in gold thread by a talented chimpanzee who'd been trained to do handicrafts; a golden goose-shaped fountain in the center of each table; small drink-refilling hovercrafts floating around, remote-controlled by Russian model waitresses. That kind of thing. As jaded as I am, I must admit I was transfixed, nearly hypnotized, by such details. I only snapped to when the hostess chirped, "Here you are. Please sit."

Lulu, stunning in Dolce & Gabbana, and I, looking quite dapper myself in Alexander McQueen, stood stupefied before the Hui family table. This had to be a mistake! I looked to the hostess to clarify, but she had already scurried off to seat the next entering couple, a top national leader and his dragon lady wife. I glanced at Lulu, who, with her eyebrows up in the center of her forehead, looked as surprised as I felt. I looked at Kelly Hui, who stared at the tablecloth as though trying to burn a hole through it. At Mama Hui swiping her iPhone like a madwoman—she's a top-ranked player of numerous mobile games, including Candy Crush. At the six other Hui family members and close friends, including a slovenly male cousin from Wuhan who couldn't be bothered to even dress up for the evening and Mama Hui's butch lady driver with whom it'd long been rumored she was having an affair. At a napkin with my name embroidered into it, and at the next setting, a napkin embroidered with Lulu's. I shrugged and pulled out Lulu's chair for her. What an auspicious mistake, what a night this will be, I thought, and silently thanked whoever had somehow screwed up the seating chart.

Boring speeches followed, you know the kind—the ones everyone desperately wants to end so that the feasting can begin. A toupeed man, the CFO, was up onstage rattling off very specific numerical figures (projections for next quarter and the like) as well as very vague ideological phrases, such as "Success is key" and "Motivation and perspiration with the State's cooperation drive enterprise." Ten minutes into this winner of a speech, Kelly leaned over to me. I wouldn't say she was being rude here—many people were whispering back and forth, some not even bothering to whisper; mobile phones were going off left, right, and center, Lady Gaga and Justin Bieber ringtones galore. So Kelly, she leans over to me, and goes, "What do you think about obesity?" And I go, "I don't have a strong opinion either way, but I suppose it's sad. Why can't they just stop eating? You know Lao-tzu said, 'A man who knows when enough is enough will always have enough.'" And she nods and goes, "Yes, of course I know that quote, I took, like, two philosophy classes at USC, okay, and yes, obesity is very sad." She goes, "I'm working on this new project. I'm going to give a speech about it in a minute and I think that—"

But then the room went pitch dark, and after a few disembodied screams, silence reigned. The lights flickered back on. Hundreds of chins pointed up, seeking the source of a dramatic whooshing sound. Eyes darted, searching, searching. And then, coming into view, the mystery was revealed: Papa Hui, attached to the rafters by cables, soared above our heads, and the bashful goose, attached by its own set of cables, soared beside him. An engine roared, and all of our heads spun simultaneously as a red Lamborghini with five yellow stars on its hood sped down the center aisle, pulling up the carpet behind it to reveal a glass floor. Below the glass floor was crystal clear water, rivaling that of the Caribbean. The Lamborghini screeched to a stop just before it hit the poor CFO, who was still stagnating on the stage, his now-crooked toupee drenched with sweat, his mouth agape. There was a buzz as the glass retracted, and then another whoosh as a mystery man, dressed all in black, soared in from the back of the room clutching a pair of jewel-encrusted scissors, which he used to snip the wires that held Papa Hui and the bashful goose.

There was a collective gasp as the two plunged downward—who was this black-clothed bandit? Who was he to send Papa Hui and the bashful goose to their deaths? These were the questions on all of our tongues, in all of our hearts.

But, lo and behold, Papa Hui did not land on a table, impaling his billion-dollar throat on a golden fountain! He landed in the water, on the back of a great white shark, and the bashful goose landed on the small yellow inflatable boat tied to the shark's tail! This bandit's cut, this fall from on high—it was all choreographed! And it didn't end there. The Lamborghini driver, a recognizable British film star, then hopped out of the car and tossed Papa Hui a wireless microphone, which he effortlessly caught, as well as a cowboy hat, which he flipped onto his head. On the shark's back as it swam laps up and down the pool, Papa Hui sang, beautifully I might add, in the voice of a saint or an angel or a teenage superstar: *As sweet as honey, your smile is sweet as honey. / Where have I seen you before? Ah, yes, yes, in my dreams!*

Yes, netizens, you can believe your eyes. I write only the truth. A fiftysomething man, our nation's wealthiest person, swooped into a banquet hall like a Chinese Superman saving his brethren from a yawn-inducing speech, landed on a great white shark, and proceeded to ride said shark while donning a cowboy hat and delivering a pitch-perfect rendition of a beloved Teresa Teng classic...

To say that Papa Hui's performance was a hit would be like saying that Chairman Mao enjoyed eating pork belly, which is to say it'd be a gross understatement. Four ambulances that had been on standby in front of the banquet hall raced off to the hospital to deliver two heart attack victims (one male, one female), one woman who'd conked her head on a chair leg when she fainted, and one man who shat himself with shock but to avoid embarrassment told everyone he'd contracted chronic dysentery on a recent trip to South Africa. I don't think the medics believed him, but they strapped him to a stretcher anyway, kindly sparing him the added humiliation of losing face.

I myself, though also physically shocked, found myself feeling a bit, shall I say, "spiritually numb" toward this performance. It was unprecedented, yes, and I wanted to like it as much as everyone else seemed to, but... I don't know. I don't want to say that he'd made a mockery of his empire, but I couldn't help but feel the whole thing was just a bit over the top.

I looked to Lulu, hoping that she, my best friend, would share my disillusionment, but no matter how hard I nudged her with my elbow, no matter how hard I dug my heel onto her Louboutin shoe, she wouldn't meet my eye. She just looked down, traced her finger over that napkin printed with her name. Seeking validation for my blas-phemous thoughts, I spun around in my seat, the room glittering all around me, and in that entire hall of faces, I spotted only one that mir-rored my own: that of Kelly Hui, who, poor thing, looked as though she'd coughed something up but hadn't yet found a place to spit it out.

At the conclusion of Papa Hui's performance, he cried out, "Let the feast begin!" and the speech portion of the night officially came to an end. Nude waitresses on roller skates handcrafted from designer shoes delivered dish after dish: heaping plates of sea cucumbers, steaming bowls of bird's nest soup, silver platters of tiger meat cooked with the fur still attached. Oh, a feast if I ever saw one. The eating went on for centuries it seemed. I partook in the more nutritious and growth encouraging of the delicacies, but the party got rowdy, crazy, and soon our nation's best and brightest were floating from table to table, drinking and laughing. Kelly, clearly irritated that she hadn't been able to deliver her speech about whatever her new project was, ate her feelings, going to town on everything, not bothering to wipe her grease-shiny mouth between dishes, releasing hearty belches. When her belches started sounding especially juicy and she looked as though she was about to vomit, she pushed her chair away from the table and announced she was off to "mingle," which consisted of her standing in a corner glaring at everyone, mimicking their laughs and whatnot. I watched her there across the room talking and laughing to herself like a lunatic, wearing her bursting-at-the-seams dress, an overstuffed dumpling if I ever saw one, and I remembered what she'd said earlier about obesity and I thought, This poor girl, she's clearly on a downward spiral, and has gained probably five or more kilograms in the short time I'd known her. Maybe she wouldn't be considered fat in America, where I hear that many of the afflicted must ride around in special wheelchairs because they can't walk or fit into regular ones, but here in China she was definitely straddling the line. I pitied her; what pressure to be the spawn of someone so powerful, and to be so physically disproportionate to yourself, and also, as you netizens so viciously love to speculate, to be an awkward supervirgin incapable of even online dating. She was so darling as a child—who knew she'd grow up into this? I wanted to cry for her, but I also didn't much feel like crying in public, so I tore my gaze away from this train wreck and instead started making eyes at a very handsome singer sipping *baijiu* a few tables away. Oh, how I'd like to get my hands on that thinning hair,

I thought. I know just the perfect Head to supply him with beautiful, natural-looking plugs, I—

A shadow eclipsed my thoughts as Papa Hui himself took a seat beside me. A second later, the bashful goose, never far behind, waddled up and rested its plump egg head in his lap.

"Well," Papa Hui said, giving me a hearty slap on the back, "what'd you think?"

I sat erectly, trying to give a good impression to this admirable man, not wanting to give away the fact that I'd been mentally blaspheming him and his daughter and mentally matchmaking myself to new clients.

Mustering every ounce of feigned enthusiasm in my body, I cried, "Fantastic! The show of the century!"

He stroked the goose's head with his index finger and said, "Exhausting."

I cocked my head.

"You know, son," he said, and I'll have you know I nearly wet myself right then and there—a living legend, the richest and most brilliant man in China, using a term of endearment on me! He continued. "I've spent the past three months preparing for this night. And sure, it was fantastic. But ultimately, what was the point? Waste a bunch of money on some damn party to make everyone feel good about themselves for a short time. They'll wake up tomorrow with a bad case of the shits and a splitting headache. No one leaves a place like this feeling any less empty than when they came in."

To that odd outburst, I had no response. There was a long silence, during which I caught a side-eyed glimpse of Kelly in the corner, glaring one of her trademark psychic holes through us. The goose, its eyes now gazing in Kelly's direction, emitted a low growl.

"It's all a distraction," Papa Hui said, stroking between the goose's eyes. "An important technique, to be sure. Actually, I was rather disappointed you didn't include anything on distraction in the 'Advice to Future Entrepreneurs' section of your book."

I couldn't breathe. I squeaked out a "You read it?" and I hoped there was another ambulance waiting outside because I truly thought I was having a stroke.

Papa Hui murmured a "Yes, indeed." He continued: "Ay, it reminded me of my own early years. You're a good man with a good head. I just have a feeling about you, a feeling that you can see through all the bullshit."

I didn't know what he was talking about, and I must've looked it.

"You know, there's no real point to any of this." He rubbed his eyes, ever so slightly crinkled at their corners.

"To any of what?"

"You'll understand one day," he said, and he left it at that. He looked down, stroking the goose, bringing it to purr, to rest its beady little eyes. Comforted by these loving movements, I finally caught my breath. There were a million questions I wanted to ask, was going to ask, but then a tall, slim man, the founder of an Internet-based furniture company, plopped down on the other side of Papa Hui and began chattering his ear off about a new start-up, something about using the power of the world wide web to harness...

I half listened, my eyes scanning the room for someone I knew, when my phone buzzed in my pocket. I slipped it out. A new message from Lulu. I looked up. In all of this feasting, in all of this talk, I'd forgotten all about her, hadn't noticed that she was no longer beside me. I looked around—she was nowhere to be seen. When had she slipped out? Where was she? How had I forgotten about my most valuable asset? My heart skipped a beat as I read and reread the message.

Just: "I'm sorry. I can't."

But can't what?

My first thought was that she'd decided she couldn't sit at this banquet any longer when she had a harvest in the morning. Understandable, as I too was growing worried about the environment—some people in their rowdiness had begun to smoke marijuana, crack, meth, all sorts (I know I shouldn't be writing this on the Internet, but I swore to tell the whole truth here, netizens, and I'm not naming names, and nothing can be done after the fact anyway, can it?), and we wouldn't want those scents tainting her hair or my hair either. But if this were the case, why hadn't she said something? I would've happily left with her.

I alternated looking at my phone's screen with looking out at the banquet hall, searching, scanning for her. A woman performed yoga atop one of the tables, downward-facing dog, and an old man with lascivious eyes stared at her ass and hacked a terrible cough, spit his phlegm into a platinum goblet. And then I thought, Oh god, maybe Lulu didn't go home to protect her harvest, maybe she's fallen ill and that brief message was the only one she, in her fragility, could manage to send; maybe she was suicidal and this was a cry for help. I panicked. I called and called her phone, but she didn't pick up. A man stood at the edge of the shark pool, tossing sea cucumbers at the gnashing shark. Or maybe she'd meant something else entirely. Mama Hui jumped up on her chair, raising her fist into the air and shouting, "I beat the level!" I rose from my own chair, phone still pressed to my ear, and covertly combed the room. I peeked under tablecloths, but all I found there was a load of people older than my parents, crouching and performing lewd sexual acts on each other. I searched both bathrooms—golden toilets, by the way, but the sinks were mere silver. I called Lulu's phone again and again, but nothing. I cursed my luck—the week before, I'd nearly been talked into having GPS tracking systems implanted in each of my Heads, but at the time I'd thought that both an unnecessary expenditure and a violation of trust, of privacy. Regret, with its strong fingers—oh, how it strangled me! Choking, at a loss, I slipped out of the banquet hall and raced into the warm summer night.

I dove into the backseat of the waiting Audi. My mind twisted, turned, lurched. This was a large sum of money we're talking about here. I'm not at liberty to disclose how much, but trust me. Not that it was about the money. It was so much more than that. Lulu Qi represented an ideal: the ideal head of hair, the ideal woman, the yin to my yang. She represented my company, my hopes, and my dreams, and if she was missing then where was I?

We approached Shanghai from the outskirts, and soon everything was a blur of lights and I was hearing voices—voices I'd never heard outside of the comfort of my bedroom. They shouted numbers: the numbers in my bank accounts, in my stock portfolios, in my retirement funds. Loud, louder, I covered my ears with my hands, trying to muffle the cries. I writhed in the backseat, but up front, the driver didn't react, didn't appear to hear anything. He steered and accelerated and braked obliviously, his eyes fixed on the road. This driver, who had never once called me by my name, who called me "sir" and "mister" and the polite form of "you." I gazed at the back of his head in disbelief. I wondered: Is he just pretending not to hear the voices? Was ignorance such an important factor in professionalism? Couldn't he just act human for once? And then I thought: But what if he really wasn't hearing the voices? If I said something about the voices, would he think I'd gone loony? Would he bypass the headquarters exit and drive me straight to some nut hospital? Would he then sell his firsthand account of a "schizophrenic mogul" to a tabloid? Or would he just feign ignorance all over again?

Finally, I arrived. Everyone at headquarters was alerted as to Lulu's disappearance, and we searched the building high and low. I read and reread her message, recited the contents over and over again in my head, and I became convinced that it was indeed a cry for help, that she had been kidnapped against her will. I called the local police, I bribed them a great deal of money to care—to hell with principles!—and a clandestine citywide search soon took place. I accompanied the officers through the darkness, to every corner of Shanghai, and then at dawn, dejected and exhausted, I returned to headquarters with tired eyes, with empty hands, with ravenous hope that maybe Lulu had been returned.

But no.

I rode the private elevator up to my penthouse, flooded with morning sunshine, and pulled shut all the curtains and curled up in bed. I turned over, and in the dull darkness, I stared up at the ceiling for a very long time, and there I listened to all manner of voices, telling me that I hadn't done a good enough job of protecting my assets, that I'd made a critical mistake, that I'd never been good enough. I thought of what Papa Hui said about the importance of distraction, and I realized that I'd indeed been distracted, if not impressed, by all the glitter and gold and hoopla. And what was the difference, really, when both result in the same effect?

You're a failure, you're a failure, you're a failure. I squeezed shut my eyes and prayed for the voices to stop, for a moment of silence, for a second of peace.

And then there was silence, but no peace. There was a knock at the door. I stumbled over and opened it to find Stefan, an on-staff stylist from the south of China who'd studied cosmetology in Australia, and who still went by his English name, and who both harvested crops and traveled around the province outfitting clients with extensions. He was one of the best hairdressers in the country, I'll admit—that's why I hired him—but he also annoyed the hell out of me. Big googly eyeballs, smiling all the time, always speaking in a whisper. He peered at me with eyes as red as mine felt and said he had something to tell me. We sat on my sofa and in that stupid murmur he said, "Lulu wasn't kidnapped."

Now I know what you might be thinking: I had a crush on him. There was something between us. I'm acting like a schoolboy, teasing and taunting when I want to be loving.

But you're wrong. Aside from the fact that I could never be attracted to someone with a smile that gummy, here's why: there is something I disdain about people who choose to work for someone else. There, I said it. Wrote it. Whatever. And what does it matter now what I say or write? I'm a man in chains!

Look, since I know you are all going to dissect my meaning and try to decode it, I'll save you the trouble. All I mean is that there is so much opportunity out there in the world, so much uncharted territory, and to me it seems foolish not to explore and exploit it. That's not to say I don't see the necessity of employees, and it's not to say I don't treat my employees well. I do. Their salaries are quite high, their Spring Festival bonuses are generous, and they have on-site housing, or if they choose to live elsewhere, I have drivers deliver them to and from work. But I don't give them my respect, not truly, not wholeheartedly; they don't deserve it. And Stefan irritated me beyond my normal irritation. He didn't just seem happy with his job, with what I provided, but with something beyond that, something out of my reach. Happy to his very depths. Way to set your sights low. To me, such people aren't merely irritating; they're dangerous. These are the types of people who fill the future generation's heads with ideas that complacency is okay, that you don't need to attend after-school lessons or start a business or strive to buy your own iPhone, that China will be just fine without innovators and executives and tycoons. These are the types of people who are satisfied with the status quo, satisfied with second place; the type who give runaways a safe place to hide...

Let me be clear again: no, I don't mean to say that all salarymen moonlight as fugitive aiders. I know better than that, and I therefore cannot speak in such absolute terms. But in this specific case, my statement holds true.

I ordered him to take me to her, and when we reached his apartment—you know, the one Hair Inc.'s housing allowance provided him, the traitor!—I pounded on the door, my fist possessed, but Stefan grabbed my hand and gently dropped it by my side. "Patience," he whispered. "Think this through. You don't want to scare her."

We stood there for a very long time, and the motion-detector light kept turning off, and I kept stamping my feet to get it to turn back on, and I was left alone in that alternating light and dark with Stefan, with his mouth-breathing, his musky cologne, his shiny leather shoes, until at last I heard some movement coming from the other side of the door. The sound of a lock turning. The door creaking open slightly.

A small gap from which a familiar eye peeked out.

"Hi, sweetie," Stefan whispered. "Are you okay?"

"Lulu," I said. I could hear that my voice was frantic, manic, crazed. Still, I spoke on. "Let us in. Please, let us in."

Upon hearing my voice, she shut the door.

An hour later, we managed to coax our way inside, and I took a good look around Stefan's apartment. It was a startlingly normal place. I don't know why this struck me as so unsettling, but I guess it's because if I'd had to imagine it—not that I spent my valuable time daydreaming about his life or anything—I'd have imagined something more flamboyant. Zebra skins and feathers and sequins everywhere, you know. But his furniture was your standard IKEA fare: plywood, cheap metal. It reminded me of my parents' home. TV set. Short bookshelf filled with some not particularly interesting looking software manuals and a few classic novels, standard concubines and swordsmen fare. A couple of fashion magazines on the coffee table.

And then there was Lulu, sitting on the sofa. Also normal, hardly the goddess I'd in the past twelve hours built her up to be. Her face was pale. She'd been crying. She sat with her feet on the sofa and her arms and head resting on her knees. I sat beside her. She didn't move or even look at me. She had changed clothes, was wearing a T-shirt, jeans. I reached out and took a lock of her hair into my hands and then released, letting it fall. Oh, the swing, the body! This was the finest hair ever grown, no doubt about that. My lungs surged with pride. I exhaled, releasing a tiny bit of air, and I stroked her bony back, and I looked at her, my best friend, my most valuable asset, and I tried Stefan's whispering trick on for size. "Lulu, you don't want to do this."

She turned her head, still resting on her arms, and peered at me from the corners of her eyes.

"Or maybe you do. I don't know. But let's just harvest this crop, and then afterward we can discuss the future."

There was no change in her expression. Her pupils did not sparkle; they were blank. Her whole face was utterly unreadable.

I took a deep breath and continued stroking, whispering. "I want you to be happy, you know that. Your happiness is the most important thing."

I know, I know what you're thinking, netizens: this girl wanted to keep her hair so badly that she fled the most decadent banquet in our country's history, hid from me, hid from the Shanghai police, sought refuge in a colleague's apartment, and yet I still tried to convince her that doing it would make her happy, that I cared about her happiness.

Yes, I know.

And well, she caved. She finally nodded in agreement, and I gave Stefan, who had been politely waiting in the bathroom, the agreed-upon signal, which was a particular Morse code—inspired flash of light from my Audemars Piguet watch. Scissors in hand, he emerged from the bathroom doorway. He took a step and then another and another, and then he tripped over his own pink-socked foot. He caught his balance before he fell, but his facial expression, icy before, gave way to an embarrassed grin. To say this guy was clumsy would be like saying that the Gang of Four caused a teensy-weensy bit of damage to our country's morale, which is to say that it'd be a gross understatement. Luckily though, he was nothing but graceful when it came to cutting hair.

Lulu sat, her head bowed, at Stefan's cheap kitchen chair with a leopard-print towel—see, I wasn't totally off base regarding his taste—draped across her shoulders.

"All off," I ordered. A familiar adrenaline coursed through me. I lived for this feeling, which I always got just before a big harvest. "Tell him, Lulu. Tell him that's what you want."

She took a deep breath, that leopard-print towel rising to graze her earlobes, and then looked up, directly at me. Through me, even.

"No," she said. Her voice was firm.

My hands trembled—I thought it was adrenaline at the time, but now I think maybe it was pure fear. "No what?"

"I'm not cutting it off."

My eyes widened. My mouth fell open. But hadn't she just agreed? Hadn't she nodded? Hadn't she sat down? Hadn't she let me drape that towel on her back? What game was she playing? These were the questions that pounded in my heart.

"Like hell you're not, you traitor!" I spat. "It's *my* hair."

Eyes soft, she gazed straight ahead, unblinking—was she meditating? Stefan stood a few steps away, frozen, scissors poised.

I wasn't finished. I was a man possessed. "Well, what are you going to do with it still attached to your head?"

"Go to Beijing and become an actress," she murmured. "Or, I don't know—"

"Oh, please," I said. "Your only talent is looking pleasant."

"Then I'll become a model." Her voice had picked up strength. *Om*, she chanted under her breath.

"Models these days need to be more than pleasant. They need to have an edge."

It went on like this for quite some time, and as we argued, Stefan unfroze, his head whipping back and forth, his googly eyes darting like those of a cartoon character watching a Ping-Pong match. On it went until Lulu jumped up, tore off the towel and threw it to the floor. "I'm not cutting my hair and that's the end of it!"

Something swept over me then—that same something that famously made me grab the scissors from the stylist all those years before, the same longing that had launched my career—*I fucking wanted it, that's why!*—and I reached for her hair. But I wasn't as strong as I'd been in my youth, wasn't as cunning. Stefan, that weakling, that sissy, that klutz, somehow positioned himself between us, blocking me, and shouted at Lulu to run.

Oh, poor little rich boy, I heard a voice whisper, *who's on your side now?*

Stefan tackled me to the floor, pinned me down, but he couldn't keep me there forever. I struggled and fought with all my might until at last I broke free and fled out the door, down flights and flights of stairs, through the building's lobby, and outside. The enormity of the city weighed down on me as I spun around and around on the sidewalk. Here there wasn't a skyline, but a skycircle. Buildings in every direction, people in all of them. Buses, cars, airports, train stations. A million roads that had made the maps, and a million more that hadn't yet. I realized, fully realized then, that she, this traitor, could be anywhere. Dizzy, I was, losing all balance, and then there was a steadying hand on my shoulder. I turned my head and looked straight into Stefan's bulging eyes.

"Let it go," he spoke in that whisper of his.

"No," I said, my voice that of a small, manic child. "I need that hair."

"It's her hair, and her choice."

"Don't give me that philosophical bullshit. I supervised the hair, I grew the hair, I paid for the hair. It belongs to me." I stomped my foot on the ground. I was six years old again, just with a more advanced vocabulary and more complex thought processes.

Stefan bit his lip. "Your parents did all of those things for you, and you don't belong to them."

I rolled my eyes.

"Don't you have enough money? Why does she matter?"

"Everyone matters," I said in a whispery voice, mimicking his own.

"Cute," he said. "But really. Are you in financial trouble or something?"

I stared blankly at him again—me, in financial trouble? Please. I didn't *need* the hair. I *wanted* it. There was a difference—or at least there used to be. I stomped my foot again.

"If you love something, set it—" he started to say, but I interrupted, snorting, "Oh, come on. Don't give me that. That's a fucking stupid saying. So if I have a kitten, I should just set it free and let it get run over by a truck, and if it loves me, the breeze will blow its flattened corpse right on back to me? Or maybe a nice restaurateur will find the poor little bastard and serve its gamey meat up to me in a delicious soup? Set it free, yeah, that's great advice." I kicked a pebble, which flew into some old man's bicycle tire spoke. He wobbled for a moment, shouted a curse at me, and then pedaled off, rode on as though none of it had happened.

Stefan placed his hand on the small of my back and whispered, "A man who knows when enough is enough will always have—" But I didn't want his touch and I didn't want to hear it. I ran. I ran and I ran, scouring the city, making phone calls, bribing police, looking for my lost Head. But in a city of sixteen million, it's easy, too easy, to just disappear...

Why am I telling you all of this? What relevance does a runaway head of hair have to do with the brutal murder of a great tycoon? Well, relevance is relative. And everything has everything to do with everything else. Frankly speaking, I'm in jail for two reasons. The first is that heiress Kelly Hui is a jealous and vindictive young woman. The second is that I'm a mental case, and it's easy to pin a murder on a mental case, isn't it? Madness in the mind leads to madness in action, that's what everyone thinks. Every day you netizens are posting and commenting on articles about crazy old ladies with unnatural strength who pluck innocent passersby up off the pavement and hurl them into polluted rivers, or knife-wielding men who burst into kindergartens and train stations, slaughtering innocent children and ticket-holders, respectively. Hell, even Lu Fun, our China's most beloved writer, came to fame with a tale of a lunatic cannibal. We are a people, a country, a world who love to vilify the mad!

But, I ask, is it not also mad to seek riches or stardom? Is it not also mad to hold up the rich and famous as examples of what it really means to live?

Vilify, worship; villain, hero. Oh, these fine lines we draw. Coming out as gay, that was easy. But coming out as mad? How difficult! I can hear the police marching around outside, I can hear them giving orders, I can hear them going about their business, plotting their punishments—I don't have long, I know, so I want to give you my all, you helpful netizens, to let it all out, whatever the repercussions might be. Here I am in a veritable cage, four concrete walls, crouched in a corner, typing my plea to the world on an iPhone I hid between my ass cheeks. If these aren't the actions of a madman, well, then I just don't know...

Now enough with the confessions and back to my plea: after Lulu left, after my reputation was damaged by her flight response, you'd think it would all be over for me. But it was—is—hardly over. I still had—have—billions of yuan of inventory. I'm fine. The actress who was set to use Lulu's hair, sure, she severed ties with us and wound up getting her extensions from some third-rate company in India, but she'll get what she paid for with that choice. Village girls who have to sell their hair in order to pay for their abortions after they've been raped? Oh, that's great, ethical, moral. Good call, Ms. Famous Actress, believe you me, the Western media is going to have a feeding frenzy with that one.

After all that mess, after Lulu left, I asked myself: What would Papa Hui do? And the answer came easy: Keep up with his regimens, that's what. Business as usual, that's what.

So I swallowed my vitamins. I drank my water quotas. I did my exercises. I supervised my remaining Heads in all of their routines.

But maybe, if I'm being honest, that was actually when everything ended for me.

You know, I never told anyone this, but I finally did find her—in the background of a terrible TV period drama set in the Qing dynasty. She played one of the emperor's many concubines, a nonspeaking role, essentially an extra, and she stood there in her cheap polyester getup with an eager look on her face, desperately eager, and I knew then that a girl that eager never becomes anyone, and something in my mind unhinged—or rehinged—and suddenly I found myself on the other side of...

What?

Forgiveness?

No, not quite, that's an awfully strong word.

I later heard she became some government official's real concubine. What a waste of talent. Okay, sorry, so I'm sure that's what you netizens were dying to know, right? About how I got into this mental state in the first place? How I went mad? Well, there it is, isn't it? That's how I lost my damn Head.

Why did she leave me though? What exactly drove her to quit? Did I ever figure that out? Again, again, I don't know. Maybe she became a Christian or a Muslim or whatever and adopted the belief that selling a part of your body is wrong. But then why was she on TV, selling her image? No use speculating though. In the case of such an outlier, it's not the cause that matters, only the effect. It'd be worth trying to figure out if there were others like her, other traitors, cowards jumping ship, but—

But back to the murder. I'm in jail. The police have locked me up, and they won't let me speak to any of the aliens, and I have this feeling that there is a spaceship outside waiting for me, but I think they've sent the military in to attack it, and these officers won't even come in and talk to me so that I can explain my side of the story.

Oh, my story. My side. That's why I'm writing this, isn't it? So you want to know what I know about Bashful Goose? About the murder of Papa Hui? Well, I'll tell you. Here it is, everything: How the hell would I know about that?

Okay, okay, I'll tell you what I do know. After Lulu took off, my world as I'd known it, as I'd built it, slowly collapsed. I kept up with things at first, but then, well. Every night, I was kept awake by voices. No, I don't think my apartment was bugged. I think these voices were in my head, but that they were also coming from somewhere outside of me, do you understand my meaning?

One morning, maybe a month or two ago, I was at headquarters, overseeing the exercise routine of a new set of Head recruits. Admiring their beauty, I ran my fingers through my own hair, the hair that launched a multibillion-dollar empire, and I almost leaped out of my skin. I kept my cool in front of the recruits, but as soon as I could steal a minute, I stepped out and into my executive washroom, where, inspired by the banquet, I'd had gold-plated toilets *and* sinks installed. I inspected my scalp closely in the mirror and noted that my hair wasn't as thick, as luxurious, as it had once been.

Lack of sleep—yes. Inability to muster up the motivation to properly exercise—yes. Insufficient exposure to sunlight—yes. I had been breaking all of my own rules, and now I was suffering the consequences. But it seemed to me more serious than that.

The next morning, I donned a common-man disguise, and a hospital doctor—I was too embarrassed to have my on-staff physician perform this examination—confirmed my fears. "Well, kid, I'd say you're going bald," he said with a shrug, and then strode out like it was nothing. And maybe it was nothing. There were people in this same hospital fighting cancer, plagued with tumors—people who were truly physically suffering. Who was I to complain? Well, I was rich. And as the ancient saying goes, where there's a condition, there's a highly priced cure. But I'd made my fortune advertising and selling organic hair. Taking medicine or rubbing ointments into my scalp might yield me a crop, but it'd also render me a liar.

I'd shot my ammunition off early, grown a whole lifetime of hair in only twenty-four years.

It was a brutal diagnosis, and I wanted nothing more than to curl up and die. I put Kai, my number one assistant, in charge of the day-to-day operations of the company, and I hid out in my apartment alone, sucking sadly on Bashful Goose Red-Bean-Flavored Tongue-Tickler Ice Lollies and watching DVDs. Romantic comedies.

Korean, American, French, British, quirky, straight-forward, poignant, prickly—they all had love in common, if not laughs, and they should have done something to lift my sinking spirits, but to be honest, the beautiful actors and actresses just gave me hair envy. I knew not everyone could grow the perfect head of hair—if they could, I wouldn't be in business in the first place. But me? Not me. I was a pioneer of hair engineering. A trailblazer.

This watching-crying-watching-sobbing routine continued up until a couple of nights ago, when I turned that particular movie off and, seeking something slightly less depressing for a change, turned on the news. This always cheered me up. Newscasters have notoriously bad hair: the spray, the gel, the fringe, the lumps, the frizz! As luck would have it, just as I flipped it on, the reporter with the very worst hair—resembling on one side the Eiffel Tower and on the other a misshapen octagon—was on-screen delivering a breaking story: Papa Hui of Bashful Goose Snack Company had been murdered, apparently by his own daughter!

I did then what every selfish human does when someone he knows dies, and I thought back to the last time I'd seen him, replayed the last things he'd said to me over and over in my head, scrounging for some meaning or message in his words, but there wasn't one, was there? Nothing is holy unless we grant it that power. Everything is inherently meaningless.

To say I took the news of Papa Hui's death hard would be like saying that China is a tad bit crowded, which is to say that it'd be a gross understatement. I was devastated. First, I'd lost Lulu. Then I received my diagnosis. And now my idol, the one who had inspired me in my youth, and whose onward attitude had given me the strength to push forward (if only for a time), despite the depths of my depression and despair, was dead. Not just dead, but slaughtered like a common chicken.

I paced my penthouse, rubbed my hands on my balding scalp, whispered to myself, trembled. My phone rang. At first I wasn't even sure if it was really ringing. What was real anymore, and what was delusion? Was there a difference? The phone—was it really a phone?—read that it was Stefan calling. I had no desire to speak with him. I'd fired him after the whole Lulu incident. Well, technically he voluntarily resigned, but given the opportunity, I would have fired him. I pressed Reject Call. He called back. I rejected again. Over and over, until I grew weary and bored and just answered.

He opened with "You heard the news?"

I choked back a sob. Was this really him on the line, or was it an alien? Were the aliens calling me home? Was my borrowed time on this polluted, messy planet finally over?

"Congratulations," the Stefan-Alien whispered.

I must have misheard. I pulled the phone from my ear and then pressed it back again. "I'm sorry, what did you say?"

"I didn't know you two were so close," its voice said.

I wobbled over to my desk and looked down at my computer, where I saw on the screen a new microblog entry: "Wang Xilai to Be Named Next Bashful Goose CEO?"

My kingdom had come, the voice said, *your kingdom has come.*

But was this an empire I was willing to inherit?

I swear to you, netizens, that is how I heard the news of Papa Hui's death, how I discovered that he had left the company to me. I did not orchestrate any of this; I had no prior knowledge or involvement. There was no master plan. I was just a bystander, as stunned by the events that transpired as any of you.

It comes as no real surprise to me that Kelly Hui would tell police that I blackmailed her into killing her own father. That girl is a real piece of work. I hate to play this hand, but is she even really Chinese? She could well be an American spy. She has an American passport after all. Perhaps the CIA set her up to take me down. This kind of thing happens all the time. Look around you, netizens, at least one person you know is a CIA spy! At least. Look into this, netizens, look into Kelly's background and perhaps you will uncover some pertinent evidence. I will reward with vast sums of money any and all of you who can prove this to be true.

I never met Kelly in an alley—I hardly ever leave headquarters. For whatever time she claims I did, I have an alibi, I'm sure of it. Check the cameras in my building. Ask my employees. Ask Stefan.

Yes, I will publish my phone records, I will publish all of my e-mails. I have nothing to hide! Here, I've bared it all anyway! I'm a madman who hears voices! I'm a madman who dances with aliens! I am utterly and completely mad! I don't care. I don't care. Just get me out of here. Wage war, netizens, wage a war against the powers that hold us down! The government is trying to kill all of us. Kelly Hui is a demon sent from the bowels of hell. I know all of this to be true. I could just prove it if these police officers would let me speak to the aliens. The aliens know everything. They want you to know that everything we think is true is a lie. But I can't go talk to them because I'm here in this room, and also my iPhone is about to run out of battery so I can't keep typing for much longer, but please, netizens, I beg you to beg for my release. Take to the streets! Call all the major global news networks. Ask NASA for help; they might be the only ones who can truly help us. Kelly Hui has the Chinese National Space Administration in the palm of her hand—don't trust them. Call NASA for help, netizens, please!

Let me make it clear again: I never told Kelly Hui that I'd give her a billion renminbi if she killed her father and that if she didn't I'd kill her and her mother and expose their family secrets or whatever it is she's telling the investigators. What do I know of their secrets? What do I care? I'm not a killer, and I've never even had a real conversation with Kelly Hui, except at that one banquet, and I told you everything we said. Yes, she wore my products, but Stefan was the one who out-fitted her. I never had any other personal contact with her. And why on earth would I want Papa Hui dead? I'm telling the truth when I say that I didn't even know he'd willed the company to me—how would I know that? How could I even dream that was possible?

5.

I HAD JUST PRESSED POST WHEN A TEAM OF PERHAPS TEN UNIFORMED officers burst into the holding cell. These brutes didn't bother with an interrogation—though I supposed they, like the rest of the world, would read my account soon enough. Although the government quickly removed my original post, dismissing it as "spiritual pollution," it was too late. Netizens had already copied and pasted. They circulated. They translated into dozens of languages. They laughed. They worried. They discussed. They didn't talk about my innocence; they talked about my money, my madness, my mind. Hair tycoon on a rampage. This is what happens to the too rich. A cautionary tale.

No, those police officers didn't ask me anything. They beat me. Whacked me with clubs, with flashlights, with their fists. It hurt, well beyond any pain I'd ever experienced, and I moaned and I screamed and I flinched, until I lay still, silent, and it didn't hurt anymore. Until I saw a white light and, in that light, the silhouettes of almond-headed figures. Voiceless figures. They came closer and closer to me, until they were no longer just silhouettes, until I could make out their features. Their nostrils. Their diamond eyes. A warmth enveloped me, held me tightly. I began to sweat. I wiped the sweat from my brow and then I held my hand out in front of me and saw that this sweat was red. When I looked out again toward that light, there were no more figures, and then too there was no more light. Everything went black.

I woke up in a white hospital room to mechanical beeping. How I survived, I don't know. I wished I hadn't. Broken ribs, bruises, blood. I was laid up in that bed for what felt like years. When I was released, the judge took pity and granted me permission to leave Shanghai for a brief period to "rehabilitate" and "rest" before the trial. I still don't know why he didn't put me on house arrest—anyone else in my position might have made a permanent run for it, might have sought refuge in a foreign embassy, might have fled to Singapore or the United States or South America. But not me. I kept my word. As soon as I could drive, I drove cross-country to Yunnan, bought a house, focused on healing and on forgiving. How is it possible for a man such as myself, who has been framed for murder, who has been beaten, who has lost his business, who has had to hide most of his remaining fortune away in overseas bank accounts; how is it possible, I ask you, for such a man, a man who perhaps has never loved another person, never even loved a clever concept or a turn of phrase, never loved anything at all but maybe the illusion of wealth; how is it possible for such a man to so blindly, so foolishly, love his own country? Well, to that I say: *Anything is possible.* Or is it this at all?

I sit at the table, still reeling from my reading. It's been a long time since I clicked that link, a long time since I remembered that particular chapter of my life. I put my arms on the table and then I rest my head inside my arms. This is how I might have napped on a desk as a child had I ever napped at a desk as a child, had I been not a tycoon-to-be but a regular ne'er-do-well. What moral, I wonder, can I glean from this blog post, from these sentences I once formed, these feelings I once experienced, this account I once gave? That I'm a sociopath? That I'm incapable of compassion? That I was selfish, greedy, and that I got what was coming to me? Will I ever gain enough distance, enough perspective, to feel like I've learned a lesson here? The moral is supposed to come at the end, but the problem with real life is that our stories don't end. They go on and on.

The rain beats down on the roof, rhythmic except for the few out-of-sync plops. Then I realize that those aren't plops I'm hearing. They are footsteps. I leap up, my heart rattling in my chest. I blink and I am standing on the roof of my house, soaked, shivering, barefoot. How did I get up here? Before me, next to the chimney, stands that black-clad figure, the shape of which I can barely make out through a sheet of falling water. Maybe I've suffered an aneurysm, a stroke, a heart attack. Maybe I'm dead. Maybe this is the lesson, the moral: You cannot escape the suffering of this world until you...

Until you what? I'm not dead. This figure isn't one of the death figures; it doesn't have an almond head, and there is no white light behind it. This figure stands in the rain, the unrelenting rain, and it throws back its head and, gargling raindrops, it releases a scream.

We are inside now, me and the figure. Everything went black and now we are inside. I turn the heating on—this is not a farmer's house. I sit at the kitchen table. I lean onto the tabletop and I cradle my head in my arms.

The figure stands before me. It speaks. It says, *They blamed it all on greed. Literally, on Greed. They've pressed charges against Greed and now Greed must stand trial for the crimes it has committed.*

I imagine Greed as a spindly demon, as Gollum from *The Lord of the Rings*, as a badly burned beggar I once saw outside a train station.

What do you mean? I ask. *That sounds awfully philosophical. I am a simple man now, haven't you heard?*

The figure says, *I mean that Kelly Hui has been let off the hook, that the powers that be have determined that she wasn't the one who killed her father, that it was Greed who chopped Papa Hui into bite-sized meat morsels, that the will that left the company to you has been declared a fake, that Kelly Hui is the rightful heir to the Bashful Goose Snack Company and accompanying fortune, and that she should be the one to lead our great nation forward. What I'm saying is...*

The figure pulls off the ski mask. It—no, he—says, "You are free."

I remove my head from my arms and I sit up straight. Is this really Stefan standing before me or is this someone who's had plastic surgery to look just like Stefan? I've read *1984*. I've traveled to Bangkok. I know what's possible. Anger overcomes me. Anger that my solid mind, my principles, my belief, and my once immovable trust in myself have been eroded. How did I get from the roof to the kitchen table? How did he get here? Why was he on my roof? How did I get on the roof? Wasn't this whole mess his fault in a way, wasn't he the one who helped Lulu run away, who sent me spiraling into madness, a madness that made it easy, too easy, for someone to pin a murder on me?

Maybe he can read my thoughts. Maybe the way my eyes are darting back and forth gives them away. He stares at me, this Stefan or Not Stefan, looking down on me.

I want to scream at him. I want to scream, "Isn't it your fault that I got dragged into this disaster in the first place, fate unwilling to let me have peace when I needed it most?!"

I don't scream. I stand up and, with both hands and with all my strength, I shove the unmasked figure. He lets out a surprised yelp and flies backward. There is the hollow sound of his elbow hitting the kitchen counter. Silence. Then he starts to laugh—a maniacal laugh, a laugh uncaged, the laughter of a man who, after many years of toiling, of despair, of hopelessness, has been set free.

Stefan sits down at the table with me and asks me to get him a cup of water. He drinks this water and then something behind his eyes changes. His head whips around, taking in this strange home of mine and, finally, taking me in with recognition. His whisper-voice is shaky. "Where am I?"

I stare at his ghostly white face, and all at once, I remember again that Village Witch story my great-grandmother told me, one I'd always half assumed was little more than a fairy tale, and maybe he can read my thoughts because he begins jabbering, saying that he remembers cutting hair and then glancing up in the mirror and seeing a Pomeranian looking back at him from some woman's Gucci bag, and then he remembers nothing else. He wonders how that haircut turned out ("Probably stunning," I say, because his work is always stunning). He says his arm hurts and I apologize for pushing him, and he says, "Don't be sorry for something I can't remember."

When he is finished tracing his path, I tell him my great-grandmother's story.

His eyes widen, and he remains silent for a long while, and then he takes another sip of water and says, "But if the weasel is a fairy working on behalf of baby spirits, who does the Pomeranian work on behalf of?"

"Rich spirits," I say, and even though he laughs, even though he says, "Like they need anyone to work on their behalf!" and even though I laugh too—an uncaged laugh, the laughter of a man set free—I'm still not quite sure if I'm joking.

What's next is that we pack up everything into the Bentley and speed off, kicking up mud as we zip away from this country house, and I settle into my seat and I flip on the radio, which comes in staticky. A man speaks in a thick Beijing accent, announcing, "It has been mere minutes since the verdict that rocked our China! In case you've been living under a rock and haven't heard, investigators determined that it was in fact Mama Hui—who 'mysteriously' committed suicide yesterday—who murdered the Bashful Goose founder, framing both her daughter and Hair Inc. CEO Wang Xilai for her crime. The judge, fearing ghostly vengeance, has opted not to posthumously charge the old bat, and the case has been dropped. Thank heavens this mystery has been solved! Now our nation can breathe easy at last! In other news, officials from the Health Ministry warn children, the elderly, and any individuals who may have medical constraints including but not limited to frequent common colds, sleepiness, and/ or possession of one or more lungs to avoid any outdoor activities today, including opening windows, due to undesirable air quality. Thank you for your cooperation. We will return with a special two-hour *Cross-Talk Comedy Extravaganza* after a brief message from our sponsor." The man had hardly finished speaking when a nasally child's voice blasted from the speakers: "Pirate Liao, you sure look like you've got a bad case of scurvy there. How about a Bashful Goose Tangerine Treat—"

What's next is I shut off the radio. So it was almost all true, what Fairy Stefan had said, but was it enough? I'd wanted Greed to be found guilty; inexplicably, above everything else, I'd wanted that part to be true. But that kind of thing only happens in stories. I'm not a gullible child; I'm an adult and smart enough to know that a concept, like a body, is an empty vessel, dependent on human spirit to carry out its will.

What's next is I turn the radio back on, and I change the station, and I look at Stefan, who smiles back at me, and together, we hum and then sing along.

What's next is that I should be paying attention to my driving, but as I sing, I can't help glancing over at him again and again. His lips curl in that familiar smile, a smile that is no longer vile to me. But which one of us has been transformed here? Or have we both? I am not the boss now. He is not an employee. We are just two people on an unpaved road. We are just two people with a third person tied up in the trunk.

What's next is we sing louder. Our voices fill the car until it feels like it's going to burst, and I roll down the windows to set them free. To set us free. What's next is no one falls in love like this, in an instant. Love is a process. A journey. It is one of those things that takes a very, very long time. But here, here I have a start.

iN THE NEWS

MAMA HUI, 53, DEAD OF APPARENT OVERDOSE

WUXI, CHINA —...and our great nation will not miss Mama Hui, not for a second! How could we force even a single tear from our collective eye for the old, shriveled-up murderess who attempted to frame her innocent, virginal daughter for a most unspeakable crime...

Though not a known drug user, Mrs. Hui, an avid gamer, did display the addictive behaviors that might plausibly lead her to blend an entire bottle's worth of sleeping pills into a banana-berry smoothie. Authorities vehemently deny any allegations of foul play...

KELLY HUI ACQUITTED, RELEASED FROM HOUSE ARREST

WUXI, CHINA —...Judge Li acquitted both Kelly Hui and Wang Xilai of all charges pertaining to the murder of Bashful Goose CEO Papa Hui. The dishonorable judge, who has since resigned, issued a formal written apology to Ms. Hui and Mr. Wang, and was made to deliver a self-criticism speech before a stoic audience of government officials...

YANG NAMED NEW BASHFUL GOOSE CEO

WUXI, CHINA — Last Tuesday, courts named Kelly Hui the rightful successor to the Bashful Goose throne. Ms. Hui, however, failed to appear at four different summonses. Sources close to Ms. Hui claim she has all but disappeared, failing even to answer phone calls or e-mails. "Grief," a psychological expert explains, "is an inexplicable journey, and it is not uncommon for those affected to react in mysterious ways."

Meanwhile, Mr. Yang, Bashful Goose's former CFO, is thrilled about his new position. "I will take up where Papa Hui left off," he told reporters. "I will do my best to ensure that Bashful Goose Snack Company remains a beacon of hope."

LOCAL PARENTS GIVEN SECOND CHANCE

NANJING, CHINA —...Ten months after their daughter lost her life to a tragic fire that obliterated a provincial fat camp, Mr. Feng and his wife welcomed a new baby boy to their family...

"Our only hope," Mr. Feng says, "is that this one doesn't develop that awful obesity like the last."

...In addition to the lifetime supply of Yam Jam Snack Cakes given to all fat camp families as part of a larger compensation settlement, the Bashful Goose Snack Company has generously donated a one-year supply of its new Mango Madness Milk Powder...

BASHFUL GOOSE CEO YANG RESIGNS
IN LIGHT OF BERRY SCANDAL

WUXI, CHINA —...a tainted batch of Blueberry Bubblers led to thousands of hospitalizations throughout the country and has resulted, thus far, in 17 deaths...

It is rumored that Mr. Yuan, currently an operations manager, will take his place...

KELLY HUI AND WANG XILAI:
WHERE ARE THEY NOW?

NANJING, CHINA —...with not a single sighting of either Ms. Hui or Mr. Wang since the pair was acquitted of charges in June of this year...

Some sources speculate that Ms. Hui may have returned to Los Angeles, where she is undergoing extensive plastic surgery in preparation for a role on a reality TV show in which previously unsightly contestants attempt to land a hunky husband. Others speculate that Ms. Hui has become a woman of the robes, giving up all earthly desires and praying daily in a monastery. Still others believe that Ms. Hui may be...

THE
TURTLE

*I believe that the purpose
of our life is to seek happiness.*
—DALAI LAMA XIV

To get rich is glorious.
—DENG XIAOPING

Lulu pursed her lips. She studied herself, the wrinkles around her eyes and mouth, in the rearview mirror of her Land Rover (a "gift" from Government Official Xia) and waited for the light to change. A bead of sweat trickled down her back. She rifled through her bag, reapplied her lipstick for the sixth time that morning, and realized in that moment that she had never been more bored in her entire life. It was time to end it once and for all. To just push the gas pedal. To invite some speeding car to plow into her own in the middle of this intersection.

She lifted her foot from the brake and positioned it over the gas. The car inched forward. She gasped and then slammed on the brake—she wanted to be gone, but she had no desire to take anyone else with her.

This was the longest light in the history of the world.

In some ways, signing up for the agency (Beautiful Girl Talent Ltd.) that government officials used to find mistresses had been the best decision she'd ever made. What a terribly dismal thought that was. Sure, she received a massive stipend and was set up in a nice apartment and had even happened to get matched with the rare official who actually wanted to remain loyal to his wife but had to maintain a mistress on paper to keep up appearances and deflect homophobic slurs at banquets. Regardless of her "good fortune," she was tired, the type of tired that sleep couldn't cure, and she was bored to her very core.

"Life," she said aloud to no one, "sucks." She tasted lipstick on her teeth. She was one of *those* girls now, one of those poor little rich girls: claustrophobic, cornered in by the meeting of these streets, by the meaninglessness of traffic's steady stream, by the waxy taste in her mouth. She considered again just gunning it, but stopped herself once more, this time to watch in fascination as a toothless woman with a face twisted and tan like a sweet potato hobbled over and tapped on her passenger-side window. Though she knew this knock was coming, Lulu jumped in her seat. She peered out with trepidation. The woman held up a turtle by its dinosaur-like tail, held it like victory. Not an unusual sight; in Beijing during the warm months, Lulu often spotted workers hawking turtles they'd found on or near the road. Eventually these workers-turned-hawkers would get lucky and some superstitious driver would buy the creature, take it home, and cook it up in a special soup, which was said to contribute to longevity and male virility—neither of which she had any need for. The woman tapped again. Lulu, now entirely detached from herself, watched her own finger pressing the button to roll down the window.

Ten minutes later, she was unable to recollect what had happened in those last few seconds at the red light, but when she took a good hard look at herself in her building's elevator mirror, she was clutching her Chanel bag in one hand and the turtle by its tail in the other.

She found an empty cardboard box in her bedroom from an air purifier she'd bought the week before in a post-romantic-comedy-DVD-viewing fit of environmental rage and then appeasement ("Why is the only sky I know gray?" she spoke aloud to no one from the sofa as the credits rolled on the TV screen. "Why don't I just move to Switzerland or something? What the hell is keeping me here?"). Now she dragged this box into the living room.

Just as she set the turtle inside and situated the box in what she determined to be an ideal location (in front of the sofa, next to the coffee table, in only partial sunlight from the floor-to-ceiling window), the door buzzed. Lulu stood up and plodded over to the video screen—pure white, as though someone was holding a piece of paper over the downstairs camera. But there was a voice. "Let me up!" After a long pause, the voice added, "It's Official Xia."

There was something different about his voice. Deeper, maybe? More serious? Perhaps the time she'd feared had come, and he was here to cut her off; no more funds, no more fun, the end. But why wouldn't he just sever ties through the agency? He was too nice, that's why; he'd want to do it in person, let her down easy. And what would she do without the income? Maybe lack of cash flow would mobilize her to do something with her life. But was she cut out for this competitive job market? No, definitely not. She never finished her degree, her acting career had tanked after an unfortunate encounter with a skeevy director, and her looks were fading fast.

Or maybe it wasn't this at all—maybe it was worse. Maybe his wife had died in some tragic accident and, knowing he couldn't get by without a woman around the house, he was coming up to ask for Lulu's hand in marriage. How might she fair as a replacement wife? Would he expect her to cook and to wear matronly outfits and to give birth to his baby? Or would he expect her to play a decidedly more familiar trophy second-wife role?

Not a feeling or emotion existed regarding these possibilities; they were merely words that scrolled marquee-style through her head.

And anyway there was no use pondering what wasn't yet real, so she buzzed him up and then cracked the apartment door open. She took a step toward the living room to check on the turtle, but a tingling in her fingertips told her to stop. She lingered in the entry, waiting for the ding of the arriving elevator, the hum of its automatic doors. There it was, and then footsteps, and then a stranger pushed her way through the door and past Lulu. This stranger—a teenage girl—plopped down on the sofa, kicked off her shoes, and settled in as though at home.

After an initial back-and-forth, the girl tucked a piece of her hair, cut into a short bob, behind her ear and gave up her game, telling Lulu who she was.

"Oh," Lulu said. She didn't know what else to say. She shut the front door and took a few hesitant steps toward the sofa. "Um, you did a very good impression of him. His voice, I mean. You're really his daughter, huh?"

"Correct. And you're a concubine whore." The girl, probably no older than fifteen, pushed up the sleeves of her hooded sweatshirt, slouched into the sofa cushions, and removed her iPhone from her pocket. She made a show of swiping at its screen.

Lulu froze, unsure of what to do or say next, but that was always the problem, wasn't it?

Luckily, the girl took it upon herself to break the silence. "My dad is a real dick, isn't he?"

A lump clogged Lulu's throat, constricting her airways. This had to be some sort of trap. This clever little devil was trying to get her to talk shit so she could record it on that phone and then play the recording to Official Xia. And anyway, it's not like there was anything negative to say really. He was a quiet man who met Lulu every week for dinner, on the same night, in the same block of time, reducing their "illicit affair" to little more than a regularly scheduled business meeting. Each time, he asked her polite questions about her week ("Fine," she'd lie) and about her studies ("Fine," she'd lie again—she'd long ago quit studying for any exams; what was the point?), and spoke not a word about himself. He always insisted she eat more and that she was too thin. When they finished eating, he'd pay the check and they'd both hop into his Audi or Benz or whatever car he was driving that week and head to the apartment he had put her up in. There, he'd say good-bye, drop her at the curb, and leave. That was it. That was all there was.

"Look, I'm not going to bad-mouth your father," Lulu said, gathering resolve from her memories. "So unless there's another reason you're here, maybe you should leave."

The girl stared intently, smugly even, at her iPhone screen. Lulu would have guessed she was now reading something, except that her eyes didn't seem to be moving.

"Um, hello?" Lulu smirked and then tossed her hands in the air in frustration. "Okay, all right, normally conversation goes one person says something and then the other person says something. But that's fine. You're just in my home, on my sofa, uninvited. It's not like you have to respond to anything I'm saying."

Still, the girl refused to look at her.

Well, this wasn't working. Lulu shifted her weight, gnawed her lip, decided to play polite hostess—maybe this would throw the girl off a bit. "I'm going to get a Coke Zero out of the fridge. I have a few of those and some apple juice and water. Tea too. Can I get you something to drink?"

Still not looking up from her phone, the girl said, "He's trying to get me to go to school in America. Utah. I don't want to go to Utah."

And there it was.

"Why would I go to America? I can hardly speak English—I hate that stupid language—and my friends are here, and I've lived here my whole life, and there's this boy I've been talking to—well, he's kind of my boyfriend now—and it's just stupid so I'm not going."

Lulu drew blood from her lip, licked it away—okay, but what did she expect her to do about it?

The girl sighed dramatically and swiped at her phone. A full minute passed. A foreign sound—claws scratching against cardboard. Lulu glanced over at the box. She had forgotten the turtle was even here.

"My name is Zhang Li, by the way," the girl said, looking up for a split second. "I already know you are Lulu."

Lulu nodded, stepped into the kitchen, and opened the fridge. Save for the drinks, it was empty. It smelled stale. She crinkled her nose. The light was bright. She squinted. Why did this girl know her name? Little girls shouldn't know about this corrupt mistress bullshit, should they? Why was she here? What did she want? Should she just call Official Xia and order him to pick the little brat up? Why wasn't there any real food in her fridge? Shouldn't she buy some proper ingredients and learn how to cook? What had she done with her life? What was she doing? Where had all of these years gone? What was there to her existence anymore beyond sleeping, watching DVDs, shopping, going on the Internet? Shouldn't she learn something, or do something, or go on a trip or something? Shouldn't she *want* to do those things? Where had her desire gone? Had she ever had it? She leaned headfirst into the fridge, breathing in the dank air. In, out. In, out. She exhaled one final time and removed two cold black cans.

When Lulu returned to the living room, Zhang Li crouched on the floor, over the cardboard box, her tiny hand stroking the turtle's shell. It was a sweet scene, and Lulu's bones softened. She set the cans down on the coffee table next to the girl's now-abandoned phone and knelt beside her. "It's a turtle," she said softly.

"No shit." Zhang Li withdrew her hand and glared up at her. "How retarded do you think I am?"

Lulu wasn't accustomed to being spoken to with such contempt—in fact, she wasn't used to being spoken to at all these days. Her cheeks burned red. "Yeah, I don't know why I said that. Sometimes I just say things." She wrung her hands. "I'm not dumb," she added. "Don't think I'm dumb. I'm not."

Zhang Li, expression blank, stared at her.

"I went to university. I studied economics." She left out the part about dropping out, about becoming a keratin farm.

"Wow," Zhang Li said, focusing her attention back to stroking the turtle. "Cool story."

Lulu inhaled and gathered her long hair, pulled it to the side, let it fall over one shoulder. "Yeah, well. I know that probably doesn't mean anything to you since you're, like, still mentally a toddler, but when you grow up you'll understand what a college degree means. That it takes a certain level of intelligence and dedication to achieve one and that only, like, ten percent of the world's population possesses that rare combination." Lying, acting like a mean high school girl, oh, she was becoming a better human being by the second. Her stomach lurched.

Zhang Li rolled her eyes. "It's more about luck and money, I think."

"I don't come from money." Out of control.

"Well, you have money now. And I don't think anyone would deny that you have incredibly good luck."

"Why are you here?"

Zhang Li stared down at the retreating turtle. She knocked softly on its shell and then said, "Blackmail." She inhaled sharply and then obviously rehearsed words tumbled from her mouth. "If he's going to try to send me to America against my will, I'm going to publicly out him as a cheater and a corrupt bribe-taker. I have social media accounts. It'd be easy as that."

Lulu's heartbeat quickened—take the man down and the woman always goes down harder. "Come on," she said, choosing her words wisely, back in control. "Let's be realistic here. I mean, what makes you think anyone would care? All officials are cheaters and bribe-takers. Not exactly newsworthy."

"Sure, but specific cases are. The public loves details. It makes things real. And what with all this Papa Hui stuff lately, everyone is on edge. The time has come for a change—that's what everyone is saying."

"What, are you majoring in PR at middle school?"

Zhang Li shrugged, removed the turtle from the box, and said, "We don't have majors in middle school." Then, not moving her mouth, she mumbled in a low voice something Lulu couldn't quite make out. Lulu raised an eyebrow. Zhang Li, speaking loud and clear now, said, "Is there someone else here?"

"No. Why?"

Zhang Li squinted. "Who was that then?"

"I thought *you* said something."

Zhang Li shook her head.

They both froze for a moment, their eyes scanning the apartment. Lulu stood. Her palms and armpits went clammy. She eyed the empty Absolut bottle visible through the kitchen door—if she smashed it on the countertop, she could use it as a jagged weapon. She took a creeping step in its direction.

That quiet, mumble of a voice spoke again. "Hello?"

Zhang Li's face drained, no color, only white. "I—I—I think it was the turtle," she stammered, holding it up.

Lulu spun around. "What?"

And from out of its shell, limbs and a head now poked out, and two beady little eyes looked back at them.

"My name is Kunchok Dawa and I was a monk in Lhasa and I died three days ago."

Lulu, dizzy, lowered herself to sit on the floor.

Zhang Li sat beside her and placed the turtle again in the box. She stared down at it and then, overstepping the oddness of the situation with adolescent sarcasm, chimed, "Okay, yeah, and you came back as a *turtle*?"

The turtle responded in a similar lilt. "Immediate availability was an issue. It was this or a dung beetle. We all make choices."

Lulu leaned forward. "But aren't you supposed to come back as something higher? Like something not used in, uh, boner soup?" She whispered the last few words, worried about Zhang Li's innocence.

"I see no distinction between one living thing and the next."

Lulu met Zhang Li's eyes and then leaned forward, resting her chin in her hands. "So, do you, like, have abilities?"

The turtle cocked its head. "Sorry?"

"What I mean is can you tell the future?"

Zhang Li's eyes flickered with interest. "Ooh"—she prodded the turtle's shell—"yeah, can you? Am I going to have to go to America or not? Can you tell?"

"Um, like am I one of those guys on a footbridge kneeling down with charts and telling every passerby with a coin to spare that they're going to strike it rich and squeeze out a fat baby son?"

Lulu nodded eagerly. "Yes, exactly."

"No." The turtle smirked. "I'm a turtle."

Disappointment washed over Lulu. "I just wanted to know if I have one," she heard herself say. "A future."

The turtle said, "Considering throwing yourself out the window, huh?"

Zhang Li jumped to Lulu's defense, strangely enough. "Well, if you really are a Tibetan, shouldn't you *want* her to kill herself? Since she's Chinese and all? And what about me? Do you want me to kill myself too?"

The turtle opened its mouth to reply, but Zhang Li charged forward with no intention of slowing down her rampage of questioning. "How'd you get into a fully grown turtle's body if you just died as a person three days ago?"

The turtle sighed. "Sometimes, rarely, soul exchanges are permitted. Usually only in animal bodies and only in the case of an emergency."

Zhang Li pushed up her loose sleeves, which kept falling. "I thought you said all beings are equal or whatever."

"Yes, but it's too complicated with human beings, too much paperwork if you will, and with people there are soul mates and emotional intelligence and any such number of complex matters to take into consideration..."

What Lulu and Zhang Li didn't know until now was that just a few days before—three, to be exact—in front of a monastery in Lhasa, Tibet, and after the morning prayers, two twenty-one-year-old monks, red robes doused in gasoline, shouted anti-China slogans and lit themselves on fire against the backdrop of a bluest blue sky.

But of course they didn't know.

Three thousand kilometers away in bustling Beijing, not a word was spoken about the charred remains dragged off by the police, the internal memos, the routine of this chaos. Not a word, not a word, not a word...

Until now.

Lulu's eyes widened. "Why'd you do it?"

The turtle blinked. "Don't get any ideas now. It's not a pleasant way to go."

The girls sat cross-legged and side by side on the floor. They lifted the turtle out of the box again, and Lulu filled a bottle cap with a bit of Evian. The turtle lapped up the water appreciatively.

"If you really want to know what happened, I'll tell you. I need to tell someone. Being a turtle isn't exactly conducive to telling stories, but I guess I can somehow talk and you can somehow understand me, so what am I even complaining about?"

So he began.

✳

Where can I start but to make it clear up front that I've always been a bit of an idiot. Not a full-on running-around-the-village-in-my-skivvies-shouting-incoherent-manifestos kind of idiot, but no real genius either. Or perhaps it's not so much stupidity; perhaps my real problem is laziness. Maybe not laziness per se—it's more that I've just never been particularly interested in scholarly pursuits. No, I guess all I really mean to say is that I always just felt like there was something wrong with me, and my true problem was that I could never pinpoint what. It could just be a matter of suffering, original sin, whatever you want to call it. Maybe that's all it is.

You might think it difficult to suffer in Lhasa, that holy city, that untouched city, that mythical city of incense-smoky dreams. Where is there room for pain, you might ask, in prayer flags and decorative ceiling tiles and *thangka* paintings and streets brimming with pilgrims and monks? But the pursuit of peace has always given rise to the most violent of struggles. And anyway, this is not a story about finding peace—you're not going to find that here. This is a story only of struggle.

How I came into the monastery is vital to understanding how all of this came about in the first place. So maybe that's where I should start. Forget everything I said before. My story begins here.

If you are very young when your father dies, as I was, the primary tragedy lies not so much in the actual death, but in your total lack of memories. I was only two years old when he fell ill and three when he passed. I can't remember his face, his voice, his character; all of that is lost. All I could ever summon was an image of his gentle, calloused hands; his bright white palms creased with dark lines. Lines like roads, like dead ends. That's it. That's all I have.

My mother, by contrast, had endless reserves of memories—of the tunes he sang, of the cigarettes he smoked down to nubs, of the contours of his body and the left-right sway of his gait, of the meals she cooked and he consumed—but she was too strong, too busy to wallow. We were vulnerable then—our relatives old and dying in villages, and us in the city, left without a male to care for us, to protect us, to provide for us. So she plowed through each day like an ox. In addition to her daily milk delivery gig, she sold sweaters by the roadside, worked as a waitress, collected discarded bottles and food wrappers and newspapers for recycling, and occasionally hawked Buddhist trinkets in front of a popular temple. This was how she came to befriend an elder monk, a jovial geezer who puttered around, gossiping and swapping jokes with the vendors, and who eventually agreed to take in both myself and a disabled neighbor's son.

I recall clearly the day our mothers delivered us to our fate: A long walk. A biting wind. Cottony clouds strewn across a placid sky. The dry heaves and sobs of my seven-year-old self, petrified at being left in the care of utter strangers. Dorjee, our neighbor's son—a sullen boy with sunken eyes. His silence, his stoicism, his bravery, I remember thinking at the time. I would soon learn otherwise. That he, with his fragile body and ever more fragile spirit, was as susceptible to weakness as anyone. But then: snowy peaks looming behind us; then, at that moment of abandonment, at that moment of handover to the gods, he glowered at his mother and spoke with a jarring lack of emotion, with a strength I'd never before witnessed: "See you later."

When it comes to friendship, children shun common ground—they don't need it, no, not even a speck of its dirt! Unlike adults, they don't demand complementary personality types and similar backgrounds and shared income brackets and what have you—such requirements are grown into, a coming-of-age gift from a judgmental world. For the very young, the mere fact of mutual existence is enough. Surrendered by our mothers to the same set of strangers, Dorjee and I naturally became best friends of circumstance. He, being a few months older than me, called me younger brother and I, being a few months younger than him, called him older brother. Together, we coasted into our new routines. We recited vows, studied, sat close in the prayer hall, devoured meals, and slept on adjacent bottom bunks in a dormitory room we shared with four other boys. Two of these boys, our respective bunkmates, were unremarkable— all quiet voices and furrowed brows, probably both from tragically poor families. The other two, a set of rosy-cheeked rambunctious twins, were another matter entirely.

There are myriad reasons families send their children into the monastery. Some can't afford to feed them and know that donning robes guarantees a meal ticket. Some are truly pious and sacrifice their sons to a spiritual path. A few others view the monastery as a last resort, a reform school, the only place that might be able to handle the destructive demons they somehow spawned. These twins, whose parents donated a large sum of money to get them in, were such a sad case.

Here's an example of their misdeeds. Very early one morning, on the precipice of dawn, I awoke to Dorjee softly crying in the bed beside mine.

Groggy, I mumbled, "What's wrong?"

He didn't answer, but pointed downward. Blurry, bleary, I rubbed my eyes: a dark patch on his sheets.

"It's okay," I murmured. I used to wet the bed quite often when I was younger. My older sister would always change the sheets, get me into fresh clothes, comfort me with stories and melodious songs, lull me right back to dreams. "It's best not to drink water so close to bedtime," I added, as a word of advice for the future.

Silent, urgent tears streamed down Dorjee's face, and I was racking my brain for more comforting words when the twins burst in, one clutching a kettle and both spewing laughter. "You really thought you pissed yourself, didn't you?! It was just a little warm water!"

Okay, so these kinds of pranks are to be expected from naughty children and, taken individually, are usually harmless, right? In this life, we each take our turn as victim; it's one of many roles we must play. But the twins' pursuit of Dorjee was so much more than that; it was unfair, bordering on absurd. It was every day. It was relentless. They hid squishy, stinky dog shit under his pillow; tied him to a tree, gagged him, and left him overnight; spread rumors that he was going to leave the monastery and undergo plastic surgery to become a girl; slipped a low-grade poison into his food, giving him terrible diarrhea.

Beyond the question of how they got away with all of this—a question I don't have an answer to beyond the obvious "they were well connected"—you might wonder why these two boys poured water on Dorjee's bed but not mine. Why they dropped caterpillars into his tea flask but left mine untouched. Why they tripped him in the corridors and spooked him in the toilets and accused him of all manner of odd offenses, including farting in meditation and giggling like a pretty princess.

One answer is: I don't know.

Another answer is: He was an easy target, the type of boy who tried so desperately to hide his vulnerability that he succeeded only in bringing it to the forefront.

A better answer is: He was weak.

Ha, but who isn't? Aren't we all but one heartbeat away from being no more? What is life by an in-vain attempt at distancing ourselves from our weakness, from the very flaw of being human? Your expensive car, those false eyelashes, that makeup, those designer clothes—aren't all of these things and all of the things like them just protective layers, fortresses we build between ourselves and our frailty? And aren't all of these things we acquire and these walls we construct to shield ourselves little more than illusions?

The truest answer is this: Dorjee had no illusions about his weakness. There it was, and there he was.

One summer evening after dinner, Dorjee and I strolled the corridors, practicing some tongue twisters an older monk taught us. Dorjee couldn't quite get them right, and each time he missed a syllable we both fell into hysterics, collapsing into a heap onto the cool smooth floor. One of the older monks peeked out from his quarters, the whites of his eyes glowing in the dark, and shushed us, told us to go the hell to bed. This struck us as funny too, and as we raced away, we mocked in whisper his overly stern voice, his words. Laughter still dribbling from my mouth, I turned the corner into our room, into an odd sight: one of the twins flat on the floor, the bunk bed's post "crushing" his stomach. Twitching in overzealous agony, flailing his skinny arms every which way, he gurgled spit bubbles. His lips opened to emit a moaning sound, but all I heard, from behind me, was Dorjee's sharp gasp.

This was a cruel joke, crueler than ever before. Compassion, empathy—these were vague concepts in my young mind, but here they grew even vaguer. Under my Buddhist robes, I was human, and when I stood there next to Dorjee, watching his expression waver between blankness and total breakdown, an anger sparked and burned inside of me. Forgive me, but I was nine years old and I couldn't help but feel, standing there unsure of how to proceed, that Dorjee, in all of his weakness, in all of his unwillingness to stand up and fight, had brought this burden upon himself. It was only a joke, and I could see that. This twin was not dying, was not hurt, was not being crushed. The other twin was probably lurking around a corner somewhere, awaiting Dorjee's reaction.

It was only a joke. Everything they did to him, everything was only a joke.

I wanted to shove Dorjee, shove him hard, tell him this, spit it in his face, shake him and demand that he remain stoic, that he not give them the show they wanted. But I remained frozen, and the "crushed" twin shouted out, "Look at me, I'm Dorjee's father," and Dorjee screamed, clutching his gut, and crumpled to the floor in a pile of snot and tears and hideous, twisted, unforgivable weakness.

I never heard Dorjee's family's story from his own lips; I heard it only in rumor, in gossip, in hushed and knowing tones. Though I may not have been a genius, I was curious, nosy even. Not knowing every detail of a story was a form of torture, and perhaps because of my closeness to its subject, this one in particular haunted me in its ambiguity. So instead of driving myself mad with speculation, I filled in the blanks myself, so that I could easily watch the entire saga play out while I sat quiet in meditation.

Dorjee's father worked as a long-distance bus driver and his mother rode along, collecting tickets, attending to passengers' concerns, and manning the bus's onboard TV. The TV was her favorite part. She loaded karaoke video after karaoke video—she was a romantic at heart and impartial to syrupy ballads. Theirs was a nice bus, with rows of comfortable seats, so much so that passengers often slept for the duration of the haul and awoke refreshed, no achy bones or sore throats or stiff necks.

The paths they traversed were bumpy, but Dorjee's father was a skilled driver. Money was tight, but their little family scraped by. From the time he was a baby, Little Dorjee rode back and forth across a treacherous landscape—mountains that shot up like spikes from the earth, steep cliff drops, unpaved and under-construction roads—forming a strong stomach and an even stronger bond with his parents.

One snowy January afternoon, with the sun burning in the sky and the white ground frozen below, while Teresa Teng wailed on about love as sweet as honey, their beautiful white metal bus careened off the side of one of those steep cliffs, rolled, flew, flipped, and came shuddering to a stop.

The music cut out, the simple melody replaced by screaming, punctuated here and there by eerie silence—many sleeping passengers had simply not woken up, had eternally prolonged their slumber.

My soul floated behind Dorjee's eyes as they saw his father's body crushed beyond recognition, flattened and bleeding and broken. My being inhabited his ears, assaulted by his mother's wails as she tried to no avail to shake her husband's corpse back to consciousness. There is nothing else to describe here. Beyond imagination, I truly saw, heard, experienced a scene so disturbing it collapsed under the weight of words.

I sat in the meditation room with my legs crossed, flattened by the burden of my older brother's karma, desperately clawing my way out from my own mind, my own creation—Dorjee's reality. Let the thoughts come, and let them go too...

✳

Zhang Li cracked open her Coke Zero and said, "Yeah, there are always people like that. Bad-luck people. Like, there was this girl at my school when I was younger who had one nostril that was much bigger than the other. Really big. You could easily fit a couple of pencils up there, no joke. Everyone teased her for it, but they also whispered that she'd gotten that way because when she was little she'd hide out in the closet while her parents fought and shove things in her nose for comfort. And then that one time she got a marble stuck up there, permanently stretching it out. I don't know. One time I called her some name, like booger-picker, something stupid that any primary school student would say. I feel a little bit bad when I think about it now, but at the time, even knowing the backstory, I truly felt nothing." She took a slow sip. "People suck."

Lulu, sitting cross-legged on the floor, leaned forward and reached for her own soda can. "What happened to her?"

"I don't even know. Her grades were really bad, no wonder, so of course we wound up at different middle schools. I do think about her sometimes. I mean, if I met her now, I'd make an effort to be nice to her, you know? And sometimes I imagine running into her on the street or at a restaurant, and I imagine myself doing something nice, buying her a milk tea or something. It makes me feel better to think I'd do better. But I know it's just 'me now' trying to forgive 'me then.' My daydreams don't actually, like, help her or change the past or how the past affects her life now or anything, do they?"

The turtle sighed. "Bad luck is an avalanche."

Lulu nodded, gazing out at the buildings and streets and cars and tiny ant people, sipping her drink, the bubbles stabbing her tongue. Remembering her manners, she lifted the turtle to give him a view too. Three sets of eyes sunk into the city scene, a bleak horizon, an impressionist painting behind a gray screen of smog.

✳

The daily life of a monk is one of routines, regimens, tasks. No one was exempt from caring for the grounds, and unlike many of the other boys who grumbled and groaned over words like "clean" and "mop," I eagerly accepted any and all unsavory chores—sweeping, cleaning, scrubbing, washing, anything. I'd convinced myself that if I performed these useful domestic tasks with enough finesse, my mother might be drawn back, might see me as more than a baby bird with a hungry stomach and a gaping mouth, might bring me home.

It was fanciful thinking, I know, but it was necessary. As I slaved over stoves and scrubbed between tiles, I dreamed up a million alternate realities, endless futures. In one, my sister raced up the monastery steps, her cheeks ruddy, her chest heaving, and fell to the landing, shouting, "Mom's rich! She's rich!" In another, the monastery caught fire and I emerged from the blaze, the wild flames, the collapse, and stumbled back to our family's rented room, no richer, no poorer, but poised, at least, to start anew. My favorite fantasy, though, was this: my mother, overcome with guilt, retrieved me one afternoon, brought me home. I knew I couldn't survive this world as a layabout, so I helped her with her various jobs, including milk delivery. Every day, we delivered to the many modest homes in our community, and then one day there was a new addition to the delivery list—an address a bit far from the others, but no matter, a new customer was a new customer, money was money. We walked, our steps uncertain, up a winding path to a grand house, grander than any house we'd ever visited, and my mother lifted her shaky fist and knocked at the door.

We waited. Our lungs ballooned. We worried the wind might pick us up, carry us away. We waited.

The light padding of footsteps.

"Hello!" An old woman with a kind face peeked at us through the crack, swung the door open fully, and took the milk. She studied us then, a mother and a son, bonded by an almost palpable love. "Say, you look thirsty. Care to come in for a cup of tea?"

My mother and I obliged, sat in overstuffed chairs with this old woman in her castle of a home, surrounded by beautiful paintings and museum-worthy artifacts. "I saved my treasures back in the fifties from the invading, looting Chinese by burying them."

Beauty buried in the earth, abandoned but always remembered, just like me.

"I dug them up only a few years ago," she added in a whisper, "when I finally knew it was safe."

As we gobbled down sweets and drank yak butter tea, she regaled us with the story of the PLA soldier she fell in love with and their ill-fated love affair, the misunderstandings, the hole that remained charred in her heart; with songs and with poems and with old fairy tales, and we became so lost in their wonder that we didn't have cause to daydream.

At last, quiet reigned and the old woman swept the walls, the floors, with rueful eyes and said, "Please don't mind the mess, it's very messy and dusty, ay, and I'm very old and just can't get around like I used to."

And my mother cleared her throat, gathered her courage, said, "You know, my son here is a very fine cleaner. He once cleaned an entire monastery."

And I hemmed and hawed, slipping into humility with ease, but the old woman saw through it, begged me to be her housekeeper on a very fine monthly salary. I accepted—oh, of course I accepted!—and my mother would quit working and my sister, now from a well-situated family thanks to me, would be able to marry any man in town, even the most handsome, maybe the man who ran the barber shop, maybe even someone from the wider world, maybe even a pop star.

One afternoon I was sweeping the dining hall, reveling in that very magical daydream, turning it over and over in my head, when Dorjee trudged in and plopped down hard on the floor.

"Move," I cackled, poking him with the broom's straws. "Don't make this old witch chase you out of here, you little rat!"

I hadn't expected him to laugh at this—his sense of humor had weakened over the previous months, worn down by the teasing, no doubt—but I also hadn't expected him to remain completely silent. He sat cross-legged, his elbows digging into his thighs and his chin cradled in his hands, staring down at the floor.

And it wasn't just lacking a sense of humor. He'd been acting more strangely all around, more forlorn, more prone to these long stretches of staring at nothing. He slept less and less, slipping from our room in the cover of night to pace the halls or study or do heaven knows what.

I swept and swept, and he sat there, and the more I thought about, the more I sensed his uneasiness wasn't rooted entirely in the twins. It had been two years already, and actually, if anything, the bullying was beginning to wane.

No, this was something bigger, more profound.

"Move," I said again, this time whacking him in the back with the straws. A tiny statue on the floor, motionless.

I didn't know what to do with my thoughts, what to do with Dorjee, so I just swept around him, continued sweeping until I was finished. I stood for a moment, the broom in my hands and across my body like a shield, waiting for him to say something, to explain what he was doing, to utter anything, but he only sat there, so of course I walked away.

I met Dorjee's silence, his descent into solitude, with a mature level of acceptance. Perhaps he would come back around later, I reasoned, and I was relieved to be free of the daily burden of worrying about him too. Time passed, relieving me also of the burden of living so intensely in my daydreams. Freedom came with acceptance.

Once I embraced the reality of my situation, life inexplicably improved. I received word that a chance encounter with a cook led my sister to love. She soon married this young man, and together they opened a successful restaurant in Chengdu. She mailed me a photograph of herself in front of the restaurant, a cozy little place with a red sign nestled in a row of shops. My heart could burst; I hardly recognized this woman with a face as round and fat and glowing as the moon. Soon, just as in my daydreams, my mother no longer needed to work—my sister sent plenty of money home. With more time to spare, my mother, healthier and happier, paid regular visits to the monastery, all thanks to my sister, who, when I was twenty, would get pregnant and send for my mother to join her and her growing belly, leaving me all alone in Lhasa.

But let me slow down a bit and back up. As I said, although we still considered each other brothers, Dorjee had largely faded into the background of my life. My teenage years were full of laughter, studying, cleaning, writing, reading, music. I developed a rebellious streak, albeit as a follower, not a leader. I joined a few others, including those naughty twins who'd long ago lost interest in Dorjee, in sneaking out to visit a nearby Internet café. The twins' father gave them money on the sly, and they generously dipped into their funds to pay the café's owner for all of our Internet fees. A few boys had cell phones, but they weren't very freehanded with them, so my youth existed largely in technological darkness. Computers illuminated my world. I scrolled through pictures, read news and short stories and discussions and arguments, played games, listened to music. One of the twins finagled a pair of headphones, which I borrowed to listen to pop, rock, and rap songs sung in Tibetan and in Chinese and in English and French too—I loved the way these foreign words sounded, beyond my comprehension and therefore easier to lose myself in.

Although all of these major shifts were under way, much of that time seems blurry, lost to me now. Thus is the effect of routine.

But I remember two moments with clarity.

The first was when I was about fifteen. I'd just sneaked back into the monastery late, perhaps around midnight. My robes had gotten stuck on a fence I'd had to climb over and were torn. I crept down the black corridor toward Jinpa's room. Torn robes became a common occurrence for those of us who sneaked out, and Jinpa, a natural entrepreneur if I ever met one, saw a hole in the marketplace and opened a robe repair side business. In exchange for his services and secrecy, he accepted cash and other valuable goods, including food. Lucky for me, I had a Watermelon Wiggler one of the twins had bought for me at the café tucked into my robes. I foolishly reached in and fingered the wrapper. *Crinkle, crinkle,* echoing in the halls. I winced and paused in my tracks, hoping no one had heard me. A low moan filled that pause. I squinted: darkness. I crept forward. Another moan. A door about a meter ahead of me to my right—a storage room for extra blankets and the like. I pressed my ear up against the closed door. I heard again an odd moan and the very quiet, very human rhythm of breath. I curled my fingers around the doorknob, listened. I don't know what stopped me from turning it— as I said, I have always been very curious—but I removed my hand, retreated, and hurried to Jinpa's room. He awoke when I entered— he always slept with one eye open these days—happily accepted his

Bashful Goose snack, and skillfully mended my robe, not waking a single one of his snoring roommates.

The second important moment, I was sitting under a tree, the sun hanging high in the noon sky, shadows short and stout. I was humming a song I'd listened to the night before and reading a literary journal I'd borrowed from one of the twin's cohorts when a great commotion rose up from the monastery's entry. I looked up just in time to see Jungney, a monk a bit older than us, maybe in his midtwenties, storming toward the gates carrying a small bag. Although we often sneaked out for our little visits to local Internet bars or restaurants, it was unheard of for any such visit to require a bag—it was too obvious, it would get you into trouble. And Jungney, he wasn't one of us. He didn't sneak out. It was midday. He wasn't sneaking out. Something was amiss.

My heart raced, absorbing the energy of late spring, of the sunshine, of the prospect of some drama, some excitement.

Commotion drew more commotion as others, startled, ran out to see what the matter was. A voice shouted out to him, "Ay, where're you going?"

Jungney didn't respond, just marched, his head high, like a stubborn soldier on his way to some doomed battle, not turning around, not giving us an answer. And then he was gone.

Slowly, the intrigued monks reassumed their positions, and our gated world was once again one of peace.

The others practiced martial arts, told jokes, napped, and I returned to my reading, an enthralling short story about a young man who was all set to travel to Beijing, work as a migrant, and earn money to pay for a surgery for his ailing father. But on the train to the capital, the young man's bag, containing his phone and money and the address of the person he was to stay with, was stolen. He disembarked in the unfamiliar capital, his existence reduced to that of a beggar. He tried for jobs, but the bosses laughed in his unkempt face. He subsisted off scraps. He pleaded with pedestrians for anything they could spare. His hair matted and dirt made its home in the creases of his skin. He lost his dignity, his mind. The story ended with him drifting to sleep beneath an overpass, still hundreds of yuan short of even a ticket home, the overhead bridge rattling under the weight of hundreds of crossing cars.

I put the story down and I sat there for a moment, immersed in that ending.

And then, from nowhere, from the ether from which all important realizations rise, it hit me in pieces: this guy, Jungney, was the one Dorjee told me he was going to study with on those nights he sneaked out. Jungney and Dorjee never interacted in daylight; they were not friends, no one would even know they were acquaintances. Dorjee wasn't up all night studying—he was barely a better student than I was. Jungney was in charge of maintenance and had in his possession keys for all the rooms in the monastery, including that storage closet.

And then it hit me all at once.

✳

"No way." Lulu squirmed, toying with her hair. "Please tell me that kind of thing doesn't happen there."

The turtle stretched his arms. "It happens everywhere, doesn't it? No environment is immune to sick people."

Zhang Li nodded, drawing her hands into her lap. "Yeah, there was this teacher at my school who gave one of my classmates a book of dirty drawings. He got fired, but it was hardly the end of the line for him. All he had to do was move to another city and start over with a new job, you know? Who would ever know? There's this line in a song that goes: *With just a little distance, a little bit of wiggle, reputations shed like skin.* It's pretty true, I think."

Lulu swallowed. "Heavens. But with Dorjee, I mean, I just really can't understand how one person can have such consistently bad luck." An instance of the exact opposite, of her own life, struck her—this ever-flowing tributary of success she'd unwittingly found herself recipient of, drowning in. What had she done to deserve it? And what was she making of it? Why was she incapable of deriving pleasure from it? Her gaze traversed the living room—flat-screen TV, BoConcept furniture, due-for-a-dry-cleaning Anna Sui jacket haphazardly tossed across the dining room table, one sleeve inside out, a crumpled tissue poking from the pocket.

"Poor Dorjee," Zhang Li said. Her empty can clinked on the coffee table as she set it down.

They allowed for a moment of silence, and then the turtle continued.

*

There were whispers for a long time after it happened, low voices around the dining hall, the courtyard, the dormitories.

"Caught touching a young boy."

"Transferred somewhere remote."

"It was a seven-year-old, I heard."

"The little guy started screaming, waking someone up."

"I hear it wasn't just that one boy. I hear there were others before him. *Others.*"

"Who do you think?"

"I would never tell anyone if that happened to me. How embarrassing. How disgusting."

"How do we know it didn't happen to you then?"

"Yeah, right. It was probably you. And I bet you liked it."

Chortles, hearty slaps on the back, full-fledged laughter.

And in the background, Dorjee, silent, as though not a broken boy but a precisely placed prop, staring into his dish, into the horizon, into the dead end lines written in his palms.

*

The turtle stopped there, slipped back inside his shell.

Lulu tapped on his shell. "Hey? You okay?"

Silence.

She lifted him from the hardwood floor and set him back into the box.

Silence.

"No, he doesn't want to be in there," Zhang Li said. "Take him out."

Lulu removed him, placed him between herself and Zhang Li.

More silence. Lulu wiped her palms on her thighs. Clammy. Was that all he had to say? Was he seeking absolution? Had they somehow given it to him? Was that all there was to this? What next?

He poked his head out from his carapace and gazed out the window. At this welcome sight, the girls simultaneously exhaled, met each other's gaze, and burst into nervous giggles. The turtle turned toward them and spoke once again: "Thank you. I just needed a minute. And after seeing this wide world, how could I bear to tell the remainder of my story to cardboard walls?"

✺

When I was twenty, I was released. Or rather, I released myself.

I'd never been much of a scholar, much of a virtuous man. I'd long been sneaking out to do unholy things, and I'd long been entertaining impure thoughts. So I guess you could say it was all a long time coming.

Of course, my disillusionment was also rooted in what had happened to Dorjee and that screaming seven-year-old and heaven knows who else. I can't go on with this story unless I acknowledge my own guilt, my own forsaken responsibility. The mental gulag in which I found myself prisoner. The questions that swarmed me like wasps, stinging, swelling my eyelids, blinding me: What had stopped me from standing up for Dorjee? What had stopped me from caring, from uncovering the roots of his pain, from opening that storage room door? What had caused me to give up so easily on him? What had made me ashamed of him? Had I somehow misinterpreted detachment? What the hell kind of brother was I?

With a head bulging with questions and no relief, no answers to be found... after many weeks of restless nights and sour stomachs... after clawing my way out of one too many daydream nightmares... I decided to leave the monastery.

I didn't want to tell my family about my decision, not yet anyway, and I didn't want to ask for their help. I discussed my predicament—no money of my own, no place to stay, a pressing need to escape—with some of the older monks, men I trusted deeply. They converged privately, while I waited in the corridor, tracing circles on the walls with my index finger. Hushed voices, determining my fate. Centuries passed. At last, they called me back into the room. I floated outside of myself, light as a wisp, as they told me the verdict—I could continue living in the monastery until I made other arrangements so long as I continued performing chores. Light-headed with happiness, I thanked them profusely and skipped, danced, twirled down the corridor. I assumed the donations my sister had sent, and continued to send, had at least something to do with their kindness, but what does it matter, really, and who am I to make such hasty judgments anyway?

It seemed probable that this goofy beanpole with only a religious education would wind up toiling as a wage employee, skipping like a stone from rented bed to rented bed, from job to job, and bound to live a life just as fulfilling. But what would be the point of seeking refuge from one unfulfilling existence in the next? I was young and I had dreams and I wasn't going to be trapped in any such cycle.

You see, I'd witnessed with my own eyes people from all over the world visiting our grounds, peering through our gates. Women with black hair and yellow hair and orange hair and purple hair too, with red dots on their foreheads, with faces completely covered; men with turbans, beards, white hair, blue hair, long skirts, pants with dozens of pockets. All of these strangers had come to see my home, and now I planned to cash in on the favor. I wanted to see the world, to be a stranger somewhere, anywhere, everywhere—this desire is the universal burden of the young, the free.

And free I was. Relieved of my study duties and with time to burn, I roamed the streets, becoming intimately familiar with the narrow alleyways, white buildings, billboards for alcohol, neon signs, shiny storefronts, Tibetan writing and Chinese characters, beggars, cranky restaurateurs, women who washed clothes in plastic buckets and women who sold vegetables spread out on cloths, vegetables I one day planned to be able to buy with my very own money.

One lazy summer night, just after the Saga Dawa Festival, when we honor Buddha's memory, when we replace the old prayer flagpole in Kailash Kora with a new one, when we set the year's fresh multicolored wishes and hopes to the wind, I strolled down a sidewalk, humming the words to a commercial jingle under my breath. The new flagpole had been set crookedly, which old-timers believed meant bad luck, but I couldn't fathom the prospect, not then. The evening was all cool breezes and smiling faces, and my world was still blooming before my eyes, and I caught sight of a man in a dark jacket struggling to pull one of a half-dozen giant plastic crates of green bottles into the open back door of a building. I jogged over to him.

"Can I help you?"

The "man," who, up close, I realized couldn't have been older than fifteen or sixteen, looked up at me with terrified saucer eyes.

"Are you a..." He spoke in Chinese and pointed at my robes, unable to complete his question.

"Yes," I said. I didn't have any other clothes, and anyway, be-cause I was still living in the monastery, it made sense for me to continue wearing them.

He studied me, his mouth agape for another twenty seconds, beads of sweat sprouting from his hairless upper lip, before shrugging and mumbling, "Yeah, sure, a little help."

Together we pushed and pulled the crates inside. Panting, I wiped the sweat from my forehead with my arm. The kid thanked me for my help, and I was just turning to leave the way I'd come when a weight pressed on my shoulder.

I turned to meet the handsome face of a tall and muscular man, long hair tied back in a ponytail. I adjusted my focus to see beyond him. This was a bar. Those green bottles were beer bottles. I had, for many minutes now, been inside a bar. My heart pounded, and all manner of thoughts ran through my head—mostly of the "am I going to be stabbed and robbed?" variety, and I didn't even own anything worth stealing.

My fears dissipated as the man's square face cracked into a smile. He addressed me with a thick Beijing accent. "You're a monk, are you?"

I shrugged—what was the right answer anymore? "Was. Am. Sort of. It's complicated."

He play-grimaced and raised an eyebrow. "All right, well, listen, I'm a bit of a Buddhist too, though maybe not a good one, and this is my bar. This might be a weird offer, but we could really use an extra set of hands around here this evening, and here you are, so how does fifty yuan for a couple hours sound? Fair?"

Questions popped into my head: Had I just walked into a job? Was this fate? Or was this trouble? I kept my questions to myself. Then I had a thought in statement form, which I said aloud. "But I don't know how to tend bar."

This was the closest I'd ever been to alcohol, aside from on billboards. Real alcohol, I mean.

The man laughed. "A monk in robes tending bar! Nah, none of that tonight. Just putting things away." He picked up a cardboard box, lifting with bent knees, carrying it into the beyond. "We're not even open yet. Hey, don't be shy. Follow me."

And that was how I, this monk in robes, wound up washing glasses, carrying boxes, and unpacking inventory in a bar with a sixteen-year-old Chinese migrant worker called Little Cancer.

Although Lhasa brimmed with ethnic Chinese migrants and tourists, working alongside Little Cancer was the closest I'd ever been to a real Han. Most of what I'd heard about the Han Chinese was in the monastery and related to a distant history of destruction and current struggles with bureaucracy: the authorities said we couldn't do this, should do this, couldn't do that. It's not that I was expecting all Han to be stubborn, difficult, and rude, but our minds become angled in certain directions based on our upbringings and circumstances.

It pains me to admit it now, but it genuinely surprised me how kind Little Cancer turned out to be, how easy to work with, to talk to. He was soft-spoken and small, like Dorjee, but had a physical strength about him, a sturdiness, a quickness, that Dorjee lacked. As we washed and dusted and organized, he told me about how he'd gotten the job at the bar (through an employment agency), how he came to Lhasa, and how he'd come to be called Little Cancer.

He began, "There was a cloth factory in the town where I'm from, and that's where everybody worked and had, since I was born, always worked. It was an old concrete structure, and it was the nucleus of local life. When I was seven years old, like everyone I knew, I went to work there too. One of the few in my work unit with arms, I was responsible for pressing the buttons on the machines and removing the cloth from the loom.

"Life went on like that—work, three scant meals a day, sleep, work again.

"But then, when I was thirteen, some plates in reality shifted. That's when my mother first discovered a tumor growing on the side of her head. It began the size of a grain of rice, but it grew, grew, kept growing. I would never see my mama looking lovely again, sure, and that was a difficult truth to accept, but in my town, we were tough, adaptable—the others at the factory didn't lose any sleep over it and took to calling her Mama Cancer. I became known, then, as Little Cancer.

"Then there was the second shift. The factory was never profitable to begin with, but the head of the township—an ugly man with jagged, turned-in teeth—always said at least it gave us something to do and, red patriotism boiling under his irises, said it contributed to our great nation's development.

"One day, out of nowhere, he forsook his love affair with busy hands, with building a better, brighter, redder future. Everyone said we should've seen it coming, that he'd been extorting taxes from all of us for a long time, making money on his door-to-door visits in the cover of night, Taser in tow. But we'd been blind in our busyness. We'd failed to come together, to protect one another, to address the problem of this robber baron. He made off with our money, fled to some city, disappeared in its depths.

"By the time I turned fifteen, there was nothing left to run the factory on and no one to sell to, even if we could produce—that township crook not only took our money with him, he took his lists of contacts and his expertise. He took our livelihood. Waste continued to pour downhill from other towns and into our dwindling water supply. No one could afford electricity anymore, and so nighttime found us plunged into complete darkness. Desperation strangled us, cutting off oxygen to our brains, and we wandered around like fools in mounds of dirt, combing through the gravel and grains for anything edible. While we were out scavenging, the factory's second-in-charge ransacked homes for TV sets and bicycles and anything worth anything, and then he disappeared too.

"Swearing to guard what we had left with her life, my mother stayed inside and nursed her still-swelling tumor. Soon the tumor became so heavy that she couldn't stand. She got around first by crawling and then by dragging herself and her tumor across the floor. I'd come home from scavenging and find her wiggling on her belly like a worm, performing chores, boiling indigo water, sweeping. As though cleanliness mattered. As though our lives mattered. Every day, this anger would simmer up inside me—she was distracting herself, kidding herself. Everyone in the town was. Why couldn't they see that we had to get out before it was too late? Before we all turned from deformed people into dust people into dust?

"For many weeks, I swallowed my anger down. It was one of my only forms of sustenance.

"But then the arguments started. Intense, unforgivable arguments. Maybe it was just because we were hungry. Maybe the radiation was driving us mad. We fought daily over my insistence that we leave and her insistence that we tough it out.

"'What will our ancestors say!' she'd shout at me. 'We cannot leave their ghosts here all alone. No good awaits us without their blessing. Tell me, what would they say?' And I'd defiantly shout back, 'Nothing. They'd say nothing because they're dead just like we will be soon if we don't get out.'

"I tried. Oh, I tried, but nothing could convince my mother to leave home, and our heated fights only seemed to exacerbate her health problems.

"Racked with guilt, and after days of eating only grass sprout soup, I'd had enough.

"With just my ID card in my pocket, I made my way through town, heading for the bus station and, on the way, passing people I'd known all my life: One-Armed Doctor, Boy-Girl, Cyclops, Fish Lady, Legless Skateboarder, Two-Faced Aunty. Here I was walking past, with two perfectly good legs and two perfectly capable arms, and all the parts I needed and none that I didn't, and I wondered: Why had I been left untouched? Or was I tainted too, but by something invisible, something inside me that couldn't be detected now, but someday would? These troubles swirling in my head, I boarded the bus. I nodded a hello to Three-Foot Driver. I was the only passenger. I looked out the window at the deserted bus station, the empty parking lot, the lonely snack shop, the muddy latrines.

"We sat there for a long, long time and Three-Foot Driver fell asleep.

"I fell asleep too and awoke, drowsy, as dawn broke. Three-Foot Driver stepped out to have a cigarette. I wondered if we would ever depart the station, if he would ever press the accelerator. I waited. I waited on that bus for days, so many days that I lost count, going outside only to piss or to steal longing looks at the one package of plastic-wrapped candied sweet potatoes in the bus station's snack shop. All of those days passed, and I grew woozy, tired, weak. I lost all of my will. I accepted that I would die there on that dingy, dirt-caked bus in that abandoned parking lot.

"One second I was slipping into death and the next my eyes popped open. The bus swayed ever so slightly. Fish Lady stepped on board. Like me, she traveled empty-handed. There was nothing worth taking, and I guess we were afraid that these things might contaminate our next life.

"I could have cheered, I was so excited. I didn't. I sat, and I waited. I held on to hope.

"And slowly but surely that afternoon, as the distant sun streaked across the gray sky, the townspeople did turn up. Driven out by dwindling savings or by the dawning realization that there was truly nothing left, the bus filled, nearly to capacity—there was one empty seat left, the one right beside me.

"You can probably guess who never came.

"Satisfied with his ticket sales, Three-Foot Driver revved the engine. And that was it. We were off, all of us freaks, to a small city bus station, where we all boarded buses and then trains bound for new places, none of us sticking together, not any of us wanting anything to do with one another any longer. We'd had enough. We were, once again and forever, on our own."

We finished drying glasses, and Boss—as Little Cancer called him—gave me my pay and told me I was welcome to come back and help any time. I nearly grabbed the big man and hugged him. I wanted to. I wanted to squeeze him half to death. It may seem silly, excitement over so little money, but this was the first time in my life that I held my very own money, money I'd earned on my own. I clutched these pieces of paper, and images of what they would allow me to buy—a portion of a rented room, vegetables, freedom—flashed through my head. I restrained myself, thanked him profusely, and under a star-strewn sky, I practically skipped back to the monastery, where I let myself in and sunk softly into a deep, contented sleep.

It's funny how everything happens one way, and then suddenly it happens another way completely. How a whole life, a whole future, can pivot so quickly, smoothly on its feet.

My fate, I knew, was wrapped up this bar, in that cancer village, in the work and the money and the people I'd meet. That next day, all I could think about was going back.

Of course, after I wrapped up my nightly chores, I hurried down familiar streets, past hawkers and holy men and sightseers, to the bar, where Boss was teaching a focused Little Cancer to mix drinks.

I stood by, transfixed, as the two poured and amalgamated various alcohols and sodas and juices. Little Cancer hunched over the glasses and bottles, pouring and measuring ever so carefully like a mad scientist with a mission relying on exactness. Boss kept smiling, telling him to loosen up a bit, but, in truth, he didn't appear to mind the attention to detail.

"Here," Boss said, finally verbally acknowledging me, breaking the spell and handing me a glass. "Try this. It's an old-fashioned."

I sniffed the syrupy concoction. I drew it to my lips and took a measured sip. My gag reflex kicked in and I panicked, desperate to spit it out. I can only imagine the face I must have been making—both Boss and Little Cancer burst out laughing.

I swallowed, fire in my throat, and then laughed too. "First time," I squeaked, and not wanting to make a fool of myself or to make an unintended statement about Little Cancer's skills, I sipped again and forced a grin.

They included me in the remainder of their lesson, and that's how I learned to tend bar. Many mixtures and sips later, we collapsed in an overstuffed booth in the corner. Boss talked, slurring a bit, about his grand plans, about the bands he hoped to bring in, about his eventual dream of operating a record label, of bringing Tibetan rock to the world. The room spun. I tried my best to listen but his words sounded far away, as though he were speaking into cupped hands and not out into the open world.

Little Cancer laid his face to rest on the table, snored, mumbled, sighed.

"Should we—" I motioned toward him, thinking maybe it'd be best to get him to bed, thinking fondly too of my own bed, how nice it'd feel to shut my eyes, to drift away.

But Boss shook his head. "He's fine. Just let him rest a bit." He was silent for a moment, his gaze traveling the brick wall, and then he said, "I don't expect you to tell me why you're only a half-monk or your life story or any of that, but I do want to ask your opinion on something, okay?"

I nodded. Sure.

"Do you think that owning a bar makes me a bad Buddhist?" Before I could respond, he chuckled. "Oh, boy. That hardly sounds intel-lectual, does it? Like praying to god about hairstyles or something. Okay, let me rephrase that: Do you think that there are other ways to show reverence and other paths to enlightenment besides just living some monastic, closed-off life?"

I peered through one of the glasses on the tabletop. Everything was distorted through it, too tall or too short. "Yeah," I said. "I hope so."

It was his turn to nod. "Yeah, I like to hope so too." He stole a sip from the glass I'd been peering through and stared firmly ahead at that brick wall. "I'm going to tell you something about myself that I've never told anyone."

I am a man who has studied holy things, but we all know by now that I'm not a holy man. Ha, and if we are going to be honest, let's be clear too: I never was a man, only ever a boy. And now I'm just a turtle.

I say that to say this: Why Little Cancer and Boss felt the need to offer up their confessions to me, their stories, I don't know. I'm worthy of no one's secrets; I feel that still.

Allow me now to confess all of my indiscretions, the sins that made me unworthy: Impure thoughts. Looking at racy pictures of women on the Internet. Masturbation. Materialism. Harboring anger at my mother for abandoning me, at my sister for not sending for me to join them in Chengdu. Jealousy. Longing. Listening to music that advocated drug use—loud, raucous music that did little to quiet my mind...

Oh, as for my sins, I could go on and on...

Boss took another sip, set the glass down, cleared his throat. "Okay, so there's this Nirvana song—old school, but they're my favorite rock band—that goes, *The animals I've trapped have all become my pets... something in the way, mmm...*"

I hummed along. I knew the one.

"So I was in the backseat of a taxi one afternoon, back in Beijing. That song, I'd heard it a million times before, but it came through my headphones then and something happened.

"Have you heard of synesthesia? Like when people have crossed wires or extra connections between their senses, hearing colors or tasting sounds or whatever? Well, it was kind of like that, but beyond that. Bigger.

"I was still sitting there, my ass firmly planted on the Volkswagen seat, but I was also outside. I was everywhere, everything. I was the mirrored glass in the skyscrapers, those red banners urging us to be patriotic, the traffic lights, girls' hair, bicycle wheels, the road, the other cars, everything. I should only have been able to feel air-conditioning and to smell the eau de toilette of the taxi, you know, tobacco and body odor and what have you. That's it. But I could feel, actually feel, the crush of traffic on my body, and I smelled broth boiling in distant restaurants, saw what was happening in each and every one of those buildings, tasted the meat of the pigeons that congregated on the sidewalk, heard strangers' whispers and thoughts and heartbeats...

"And that song. *Something in the way.*

"When it first happened, I guess I was frozen in shock. But I snapped out of it quickly. My entire body felt numb, misassembled.

I thought I must have died. I gnawed on my lip and pinched the skin on my hands. Pain receptors fired.

"I screamed. The driver glanced up at me in the rearview mirror, but didn't open his mouth. I ripped the headphones off, rolled down the window, and hurled my iPod out. Some guy at a bus stop scurried over to the road's shoulder, grabbed it, and ran off. Good fucking riddance.

"But now I want it back. Not the iPod, I mean... that feeling. I wasn't ready for it then—who literally throws a spiritual experience out the window?—and I'm probably still not ready now, but I'm—I'm obsessed.

"That feeling, I want it back for a second, a millisecond, I don't care. That's all I want. And it's connected to music somehow, I know it. The portal or whatever it was I slipped into. I tried listening to that song again, went back to the exact place in another taxi, tried everything, but nothing. Nothing." He clenched and unclenched his fists, wiped his palms on his pants, traced a character into his glass's condensation. "Mmm, I don't even know why I told you that. It makes me sound like a lunatic. Whatever. Anyway, I am going to go check out a band tomorrow after lunch. They live in an apartment not far from your monastery, in fact. Supposed to be pretty talented. We'd have them come over here, but the sound equipment won't be delivered and set up until Tuesday."

Drowsy from the alcohol and from the soothing rhythm of Little Cancer's snores, I found myself nodding.

"So, great, we'll check them out tomorrow then."

I nodded again, and then, flustered, I shook my head. "Actually, I can't."

I filled him in briefly about the details of my situation—my obligations at the monastery.

He listened, a twinkle in his eyes and a twitch in his lips, antsy to counter. As soon as I finished, he said, "I own the upstairs here too. That's where Little Cancer and I stay. There are extra beds. Forget that place. Stay here. Work here."

I instinctively opened my mouth to protest—but protest what?

*

"What I don't understand," Lulu said, "is why some Nirvana-listening rich boy from Beijing would go to Lhasa to fulfill a dream of operating a successful bar. Surely there are more happening places in the world with better scenes." She thought of the clubs around the city, around Beijing, where in her short-lived acting days she'd danced away many nights, leaving with a nauseated stomach and hair that reeked of smoke. She thought of all the clubs around the world that she'd seen in movies and on the Internet—in Tokyo, in New York City, in Los Angeles, in Seoul—clubs she would go see for herself if only she could work up the motivation, the drive, the desire to do so. "I mean, if he wanted to start a record label and become some big shot on the nightlife scene, why wouldn't he start somewhere a little more—"

"Yeah, I don't get it either," Zhang Li interrupted. Though she didn't have any experience in nightclubs, one of her classmates had traveled to Tibet on a tour, bringing back some yak snacks and tales of altitude headache halos. Based on her own limited knowledge, she told Lulu, Tibet was hardly synonymous with rock 'n' roll.

The turtle shut his eyes for a moment, considering, soaking in their doubts. "I didn't understand either at first. But here's what he told me..."

*

That afternoon, after a solid night of sleep above the bar and a dull morning headache, as Boss and I walked to find our band, he addressed these whys and hows...

"I grew up in Beijing, a typical urban son of the nineties, never wanting for anything. I was a below-average student, but my parents accrued enough wealth that it didn't matter. I scored poorly on my university entrance exams, but they paid my way into a private university.

"Most days I could barely drag myself to class. At eighteen, I was far more interested in girls and beer and partying than in listening to dull lectures in mildewy rooms. Go figure. And because my parents set me up with a generous monthly allowance, a sleek car, and an apartment, and maybe too because of my looks, I never had trouble making well-connected friends. Regular nights at the club found me falling into a group of wannabe models and other beautiful, bored entertainment types. Though I typically only heard from these friends after nightfall, one afternoon, a young woman from the film academy, the daughter of a very rich businessman, called up, asked if I'd be interested in playing a role in her thesis film. I'd never acted before, but I said sure, because who wouldn't say yes to that?

"Anyway, she sent me the script, and weeks later, we were shooting in a bar in Houhai. I played a lovable gangster with a gambling problem who had to ask his father, the big gangster, for a loan to pay for his girlfriend's abortion. The film was very arty, philosophical, false. Full of the kind of glamour that only the rich can find in grit. Utter crap if you ask me, but, regardless, it got noticed. Unfortunately for this friend, it wasn't her directing or writing that garnered the attention. It was—and I'm embarrassed to say this now, but it's the truth—it was me.

"So, to the feigned disappointment of my mother, my half-assed university career creaked to a halt. I landed a regular role in a soap opera, playing a ladies' man, a Don Juan. A couple of other small roles followed. The TV shows didn't pay much, but they led to commercial work, which did.

"And oh boy, I really thought I was hot shit. I bought ridiculous clothes, devoured filet mignon and sea cucumbers like they were going out of fashion, had a different girl on my arm and in my bed every weekend. And then there were the substances, oh, the sweet, sweet substances. I was almost always shit-faced. Drunk. High as hell. Snorting horse tranquilizers off nightclub tabletops and popping whatever pills anyone would place in my palm.

"So I was off my face as usual one morning, riding along in the passenger seat of my friend's Porsche. We dawdled in traffic, talking about nothing. We had nowhere to be and nothing to say. I glanced out the window at one point, an innocent enough glance, except that it wasn't. Staring back at me, bigger than the face I was looking from, was my face, all blown up on the side of a bus with a goose's face next to it. An ad for the Bashful Goose Snack Company.

"Panic. Pure panic. I couldn't remember even hearing about, much less participating in that photo shoot. My friend removed his foot from the brake, laughed dismissively, and assured me I'd agreed to it and done it.

"The light changed and we sailed onward. Traffic's tides eased up, and my friend gunned it, taking sharper and sharper turns. I buckled my seat belt and frantically dialed my accountant, who confirmed everything. Where were my memories going? Was someone stealing them? Who was I and who was that face on the side of a city bus?

"I spent the next three days at home, in and out of consciousness, swallowing pills and swigging whiskey and vomiting and doing it all over again. I'd been cut from sanity's anchor, set adrift, flying a flag that read, 'Who am I if I can't remember what I've done?'

"I was a terrible son, flippant and out of touch, so I didn't expect my parents to notice anything amiss, but you'd think that my disappearing off the face of the earth might spark some concern among those friends of mine. In moments of lucidity, I listened for a knock, checked for an imploring e-mail or text message, listened for my phone's once-familiar ring.

"But there were other handsome minor celebrities with drugs to snort and money to burn out there, not drowning in themselves. There were hundreds of more functional messes.

"Those awful days stretched on like years, but somehow, through no miracle or moment of clarity, I began to pull myself together. Slowed down. Stopped going out every single night. Started putting money into a savings account. Hell, I even attempted an actual relationship with an amiable, responsible girl—it only lasted a few months, sure, but it was progress.

"Above all else, in these slowed-down months, I focused on maintaining my memory. I practiced recalling events, sequences—going through everything I'd done that day step-by-step, retracing my thoughts back to their roots. I tried to remember how to say certain words in English, and I taught myself the French words for various actions and household objects—just to have something new to remember. Time passed and I was finally able to trust in my memory again, and life was looking up.

"Then one night after that girl and I had called it quits, I was at a dinner with my father, one of those business banquets. Here I was at five p.m., surrounded by middle-aged men downing shots of ridiculously expensive rice wine. By six, everyone was hammered, and my father stood up to make a toast. There had been a dozen or more toasts before this, but this time he toasted to me, to his son, following in his footsteps, becoming a rich, successful man in his own right. I cheered and guzzled my liquid fire alongside everyone else, but there was something about this statement that undid me on the inside, underscored all the progress I'd made. I looked around the table of red-faced men, overgrown lobsters, shrieking and pinching at all the things they could acquire in this world, and I felt gutted. You might just say, oh, it was the alcohol, but there was something so overwhelmingly depressing about this predictable future that was mine for the having.

"I really wish I could say that I stood up and made some profound speech at that dinner. That I walked out and emptied my wallet into some beggar's bowl. That I founded a charity, started eating organic food, whatever. But I was hardly that brave, and it was another year of bad acting and cheesy modeling and bouncing around thumping clubs, searching for something I couldn't identify and would therefore never find, before I truly found my way out.

"Some time after this dinner, I started reading up on spirituality and slowly began identifying as a Buddhist. Coincidentally, a friend of my mother's had recently gone on a photography expedition to Lhasa. She showed me beautiful pictures and told me a heartbreaking story she'd heard there, about an old Tibetan granny who had prostrated her way to a temple in Qinghai from a tiny village. Her bones were brittle and her knees ached, but this pilgrimage, this thank-you to the gods, was essential so that she could get to the temple and make a final wish.

"When after two weeks of hard travel she reached the temple, the Chinese guard barked, 'Granny, where is your registration permit?'

"The granny held up her shriveled hands. 'I've got no permit to travel. But I am an old woman and I want to make a wish.'

"No matter how hard she begged and cried, the guard wouldn't let her in.

"At the end of this story, my mom's friend shrugged and said, 'I don't know. I'm sure the guard just thought he was doing his job.'

"I was disturbed by this story, disgusted by this guard, disgraced by this friend's reaction. Aren't we all the same? Who gives any one person the right to stop another person from making a wish? What gives anyone else the right to comment upon these atrocities, to justify them, to normalize them? Tibet plagued my thoughts, my dreams. I knew I needed to go, that my life was pushing me in that direction, and as it so happened, this friend of my mother's knew a few Chinese businessmen in Tibet who were doing well for themselves and put me in touch. It was one of those guys who sold me this bar..."

✳

"Wow," said Zhang Li. "An actor. I wonder if we'd recognize him. Do you remember his real name?"

"No," the turtle said. "He was known to me only as Boss."

Lulu stared out the window. "But what about that band you went to see? Were they good?"

"Yes," said the turtle. "Boss was pretty happy with them. He hired them for the opening night and told them that if it went well they could come back and play regularly."

Zhang Li pantomimed playing guitar. She stuck out her tongue. "I wish I could take guitar lessons. Or drums. I'd love to be a rocker. But no, I must play piano." She spoke in a mock parent voice, straightened her spine, pantomimed playing piano, a dour expression on her face.

Lulu laughed. "Hey there," she said. "Cheer up, maybe you can take guitar lessons in America."

Zhang Li glared back at her. A spell had been broken. "I'm not going to America." She looked down at the turtle, who was looking up at her. Then, with tears welling up in her eyes, she too began to laugh, falling back into the absurdity of it all.

✻

That evening, after some hard work and shared drinks, I excused myself upstairs. I felt very tired from this, my first day of total freedom. I thought about how I needed to e-mail one of the twins to stop by, wondering if they were wondering about me. I wore street clothes now, clothes that Boss had given me. I'd caught sight of myself in a mirror earlier that day, in more than one mirror, and I felt simultaneously compelled each time to both gape at this strange, unremarkable man-child and to turn away. I sat on the bed now and picked up my folded robes, held them in my lap, and brushed them, dusting them, chanting the heart sutra. Old habits, you know. I didn't see Boss come in, but he sat beside me. The mattress sank under his weight. I fell silent, self-conscious. He said, "No, please continue." Shyly, I did. I watched him from the corner of my eye as I chanted. He shut his eyes and rocked ever so slightly along.

"That's beautiful," he said when I finally stopped. "What does it mean?"

"If I just translate it, it's something like 'Form doesn't differ from emptiness, and emptiness doesn't differ from form. They are both each other. And the same is true for feelings, perceptions, volition, and consciousness. They are all one.'"

He nodded, letting his eyelids fall. The way his brow furrowed with that deep crease in between told me that he really didn't understand—that he was turning it over in his head now—but was too proud to say anything. Let's just say it was a familiar experience for me, something to which I could relate.

"Let's put it this way," I said. I removed my hands from my robe, used them as tools. "Okay, so you said that in the past you really liked girls?"

Boss smiled, but he did not open his eyes.

"And girls are forms. They are beings. You can see them. But their forms exist in emptiness."

The corners of his lips rose into a sheepish grin. "Yeah, I've met a lot of girls who live there."

"Yes," I said, laughing. "Okay, so say you have a girlfriend. And the girlfriend occupies that empty space in your heart, fills it up. But then the girlfriend leaves you, and the emptiness returns. Before the girlfriend left, when you were together, was there still emptiness in your heart? Yes, of course, that empty space still existed, but she just filled it for a time. But how about that emptiness now? Now that she's gone, is there form there now? Yes, but not the form of a girl. The form of emptiness."

Boss nodded, considering. I noticed movement from the other side of the room. Little Cancer had come in too. I didn't know when, but there he was perched on the edge of an empty bed, listening intently. I gave him a grin, and then on and on I talked and talked, not recognizing these wise words that flowed from my stupid mouth.

The days and nights that followed passed in a blur of inventory and renovation and cleaning and booking and advertising, until at last, our big day was upon us. The workers had only just finished building the stage, and I frantically swept away the sawdust and other bits they'd left behind. Boss sprinted up and down the stairs, checking messages on his computer, making calls, testing the sound equipment. Little Cancer scurried about behind the bar. The sun dropped behind the mountains and the bar went from dim to dimmer. Boss flicked on the lights and loaded music on the speakers—Nirvana, of course. And we, the three of us, the core of us, waited silently to this sound track of mumbling, of heartache, of bliss.

It started with one lonesome patron, followed by another, and then a few others, and then: mayhem. Little Cancer and I stood sheltered behind the bar as the crowd swelled to enormity. Girls in false eyelashes and high heels; girls with shaggy haircuts and Converse sneakers; boys in dingy T-shirts; boys with perfectly coiffed pop-star hair. There were so many people, it was hard to remember the details of any of them, to remember which parts went to which. So that's how I saw them: in pieces.

Boss cranked the music up. The band puttered on the stage, making final adjustments and tweaks. Little Cancer and I filled order after order, accepting cash, making change.

And in this chaos of limbs and flesh and smoke, there was only one person I saw in entirety, one person who was not just pieces: a girl with honey-brown eyes and dyed red hair.

"Gin and tonic!" she shouted, pushing her way through the hordes swarming the bar. She waved the twenty-kuai note she held in her hand. I snatched it and prepared her drink, an easy one, handing it to her only seconds later.

She took a sip of the clear liquid and made eye contact with me. The scene froze as I stared back at her. I don't know how long this silent, motionless moment lasted, but I was jostled back when Little Cancer bumped into me while reaching for a box of orange juice.

The girl continued to stand firm, not backing away despite the many forceful bodies, the groping and grabbing hands. She performed an odd motion, a flick of the wrist. I looked to Little Cancer for help interpreting. He scowled in concentration, busy pouring drinks. The girl dug something out of her pocket—a cell phone. She waved it in the air. I could only barely make out her words. "I want to give you my phone number!"

My heart fluttered.

But I didn't have a phone. I nudged Little Cancer. "Let me borrow your phone," I whisper-shouted to him. He reached in his pocket and handed it over, his eyes still fixed on his work. I beckoned for the girl to slip under the bar to safety. She did and she programmed her number in, along with the name "Red Hair."

Silently, she slid back under the bar and rejoined the crowd. I went to give the phone back to Little Cancer, but he was at the other end of the bar, busy with his mad science. I slipped his phone into my pocket for safekeeping and returned to serving the masses.

I poured and I mixed and I made change, and I thought the crowd would never relent, but when the band began to play, the human sea receded from the bar and swelled in front of the stage. Jumping, screaming, dancing, the room was in action, and the band played this song that went, *Do you believe that the world lasts forever / or do you believe that the world will soon end?*

It was loud, the loudest music I'd ever heard, chords and words blasting from the speakers, drums pounding, bass pulsing, and then, right in the middle of the song, everything went silent. Everything froze.

I located Boss's face in the crowd. His smile had fallen, his mouth a dash. And he was taller. I scanned the room. Everyone was. I turned to Little Cancer, who for the first time all night looked directly back at me. He was taller! I cast my gaze downward. His shoes weren't touching the ground—they were floating. I looked out again at the crowd. Not a single foot on the floor.

I blinked, thinking surely this must be a hallucination, surely this can't be real. I looked down at my own shoes, both firmly planted, grounded. I looked out again—everyone else, their feet, their shoes, their bodies, were not.

There was a squeaking noise, high-pitched, the sound system squealing. I winced, my face screwing up, my eardrums on the verge of explosion, but everyone else maintained peaceful, empty expressions.

And then they all disappeared.

✻

Lulu's eyes widened. "What do you mean they disappeared?"

"Exactly that. One moment they were there, the next, poof, gone."

✻

I ducked under the counter and sprinted across the empty bar to the stage. I couldn't wrap my mind around what had just happened. Shock. Pure shock. There was this whole world, all of these people in it, and suddenly all of it was gone.

I darted up the stairs, three at a time, to where we'd slept. No one. I ran back downstairs and outside.

A vibration in my pocket. I slipped out Little Cancer's phone. The name "Mama Cancer" flashed up on the screen. I didn't answer. What would I have said? Sorry about your tumor and everyone you ever knew leaving you, and, oh, hey, by the way, your son just disappeared before my eyes? I rejected the call and scrolled through the directory until I found Boss's number.

A robotic female voice repeating over and over, "I'm sorry, but the number you've dialed is no longer in service."

I tried again and again only to get the same automated response.

Red Hair. Red Hair. Red Hair. I scrolled and found her number too. But there was no answer. Her phone, it just rang and rang.

These familiar streets were dark. There were passersby, but no one I recognized. Strangers stared back at me with peculiar expressions, and it occurred to me then how pale and clammy I must have looked, how mystified, how insane. I trudged on, searching in vain for a familiar face. When I realized the pointlessness of my search and returned to the bar front a few short minutes later, would you believe that now the sign was gone too?

I stepped inside. The sound system was gone. The lights were gone. The bottles of alcohol were gone. Looters? I wondered. But how had they come and gone so quickly, and how had they done such a neat job of it? I reached into my pocket and clutched Little Cancer's cell phone. It was real, what had happened. I knew it was real, had been, and I had these pieces of evidence to prove it.

I lumbered up the stairs and lay down on the bed, but I couldn't sleep. I chanted the heart sutra, lost in its form, in its emptiness, until the sun came up, and then I noticed that all the beds save for the one I lay in were gone. At a loss for what to do next and not wanting to disappear too, I shot off in a sprint toward the monastery.

As I raced through those familiar streets housing all these unfamiliar faces, a great shift took place within me and I knew I desperately needed something to anchor me to my past. Remember Dorjee? Dorjee, my childhood friend, my brother. Through the gates I ran and I found him in the courtyard, sitting there, doing nothing, looking at nothing, same as always, as though nothing had changed.

"Dorjee," I panted, my hands on my knees, sweat dripping down my forehead and neck. "I need to talk to you for a second."

He didn't look away from the ghost or whatever it was he was staring at, but I started in anyway, rehashing the whole story: the wandering, the bar, the dullness inside of me, the rock band, the cell phone, the people levitating and disappearing.

Dorjee, my big brother, my trusted childhood companion, didn't scoff or laugh or even stoop to join me in my panicked state. He looked up at me with those piercing eyes, sunken deep within his head, and he told me, as matter-of-fact as discussing the weather, about what had happened to our city in the time I was away from the monastery.

There had been an incident, a drunken incident outside of a bar. Just some alcohol-fueled fight between two groups of men—one group Han, one group Tibetan. Rumor had it one of the Tibetans had said something blasphemous about Papa Hui's ghost. Others said it wasn't about Papa Hui at all, something about someone's mother or girlfriend or the size of someone's penis. It was hard to say what had truly happened and who was to blame, but when a Chinese police officer got involved, things careened in an ugly direction. Three young Tibetans were beaten to death and the others arrested. Tibetans young and old, but mostly young, awoke the next morning to this news with hangovers and hate-filled hearts. They took to the streets in protest. They burned down Chinese businesses, smashed car windows, used knives and fists. There had been riots, Dorjee said, an eerie waver to his voice. Hundreds, both Chinese and Tibetans, had been killed.

He went on and on, and I thought he must have been haunted by what he'd seen, by the senseless violence, and I thought, Dorjee, my reasonable friend, he is one who has suffered and one who has survived... and then I realized this wasn't something he was talking about as a spectator, that this wasn't something he was going to let go.

In case you're wondering, yes, I tried to talk Dorjee out of it. I understood that his worldview was tainted by his own demons, by his own circumstance, by his own weakness. However, I knew too that I hadn't suffered the same terrible fate that he had. That I had sought out my own causes of suffering and therefore had control over the consequences. That by contrast, suffering came to him uninvited, came in the form of blood and carnage and violation.

Where had I been in the days of those riots? I had been in that bar, but there wasn't really a bar, was there? Why, I wondered, had the world spared me yet again?

He was going to self-immolate. He told me all the details in a whisper. He spoke with pride. I'd never heard him sound proud before.

I sank to sit beside him. I said, "No, no, don't do it," but my words of protest were weakened by the strong connection I felt to him. By my guilt. By the times I'd failed to intervene. I couldn't help but think again about how I should have known there was something seriously wrong when he kept disappearing at night. That I should have known. That I should have opened that storage room door. That I should have said something. That I should have been a better friend to him after. That I shouldn't have left the monastery. That I should have at least taken him with me. That I should have done my part to ease his suffering. My brother.

He smiled. "It is my fate," he said. And as those words settled into my soul, he told me about something he'd seen on the street during those riots, about a Tibetan girl with dyed red hair who bravely dragged the bloodied body of a young Chinese man out of the sight of a mob that had momentarily lost interest in torturing him. The mob, he said, regained its interest quickly and soon began beating the both of them. He spoke of another incident of that same day: of a small body that reminded him of his own, lying on a car, bleeding out, repeatedly whispering the word "Mama." He spoke of Converse shoes red with blood, of dingy T-shirts, of shaggy haircuts, of exposed muscle, of protruding bones, of bruised and broken skin.

A tear in his eye, and many more in mine.

"Don't worry," he said, patting my arm, making physical contact with me for the first time since our childhood. "We will return someday as brothers." And I knew all was forgiven and, too, that there was no turning back.

There are these moments that pluck us from our lives, remove us from everything, set us back down in a different way. Revelations. Seismic shifts that change our way of thinking, that connect us simultaneously to the emptiness and to the form.

Sometimes these events appear magical; sometimes they're perfectly mundane. But they never just happen; they never just come uninvited to us. We must take baby steps in their direction—we must find and walk their twisting paths. Eventually, sensing our effort, revelation, like a good and patient mother, will scoop us up. In her arms, we are warm, we are important, we are loved, we are everything and we are nothing too.

But we cannot live forever in the safety of these arms.

Revelation, that wise mother, sets us down, blows a kiss, send us on our way to once again wander those twisted trails. It costs us time and pain to sort out the details, the practicalities, that will help us make our way back into those arms. But this vigorous journey will someday be forgotten. We will remember only the light, the love. If nothing else, I can assure you of this.

I've recounted to you what I remember in my head, but stamped in my soul is the memory of that moment, that serene moment, in which I was held tightly; that moment in which everything floated, in which everything burned, in which everything but myself, my true and connected self, disappeared.

Into the emptiness, into the form, into the everything...

✳

The turtle opened his mouth, but this time there was no voice.

"Hello?" Lulu's voice trembled with desperation. "Hello?"

The turtle didn't answer. It retracted back into its shell.

Zhang Li shot up to a stand, speaking in a shaky voice. "He needs us to find that phone. He left it at the monastery. He must have. We have to call that Red Hair girl, figure out where she went."

"He already tried calling her, and she didn't answer, so what's the point?"

"No, it rang. Her phone actually rang, remember? If the phone was ringing, that means it wasn't shut off or anything. It's still on. She has it. It means that there's still a chance she might pick up."

"What if the people who beat her stole it? That seems pretty likely."

Zhang Li shook her head. Her voice was higher, lilting. "Thieves don't leave phones turned on. They turn them off immediately and then change the SIM card. Trust me, I've had two phones stolen before. And besides, in the turtle's version of events, she wasn't beaten. She just disappeared. That means she has to be somewhere then, doesn't she? They all have to be."

Lulu narrowed her eyes. She smoothed back her hair. She glanced at her car keys, dangling from the entryway hook. "What are you suggesting we do?" she asked, but she already knew the answer. She stood up, and the two girls, entering the warm embrace of some invisible arms, looked at each other for a very long time.

While Zhang Li was on the phone to her father, convincing him of the trip's educational merits, Lulu pulled up to the intersection that started it all. The old woman hadn't gone anywhere, was tapping on windows like it was her life's calling with a new turtle in hand. Lulu rolled down the window, shouted, "Ay, Aunty!"

The woman's head whipped around. Lulu gave her a nod, and the woman hobbled over. Lulu slipped the turtle through.

"Thank you, Aunty," she said. "But I don't need him anymore."

The light turned green. Lulu rolled the window up and accelerated. In the rearview mirror, she saw first her own face, her lips curled ever so slightly upward, and, beyond her reflection, the old woman, grinning, holding a turtle in each hand, her fortune doubled.

Zhang Li hung up the phone. She bit her lip. She spoke to the windshield. "I told him if he let me do this, I'd go to America." She drew her hand to her face and bit at a hangnail. "We're good to go."

And they were off.

They drove for a week, through Inner Mongolia and Ningxia and Gansu and Qinghai, alongside freight trucks and bread-loaf vans and luxury cars.

And at last. The city was as the turtle had described, and they prayed and kowtowed in front of many shrines, ate in many restaurants, marveled at many sights. They slept night after night in a Chinese-owned hotel with scratchy sheets. They struggled, at times, to catch their breath.

They looked but didn't see. They searched and found nothing.

Zhang Li's father rang once, and then rang more and more, speaking of limited time—he'd booked her ticket. She had two weeks.

More days passed and still, they found no magical bar, no monks who claimed to know Dorjee or Kunchok, no sign of Boss or Little Cancer.

They grew tired. They grew weary. They grew bored.

"We failed," Zhang Li said, as they tucked themselves into side-by-side Lhasa twin beds for the last time.

Lulu, eyelids heavy, reached out for the bedside lamp. "Yes, but we had a good time."

After breakfast, after one last cup of yak butter tea, they checked out of the hotel, settled into the Land Rover, cruised through the city one last time. On a narrow street, out the windshield, a flash. Lulu slammed on the brakes. A girl, her gaze cast downward, had walked out in front of them. Tires squealing. Red hair. Slow motion. Jerking to a stop. Just in time. Red hair, red hair, red hair. The girl looked up, startled. She smiled. She waved. She held up a phone. She turned around in the street, shouted something indiscernible to someone behind her.

Zhang Li reached for Lulu's hand.

A parade of people emerged from a narrow alleyway between two blocky buildings, following the red-haired girl. Girls in false eyelashes and high heels; girls with shaggy haircuts and Converse sneakers; boys in dingy T-shirts; boys with perfectly coiffed pop-star hair. A broad-shouldered, handsome man with long hair. A smaller, younger, serious-faced man. Horns blaring. A line of cars behind Lulu's Land Rover. Someone attempting to maneuver around her. Someone rolling down a window and crying a curse: "Stupid bitch! Your husband put you in that tank because he knows you can't drive?! Go already!" A curse directed at her. But she wasn't the one causing this delay; couldn't the drivers behind her see these people pouring into the street? Honking. Lulu glanced into the rearview mirror, frowned. Only a second had passed, but when she looked out the windshield again, the partygoers were gone, the street before her empty.

Lulu blinked. "Wait, did I... just... ? Did you... see... ?"

Zhang Li, wide-eyed, only nodded. They'd been set free.

And for seven days, they drove in silence, driving the very same road they'd driven before, just in a different direction. In her head, in that silence, in reverie, Lulu repeated, *Sometimes it's as easy as believing; sometimes it's as easy as going where you're called, into the emptiness, into the form, into the everything; sometimes it's as easy as...*

iN THE NEWS

RIOTS ROCK TIBET

LHASA, CHINA —...The Party urges both Han and Tibetan citizens, who are all citizens of the People's Republic, to end this senseless violence. The Party also wishes to remind citizens of the evilness of the Dalai Lama, a Satan on this earth, and to speak his name as one might speak Lord Voldemort's name, which is to say never...

KELLY HUI: HAVANA'S NEWEST SOCIALITE?

NANJING, CHINA — On Saturday, renowned gossip columnist Ma Guowei reported on his microblog that Ms. Hui may have been sighted at a nightclub in Havana, Cuba. Although this sighting remains unconfirmed, Mr. Ma notes that Ms. Hui's late father was indeed a frequent visitor to the island nation...

YUAN STEPS DOWN AS BASHFUL GOOSE CEO

BEIJING, CHINA — Yuan Wang Ping, CEO of Bashful Goose Snack Company, announced today his resignation. He steps down following controversy over tainted products and alleged food safety cover-ups. Activists purport that Mr. Yuan paid off regulatory and media entities to "make this damn mess go away..."

Mr. Yuan, who came into power after Mr. Yang's resignation earlier this year, is rumored to be succeeded by a Mr. Jiang.

"Jiang has a tough road ahead of him," said a middle-aged, balding professor of finance at Qinghua University who hails from Papa Hui's Wuxi and who spoke to us on the condition of anonymity. "Bashful Goose sales figures have plummeted. Consumer confidence is at an all-time low. Frankly, people are terrified to eat the snacks they once held dear..."

MILLIONAIRES ACADEMY GROOMS
NATION'S FUTURE TYCOONS

SHENZHEN, CHINA —...Gone are the days of Papa Hui's awe-inspiring leadership, and with the city's millionaires disappearing at alarming rates, our tycoons-to-be lack strong, wealthy role models. Spotting this gaping hole in the marketplace, Ms. Huang founded the Future Millionaires Academy. The academy, located on Dongmen Street, caters to students ages 6 to 16 and offers intensive courses such as Mind Your Manners, To Bribe or Not to Bribe?, Business English, Navigating the Foreign Corrupt Practices Act, and French Wines for Beginners...

While none of the all-star faculty members is currently a millionaire, most hope soon to be. Classes are filling up quickly, Ms. Huang tells us, and space is limited...

NATIONAL SPIRIT STAGNANT, REPORTS INDICATE

BEIJING, CHINA —...Mr. Deng, our nation's leading happiness expert, declined to comment, as he couldn't be bothered to get out of bed and answer his phone...

THE EX-MiLLiONAiRES' CLUB

In the unlikely event of my death,
the goose shall inherit the throne.
In the even more unlikely event of the
goose's death chaos shall reign!

—THE RISE AND FALL OF THE TIMID DUCK
(A MAINLAND-BANNED FEATURE FILM
DRAMATIZATION)

THE WOODS, THE SETTLEMENT, THE COMMITTEE

Let us form a committee, a committee to solve this mystery.
An elusive city.
But it's not really a city, is it?
Whatever it is, it is here before us. We can see its buildings,
  we can see its streets, and yet...
We are the finest minds in this country.
Are we?
But the city is here, here it is, what is so elusive about
  something that can so clearly be seen?
Well, where shall we begin?

LULU GAVE UP HER MONEY, HER LAND ROVER, HER APARTMENT, HER unreachable dreams, her vanity, her shopping sprees, her Coke Zero. She gave it all up until there was nothing left to hide behind, nothing left from which to run.

And now she was here, at night, in a forest thick with trees, in this overgrown forest, still running, running away from that nothing.

She sucked in her stomach and squeezed herself between two trunks, stepped over their gnarled roots, squinted to make out the path ahead. She pictured herself clambering all the way up this mountain, through its ecological labyrinth, and down its other side, dashing through orchards and fields and back, eventually, to civilization.

That would be one way to do it. But then what?

The quarter moon hung low in the sky, tilted ever so slightly—a crooked smile, offering its blessing. She peered up at it through the skeletal branches.

Snapping. Crunching. Footsteps. She gasped, pressed her back against the trunk, camouflage. Her heart pounded.

These woods were safe. These woods were hers.

Another broken branch, another step, another skipped heartbeat. She stifled a scream, her tongue bloated in her mouth.

Two red eyes floated in the near distance, staring right through her. They glowed in the dark: sharp crimson light, two evenly spaced laser pointers. No form, no else; just eyes.

Don't scream, she willed herself, don't.

But the eyes had a voice. The voice spoke her name. *Lulu.*

Set to sound, a whiteness emanated from them, cloaked her rag-dressed body with warmth. All at once, she knew, sensed deep down to her core, that this being wasn't here to hurt her, it was here to help.

She peeled her back from the tree trunk and leaned forward. She stared back into those eyes. Her limbs tingled, pins and needles. She yearned to speak, to shout, "Please tell me what to do." Her tongue wiggled, a serpent seeking escape. She clamped her mouth shut. She breathed. She listened.

What do you want? the voice asked her.

She did not allow her teeth, her lips to part. She needn't speak her reply aloud. The eye-being knew her soul. The eye-being reached inside her and pulled its answer out.

Dear Officials,

We thank you for your patronage of the social sciences and for your generous financial donations to support the continuation of such pursuits. Thank you also to Happy Mart Inc., whose own tax-exempt contribution served to make this study ever the more possible. We are pleased then to offer you the findings of our research regarding [This Settlement]:

History books tell us that [This Settlement] was once, for three weeks, the home of Confucius, who had fallen ill from food poisoning and who declared the area's tranquil mountains and streams "ideal spots for secret relief." *Lao-tzu, who also passed through, declared the famous local delicacy, fish-head soup, "damn delicious."*

Until recent years, however, [This Settlement] enjoyed no further fame, no nods from heads of greatness. In fact, when Wang Xilai and Stefan Ping arrived, it must have stood all but abandoned, a few country houses in an empty valley, its native inhabitants long gone off to cities to seek their fortunes.

Our research confirms that, earlier this year, inspired by Mr. Wang's and Mr. Ping's renunciation of wealth and embrace of simplicity, millionaires across the nation abandoned their homes, dispersed and dissolved their assets, and uprooted their lives to [This Settlement]. A number of notable CEOs, businessmen, film directors, actors, singers, and other public figures...

Months before that encounter in the forest, Lulu—weary from hazy days of trains, minibuses, cars, and hiking—had arrived at the Settlement. She stood at the base of a mountain looking out across the valley, at the village nestled within: clusters of buildings, a grid of dirt roads, plots of farmland. This, this was it. A meaty lump lodged in her throat. She was torn between laughing and crying.

She did neither. She took a deep breath.

She situated herself on the earth, dropped her bag beside her, planted her palms on her hip bones. This was the place, the place she'd overheard a woman in an overpriced coffee shop extolling, the place an oil industry acquaintance fell into drunken raptures over at a wedding reception, the place founded by her old friends Stefan and Hair Inc. CEO Wang, the place that everyone who was anyone was elevating to myth. This was Mecca, Bodh Gaya, Paradise. This was home.

Energy, electric, coursed through her veins, and she swore she heard the wind whistle welcome.

Or maybe it wasn't the wind.

"Ay!" a voice called. "Hey, over here!"

Lulu spun on her heel. Two ball-like blurs. Then clarity: two old ladies, raggedy clothes flapping on them like flags in the wind, each clutching a bag to her abdomen, tumbled down the mountain like roly-polies.

That lump in her throat dissolved. A smile crept across her face. Judging by their somersaults, these ladies must've been retired acrobats, ready to move out from the spotlight completely. What stories must be housed in each muscle, each ligament, each joint.

The lady-balls slowed to a stop, uncurled, reassumed biped status, dusted off, and limped toward Lulu.

One of the women extended her hand and sunk into a curtsy. "Hello, my name is Witch One, and this is my sister, Witch Two."

"Oh," said Lulu, taking the woman's hand. Odd names. Stage names, perhaps. "I'm Lulu."

"Well," Witch Two said, "shall we then?"

Lulu nodded, her head on an independent streak—she wasn't sure, with that nod, to what exactly she was agreeing. But this was a new life, a new start. She didn't need to know everything. She needed to trust.

She grabbed her bag by its handles. The women linked on to either of her arms. The three of them tromped toward a structure on the western edge of the mountain's base.

"We knew," Witch One said. She tsked. Her eyelids drooped to half-mast. "Oh, yes, we knew."

"Indeed," Witch Two took over, "we knew that when we arrived here, our new sister would reveal herself."

Lulu fixed her eyes on the mystery structure, the goal without purpose, or at least a purpose made clear to her, and on the vast golden sky behind and above and all around it. Her brain produced thoughts in slow motion. They're not acrobats. They're witches. They rolled down the hill not for the sake of athletics or aesthetics, but because it's easier to roll down a hill than to walk. And because they could. Because they're witches. And they seemed to think she was a witch too.

Witch Two continued: "Our sisterhood is once again complete. Funny, our last sister died only a few months ago, but you must already know that—"

Witch One interrupted. "Ay, she was just minding her own business when she was bitten by a wolf."

Lulu's eyes, still moored to the horizon, widened.

Witch Two cleared her phlegmy throat. "Yes, that's right. A wolf. She'd traveled to Inner Mongolia to collect a very special kind of herb that we needed for a potion—"

"And she made it almost all the way, but then a wolf grabbed hold of her leg. She managed to fight him off and escape before he gobbled her up completely, and she staggered into a nearby village, if you could even call it that—"

"They live in tents there, you know."

"Of course she knows. Everyone knows that."

"Yes, those horsemen. Nomads. They pack up their tents and move on and—"

"So anyway, when she staggered in, her mouth looked like a bubble bath in one of those French films."

"Foaming at the mouth! Rabies! Ah, cruel fate!"

"Ay, yes! Who knows how long it'd been since that wolf had sunk its teeth into her tender leg meat. Days, maybe. Staggering around like a right lunatic—"

"People meat is a delicacy for wolves, you know. It's like puffer fish is for the Japanese or—"

"But anyhow, how impressive that she hadn't just given up."

"She spent heaven knows how long dragging her ailing, poisoned body to civilization—"

"When she could've just given up the struggle altogether, laid down and died—"

"Ay, yes, it'd have been much easier. But she didn't. She continued on for us. She gave the nomads our information. She wanted us to know what had happened to her. To not waste time wondering, searching—"

"So the nomads sent us news that she'd fallen ill and died—"

"And we sent a *ganshiren*, a corpse walker, to bring her body back to us—"

"Most people would be afraid to keep a rabid body around, but—"

"The nomads whose tent she crashed put her outside, away from anything that could be infected, kept a distant guard on her body day and night until the *ganshiren* arrived."

"But those *ganshiren*, they're trained for that kind of thing. They sleep with dead bodies in their rooms. They aren't afraid of rabies! So he lifted her body under the armpits and then he did his rhythmic call—*ho, ho, ho, ho!* And he took away his arms and she stayed upright on her own and her dead feet began to move to the beat. *Step, step, step, step.*"

"Suddenly, Ms. Two Left Feet can dance, imagine that! And like that, she followed him across the plains of Inner Mongolia and back down to where we were living in Shaanxi, and we gave her a proper burial."

"We thought we'd done everything right, but—"

"But then her ghost turned up."

"In broad daylight."

"We were cooking porridge in the morning and there she was, clear as bone broth, and she spoke in her living voice, a terribly shrill voice she always had, mind you, and told us—"

"Told us to head south, to Yunnan."

"And she said once we arrived in Yunnan, everything would become clear."

"Then she just disappeared! How were we supposed to enjoy our breakfast after that?"

"So we packed everything up and took a train to Kunming, and outside the station, we camped out, waiting for her ghost to send us a sign. We sat there, nothing to do, for days. *Bor-ing.*"

"Embarrassing is more like it. Some passersby mistook us for bums and left coins in our teacups!"

"Ay, hardly embarrassing. I told you, it was a compliment. It speaks to our fashion sense. I've seen magazines. Nowadays it's hard to tell who's homeless and who's filthy rich."

They both cackled.

Witch Two waved her hand, continued. "But we're just joking. We know we're not fashionable. And anyway, sitting outside that train station like common vagabonds, we began to worry that maybe we'd made a mistake."

"Or that Witch Three was just playing a trick on us."

"Ay, she always was a trickster. Maybe she'd sent us to Yunnan for no good reason, just for laughs."

"That was the kind of thing she would do. Once, at a wedding, she slipped an herbal oil into the philandering groom's wine so he wouldn't be able to perform in the bridal chamber. Flaccid as an earthworm. His bride divorced him within the year, and his mistress left him too!"

"Actually, when we first caught wind of her death, we thought it was a joke—talk about the witch who cried wolf!"

They cackled again.

"And she was always slipping dead mice into our shoes and—"

"Don't give this new one any ideas."

"Ay, right. So, surrendering to a joke well played, we tossed back our heads and laughed and laughed outside the train station, and we shouted to the heavens, 'Good one, Witch Three!' and we gathered our things and decided to head out, to find some sort of a tour group to join, figuring we may as well enjoy the sights—we're not getting any younger—when a young man talking on his cell phone stopped directly in front of us, paced the same couple of steps, back and forth, back and forth, rattling on."

"At first we were annoyed. Young people on those damn contraptions, shouting, not paying any mind to their surroundings or to the affairs of others. But when the words of his conversation began to take form—"

"He was talking about a village he'd heard of, some new sort of commune where its citizens rejected modern ways."

"Imagine that, a young man in a business suit, a very fancy-looking man, mind you, speaking and philosophizing in awe about a place where people rejected everything he was, everything he stood for!"

"And crazier yet, he was saying he was thinking about going, about joining them!"

"He ended his conversation abruptly—the person on the other end of the line must've had something to do—and then he faded into the throngs. My sister and I just looked at each other—"

"And we allowed Witch Three's ghost to guide our feet. Now she was the *ganshiren* and we were the corpses. *Ho, ho, ho, ho.* We stepped in sync, not knowing where we were going and—"

"Not needing to know. We walked and walked until at last we reached this mountain. Insurmountable, it seemed, but we had a feeling in our bones, in our guts, that told us that the village commune lay just on the other side, that this climb would be well worth it."

"And when we finally reached the top, when we saw that we were correct, we were so excited, and exhausted, that we decided to just curl up in balls and roll down!"

"Wheeee boy, that was fun!"

"And, I swear, I heard Witch Three's voice again as we rolled down. She shrieked, 'Farewell, my loves! Your new sister awaits you on the other side!'"

"I heard it too!"

"We both heard it, and then we began to slow down, and that's when I saw you and—"

Just when Lulu had finally mustered the courage to open her mouth and object, to tell these witches that they had this all wrong, that she didn't come here to join a coven, she came here to make soap and grow vegetables and inhabit happiness, or whatever it was these ex-millionaires did, Witch Two said, "Oh, don't worry. We'll teach you everything we know. When we're done with you, your spirit won't long for anything your mind can't provide."

At last they reached the structure: a quaint cottage surrounded by a low stone wall.

"Hey!" Witch One cried, releasing Lulu's arm and hurdling over that wall. "Anyone home?"

No answer.

Witch Two released Lulu's other arm and pushed the gate. It creaked open. She nodded, and Lulu followed her through. Lulu's shoes sunk into the plush black dirt—the ground inside the wall was markedly different from that outside.

Witch Two crouched down and scooped up a handful of soil. She spread her fingers, watched the clumps fall through.

"Ah, perfect for growing flowers!"

"Oh, for, uh, potions or medicines?" Lulu asked, half interested. She was more concerned with Witch One, who first pounded on the house's front door and then, receiving no answer, threw her shoulder into it, forcing it open and making her way inside. "Should she be—"

"Some of them we use for potions. But mostly they're just pretty."

Witch One wedged the window open, poked her head out, and cried, "And they smell good!"

Witch Two plucked a beetle from the dirt, held it in her cupped palm. It stopped moving and stood on its back legs, staring up at her and making a hissing sound. "We like flowers," she said.

"Lesson number one," cried Witch One, her head now sticking out a different window. "Purpose is objective! It's something we give, not something we get!"

Witch Two set the beetle down. It scurried off, six legs in sync. She teetered to a stand and wiped her dirty hand on her tunic. "Ay, but she already knows that!"

We of the Committee adopted an etic approach in our field research, observing the culture of [This Settlement] from afar over a two-week period. Although it would have been ideal, both anthropologically and socially speaking, to live among the ex-millionaires, we, as career academics, clearly lack the social graces, flawless skin, and cocky swagger necessary to have gone unnoticed among [This Settlement's] elite population. Furthermore, we of the Committee would like to note that although our dear government leaders may have deluded themselves otherwise, we are ill equipped, as well as inadequately compensated, to partake in dangerous covert operations. Moreover, we must point out that nine-tenths of the Committee expressed their heartfelt discomfort at participating in group sing-alongs, of which in [This Settlement] there are many.

In any case, from the safe distance of the small foothills on the outer edge of [This Settlement], we observed and noted patterns, anomalies, and other occurrences with the aid of binoculars and night-vision goggles and the sporadic use of a drone camera generously donated by Happy Mart Inc., where low prices are an everyday phenomenon...

The cottage, empty save for a few sturdy pieces of furniture, felt as though it'd been custom designed for them: its fertile yard, its strategic location near the wooded mountain where medicinal herbs and roots grew in abundance, its three identical cots in the bedroom, its cozy brick fireplace, its long dining table ideal for spreading out and sorting through forest findings, and its bookshelves aching to be filled with tomes on divination and herbalism and fortune-telling and the I Ching.

Despite their initial explorers' enthusiasm, the witches insisted, for decency's sake, on spending the first week camping outside the walls. Lulu hovered on the scene's periphery, an observer to their small twig-fueled fire and message scrawled to the universe on a scrap of paper: *If within one week this house's owner doesn't appear to claim it, we shall become its rightful tenants.*

Witch One fed the paper to the flames. The hungry blaze devoured their words; the edges curled in, the fire crackled, the wish turned to ash. The witches laughed. Lulu smiled. They danced. Lulu swayed. They blew kisses to the moon. Lulu hesitated—this wasn't why she'd come here, was it? but, then, why had she come?—before muttering her resignation, diving in, puckering up.

Their legs pudding, they collapsed to sleep on the firm ground, stars shining down upon them like night-lights in a child's bedroom, comforting in theory but in actuality only illuminating danger's lurking possibilities: monsters and bandits and wolves and worse.

Still, they slept untouched, night after night.

Twigs and leaves and even a few bugs made makeshift homes in Lulu's tangled hair. She plucked out the intruders, placed them on the ground, wished them well. Once, she swore a caterpillar gave her an appreciative nod, but this might've been a product of her wild imagination, a delusion born of peculiar circumstance.

She followed after the witches as they gave themselves daily to the mountain's woods. They were enthusiastic teachers, filling Lulu's head and heart with innumerable new nuggets. What relief not to retire from the day neurotic and insomniac, tossing and turning on some overly soft bed, legs twisted up in high-thread-count sheets. What relief it was to rest her head, heavy with information and ideas, on that terra firma, to drift contentedly into well-earned dreams.

That week passed in a flash. No time to think; only to learn.

On the seventh day, Lulu politely opted out of her lessons and ventured down to the valley, to the commune village, for the very first time. She met all these people she'd once read about in magazines and watched on TV, and she reconnected with a few she'd known in lives past. She dropped in on Stefan, so delighted to see her that he wept, squeezing her tightly. Friends new and old fed her homemade stews, shoved cups of mint tea into her dirt-caked hands, greeted and gossiped and sang.

She asked everyone, but no one knew anything about the former occupant of the cottage on the mountainside.

She returned. She ceded. She accepted.

And on that seventh night, the witches and Lulu, repacked bags in tow, burst through the gate, glided across the garden, threw open the doors. They lined their shoes in the entry, hung their clothes in the wardrobe, beat the dust from the wafer-thin mattresses, wiped down the table's unfinished top, unloaded their books onto the shelves, and burned sage, tearing through the house like banshees, crooning and shouting, hooting and hollering, clearing out any lingering spirits, making this house theirs, all theirs, making this house their home.

Although its population has swelled in recent months, [This Settlement] does not suffer from the usual negative consequences linked to rapid urban development. Here, there are no cranes, no noisy building sites, no iron bars clanging against the ground, no jackhammers humming into the night. There are indeed new buildings, new structures, but they are constructed slowly, steadily, almost stealthily, all by hand.

In [This Settlement], there are no legless beggars on the corners, no men squatting on the pavement praying for work, no tenements where old Tibetan women stir simmering gruel atop hot plates. There are no banks, no monetary transactions, no indications of poverty or of wealth. Citizens farm their own food, make products by hand, and engage in occasional trade and barter.

[This Settlement's] streets play host to not one half-smoked Zhongnanhai cigarette, not one steaming pile of dog shit, not one discarded Bashful Goose Watermelon Wiggler cellophane wrapper, not a single hacked-out phlegm oyster. Each morning and evening, a brigade of citizen volunteers take to the streets to sweep and tidy what little mess there might be—a leaf here, a wind-surfing wadded-up tissue there.

In our observations, we of the Committee noted not a single instance of shoving, belligerence, line cutting, or the similarly stress-induced behaviors so often exhibited in our great nation's populous centers. During daytime hours, [This Settlement] remains peaceful, near silent. Citizens write, paint, craft, garden, and exercise, among many other leisurely pursuits. When they sleep, they leave doors unlocked, in case anyone need come or go, and they leave windows open, inviting the cool breeze and the fragrance of cherry blossoms to waft into their dreams, completely unmoved by the prospect of burglars, rapists, or machete-wielding murderers...

And now, in the present, in the after *after* the after, Lulu dusted her hands on her tunic and set to work clipping the pile of laundry she'd just washed in the stream to a clothesline. She performed the movements with a precise, practiced rhythm—bend, lift, shake out, hold up, pin, repeat—and in this cadence, she found comfort.

This was life now, this was life eternally: sun-bleached moments, serenity.

She clipped the final sheet to the line, sat on a stone to rest her sore back, and gazed at the country cottage, her home. Framed within the window, the old witch sisters hunched over the table, shoveling porridge into their papery lips. Lulu smiled—a real family at last—and turned her focus to the mountain. Endless angles, views, landscapes—if she were an artist, this tiny world would be her muse—

She sprung to her feet: movement at the base of the mountain. She squinted into the sun, shaded her eyes with her hand.

It wasn't uncommon to spot someone crossing the border to renounce his or her old way of living. New commune members arrived every day, but no one—the witches aside—had climbed and then descended this mountain. Most went around it, or approached from the other side of the valley entirely, where the mountains rose mildly, more akin to hills.

This, *this* was uncommon.

She blinked. A flash: her night in the forest; her moonlit wanderings; those red eyes.

But this was only a man.

He spotted Lulu, jumped in place, waved both of his arms over his head, and veered to the right, re-aiming his path toward her. His run was unsteady, desperate, flailing. Lulu wrung her hands. She looked down, hoping that when she raised her gaze, she'd be alone, a victim of illusion, of mirage.

But this was what she'd wanted, wasn't it? This was the one obstacle in the way of total peace. This was what she'd soundlessly asked for from those red eyes. This was it.

When she raised her head, the man was nearer still, more real, close enough that, with focus, she could differentiate his irises from the whites of his eyes. She rotated on the balls of her feet, abandoning the hand-woven laundry basket, and scrambled inside the gate, into the house. She slammed the door shut behind her. The witches, their porridge bowls put away now, looked up, startled, from their piles of herbs.

"There's a strange man out there," Lulu said, floating outside herself.

Witch One, reclining in her chair, said, "Mmm, yes, I had a feeling we'd receive a visitor today."

Witch Two murmured in agreement, nodded knowingly, drew a sprig of lavender to her nostrils, took a slow whiff.

Lulu kicked a stray clump of coal toward the fireplace. "You didn't think to mention that to me?"

Witch One shrugged. "We thought you knew."

They often assumed she knew more than she did, felt more than she did, overestimated her limited abilities. Lulu ran her fingers along the spines of the books on the shelf. How could she make them understand? "He was heading straight for me," she said, "a madman."

The witches didn't respond. They tinkered with their sprigs and leaves and stems and roots, unconcerned, unbothered by her sweaty, unbridled fear. She paced the room, touching everything, and breathed in, out—trounced by a cocktail of panic and sadness, that all-too-familiar feeling she hadn't felt in a very, very long time.

Not a moment later, there was a knock at the door.

In his essay "The Gospel of Wealth," the great American capitalist-roader Andrew Carnegie famously set forth the notion that the wealthy bear a philanthropic responsibility to the society in which they live. The ex-millionaires of [This Settlement], who have presumably donated their sizable assets to charities and worthy organizations (Ed. Note: We of the Committee were unable to unearth actual records of any such donations) and adopted a back-to-basics lifestyle, must believe then that they are fulfilling their utilitarian purpose, contributing to a greater good.

However, we of the Committee disagree.

More than their money, our nation needs their presence. What right do these tycoons have to disappear, to leave us out in the cold? It is one thing to take their riches and flee abroad, where great freedoms and luxuries and breathable air await, but to renounce money's religion and remain within our country's borders?

Audacious. Outrageous. Disgraceful.

Think of the children, growing and aspiring to waste; of the skyscrapers, longing to be built and filled; of the corporations, never to be established; of the roads, crying to be driven on.

Think of the people, without hope.

In a country such as Canada or the United States, [This Settlement] might be named a model city, might be held in esteem as a national, or even international, example of the "right way to live." However, we of the Committee fully support the scrutiny, disapproval, and distrust with which our dear government has elected to view [This Settlement].

We of the Committee hereby recommend that the government and its affiliated entities sponsor the insertion of an undercover agent to attempt to break the town of its non-capitalistic habits, which are indeed harmful to the stability of the Party and the State...

THE BASHFUL GOOSE DIARIES, SELECTED EXCERPTS, PART 1

DEAR DIARY,

Today, I begin anew.

On the heels of a lifetime of caviar and private chauffeurs and riches beyond imagining, I have reached a new road, settled upon a new purpose: to serve the people.

Yes, the people, who have wept and wailed for heroes lost. The people, who have suffered immensely, but who have labored onward, building a new future, which—judging by our past—will only be destroyed by some foolish future generation.

Yes, the people, who labor on.

Some may call their persistence stupid, indolent, foolish, idiotic, naive. Some may say that to press forward in the face of inevitable failure is indeed humanity's biggest downfall.

But, dear comrades, I propose now a different view.

I cry, shout of the unbreakable spirit, of bravery unlimited! In a former life I might even have raised a glass: *To the people! Who persevere!* But no longer do I partake in drink, a bourgeois proclivity of intellectual life. No longer do I allow my petty physical desires to seize control of my prodigious Communist spirit.

Today I am a new goose, born again to serve!

But I digress. Allow me now to begin where everything should: at the beginning.

The night before we were to be bid farewell, the sky drooped, weighty and wet, bloated with clouds, buzzing with electricity, with imminent thunder and lightning and rain.

They'd transported our bodies from Wuxi to Beijing on military aircraft for a State-sponsored corporate funeral, the first of its kind. Under these special circumstances, authorities permitted Tiananmen to remain open through the night, and many tens of thousands of mourners poured onto the square from the underground entrances, swarming like ants, holding vigil on the concrete.

Some held signs. Some chanted slogans. Some delivered heartfelt speeches. Some stuffed Bashful Goose snack cakes into their traps. Some chewed slowly, deliberately. Others chewed quickly, their canines gnashing, their molars grinding. A few didn't chew at all, swallowing their sorrow whole. Still others forwent the snacks and wept silently, fat-free, calorie-free, into their own arms.

And oh, there was sobbing and moaning, weeping and wailing. Men and women alike pounded at their chests, fell to their knees, collapsed into heaps of pity and remorse and crumbs. This wasn't only about a couple of dead bodies in caskets, just flesh after all, but about the hope that would be laid to rest with them. What man or women didn't aspire to be, in some way, like Papa Hui? How glorious to be rich. How wondrous to be successful. And how virtuous, in the face of these coups, to remain humble.

And now that I've painted the picture outside, let us move to Zhongnanhai, the top secret compound where our leaders live and sleep and dictate from on high and masturbate to thoughts of all the women who aren't their wives, and where two gold-plated, silk-lined coffins rested, side by side, one bigger, the other smaller. The two sacks of meat and bones the coffins contained were to be pickled and placed in a state-of-the-art mausoleum at the Bashful Goose headquarters. But first, the mausoleum had to be constructed, and who possessed the mind to oversee such a precarious project but the man who lay in the coffin it would someday house? A conundrum indeed.

Papa Hui, how the hungry nation longed for one more declaration, for one more day, for one more bite!

Ay, all over the country, people cried, "Bashful Goose, come out, come out!" And what they meant was this: Papa Hui, come back to us, you kooky tycoon! Come back and tell us where to go from here!

They were not calling for me, you see, but for my master.

Anyhow, it didn't matter what they meant. Because Papa Hui couldn't hear them. Because Papa Hui was dead. Because so little ever really matters. Because inside the smaller coffin, there was a stirring, and in that Zhongnanhai compound, behind locks and barbed wire and great red walls intended to keep everything noisy and disruptive and ugly and real at bay, I awoke.

No time to waste, to contemplate, to hesitate. I whacked the top of the coffin with my bill. Again and again, I hammered, until, at last, the blasted thing cracked open. Light streamed in. I sat upright. A stiff ache reverberated in my neck, where the knife had sliced through, but my wound had closed, my throat had healed itself. Ay, I'd suffered a blow for sure, but we all know there are things in this world that can never be fully destroyed, and apparently I was one of them.

I stretched, climbed out, and waddled toward the bigger coffin. I paid little mind to the room's rug, woven from the highly valued hair of Nepalese virgin orphans, nor to the wallpaper, specially infused with platinum and saffron. I had but one focus: my master.

I opened the lid.

I knew, logically, that there was not just one master in the world. Oh, comrades, I knew I would move on to serve someone or something else. But forgive me now for my lapse into weakness. Suffice to say, when one is set free after a captivity in chains, one experiences mixed emotions. Freedom is a carnival: in the early evening all multicolored lights and melodic laughter. But as the night wears on, the scene turns garish, sinister. The lights dim, burn out. The laughter belongs to demons. The rides assume lives of their own. You come to understand that no one can guarantee your safety, that you walk the midway alone.

Over that golden casket, I mourned my past, my present, my future. Memories that would grow fainter and fainter over time: his husky voice, the scratchy touch of his hand stroking my head, the bedtime stories he read aloud, guiding me to dreams. I mourned moments of perfect sunshine, warm and alluring, on late-afternoon strolls across headquarters grounds; moments of belonging; moments of love; moments of genius and triumph in product development conference rooms and laboratories. These moments were all I had.

Time ticked on.

Footsteps from the other side of the door. Hollers. Whispers. Pleasured moans.

I craned my neck, bowed into the coffin, and lay a final peck on my master's waxy cheek.

A tiny tear fell from my eye.

But my tear, sincere as it might have been, would not bring him back.

At dawn, there'd be a commotion, a realization, and then there'd be the well-greased gears of cover-up. Our dear government leaders would replace my body, find a new goose to lay to rest. As was always the case, the public would be none the wiser. Time, as always, would tick on.

I crept through Zhongnanhai's majestic maze, maneuvering around mahogany desks and deluxe soda machines and taxidermic cryptozoological works of art. I tiptoed along the walls of a storage room containing the cryogenically frozen heads of a number of deceased world leaders and sports stars, slunk through hallways and passageways and underground tunnels. I overheard our voluble leaders, ranting and raving on and on: talks of tanks and military personnel stationed outside the city, in case the mourners got out of hand; talks of Papa Hui's business model finally going down in the metaphorical ground with him—no more of that "no bribe" bullshit—let freedom ring. There was dancing. There was laughing. There was cake.

THE WANTS AND NEEDS OF LULU QI

IT BECAME CLEAR THAT THE KNOCKING WASN'T GOING TO STOP, SO AT the witches' urging—never deny someone in need, they always said—Lulu cracked open the door.

Words flew at her, spit in her face: "Excuse me, miss, hello, are you Lulu Qi?"

Lulu leaned away from the man. From behind her, once-busy witchy fingers ceased. No more scratching or sorting or rustling. Just silence, loaded with questions: Who was he? How did he know her? Why didn't she seem to know him?

The man cleared his throat. "Sorry, I don't mean to frighten you. I'm just a bit winded from my trip. Allow me start over." He sucked in a deep breath, his beefy chest visibly rising under his shirt. "My name is Liu Wei, and I have come to join this commune, and I would very much like to have a word with you, Ms. Lulu Qi, if you could spare a few moments."

Lulu crossed her arms over her chest. She studied the man, who was at once familiar and strange. She looked to the witches for an answer, for advice, for anything; as per usual, they just smiled, nodded knowingly. This was a new life—trust. She permitted her arms to fall to her sides. Purpose is objective; fate gives us nothing to fear.

"Yeah, sure, okay," she said. "Please, do come in."

The witches, all raised eyebrows and girlish giggles, excused themselves outside for a walk, leaving Lulu and the man alone. He was, Lulu determined as she boiled water, most certainly a former businessman. Only a businessman could sit, as he had, without hesitation in a stranger's home and appear completely at ease.

She removed the kettle from the heat and poured water into two cups. She pushed one cup toward the man and pulled the other toward herself. "Drink," she urged. "Please drink."

The man lifted the cup to his lips and took a careful sip.

She lowered herself to sit. He stretched, his eyes occupied, traveling the room, lapping up the scene. She didn't want to be rude, to tell him to get on with it already, to tell her who he was and where'd he come from, but it wasn't every day that a strange, handsome, man showed up at your door, a man who knew your name and wanted to speak with you about some seemingly important matter. And there was that whole business about the woods two nights before. The glowing red eyes. The question. The "What do you want?" Her answer. Her answer. Her answer.

✳

Once upon a time, Lulu Qi had wanted, simply, to lead a normal life. She wanted a normal mother who'd take her to the cinema and to the playground, who'd cook elaborate dinners at holidays, who'd sit beaming in the audience during school performances, who didn't spend most of her waking hours faking maladies and rotting away in bed. She wanted a normal father who'd take the family on weekend trips, who'd return from work in the evenings grumpy but satisfied, who didn't go missing for days at a time, who didn't gamble away his paychecks, who didn't return to their apartment one night with a strange woman who smelled like the dumpster behind the flower market near their home.

And oh, the things she didn't want: For her mother to scream at her father as he clung to the strange lady's noodle arm. For him to take a swing to silence her mother's shrieking mouth, to miss, to accidentally clock the strange lady in the side of the face, to send her to the floor, squealing like a pig, "My nose, my fucking nose!" For her mother to shove him and his whore out the door. For her to order him never to set foot in that apartment again, or may he be stricken down by a thousand vengeful deities. For him to listen, to heed, to disappear forever. For the last memory she had of her creator to be drunk, slurring, swinging, fly undone, pocked cheeks glowing red.

For a long time, she didn't want anything. She'd stare at television commercials, unmoved by their emotional pleas. She'd sleep at night and dream of nothing. At school, the bored cafeteria ladies would give her a choice between topping her rice with one kind of slop and another, and she'd stand there, bowl in hand, face blank, not answering, until, frustrated, they'd pick for her, slap a ladleful down, curse her for wasting their time. In class, she would hurriedly circle answers on quizzes and exams, not sweating a drop over scores or rankings, and as the other students deliberated and stressed themselves into earlier graves, she'd stare out the window at the desolate grounds and concrete basketball courts without purpose or desire, absent of want.

It went on that way until things, as they so often do, went another way entirely. One afternoon when she was nine, two years after her father left, her bedridden mother sent her, as she so often did, on an errand.

Lulu dawdled over to the same corner store where she bought her instant noodle and chip rations. She dawdled through the narrow aisles and finally happened upon what she'd been sent for. She dawdled to the register. She set the package on the counter.

The cashier, a woman with severe, tattooed eyebrows, chortled. "A bit young for this business, eh?"

Lulu glared. Child bullies she could tolerate, but grown-ups should know better. "They're for my mother." She spoke with a biting tone, an attitude she dare not cop around her school-aged tormentors. "Not that 'this business' is any of your business."

The woman blinked slowly, unimpressed. She turned up her nose and robotically announced the total. Lulu paid and tucked the change and the small package into her jacket pocket, out of sight.

She stomped down the street, dodging bicycles and pedestrians and motorbikes, all enemies, all trying to hit her, all trying to take her out for good. It was bad enough that her mother had sent her to buy these stupid, embarrassing things, but to have someone make fun of her for it, my god. Lulu ran through all the derogatory names she would call that wretched cashier, if she ever had the chance: Sausage Fingers, Fat Watermelon Head, Mean-Spirited Devil, on and on. She finally stopped herself at Useless Rice Bucket and decided then and there that she would never go back to that convenience store again as long as she lived. There were other stores. Farther away, yes, but what was her time? She didn't have a better way to spend it.

She rounded the corner and stopped at the newspaper stand. She issued a friendly hello to the old man who sat inside. Sometimes he'd give her a White Rabbit candy, tell her, "Shh, don't tell, you're not supposed to accept candy from strangers." She sometimes allowed herself to imagine that he was her grandfather.

"I'm fresh outta candy"—he grinned a toothless grin—"but swing by tomorrow, and I'll have two pieces ready!"

Lulu turned to continue on her way, but a magazine cover caught her eye. She froze. A mirror, her own reflection. A face with the same pale skin, the same smattering of freckles, the same button nose, the same bright eyes, the same cherry lips, wearing the same two framing black braids. There was text across the face, text that assured her that this wasn't actually a mirror, text that read: "Meet Li'l Goose Girl, Our Country's Most Darling and Perfect Child!"

She paid for the magazine with her mother's change and sprinted back to their apartment's courtyard. She plopped down on a planter box, rested the magazine in her lap, and shoved the entire free-with-purchase Bashful Goose Guava Goober into her mouth. Once the goober was melted, gone, she opened the magazine: a special edition of a children's monthly, devoted entirely to the Bashful Goose heiress, Kelly Hui.

As Lulu read and read, the world fell away. There was no mean lady at the convenience store. There was no convenience store. There was no dog taking a leak on the edge of the planter box, dangerously close to her leg.

There was only the behind-the-scenes peek at a television commercial shoot for a top secret new Bashful Goose product. The article stated that an eight-year-old Kelly wrote, directed, and starred in the commercial, and even composed and performed the jingle at the commercial's end.

There was also an essay the little darling had written at school about patriotism: *I'm proud to live in China because there are people here I can trust!* Printed alongside were the teacher's comments: *What a remarkable gift this young lady possesses! What love she has for our great nation! It is with a pride-bursting heart that I have decided to resign from teaching. I have nothing further to offer this world! May this young lady continue to give it her all!*

There were excerpts from Kelly's daily journal. *Today I helped my mother with the household chores. We cleaned up the goose's bedroom because Papa says the little guy is too busy with molting season and business deals to clean it up himself. We swept and vacuumed and scrubbed the floor, and Mama even let me use Clean-It-Up brand bleach! [WARNING: Bleach is a hazardous chemical, and use or consumption of bleach by children is in no way condoned by the Bashful Goose Snack Company.] Finally, we made up the goose's bed. Mama says he gets to have high-thread-count sheets because he's a national icon. She says when I start contributing to the household in a meaningful way, maybe I can have a super-king-sized bed just like him. What a great day!*

There were drawings Kelly had completed in art class, masterpieces all of them. There were bulleted lists entitled "Kelly Hui's Tips for Badminton Masters" and "How to Have the Table Manners of an Heiress." There was a column called "Dear Kelly," in which wayward youth wrote to Ms. Hui seeking advice for such issues as incurable chronic hiccuping and what to do when your mom won't let you keep your hamster in the house because she's uptight and afraid of the plague and the poor little guy freezes to death on the balcony. There was a photo of Kelly planting trees at the Bashful Goose headquarters for Earth Day. There was another of her distributing Bashful Goose snacks to AIDS orphans on a relief trip she took with her parents to Africa. There was a full-color, pullout wall poster in the magazine's center, titled "An Ideal Girl," featuring illustrated reminders for all the nation's imperfect but improvable children: A cartoon Kelly sitting, pencil poised, at a desk. *Complete your homework.* A cartoon Kelly kowtowing before her cartoon father and a cartoon goose. *Listen attentively to your elders.* A cartoon Kelly, under a wall clock, using a knife and fork to cut into a Bashful Goose Watermelon Wiggler. *Take your snacks on time.*

Daylight waned. Lulu realized, as she licked her finger and turned the last page, that she'd been consuming only necessary air, breathing shallow. She gulped up a lungful; she wanted to breathe. She shut the magazine in her lap and sunk her eyes into the twilight horizon. She was alive; she wanted to be alive. She was awake; she wanted to be awake. She wanted; she wanted to be that girl.

❋

Lulu listened intently, tried to center all of her empathetic energy on this Liu Wei, on his tragic story of losing his wife and daughter to a car accident, of losing his faith in his corporate consulting business and in the merits of the money it provided.

But questions and doubts wiggled in her mind, distracting her: Was this a coincidence after all? Was this nothing to do with those red eyes, with her wish? But then why did he know her name? And why was he telling her all this? If he simply needed someone with whom to share his sorrows, there were a billion other warm bodies out there with ears attached. There were people with whom he had to have a personal connection, and still other people who had made it their profession to deal with grief. There had to be a reason he'd chosen her, a reason he knew her name, and yet, when he finished his recounting, she couldn't bring herself to ask.

His eyes glistened with weary tears, lacking the energy to fall.

"I'm very sorry for your losses," she said softly. She cast her gaze to the tabletop, to the piles of herbs she'd pushed to one end, out of their way.

"Thank you." The timbre of his voice housed a complexity, a peculiar layer that nearly urged her to inquiry. Perhaps he'd seen those red eyes too. Perhaps they'd told him her name.

She clasped her teacup, a tiny heater in her hands. The noontime sun would soon sweep across the sky, shining into their windows and warming the place up. But not yet. Goose bumps rose on her forearms. She tried to formulate a delicate question in her head, but everything she cobbled together came out inappropriate, crass.

"So, anyway, I came here," he said, as though hearing her desperate intent in the silence, "looking for a fresh start. I don't know what that entails, exactly, but it doesn't matter. That'll all come later is how it works, is how I understand it. A friend told me about this place and mentioned you, showed me a picture. Kai. He said he worked with you at Hair Inc. And, I don't know, you were the only thing about my future that I knew by name, and I nursed this funny idea you might be the one who could help me start this start." He smiled slightly, sadly, with pale pink lips. His cheeks flushed. He looked down. "Ah, anyway."

Lulu's kneecaps buckled, melted into her calves—had she not been seated, she would've melted straight to the floor. She opened her mouth to say something, anything, but was stopped by footsteps, voices, a creak. The witches burst in, laughing and chattering, their baskets ripe with the day's harvest.

Witch Two, though grinning wide, winced with each step. Recently, Lulu had taken over most of the physical labor on the mountain, bending, rooting around, maneuvering over rocks and brambles and other obstacles—though spritely of mind, the witch sisters were no spring chickens. A wave of guilt crashed against Lulu's stomach's walls, and she jumped up, thankful her wobbly knees held out, and rushed over to help the witches with the baskets.

The witches retook their seats at the table, sighed with relief, pushed aside the lukewarm teacups, and rolled up their sleeves. Whether Liu Wei was there or not, there was work to do: sorting, packaging, and preparing potions and medicinal mixtures for the villagers down below.

Lulu joined in this familiar task, her hands occupied, but her head still stuck on this man. "Well, look, we're on the outskirts here, as I'm sure you know. Maybe tomorrow I can take you into town. And, uh…" She looked to the witches for approval, which they issued with a slight nod each. "You can stay here tonight if you'd like. I just did some wash, so there are fresh sheets. We can make a bed for you on the floor in here."

Lulu looked up, awaiting an answer, and watched him watch their busy fingers working their magic. He furrowed his brow, frowned. She set down the jar she was packing with mushrooms. The glass clunked against the wood. "I'm sorry, have I said something wrong?"

He jolted, genuinely surprised. "No, no, not at all. It's just that you're so kind. I'm very touched. And," he added, pointing at their mess of colorful, earth-coated nature. "I would love if you ladies could explain all of this to me."

Witch One raised an eyebrow. Witch Two grinned. They cannonballed into an explanation of traditional medicine, of healing properties, of herbs and mushrooms, of blends and teas, of theory and practice. Liu Wei listened receptively, an eager student. Out the window, the sun streaked across the canvas sky.

✳

The question. The "What do you want?" Her answer. Her answer. Her answer.

All those years ago. The night of the Goose Girl's commercial debut. Every action felt imbued with new meaning. Lulu poured boiled water over her instant noodles: an offering. She leafed through the magazine, dog-eared and worn: worship. She chugged a bottle of iced tea: a prayer. She parked herself in front of the TV: transcendence.

The commercial was scheduled to run during an imperial soap opera. Eunuchs and concubines schemed. The emperor issued decrees. The second wife chunked a piece of jewelry into a still black pond. *Plunk.* The camera panned back to the second wife's face. A single tear leaked from her twitching eye.

And cut to black.

This was it. Lulu inhaled sharply, clutched a pillow to her chest. She pressed her sweaty palms into her stretch pants.

Lights, camera, action.

Kelly Hui, in the filmed flesh, sitting before a table, looking ahead, her anticipation clear. She was waiting, waiting for something important.

And then a deep, booming voice, a voice like God's: *Bashful Goose snacks! You won't even know what hit you!*

Still, she waited.

A second passed.

A pie flew into the frame.

"Duck!" Lulu jumped to her bare feet, shouted at the screen.

Smack. The pie caught Kelly square in the face.

A second passed.

Kelly ran her finger across her creamed cheek, popped her finger into her mouth, grinned. "Bashful Goose snacks!" she chirped in her sugary voice, addressing the nation, a vast nation, a nation that included Lulu, who lowered herself back down to sit on the hard wooden sofa. "They're finger-licking good!"

Notes, a tinkly tune. Kelly rose, bounded atop the table, and, face still covered in cream, tap-danced along: *Bashful Goose Cream Pies / Bashful Goose Cream Pies / Don't be a clown / Don't be a clown / Just eat them down / EAT. THEM. DOWN!*

"Honk, honk!" she added, giving a heartfelt thumbs-up, as the camera zoomed in on her face.

God again: *Bashful Goose Cream Pies, available where all fine snack products are sold!*

And that was it. The next commercial began: *If you don't wanna be a chump, you'd better buy a European car, blah blah blah.*

Lulu picked up the remote and turned the TV off.

Silence. Toilets flushing in other apartments. Sinks running. Water washing through pipes. From the next room, her mother's snores—Lulu had long ceased deriving any comfort from their rhythm.

She fiddled with a thread that'd come loose from her sock. She replayed the commercial in her head. She loved it, loved it with all her heart.

But for one part: just after the pie in the face, there was a moment, a flash of something dark in that Goose Girl's eyes. A familiar flash. Unhappiness? Discontent? Boredom? The acidic pain of being someone's child, a someone not of the child's choosing, of being forced to occupy a preordained place in this world? Lulu stuck on this moment, picked at her socks, lingered uncomfortably there. She'd wanted to be that Goose Girl, yes, but what if that girl wasn't who she appeared to be?

Fifteen years later, she'd all but forgotten about that commercial, the passion and turmoil it had stirred within her. She'd since moved on to and away from countless other loves and wants and fixations: books and movies and coconut oil; men and friends and meditation; jobs and dresses and soy milk lattes.

If she'd known as a child that fifteen years later, she'd meet the Goose Girl herself in a banquet hall's bathroom, that she'd witness Ms. Kelly Hui march to the sinks and hold her hands under a faucet like a mere mortal, that she'd ogle and gape like a damned fool...

If she'd known as a child that someday she'd stand beside her, studying that Goose Girl's zits and the way her pudge poked out beneath her dress's cap sleeves; that the Goose Girl, grown up, no longer cute, no longer her spitting image, would meet her eyes in the mirror and sneer, "What are you looking at?"

That she'd smile, say, "Oh, I—sorry, this is just a weird moment for me."

That Kelly would shut off the faucet, mutter, "Join the club."

That Lulu would laugh an ugly, unbecoming, but entirely authentic laugh. That this would bring a smile to Kelly's round face. "Are you one of those hair extension girls?"

That Lulu would nod, owning her lot in life.

That Kelly would flip her own long locks over her shoulder. "This is the Lulu batch. Expensive as unicorn shit, and I hear it won't be available to non-superstars like me anymore. Movie stars only from here on out, or whatever."

"Actually, I'm Lulu."

That Kelly would peer at her. "No way."

"Yep."

That she'd say, "Well, fuckin' sweet." That she'd raise her hand, her palm out to Lulu. That Lulu would flinch, believing for a moment that Kelly was aiming to hit her, but then realizing that she was only asking for a high five.

That as their palms slapped together, Lulu would feel something leave her body. A weight she hadn't known she'd been carrying. A weight she'd been carrying for a very long time.

If she'd known all this, fifteen years before, as a child, belly full of chemicals, pretzeled on the sofa, picking at her lint-bumpy socks, she would've laughed, she would've cried, she would've shut off the TV, torn that magazine to shreds, run to the mirror, told herself this: none of these snacks will ever fill you up.

*

And that was how life went: unfathomable possibilities actualized in sequence. Lulu and Liu Wei and the witches spent that evening around the fire pit out back, the four of them alone together, plucking and strumming a *guzheng* and chatting about the villages and neighborhoods of their youths, weaving from memory tales of deprivation and starvation and innocence and simpler times.

At eleven, the witches retired to their sleeping quarters with winks and nods, leaving Lulu and Liu Wei alone beside the dying fire. They sat, not speaking, lost in their own thoughts. This quiet was comfortable, intimate, and Lulu reveled in it, thinking back with nostalgia to her recent night in the woods, grateful for that red-eyed creature's gift, for its warmth, for its ability to quell the inherent flight response that had threatened to lead her away from the best life she'd ever lived. She stole the occasional sly glance at Liu Wei, lost to his own mental meanderings, and struggled to suppress the goofy smile that threatened to seize her face.

She allowed her gaze to linger too long on his cheekbones. He caught her eye. He smiled.

"Well," he said, clearing his throat, motioning at the waning fire. "We'd better do something about this, eh? Action, I say!"

He hopped up. She followed him through the gate and around the outer perimeter of the wall, helped him gather dry brush and branches. Once they'd amassed a sizable collection, they returned to the fire and fed the flames.

"This'll keep us going for a while," he said. She nodded, grateful this night would stretch on.

Liu Wei retook his seat. Lulu hesitated, wanting very badly to sit beside him on that same log, but opting instead for an adjacent rock. There was no rush. They had a lifetime.

"So," he said, clapping his hands on his thighs, a child eager for a story. "Tell me more about the commune, the citizens."

Lulu surrendered to her goofy smile. "What do you want to know?"

"I don't know," he said, resting his elbow on his leg and his chin on his palm. "Everything. This place is a mystery to me, as I'm sure it was to you when you first got here. Blind faith led me. And now I'm asking you to be my eyes."

"Well," she began, "the first thing you need to know is that right now everyone down there fancies him- or herself a beatnik. They've all read this same copy of *On the Road* in translation—some ex-investment banker runs a lending library out of his room—save for the super-elite who claim they read it in its original English back at university."

He laughed, and she continued, regaling him with tales of the commune and its whacky citizenry. Of the ex-chef who kept a cow in his living room, claiming he shared a telepathic wavelength with this cow and, more recently, asserting that the cow was his wife, although not officially because of bestiality laws, but "in spirit." Of the gaggle of gangly ex-models who lived together and had become master picklers, taking their craft so seriously they demanded it be called an "art" and, to prove their point, held a pickling exhibit in their neighbor's living room-cum-art gallery, in which they displayed fifty varieties, none of which anyone was permitted to actually taste. The ex-CFO who got around on a unicycle he'd somehow cobbled together from bamboo and chewing gum. The creepy shed next to Wang and Stefan's house that they kept locked at all times and that nobody but them ever stepped foot inside.

"Well, what'd be worth seeing in a shed anyway?"

Lulu poked a twig into the fire, lifted it, watched its end burn like a sparkler at Chinese New Year. "I just think it's weird," she said, twirling and dropping the stick into the fire. "There are citizens who have sheds and stuff for woodworking or crafting, and there are a few who've constructed these tiny temples in sheds, but all of that is whatever. It's no secret, I mean. Neighbors come in and out."

"What do you think they're hiding in there?" He spoke these words with a stilted nonchalance that gave Lulu pause, that broke the night's spell.

"Nothing," she said, desperate to veer back toward the magic. "It's probably nothing. I'm just nosy, is all." A cicada chirped. Liu Wei gazed over her left shoulder. Get back on track, get back on track, back on. "Oh, and here we are sitting in front of a fire and I didn't even mention the ex-TV host who has taken up fire-breathing!"

The fire crackled, the moon smiled, and Lulu and Liu Wei plunged back into the sorcery of stories well told.

She told him about the trip she took to Tibet with a middle schooler, her days as a human hair factory, her lonely childhood, her lonelier apartment in Beijing. She'd never spoken so freely, never been with someone who listened so attentively, who asked all the right questions—someone genuinely interested in what it was she as a human being had to offer this world.

Yes, what good was a book without a reader? A play without an audience? A song without an ear? What good was a life without someone with whom to share it?

Time slipped away, and their yawns grew more aggressive, and the black sky lightened, purple and gold. They doused the fire with a bucket of water and shuffled inside to catch a few hours of sleep.

"Like I said earlier, when you're ready," Lulu whispered, padding around the pallet she'd prepared on the main room's floor. "I can show you around the town and help you find a place to settle in. There are some people who are looking for roommates, and, uh, I'm sure you could find a really—"

He stood now in front of her, against her, a wall, a shield. He pressed one finger gently to her lips.

Electricity jolted, shooting up from the base of her spine.

They paused there, bodies close, for a long, heavy moment.

They did not kiss. They said good night

A couple hours later, Lulu—unable to sleep, restless, and uncharacteristically irritated by the witches' rhythmic snores—stumbled out of the bedroom. She would cook up a big breakfast and she and Liu Wei would sit at the table, talking in hushed voices, until the witches awoke, and then perhaps they'd all go out into the woods together, come back, get the sorting done quickly, and head down to the commune in the afternoon.

Lulu looked around. "Liu Wei?" she spoke to the lifeless room. There was no answer.

"Hello?"

Nothing. No one.

He must've gone out for a walk. He probably couldn't sleep either, too energized by whatever this was blooming between them.

She stepped into the kitchen, took stock of the food situation— plenty of rice, a head of cabbage, what else?

A creak. She spun her head around. The front door swung open.

She exhaled. Liu Wei. Thank you, spirits.

"Good morning!" he called. She drew her finger to her lips to shush him and blushed when she remembered his finger in that very spot only hours before. She spun back around to hide her reddening face.

"Good morning." She bent down to retrieve a pan from a low shelf. "So, there's a wild chicken or something that hangs around the woods, leaves eggs here and there. I was thinking I'd go out and collect a few and cook us up a big breakfast. Porridge, fried egg, maybe some—"

He interrupted, his voice low, subdued. "Lulu, I'm terribly sorry, but I'm afraid I won't be able to stay for breakfast."

She set the pan on the counter and stared into the cast iron. "Okay, no problem. How about I just quickly cook up some—"

He wasn't in the doorway any longer. He stood behind her. His hands appeared, clasped around her abdomen. His arms pressed into her and then his whole body. Her knees buckled. It didn't mat- ter. He wouldn't let her fall. He leaned in. His lips caressed her neck.

"I've got to go down to the commune," he whispered, inciting full- body goose bumps, his lips brushing against her earlobe. "It's calling me. Spiritually. Mysteriously. I don't know what it is. I need to go today, alone. I can't explain it. There's just something I'm called to do. You know. You understand."

She sighed yes and, seconds later, watched, as women are destined to do, helpless and hopeful as her man marched off to war.

THE BASHFUL GOOSE DIARIES, SELECTED EXCERPTS, PART 2

I WRITE TO YOU NOW FROM MY HOME FOR THE NIGHT, AN ABANDONED grain silo. Only hours ago, I alighted from my first cross-province train ride. This was an authentic train, a people's train, my car packed with peasants and farmers hauling overstuffed plaid sacks and canvas satchels.

We shouted. We cursed. We sang.

Oh, we sang old Maoist ditties. We sang Teresa Teng's greatest hits. We swigged *erguotou*, huffed unfiltered cigarettes, spit sunflower seeds out the windows and onto the floors. How warm, how right, how enveloped I felt among the masses. How my spirit swelled amid the booze, the seeds, the smoke, the song. My one tiny mouth, it cried out, but one voice of many in a wide, wild world.

Finally, hours and hours in, the singing stopped. The car grew quiet. The train chugged along, metallic, rickety. Though it'd been dark for hours, only now did the blackness, its presence, its existence, even register. From all around me, stares. Side glances. Cloudy eyes.

A nervous chill radiated through my wings. A lump lodged in my throat.

The glower of one woman in particular unnerved me, her body solid, her face a broad and wrinkled map of lives past.

She knew.

Of course—did I really expect to travel without someone recognizing me? I am *the* bashful goose, and this is the age of the cult of celebrity, an era of obsession with the rich and famous. Anonymity is a delusion of the past!

The broad-faced woman licked her white chapped lips and whispered to the rumpled man squatting beside her—and I use that word loosely. As the old saying goes, you can hear a peasant's whisper from a *li* away. "My god, can you imagine that plump little thing braised and cut up over rice?"

A wave of initial relief; a cacophony of growling stomachs; an endless sea of longing looks; a goose trembling with realization of a whole new terror, fleeing grabby hands, squawking, tucking and rolling alongside the tracks; many peasants following suit, rolling like hedgehogs down the steep embankment, some cracking their skulls, others more agile simply missing their ride home; a goose taking off in flight, leaving the world hungry once again.

Make your intentions clear, clearer still!

"Ah, cruel world," I cried to no one as I landed, and raced through a field of corn, "I said serve the people, not be served!"

✻

It occurred to me today, after weeks of failures and mishaps (the station in Henan where a boiled egg vendor, surprised to see a goose waiting in her line, knocked over her cart, cursed to high heavens, and incited a riot that resulted in one young man, eager for a free lunch, jumping in front of an oncoming train in an ill-fated attempt to catch an egg that had been sent airborne; the blind massage parlor where I accidentally tripped a masseuse, causing him to drop a vat of scalding hot water onto a female customer texting on a poorly assembled cell phone that electrocuted her; the karaoke girl who, after a strange and complicated series of events, may or may not be dead in a cage at the bottom of a lake—among other notable examples), that perhaps my inability to properly serve the people stems from my lack of understanding of the people. What do I know of toiling, of suffering, of truly living?

I happened upon a village last week, deep in the countryside. The citizenry was sparse, primarily comprising children and seniors—

only those too weak or old or young or stupid to leave would remain in a barren wasteland such as this.

There I stood outside a small snack shop, awaiting a new path to reveal itself. Packages of Bashful Goose snacks, production dated well before my tragic death, lined the store's dusty shelves, providing the only color in this otherwise bleak landscape.

I waited for hours. The old clerk shuffled out to study me a few times, muttering each time, "Well, free advertising, eh?" and then returning to his post.

Just when I was about to give up, to go find a pond or a creek in which to wash myself clean of this mess, a young man, donning a raggedy backpack, radiating Lei Feng's selfless spirit, waltzed past and into the shop.

"Ay!" he cried to the clerk. "I'm going."

The old man jerked awake, dragged his head up from the counter. A puddle of drool gleamed atop the filthy glass. He smeared it away with his sleeve. "That's it, then?"

"That's it!" the boy cried cheerfully.

The man stood. "Good luck," he said. "May the gods look favorably upon you." He reached to the shelf and handed the boy a Watermelon Wiggler. "This one's expired," he said. "But I imagine you'll make do."

Ah, the roads we walk, the strangers we follow!

Many minibuses and stretches of railroad track later, I found myself in a city as dusty as that village, on a building site dustier still.

I watched from the doorway as the boy I'd followed all that way marched into an office. A man sat in a computer chair, his feet propped up on his messy desk.

"Is Subcontractor Hao in?" the boy asked the man.

"I'm Subcontractor Hao," the man said. "Whaddya want?"

The boy, named Little Warrior, introduced himself and announced his vague connection to two workers already on the project. "I'll work as hard as possible," he said. "I've got to earn extra money to pay for my grandmother's medicine."

The boss, after some prodding and convincing, agreed to hire Little Warrior. He gave him directions to the dormitory and told him to be ready to work after lunchtime—"And no, you cannot join us for lunch today. Work first, then eat. Dinner is at six."

Little Warrior smiled and marched out, head held high.

Deciding that some hard labor might do me good, and wanting to follow Little Warrior's noble example, I waddled up to Subcontractor Hao's desk.

"Ay, another one," he muttered. He gave me a slow once-over. "You'll do," he finally said. He shook his head. "Ain't got a hard hat that'll fit that strange little head of yours, but you'll do."

✳

Forgive my poor penmanship. I write in the dark of night, the moon my only light source, my only companion. My days of toiling among the workers are finished, dear diary. I sing my lament now to you!

You see, after some initial growing pains at the building site, I discovered my true talents resided in messengering and assisting. I soared up to the top floors and performed checks, inspections, deliveries. I passed on messages between those working on the top and bottom of the building. Additionally, my bill served as a most excellent screwdriver.

Subcontractor Hao was eager to get everything wrapped up before we all headed home to celebrate the new lunar year with our families, so in the weeks leading up to the Spring Festival, we labored well into the night. We kept ourselves alert guzzling cans of coffee from the on-site commissary, where snacks, toilet paper, and other essentials were available for purchase, no cash necessary—our expenditures were deducted from our pay, which we would receive at the end of our work period.

We consumed can after can of bean water and cream and sugar, and the blackness under our eyes darkened by the day, and our meat seemed to separate from our aching bones, but our hearts grew fat with excitement, with anticipation, with dreams of impending freedom.

Payday morning arrived before we knew it. We waited, breath bated, outside Subcontractor Hao's office. We waited for the familiar crackle of his BMW's tires on gravel.

Time ticked on.

Cold sweat coated us.

We waited.

Only silence near us; in the distance, the sound of passing cars.

When we couldn't wait any longer, we banged on the door. We shouted. We waited even more, and when we couldn't wait even more anymore, Old Meng kicked in the door. Someone else smashed the windows. We raided the office. No signs of Subcontractor Hao.

We waited.

The photographs he kept on his desk of his heavily made-up wife and his beloved German shepherd were gone. Only the photos' frames remained, containing blank white sheets of papers. We examined the emptied frames, removed their cardboard backs.

We waited.

Opening drawers and peeking inside soon gave way to full-fledged looting—smashing glass, shoving into pockets anything worth a damn: Post-it notes, nubby pencils, individual wheels from Subcontractor Hao's computer chair.

When the door flew open, the wind seizing loose papers and scraps, sending a chill down all of our spines, we held our breath.

We waited.

Many of the workers had train tickets home, paid for with money borrowed from friends or relatives with the intention of paying the money back as soon as they received their salaries. Many of the men nursed well-earned visions of returning home with fat wads of cash, of paying for electric fans and new cell phones and hospital bills and tuition fees for their mothers, fathers, sons, daughters.

These intentions, these dreams, hung palpable in the air, the strong winter wind no match for their sturdiness, nowhere near powerful enough to blow them away.

Old Shopkeeper Lu, who operated the commissary, strode through the blown-open doorway, his round cheeks red. "Where's that rat bastard? He owes me five hundred yuan!"

Little Warrior, holding a smashed lamp, explained the situation.

Old Shopkeeper Lu pondered for a moment. "Well, if he disappeared then it's you bastards who owe me money! You inherit his debt! It's the law!"

Oh, dear diary, I didn't care about my own pay. What would a goose like me do with a few thousand yuan anyway? I'd been the beneficiary of billions. I'd tasted life's luxuries.

But for these men, these hopeful men!

I devised a plan, whispered it to Little Warrior; he alone could understand me, had served as my translator for all those weeks. We would protest, demand that the bastard boss come back and give us what was rightfully ours. We would draw attention to the crime that had been committed, to this atrocity. We would lay down in the busy road in front of the site until the police listened to our complaints and tracked the bastard down, shook him down for all he was worth.

The majority of the workers stood with us; the remainder camped out in the dormitory, prepared to miss their trains, hanging on to the false hope of Subcontractor Hao's return.

We waited until the light turned red, walked to the middle of the street, and lay down on the chunky white stripes. Honks rang out in reaction, car horns wailing. Their light was still red.

We didn't move.

The light turned green.

We didn't move.

Shouting heads popped out from car windows. A few drivers attempted to maneuver around us, onto the sidewalk, where bicycles had already staked their claimed. One car, a Volkswagen, crashed into an electrical pole.

The workers murmured encouragement to one another. A dense crowd of onlookers assembled. I stared up at the sky, coal gray. The city police turned up in full riot gear. One of them pulled out a spatula-like tool and attempted to pry Little Warrior's head off the pavement. Little Warrior jerked away.

"Whaddya want?" the cop spat.

"Money!" Little Warrior shouted, vigor in his voice.

Old Meng, next to him, piped up, providing a more intellectual explanation, detailing the months on the job and the boss's sudden and convenient disappearance once pay came due.

The cop feigned interest, hacked a phlegm oyster onto the ground beside my bill. A belligerent driver swerved onto the sidewalk, taking out an old lady riding with a flat-faced Pekingese in her bicycle's basket.

Things weren't going well. I prayed to the gods for an idea.

They answered.

I whispered to Little Warrior, "Tell him that if he doesn't do something, we're going to burn the building down!"

Little Warrior gasped, barely audible among the sounds of blaring horns. The cop somehow heard it and turned to peer at him.

This was my cue to slip away. I flew onto the site and found the cans of gasoline Subcontractor Hao stored at the eastern edge. We had to show the world that we were serious, that our threats weren't empty. Subcontractor Hao's office was easy. A bit of gasoline, a lot of papers, a knockoff Zippo lighter, boom, done.

My plan may have been ill conceived. Admit your mistakes! Own up to them. Cherish them. They are your most honorable teachers.

Yes, I failed to calculate the wind's strength or direction, and I didn't intend for the fire to spread, but oh, spread it did. The few foolish, camped-out workers sprinted from the dormitory, clutching their hastily gathered belongings to their chests.

Stunned, I flew back to the street junction, where the protestors remained flat on the pavement and where those dozens of SWAT officers now stormed, armed with batons and handcuffs and pepper spray. A mass struggle and arrest session followed. Even the wind took sides, as the building we'd spent so long piecing together went up in flames. Sirens moaned. One of the steel support beams came crashing down onto a neighboring shopping mall, killing dozens standing in line at the ice-cream window outside a McDonald's.

I followed the white cars and flashing lights to the police station, where I attempted to turn myself in. The officers paid my confessions no heed. *Honk, honk, honk* was all they heard, was all most anyone heard, everyone but Little Warrior.

I met his eyes. I remembered the first time I saw him, wearing that ratty backpack, waltzing into that snack shop, a child. He sat now on this bench, handcuffed and sedated, a man. He shook his head, dismissing me, urging me onward.

His goodness, the goodness of the people! The people who took the fall!

Forgive me, dear diary, as I've written many times of maintaining an honest record. I must therefore retract some of my earlier claims. I must admit that, yes, Little Warrior tried to turn me in. That all the arrested workers tried with him.

The detectives responded in increasingly incredulous tones. "A goose? A goose made you do it?"

"What, bird flu go to your brains?"

"I've heard some crazy things in my time, but this!"

Laughter erupted throughout the station, much the way my fire had started, born in crackles and sparks before erupting into a glorious blaze. The entire station chortled and guffawed, falling on the floor, clutching their overfed bellies, laughing and snorting and farting and crying. Even—after sufficient time had passed—even our arrested men couldn't help but smile.

Fifteen of the workers were handed life sentences, sent to labor camps. Five more, who were deemed ringleaders, were handed the death penalty. Destruction of private property, arson, manslaughter, obstructing traffic's natural and steady flow, illegal employment, use of an unapproved fuel source to start a fire, general mischief and hooliganism, illegal migration/residency, disturbing the harmonious society, public gathering without a proper permit—the list of their crimes, oh, it went on and on.

5.

THE SHED, THE SECRET, THE TREATISE

We are disillusioned. We are burned out.
We hail from near and far.
We step forward, hiding no longer behind masks of cash
   and clothes and luxury cars.
We come unveiled.
We seek new truths, new paths to fulfillment.
   We seek avenues unexplored.
We are the ex-millionaires, and we would be the future of this great
   country, if we gave a damn about this great country's future.

It came to Wang in a dream. His dream-self, poised atop the roof of his old Hair Inc. headquarters in Shanghai, on a cushion, meditating, breathing in, out, existing within the present moment but remaining keenly aware of his Heads, exercising and swallowing vitamins and sprouting strands in the building below. In, out. Something fluttered before his face, landed in his lap: a red autumn leaf, written upon with ink, sent for him. *June 5,* that was the message, the entire message, and upon receiving that message, he jolted awake in bed.

He would've forgotten it, dismissed it altogether, but this was modern times and this message wasn't to be contained within one medium. He received it afterward also in the waking world: he became strangely fixated with a stone on an afternoon walk, one of a thousand stones, and when he turned it over, he found nestled in the damp ground below it a folded-up note bearing only: "June 5." One morning, on his way to pick up bread from a neighboring baker, he came upon two villagers playing some game of their own invention, something involving throwing a stone and singing old commercial jingles, and just as he walked past one of them announced the current score, six to five. Six five. June 5. He'd wake as dawn broke, jolting from one of those falling dreams—body tensed, wet with sweat— and always at the same time, 6:05. June 5.

He understood the message the instant he received it. This was the date he was to be removed from this earth, to be reclaimed by those shadow people with their white light, their loving warmth.

Until that date, he waited.

The ethos that underlies our actions is simple: We believe every act of corruption spawns immeasurable evil, and we spurn its dark practices. We reject the notion that life, in order to be meaningful, must be oriented toward the setting and achieving of goals.

June 4. Morning's sunny fingers reached through the windows, shook him awake. It was late, seven or eight. A damp earthiness hung in the air. Next to him on the kang, Stefan snored peacefully.

This cozy home they shared was truly a farmer's home, a nest where they'd lived out their past months, fully intending to remain alone. But life had other plans, and there's no real way to get lost anymore. Like pigs to a feast, others appeared, their eyes desperate, their mouths drooling, their intentions clear. A veritable city had sprung up around this simple home, fantastic flames born of a modest spark.

He rose, crawled over his corpse sleeper of a boyfriend, stretched, and hobbled outside toward the outhouse. Birds chirped. A breeze blew. From somewhere far away wafted the faint song of some happy couple making love and enjoying it immensely, judging by the over-enthusiastic timbre of their moans.

To be fair, what was there not to enjoy? It was a paradise, to be sure. Everything this village had, aside from a few dozen of the original mud houses, its people made themselves and enjoyed making. They grew and raised and preserved and cooked their own foodstuffs, sewed and patched their own clothing and linens, tended to their own scrapes and wounds. Here, there were no worries about money, no blood-pressure-spiking competition, no scrambling for limited resources.

Just laughter, music, art, joy.

His healthy stream dribbled to a stop, and he shook himself dry, zipped, spun, took a step. Or *tried* to take a step—his foot slipped out from underneath him, slid back, sunk into the trough. His body careened toward the ground. He braced for impact, caught himself evenly with both palms. He lay there on the outhouse floor, unmoving, his bare foot immersed in a swamp of human shit and piss. A second passed before shock subsided. He stabilized his torso and pulled his poor appendage from this quicksand. He didn't get up.

He blinked. He saw red.

He was in no state to make decisions, but luckily, his voice took the lead. He bellowed first as a way to claw out from what shock lingered, and then out of agitation, and then one final time, just for drama's sake. He roared Stefan's name, but that was a man who could sleep through the end of the world.

He was on his own.

His wrists ached. The skin on his palms stung. His mind spiraled. He shouldn't have come in here, he should've just pissed in the yard like Stefan always did *if we're going to live like farmers...* If we're going to live like animals is more like it. But even cats keep it in a box.

He lugged himself upright, grimaced, and stepped, carefully this time, from the outhouse. He scurried past the shed, grabbed the metal bucket, and bent over to turn on the water spigot. The rusty faucet sputtered. Nothing. More sputtering. Three fat drips, taunting him, plopping one after the other on the grass below. *Ha, ha, ha.* And then more nothing.

A sigh rose from Wang's lungs, escaped his lips, burdened the air around him.

This, it was *this*.

All was fucking paradise until you went to take a piss, slipped, and fell into slimy shit slop like a common hog. Until you wanted nothing more than a wash and couldn't even get your goddamn water to work. Until you craved a succulent bite of hairy crab and were left to make do with some old hag's bitter berry jam or some other similar DIY snack atrocity. Until you longed to unwind with some luxury shopping followed by a cocktail at a swanky hotel bar with a glittery city view—as if that were so much to ask—but were left to alleviate your stress by chanting out your feelings in a drum circle. *This*. He was fucking sick of *this*. The inconvenience, the filthiness, the haughty and delusional people who acted like their semi-self-deprivation deserved a Nobel Peace Prize. If they really wanted to live like peasants, how about they hop in a time machine and replay some famines. How about they go around beating and humiliating each other for not being Nationalist enough or Communist enough or whatever-the-political-flavor-of-the-day-was enough. How about they really do without.

And surely none of these neo-peasant jokers was stupid enough to truly relinquish everything, to actually "do without"—certainly they still retained deeds to their multiple properties and access to bank accounts in the Virgin Islands. Their real lives hadn't been ejected; they were just on pause. All of these people were posers, this paradise a fraud.

And if he was going down that road, well, once upon a time, he'd felt something like love for Stefan, some pattering in his chest that could well have been explained away by heart palpitations, but lately that warm, excited feeling had devolved into something resembling dread. The bastard was always so cheerful, so far and obnoxiously removed from the reality of any given situation. If Wang dared complain about anything, Stefan responded with a chirpy "Look on the bright side of things." Please. If he wanted to feel all optimistic and wonderful, then why would he be complaining in the first place? There was something to be said for the power of commiseration. Commiseration was an important bridge between human beings.

Suffering could not always be allayed, but at least it could be understood, empathized with. The ability to complain and feel as though your complaints were heard and comprehended—all too often that was better than being handed a solution.

Though right now, with fecal matter caked between his toes and sweat pooled on his upper lip and this goddamn water spigot blowing air, he had to admit that a solution would also suffice.

We believe that wealth is both our greatest liberator and our greatest oppressor. That money is but a clever dictator and master propagandist, filling our hearts with hope and our minds with fear.

He stomped back to the house—huffing, puffing, and unwashed—and threw open the door. Stefan's snores rattled the floorboards.

Wang hopped on one foot to the south wall, where a towel hung on a hook. Stefan's towel. He yanked it down, spit on it, and used it to wipe clean his foot. Let him get conjunctivitis, he thought with a sneer. Look on the bright side! Struggle makes us stronger.

Two more hops and he scoured the bottles lined up on their chopping block, poured some homemade *baijiu* onto the unsoiled side of the towel, and gave his foot a second, antibacterial rubdown.

Sufficiently sterilized, for now anyway, he rehung the towel on its hook and limped to the corner, to the desk where they stored their shared laptop computer. They didn't use it much, tried to keep their electricity usage to a minimum, and the Internet was so slow here besides, but this was an emergency.

He drummed his fingers on the desk, waiting for the page to load. Slow, slow, slow. He clicked the X, stopped the browser. Why run a stupid search for how to repair a broken water spigot now? He could do that once Stefan was awake. He glanced down at his shit-foot. What if there were still particles? Could they enter his bloodstream through his skin? Was that science? How long had it been since he'd truly felt clean?

His hands trembled. He took a deep breath, glanced over at Stefan, who slept peacefully—did he sleep any other way?—and satisfied by the steadiness of breath, he typed his own name into the search engine. He pored through the results, pausing every so often to ensure that Stefan remained unconscious. "Hair Tycoon Disappears, Rumored to Have Renounced Riches"... *Wang Xilai, once a national superstar entrepreneur and a hero to many... disgraced and disillusioned by a murder charge, which was later dismissed...*

The man he used to be was a mystery to him now. Why, after just one lousy nervous breakdown, did he decide to get in a car with a fairy-possessed fairy and uproot his entire life, an entity he'd given pulse to for twenty-some-odd years?

Stefan stirred, the sheets crunching under his body like potato chips. Wang jerked in his seat, exited out of the browser, slapped on his best virtuous face.

Stefan rolled over to face the wall, his eyes shut all the while. He smacked his lips and resumed snoring.

Wang shook his head, sighed, reopened the browser, deleted the history, shut it again, stood up.

We believe that happiness is not a product, manufactured by corporations and advertising agencies, attainable only through purchase. We believe that happiness is for free; that it is a feeling, an action, a choice.

He schlepped outside to the shed. What he needed now was reassurance. One more day, one more day, one more day. He needed to see her. So long as she was still under his control, he was in control. He reached for the padlock.

Rustling. Rattling.

He retracted his key, shoved it into his pocket, spun around. "Who's there?"

No answer. More rustling.

He stole a glance at the shed's door, which appeared untouched.

Trying to keep his cool, he crept along the shed's wall, hackles raised, preparing to punch or to be punched.

He rounded the corner. He rolled his eyes. "Oh, hell no," he muttered.

A man and a woman, naked in the grass next to his shed, giggling, groping, copulating.

He cleared his throat, hoping the hacking would draw their attention, their apologies.

They stopped thrusting and grunting. They fell still. They turned to look up at him with wide eyes. Their sweaty bodies glistened in the sunlight. They didn't say anything, no sorry, no nothing.

He couldn't just keep standing there; he had to speak. His voice came out high-pitched, foreign.

"What the hell are you doing?"

Still, they didn't open their mouths.

He squinted, frozen. He couldn't bring himself to look away from them, their shimmering skin. He recognized not their faces—perhaps newbies to the community, people who didn't yet have a firm grasp upon its boundaries and rules—nor the curious emotions those faces housed. Surprise never surrendered to shame. As though they were waiting for him to leave so they could continue their tryst. As though he was the one in the wrong. As though stumbling upon them had been some sort of sin.

He considered his next move. He blinked. They were gone.

He cocked his head; no more rustling—just birds singing, cicadas chirping.

He rubbed his eyes. Still gone. Perhaps some shit-borne illness had indeed entered his bloodstream, leading to hallucination. Perhaps the stress was cracking him up. Perhaps these naked fornicators were just really fast runners.

He blinked again, checked that the coast was clear, and returned to the shed's entrance. He turned his key in the lock, opened the door, stepped inside.

We believe that the desire to accrue wealth is but a symptom of a greater malaise. That discontent and dissatisfaction breed greed, and that greed breeds discontent and dissatisfaction, and that this is a cycle in which innocent souls can so easily become lost, crushed.

We believe that the best way to cure society of its cancer is to remove its tumors. That we are its tumors.

A lifetime ago.

When love bobbed on the tranquil horizon, when Stefan and Wang's songs whirled to the sky, when they cruised down bumpy country roads, endless, it seemed, an eternity before them, an eternity to go.

This was a lifetime ago.

When their hearts became too full, they expanded them. When their voices went scratchy, they sang through the pain. When their eyes drooped, they switched spots—driving, riding, it was all the same.

If only life could go on this way forever, if only, if only. This was a song they sang.

At dawn, on a stretch of straight gravel road beside a rubber tree plantation, they stopped to take a leak. Side by side, in silence, they relieved themselves, eyes fixed on the evenly spaced rows of trees.

There was a rattling then too.

Wang shook himself off, zipped up. "Do you hear that?" He paused, craned his head to the car, and then said, though the words tasted ridiculous in his mouth, "Is someone in the trunk?"

Stefan zipped up his trousers. He hacked out a loogie, squared his shoulders, and sauntered around to the driver's side. The way he was now, it was unlike the sweet self he'd been before, belting out ballads at the top of his lungs. The way he was now was more like the black-clad figure he'd been on the roof: fierce, startling, unsettling.

He continued around to the car's rear. "Look, I don't want you to be mad at me, but I think I may have kidnapped someone when I was under that fairy spell. I did, I mean. I know I did. Before I drove out to see you and all of that."

"What?" Wang wiped his clammy hands on the front of his pants. "Kidnapped someone?"

Stefan shrugged. He spoke, his voice gravelly, half him and half somebody else. "I, um, I started to remember as we were driving. She was watching a DVD in her apartment and I burst in and I just, uh, kidnapped her. Put her in my sports car. Drove. And when I got to your place, I moved her into your trunk."

"Who?"

Stefan coughed. He fell back into whisper, desperate. "I was trying to avenge you, I guess. Seeing as how she framed you. Seeing as how she sent everything spiraling out of control, saying you paid her to murder her father, driving you mad, ruining your business, devastating this country. I only wanted to help, is what I think, but I wasn't exactly in control of myself, was I?"

A familiar sentiment, and at once, Wang knew.

"I suppose it's up to you, what we want to do now." Stefan sighed, his shaky hands on the trunk. "But this part, at least, is done."

He popped it. The door sprung up, bounced a little, settled.

Wang stepped over, reluctant, afraid, not ready to accept this new fate. But what choice did he have? Here it was before him, hog-tied and gagged in the back of that Bentley: none other than the devil herself.

This, we believe.

THE BASHFUL GOOSE DIARIES, SELECTED EXCERPTS, PART 3

TONIGHT, I WALKED AN UNPAVED ROAD. DUST FLEW INTO MY EYES, stinging, burning.

As I made my way, I considered all the damage I'd done in the name of good: death and imprisonment and family feuds; illness and lovelessness and old evils renewed.

Oh, how I tried!

I'd given money to a limbless beggar, who was immediately mugged and beaten by a teenage gang. How was I to know of turf wars, of unseeable borders, of the gangsters' limitless cruelty?

I'd served tea to some soldiers whose convoy was broken down, and gave them all a bout of *E. coli* their torn-up guts aren't ever going to let them forget. How was I to know the water hadn't been boiled?

Oh, how I tried.

How little I learned in these months of the world and how it works. How little I learned of how to weave kindness into everyday acts. For kindness and goodness, these are not to be given freely anymore. There are rules, mores, accepted practices.

This is civilization, after all.

On that dusty road, I stepped, one, two, and something stuck to my foot. I stopped, looked down, bent over, picked it up. A cellophane wrapper bearing my face, my wing, my name.

Indeed, how could someone like me, someone who'd led such a pampered life, someone whose image is mass-produced and mass-loved, ever know suffering? How could I ever hope to understand the people, much less serve the people?

Perhaps I'd misread my second attempt at life's purpose. Perhaps the truth was I had no purpose at all; perhaps my rebirth had been a fluke, perhaps my initial birth had been too. What good had I ever done this nation? I'd given the people snack foods, empty calories. I'd given them jingles and songs. I'd given them, in essence, nothing.

A single tear burst from my duct. I hadn't cried for many months, not since my good-bye to Papa Hui, and I could've blamed it on the sand. I could've pushed that pathetic tear aside.

But I didn't. I dropped the wrapper to the breeze, and I walked on.

Ay, but, this tear, and the others like it that welled up in my eyes, they nearly blinded me from seeing something important—a shadow, a long shadow—its object behind me, descending, quickening.

A telephone pole, falling, falling toward me, aiming to fall on me.

This could've been my end, the end I deserved.

But ay, to die or not to die? That is truly the question, and one to which most are given no choice.

But I had one.

To allow my legacy to be tarnished, to let my legacy go, or to rise to this new occasion, to this new dawn—to claim a new dynasty of snacks?

The heavens whispered in my ears, whispered of truths and secrets. Perhaps I did not give this nation nothing. I'd given it my sustenance after all, and I'd given it my spirit, and I'd given it my all!

So I lifted my wing to wipe away those tears, lifted my wing into my signature pose, and, holding on to but a glimmer of hope, I cried out, "I am no Lei Feng, and I won't die like one!" and I sidestepped that black shadow and I ran, ran like hell.

✳

Out in the woods, on the other side of an important moment, if you listen very closely, small footsteps are audible. The sound of twigs bending, but not breaking.

Listen.

Those footsteps, they belong to me. After nights lurking among shadows and trees, I am walking toward this community, this dangerous rebel holding ground. I am approaching the place where many men and women have given up the ghost of greatness.

The land that stretches out before me, somewhere beyond this forest, is a graveyard of dreams. Oh, it sounds melodramatic, but it is true!

Hear me now: greatness resides outside the body. It does not belong to any man or woman. It is something we borrow, something that calls to be shared.

There is no such thing as a self-made millionaire, for instance. This is lore, and one we love to believe: that any one man can rise up and become an icon. But a "self-made" millionaire carries genes from his mother and father and all the ancestors who came before. He uses language, developed by people long since buried in the ground, and language is also evolving, we contribute even now to its evolution. He lives within a society created by others, is governed by laws passed and enforced by others. He spends, and eventually earns, money dirtied and worn by others' fingerprints and lint from others' pockets—and that's not to mention the entire economic system of which money is a part, this great mess of wants and needs and bartering and trading and currencies both monetary and electric. He learns lessons from his parents and teachers and friends, but no need to get hokey here. It is from others that we learn kindness and honesty, sure, but also from others that we learn to exaggerate and to hunger for more and to swindle and to partake in all of those devious, wonderful activities that millionaires and dictators do best.

And society, how it despises wandering ghosts. How it longs for greatness embodied. How it starves for the myth of the millionaire. How the people crave someone to pin their hopes upon, to worship in church or in the supermarket or in Tiananmen goddamn Square.

We want to believe that we can get better, together, alone, whatever. We want to believe that we can become something more than what we are.

But we should know by now: what we are is all we are.

And now I'm veering dangerously off track. Forgive me for my slight swerve onto the scenic route. Let us get back on course. All I mean to say is: self-made my ass!

Greatness is a ghost. But not for long. I'm here to guide these bastards home.

And with that, I will leave you, dear diary, as it is here I take my final step out of the woods, raise my beak to the crescent moon, and release a hearty honk: *Hey, fuck your mothers, the bashful goose is back!*

THE WANTS AND NEEDS OF WANG XiLAi

FOR THE REST OF THEIR DRIVE, THEY DELIBERATED. THERE WAS NO MORE singing. There was no more balance. There were only options.

As far as Wang was concerned, there was no good that could arise from letting her go. She'd tell the world she'd been kidnapped, or worse, she wouldn't say anything, but return to her life, appear in court, claim her father's company, and hold this whole kidnapping thing over his and Stefan's heads, sparking an inexhaustible game of blackmail.

Killing her was also out of the cards. He'd already gotten away with "murder" once. Could the public forgive him again?

The only option then was to keep her around until a better option presented itself. This option became all the more appealing when, upon their arrival in this weird ghost village, Wang was given his expiration date, June 5—yes, he'd subdue her until then, and after that she was somebody else's problem.

As soon as they found the house they were to settle in, Wang connected to 3G Internet on the laptop they'd brought along in the car. He researched. He recalled a story his grandmother once told him. He found an online shop that sold *gus*, tiny worms that could be slipped into food and that allowed one person to mentally control another. He lied his way through an e-consultation, told the black magic pharmacist that he needed to maintain control over his daughter as she studied for the university entrance exams, help her keep her head on right. The pharmacist typed that he understood, but for safety's sake, he could dispense only one *gu* per patient per month, and asked if that was all right.

"Fine," Wang typed back, "I'll need one per month for the next six months then."

He couldn't have the worms delivered to his new home—no post office in range, and too risky besides—so he used a convincing fake ID card leftover from his checking-into-love-motels-with-closeted-pop-stars days and a credit card registered to the same ID, and arranged for the package to be delivered to an old man in a village three hours' walk away.

"Do what you have to do," Stefan told him, absolving himself over time of any responsibility, as mere mortals are wont to do. "But from here on out, please keep me out of it."

Wang held his tongue.

He rendezvoused with the old man at a halfway point, on a narrow path beside a wide, stony creek. It was a pleasant walk through wide fields and rolling hills, made ever the more pleasant by its solitary nature. Once the annoying ex-millionaires arrived, he anticipated the monthly trek even more. Peace and quiet.

The ex-millionaires, however, all viewed it as some sort of a spiritual exercise, their leader's monthly pilgrimage to grow closer to the mysteries of the universe. As though writing one lousy treatise and living in filth had transformed him into a sage. One morning, a group of them cornered him as he was picking mint leaves in the garden and asked if they could tag along.

"We'll be quiet," one said.

"Utterly silent!" said another.

Wang gripped his handheld spade, dropped his gaze, and shook his head in feigned resignation. "I'm sorry, my children, but this is one path I must walk alone."

It struck him how easily deceit was mistaken for wisdom.

So his walks remained an interlude from his otherwise bleak waiting period. Each month, at the meeting point, he tucked the new package away in his pocket and paid the old man for his compliance, a pittance really, from some money he kept stashed away, buried in a tin can in the shed.

What killed him, what threatened to break him down, what detracted from the journey's joy was the way the old man clutched the bills, as if they were gold. When he turned and departed the scene of their transaction, there was always a spring in his step, a joy radiating from his bones. Wang learned his lesson quickly, made it a point to turn away first. He couldn't watch. He couldn't bear the fallout.

And he couldn't tell the old man about the date, about the lurking drought. He couldn't tell him that the orders would stop. That the money would stop. That he'd be back to his old poverty, his old boring life, until he found another way.

He tried not to concern himself with this, tried not to waste precious time wondering what would become of that old grinning face, those bowed legs, those rough, weathered hands.

The world was full of ways. That old coot would find one.

✳

Wang shut the door behind him. A sliver of pale sunlight filtered in through the shed's one tiny frosted glass skylight. "Kelly?" he whispered into the dingy room. "I'm leaving soon, forever, so I need to speak with you about something urgent."

"Oh, really?" a man's voice replied. "Is that what you need?"

Wang's head turned this way and that.

Singsong: "Yoo-hoo, I'm over here!"

His gaze scaled the walls, traveled the floors, and finally, Wang located the voice's owner. A man, perched on a haystack, one leg crossed over the other, spine erect, poised but casual, as though waiting for his maid to bring afternoon tea.

"Are you Wang Xilai?"

Wang felt his head move vertically on his neck. Nod, nod, and then an involuntary burp of questions: "Who are you? What the hell are you doing here? How did you get in?"

The man smiled, revealing a straight line of bleached teeth. "Well, what kind of master spy would I be if I couldn't pick a simple lock?"

Wang gaped, whimpered, composed himself. "Where's Kelly?"

The man waved his hand. "Ah, don't worry about that."

He spun around, eyes searching for his hostage until a realization hit. "Oh. Did the aliens send you?"

The man squinted. "Aliens?"

Want squinted back.

"No," the man said, uncrossing his legs.

Wang squinted harder, his eyelashes obscuring his vision.

Outside, there was a loud thud—the sound of something very heavy crashing to the ground.

"Yes," the man shrugged. "Sure, whatever you'd like to believe."

Wang walked over and sat beside the man on the haystack. He inched closer. He placed his hand on the man's milky-white forearm. The man didn't pull away, but smiled a pitiful smile, the kind of slight upward lip movement typically reserved for the very old and the very young and the very mentally deranged. Wang retracted his hand.

"Now, Mr. Wang, I can't for a second fathom that a man such as yourself—a rich man, a successful man, a man of power and means—might truly be happy in such a"—he traced his finger along the grime on the wall, frowned at his blackened fingertip—"forgive my language, but such a shit-hole." He stood, his speech gaining momentum. "Now, I don't know how you ended up here, though I imagine some rather dire and inescapable circumstances must have caused you to, shall we say, hit rock bottom. But what I do know is this—"

Outside, there was a loud commotion. There was crashing, banging, screaming.

"Mr. Wang, when I found Ms. Hui in this shed only a half hour ago, she was delirious, muttering about UFOs and humming to herself a song from the Broadway hit *Annie*."

"*Tomorrow, tomorrow, you're only a day away?*" Wang sang.

The man respectfully lowered his gaze. And that damn smile again. "Mmm, yes. And a sack of bones, she was. I imagine it was difficult for you to sneak into this shed the massive quantities of processed foods that once composed her diet without the neighbors growing suspicious. Honestly, she's never looked so good."

Wang suppressed a snort.

"Now I know, Mr. Wang, that you and that boyfriend of yours must have kidnapped her, dragged her here, drugged her up with heaven knows what—"

There was another loud sound outside, something like fireworks, and then there were shadows flitting on the wall, shadows without a source.

"We used a *gu*. I used a *gu*," he said, and he wasn't sure why he said it. "Mind control."

"Oh, perfect." The man rubbed his palms together. They didn't even make a sound, that's how soft, how moisturized they were. "All the better to pin it on the witches then."

Wang felt dizzy. "What?"

"Mr. Wang, your boyfriend, Stefan Ping, kidnapped Kelly Hui and conspired with those witches on the outskirts of town to keep her drugged and mind-controlled, so that they could throw the Bashful Goose company's leadership into chaos and establish this awful commune in hopes of subverting the Chinese Communist Party. Did you know that those witches are Falun Gong practitioners? That they've long sought to overthrow Party rule? And did you know that the young woman they shack up with, Lulu Qi, is an avid supporter of the Dalai Lama and of the Tibetan independence movement? That she traveled to Tibet just last year to involve herself in an uprising?"

Shadows appearing, swaying, disappearing.

"I don't think that's—"

"Your boyfriend, Stefan, in addition to drugging Kelly, also administered *gus* to you, betraying your trust and forcing you to lead this commune against your will. He coerced you into authoring a treatise. 'We believe...' Yeah, sure, we believe it's all bullshit."

Wang tried again to interject: "But I wrote—"

"Luckily," the man went on, his voice booming now, "as the nation already knows from your bestselling memoir, you possess an unbreakable spirit, and after many months as prisoner, you managed to escape the *gu*'s influence by secretly vomiting it up. You broke free from Stefan's reign of terror, forced your way into the shed, poured a cleansing herbal tonic into Kelly's mouth to rid her of the *gu*'s last grip, and then you set her free."

Outside, there were howls, crackles, booms, pops. Kelly's unmistakable banshee wail. A long-overdue wave of terror, of murder, of destruction.

But he, in this shed, was safe. And he could stay safe.

Shadows skipped, their dark limbs long, urging him a certain way.

Wang turned the story over in his head.

The man cleared his throat, ground his heel into the floor, inhaled through his nose. "Well, I suppose I'd better attend to whatever's happening out there. There are only so many deaths we can attribute to suicide, you know—once the quota's filled, it's filled. And we need some of them to return, keep the gears turning, as it were. I'll have to brief them, get them on board, but I'm sure with your help that won't be a problem."

He strode over to Wang, still sitting on that haystack, and gave him a friendly slap on the back. "At midnight, we will alert the media. Stick to the story, Mr. Wang, and you will be rewarded. Your kingdom, as they say, awaits."

He turned, he opened the door, and he left, swallowed up by light.

Behind him, the door creaked shut.

On the wall, the shadow people, fully formed now, limbs and bodies and beating hearts, danced. And they danced. And they danced and they danced.

*

There would be no spaceships.

There would be an heiress to a fortune coming to, coming loose, and, with all her strength, tearing through the commune, shouting out her own name.

Citizens would rush to their doors. "Is that—?" they would say. "No, it can't be—" But they would know it could.

There would be journalists pouring over the hills, with cameras and microphones, poking their snotty noses where they didn't belong, asking honest questions, printing lovely lies.

There would be police. There would be guns. There would be tanks.

There would be a goose, emerging from the woods, eyes still aglow, honking and hollering. Running toward his old enemy, his new master. Soaring into her open arms.

There would be no more dancing shadows, no more messages in dreams, no more stones crying to be overturned.

There would be a young tycoon who would work forever to forget the look in his boyfriend's sleepy eyes as the police closed in. A tycoon who would work ceaselessly to forget the words Papa Hui once spoke to him, to overlook the meaninglessness in all of this, to distract himself from the restless soul that resided in his hungry body. A tycoon who would henceforth serve as Kelly's right-hand man, advising on a number of critical carbohydrate decisions, retelling the same story again and again until he believed it, ghostwriting a stirring memoir of a reincarnated bird, reveling in riches yet unimagined.

A young man who would never be abducted by aliens, but who would, indeed, be taken home.

There would be a grand gathering of people around this young man and the girl and her goose. There would be a speech, a grand speech, that would be immortalized in poems and in jingles. *Yes, ladies and gentlemen, that's right, the heiress herself has returned! The mandate of the goose is mine!*

There would be cheers. There would be sobs. There would be mur-murings about the state of the heiress's hair. There would be many ex-millionaires rushing home to charge their long-dead cell phones and to log on to the snail-slow Internet, to contact family about returning to their cities, to their companies, to their bank accounts. There would be not a word spoken about what frauds they'd all been, how poised they'd remained all this time to slip back into their old ways. There would be chauffeured Audis and Land Rovers and BMWs and Maseratis and Lamborghinis kicking up dust as they descended upon the once-tranquil valley.

And there would be no enlightenment, no absorption into its warm white light, into the nothing, into the everything.

There would be a man whose job was simple, to liberate the nation's millionaires from their self-inflicted chains; a man whose task had been successfully completed and in minimal time. For him there would be congratulations, endless toasts over endless feasts, a promotion, a raise, an inexhaustible network of favors owed.

There would be a young woman to whom this man would rush, issuing a warning to be gone before the police arrived at her cot-tage and to take those witches with her. But her sisters had already sensed something amiss, were already long departed. "Magic," Witch Two told her, unbothered, untouched, as she stuffed the last of their books into her bag, "is always on the run."

A young woman who had chosen not to join them.

Who had waited here for him.

A young woman to whom this man would urge, "Go. Go now before it's too late."

A young woman who, unsettled now, couldn't quite bring herself to thank him for his mercy, his hormone-driven concern. A young woman who had truly believed that this man was someone he was not, that he was what she'd wanted.

What she'd wanted, all she wanted, was something that would stick. A love that would last.

To whom he would give a dismissive wave of the hand and speak the bitter words, "Please. Love is an illusion."

A young woman who had come to her senses, who had realized the truth about the red eyes in the woods—they had seen her, yes, but they would never know her. Who would spit in reply to the man, "No, you're just an asshole." Who would strut into the woods, disappearing into its thick of trees and bushes and roots and shadows, not to be seen again.

There would be a nation that would speculate not for her whereabouts, cry not for her absence.

There would be another way for her. She'd find it. She would.

ACKNOWLEDGMENTS

First and foremost, thank *you*, reader!

I owe a great many more thanks, and so here we go, in list form...

Chris Heiser, Olivia Taylor Smith, and everyone at Unnamed Press for taking a chance with this book.

My family: Paula Hallman, the most talented artist I know. Scott Hallman, the glue that holds us all together. Shawn Hallman, a.k.a. Rock-N-Roll Jesus. Tristan Hallman, who will someday write a serious and respected journalistic tome and make me look a fool. Harpo, that little rascal.

Paul "Moon" Harding, my life-partner-in-weirdness and co-creator of the Bashful Goose Snack Company.

Mia and Bean-Bean, my familiars.

My writing teachers at St. Edward's: Beth Eakman, Doug Dorst, Dr. Mary Rist, Kelly Mendiola, Dr. Drew Loewe, Dr. Catherine Rainwater, Michael Barnes, and the late Marcia Kinsey.

My students and professional contacts in Beijing, who taught me more than I ever deserved to know.

Frey Miremadi, for friendship, café work dates, and Korean waffles.

JY, for teaching me all about corpse walkers and Chinese magic.

Zejian Shen and Claire Hsu for horror movies and cat photos.

The authors and booksellers who very kindly wrote blurbs, including Annalia S. Linnan, Amelia Gray, James Fallows, Peter Mountford, and Mark Haskell Smith. I remain humbled.

Additional thanks to Houston Holmes, Cherry Kow, Mary Ky, Caroline Morris, Sheryl & Ken Lehnig, Cherry & Frank Harding, Oskar Eastwood, Jemma & Simon Eastwood, Leslie Reese, Contina Pierson & Michael Graham, Lu-Hai Liang, Cassie Woods, Jena Heath, Bryce Pearcy, Mike Dardzinski & Echo Sun, Ivy Taylor, Lisa Marie Ivarra, Valerie Villarreal, James David Wade, Christian Brady Spence, Jimmy McGuffin, Katy Larsen, Sandra Jeffrey, Vincent Galbo, Christina Ayers, Virgenta Lane, Fei Dee Tsing, Jalesa Daniels Jones, Susie Celis, Harold Owens, all the APSA kids, everyone at GlobalTrack, and the whole AIFS 2006 crew.

...And if I've foolishly forgotten to thank you, please forgive me and know that you've given me the perfect excuse to go write another book. I'll get you next time, I swear.